YINZER GOLD

YINZER

GOLD

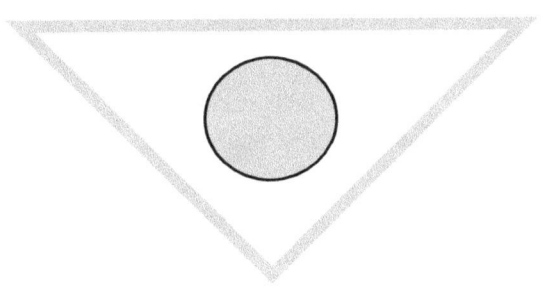

WRITTEN AND ILLUSTRATED BY

ROBERT EMMET CONNEMARA

STEEL PENNY BOOKS LLC

Steel Penny Books LLC

Pittsburgh, Pennsylvania

ISBN 979-8-9908372-0-1 (paperback)

ISBN 979-8-9908372-1-8 (hardcover)

ISBN 979-8-9908372-2-5 (eBook)

TO MY MUM

Oscar Wilde: "We are all in the gutter, but some of us are looking at the stars."

For the reader,

To truly understand life in America during 1979, you must be completely immersed in the popular culture of that time. Therefore, to fully convey my story, you will be inundated with nonstop name-dropping of historical people, places, products, songs, movies, TV shows, and events. A stark reality based on spitting facts is imperative. All maps depict real locations. This is not a fantasy tale about an imaginary universe inhabited by other-worldly characters with magical superpowers. If you want to read a make-believe novel about kids flying around on broomsticks, then go and look for one in the dusty pile under your bed. In contrast, this book is based on actual bloody battles in which real warriors either ferociously fought to live another day or tragically perished from the earth. I want to be clear: The lives and legacies of these lost warriors are far more important than what transpired with me and my friends on the last days of summer in 1979.

Robert Emmet Connemara

Contents

Introduction: Yinzer 101

This is a tale about real people, real places, and real events. The adventures that await you are rooted in authentic American history and are not solely based on local legend and folklore. Likewise, my story is not just one long string of esoteric allusions that only a "Yinzer" would understand. Alas, it would be a disservice for me to not provide a crash course that answers one big question: "What is a Yinzer?"

I am a Yinzer. The word "Yinzer" refers to someone from Pittsburgh who uses the unique word "yinz" in conversation. Yinz is simply a pronoun that is used to address two or more people. For example, a Yinzer greets a gathering of friends with a cordial "How yinz doin'?" Yinz is a curious cousin to the much more familiar "y'all" which is widely engrained in common speech throughout vast swaths of the American South.

Today, the term Yinzer is more broadly used to describe anyone who resides in or is native to the region around Pittsburgh, Pennsylvania. When I was young, Pittsburgh was well known as a blue-collar American town that long prided itself on two things, steel and sports. As a kid, I wasn't even aware of my Yinzer upbringing. But when I look back, it smacks me in the face like the delicious aroma of Potato Patch cheese fries when you step out of Noah's Ark at Kennywood Park. (Okay, it's more difficult than I thought to avoid using inside Yinzer references.) I grew up within sight of the city's towering U.S. Steel Building. In my youth, I played along the Allegheny River in between the steel mills that employed my father and his father before him. Every day, I wore at least one article of clothing that had a Steelers, Pirates, or Penguins logo. (On some days, I wore all three.) I thought every sandwich was supposed to be topped with a big pile of fries and coleslaw. When it came to meeting the geographical and cultural requirements of the descriptor, I was a bona fide Yinzer.

But there was more to it than that. I spoke like a Yinzer. When I was in elementary school, I was placed in a remedial speech class. At the time, I couldn't fathom why I was pulled from regular classes to visit with a speech pathology teacher. It was embarrassing because I generally earned high marks in school. But in retrospect, it's clear to me that the experts in my early childhood education deemed my locally influenced speech patterns to be an impediment to my future scholastic endeavors. I can distinctly recall how the speech teacher would peek her head into my second-grade classroom and whisper, "Can I please see Bobby Connemara for fifteen minutes?" To my dismay, I would always get yanked out of the fun activities like finger painting. I hated the hassle of taking off my painting smock, an old flannel shirt that we had to put on backwards. Even worse, sometimes my speech instruction cut into free playtime or recess. Never would Mrs. Viola excuse me from multiplication table practice or the weekly spelling test.

To be fair, Mrs. Viola was a very likeable teacher who cheerfully rewarded her students with gold coins when they achieved mastery in a speech lesson. I always had an affinity for gold, even fake gold. With hopeful eyes, I would constantly glance at that mound of cheap plastic coins resting in a small cardboard treasure chest on her desk. The gold tokens could be used as currency in her classroom "store" to purchase small prizes like colored pencils or Scratch 'N Sniff stickers. I set my hope on a little blue eraser in the shape of the Scooby-Doo gang's van.

I remember everything about her classroom. It was small and stuffy. It didn't have a single window. I always wondered how her little green ivy plant even stayed alive in there. I also remember the exercises that she would make me do. On the board, she would prepare a diagnostic test that was just waiting for me to butcher. For example, she would ask me to read aloud these three terms written in yellow chalk:

Down   Town   Crown

I would say all three words with ease and look around in disbelief. I was clueless. My kid-self thought, "How's come I'm missin' out on finger paintin' 'at awesome purple elephant for this crap?" While I would be checking around the room for a hidden recorder like on a *Candid Camera* television episode, a concerned Mrs. Viola would scribble down another scathing weekly progress report on her clipboard.

In hindsight, I realize that she was not evaluating my reading skills. It was my pronunciation skills that greatly bothered her, as well as my teachers and principal. In my thick Pittsburgh accent, I had quickly mumbled out her list of words.

Bobby: "Dahn. Tahn. Crahn." (Spelled how it sounded.)

After I said the terms out loud, Mrs. Viola would lightly shake the beehive hairdo on her head and record her notes with a discouraged look on her face. While most Americans would say that she was "frowning," I would say that she was "frahning" in my native vernacular. Although in the local dialect words with "ow" were commonly pronounced "ah," my speaking habits stood out even among the other young townies in school. My strong Yinzer accent was thicker than the foam on a freshly poured Iron City beer. It was deeply ingrained since birth. She couldn't break me. It goes without saying, but I was a very rare customer at Mrs. Viola's classroom store.

Yinzers have a noticeably distinct form of communication. To fully comprehend the story ahead, you will need to learn a little bit about how a Yinzer speaks. Once described by a writer from *The New York Times* as "The Galápagos Islands" of regional American dialects, the Pittsburgh language and accent may seem utterly foreign to many English speakers, even to those within the United States. Depending upon the Yinzer, the peculiar accent might range from slight to unintelligible. The local lingo also contains colloquial words that are only used in this small metro region.

Here are just a few of the unique Pittsburgh words, matched with respective definitions, that you will find in conversations throughout the narrative ahead:

<u>yinz</u> – second-person plural form of "you" (*pronoun*). Used to address two or more persons, yinz is a contraction of "you ones."

<u>jagoff</u> – a jerk (*noun*). Can also be a descriptive adjective used to describe a person ranging in tone from playful to mean-spirited.

<u>jag</u> – to jokingly tease someone (*verb*).

<u>nebby</u> – nosy or prying into one's business (*adjective*).

<u>redd up</u> – to clean something (*verb*).

<u>worsh</u> – to wash something (*verb*).

<u>slippy</u> – slippery (*adjective*).

<u>dahntahn</u> – downtown (*noun*). Some words will be phonetically spelled to aid in comprehending the local accent. For example, "down" will be spelled "dahn."

<u>Picksburgh</u> – Pittsburgh (*noun*). In the thickest of Yinzer accents, even the name of the city itself is unbelievably pronounced this way.

<u>n'at</u> – contraction of "and that" (*noun*). Often used at the end of sentences to allude to various other things or ideas.

The accent is rough and curt. For instance, an ingredient used to make steel, called "iron," would be pronounced "ahrn" and not pronounced "eye-urn" with two syllables. Words like "power" would be pronounced "pahr" in one syllable and not "pow-er" in two distinct syllables. "House" sounds like "hahse" while "out" sounds like "aht." The word "real" is pronounced as "ruhl." And "mom" would be endearingly pronounced "mum," similar to a Scottish accent. In fact, the word "yinz" is believed to be derived from the town's original Scots-Irish settlers, who would say "you ones" when directly referring to a group of people.

In addition, there are many grammatical liberties that Yinzers use when speaking. Double negatives are commonplace. Most native Pittsburghers simply condense or eliminate words that they consider unnecessary in communication. The most frequent elimination are the words "to be" when referring to an action. While some only jokingly speak in Yinzer, many locals do not even realize their unique grammar. Even highly educated Pittsburghers tend to use some of these grammatical functions.

For example, in many parts of America one would say the phrase:

American English: "Those dirty dishes need to be washed."

A person from Pittsburgh would eliminate the "to be" and say:

Yinzer: "Them dirty dishes need worshed."

Likewise, one from many other regions of America would say:

American English: "The lawn needs to be mowed."

However, in Pittsburgh, even a doctor or lawyer would likely say:

Yinzer: "The grass needs cut."

Here is an example of a Yinzer double negative along with a word reduction.

American English: "I don't have any more money to spend down at the casino."

Yinzer: "I ain't got no more money to spend dahn a' casino."

Often "at the" or even "the" is condensed to "a'" when referring to a location. Additionally, many short words are shortened even more in the spoken Yinzer language. For example, the adverb "really" is almost always compressed to "real" when used as a descriptor. Also, the word "that" is often conveniently shortened to "'at" by Yinzers. For example:

American English: "Is that your dog? She is really playful!"

Yinzer: "Is 'at your dog? She's real playful!"

And then there is a Yinzer word that I can only very loosely compare to the Hawaiian Pidgin term "da kine," which can informally refer to just about anything and everything. This anomaly of a word is "n'at." Widely heard in everyday conversation in Pittsburgh, it is a fusion of "and that." Here's an example:

Yinzer: "She'll stuff ground beef n'at in the green peppers before bakin' 'em."

In this case, n'at could be referring to sauce, spices, or rice. But n'at could also mean sausage, onions, or cheese. This nebulous contraction can refer to anything from inanimate objects to abstract ideas. Like "etcetera," n'at is more often added as an extension to a spoken sentence and translates to "and other things" or "and so on." Yinzers have the habit of tacking it on to the end of comments like so:

Yinzer: "Our nebby neighbor knows all the latest tahn gossip n'at."

Do not be intimidated. Only when I am quoting direct spoken dialogue will the local dialect and jargon be utilized. By the way, most Pittsburghers now refer to their native spoken tongue as Yinzer, and not Pittsburghese. The baseline word to comprehend is "yinz." Once you understand that yinz means "you guys" or "y'all," then you will be good to go. The conversations between characters in my story will not be beyond your grasp. However, before you continue reading this book, I want to give you a sample of Yinzer translations in order by increasing level of difficulty. The translations will be presented in a format resembling a modern language learning app. As previously stated, I will take the liberty of using some phonetically spelled words in order to more accurately portray the local accent.

Let's begin...

<u>Easy</u>

Yinzer: "How yinz doin'?"

Translation: "How are you guys doing?"

Medium

Yinzer: "Yinz goin' dahntahn to watch 'at Stillers game?"

Translation: "Are you guys going downtown to watch that Steelers game?"

Difficult

Yinzer: "Git ahtta tahn! Yinz jagoffs jaggin' me? How's come yinz worshed my new wheels wit' water yinz got from dahn 'ere in a' crick?"

Translation: "You cannot be serious! Are you jerks kidding me? Why did you guys wash my new car with water that you have taken from down there in the creek?"

Borderline impossible

Yinzer: "My jagoff mum's so nebby n'at. And 'sides leavin' 'em worshed floors all slippy, she's ruhl into reddin' up the hahse wit' 'at sweeper."

Translation: "My rude mother is very nosy in my affairs, among other things. And along with leaving the washed floors very slippery, she is really concerned about cleaning the house with that vacuum cleaner."

Finally, I want to add two more random details about the Yinzer language. As seen in prior example sentences, the word "jagoff" is a very commonly used word in Pittsburgh. The word refers to a "jerk" or "idiot" in Yinzer and does not have a crude innuendo as some may assume. Also, inexplicably, instead of simply using the word "Why?" Yinzers often say "How come?" or even "How's come?" to ask a question.

To be frank, outsiders often find the Yinzer dialect and accent to be completely bewildering and even ugly. Like I mentioned before, none of the dialogue in my story will go beyond comprehension like that of the "Borderline Impossible" example above. The word "yinz" will obviously be used often. However, in normal talk between characters, I will only phonetically spell a few words such as "dahn" for "down" and "tahn" for "town." Yinz will be fine n'at.

But there is much more to being a Yinzer than simply how one speaks. Yinzers have close bonds to their city. They are obsessed with their hometown and its history and culture. Yinzers love being Yinzers. Getting called a "Yinzer" was once derogatory. It was belittling. There was a stigma attached. Now Pittsburghers embrace it with extreme pride. This intimate connection will be vividly detailed in my childhood adventure so I will not delve too deep into the heart of the Yinzer at this point.

However, I did create two simple checklists for you to review and analyze. The first one is to see if you are indeed a Yinzer yourself. The second checklist is to see if you are in fact a Super Yinzer who holds distinction over all other Pittsburghers.

10 Point Yinzer Checklist:

- ☐ A Yinzer always wears at least one Steelers, Pirates, or Penguins item on them, even while sleeping. (Tattoos count.)
- ☐ A Yinzer dips almost everything they eat in Heinz ketchup.
- ☐ A Yinzer has enjoyed the Jack Rabbit, Racer, and Thunderbolt roller coasters at Kennywood Amusement Park all on the same visit.
- ☐ A Yinzer always refers to the three most beloved local sports heroes by first name only as Roberto, Franco, and Mario. And one other by a partial last name, Maz.
- ☐ A Yinzer has eaten leftover pierogies for breakfast. (If you don't know what a pierogi is, then you are not a Yinzer.)
- ☐ A Yinzer puts a folding chair outside of their row house to reserve their parking spot. (If they are wealthy, then they put a folding chair outside of their townhouse.)
- ☐ A Yinzer has dipped their feet into the Allegheny, Monongahela, or Ohio River (or all three).
- ☐ A Yinzer has ordered a kielbasa sandwich at Primanti Bros. Restaurant and pronounced it "kah-bossi" while ordering.
- ☐ A Yinzer has his or her own personal Terrible Towel… and a spare one just in case.
- ☐ A Yinzer can fluently communicate in Yinzer with others, even if in jest.

Many of you might be able to check off a few of the boxes from my Yinzer checklist above. If you can check all 10 boxes, then you are most definitely a certified Yinzer. Next, here is my more rigorous Super Yinzer checklist with only 3 checkpoints.

3 Point Super Yinzer Checklist:

- ☐ A Super Yinzer has never ventured outside of Southwestern Pennsylvania and only vacations at nearby State Parks with lakes.
- ☐ A Super Yinzer has tattoos of all three Pittsburgh professional sports team logos, a yellow bridge, and the city skyline… on their left arm tattoo sleeve.
- ☐ A Super Yinzer has eaten the complimentary peanuts at Jack's Bar in the South Side… for their Thanksgiving dinner.

Most importantly, if someone truly happens to meet the strict criteria governed by the Super Yinzer Checklist, then they likely were completely unaware of their status as a Super Yinzer.

Finally, if you are a true Yinzer, then you're extremely frustrated that I did not create more checklist options. At this moment, you are thinking or talking out loud to yourself:

You: "This jagoff writer forgot about... "

Okay, now that you know some of the basics of who a Yinzer is and how a Yinzer talks, I am going to tell you all about my Yinzer odyssey. My story takes place in the waning days of summer break in 1979. It was a moment in time that feels like yesterday at one instant and light-years ago the next. In those days, many Yinzers (including myself) didn't even self-identify as Yinzers yet. I was a wandering 14-year-old trying to make the most of my last fortnight of freedom before entering high school. I vividly recall the details from the events of that two-week period, as one usually does with the most exciting adventures of one's youth.

For me, this book is a bike ride down memory lane. A memoir of my golden days. But this yarn is not just about me. This two-week escapade was well over 200 years in the making. This is a tale about countless Yinzers who have ever made a home in Pittsburgh. Some were permanent residents while others were temporary visitors. But they were all Yinzers in some way, from the newest arrivals of hopeful immigrants to the earliest generations of emboldened steelworkers. My story is about young Yinzers and old Yinzers, from the poorest kids in the alleys to the richest tycoons in the world. Wrapped in it all, this saga involves the origin story of the first Yinzers, from a great Native American Chief to the first President of the United States of America.

Oh yeah, and there's a hunt for a hidden gold treasure too.

YINZER

GOLD

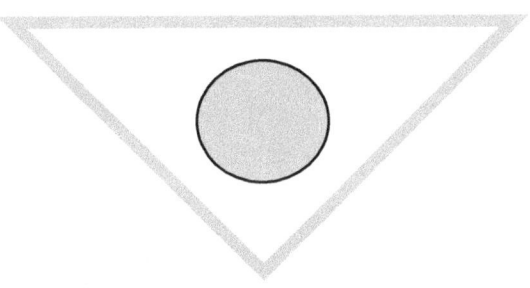

ROBERT EMMET

CONNEMARA

Chapter 1: Urban Warfare

It was a hot summer day in August of 1979. I was in grave danger.

Enemy Soldier: "Freeze! Yinz are dead meat!"

His voice came from behind me. I knew his gun was ready and aimed. That was certain. I just wondered how he snuck up on me. Frozen in my tracks, my eyes darted around as I frantically tried to calculate how I could possibly escape from a rifle that was trained squarely at my back. I was in point-blank range, and he was dead set on eliminating me for good. That would finally put an end to this dirty street war. He began to press the business end of the cold steel barrel between my shoulder blades.

Enemy Soldier: "Surrender or else, dirtbag!"

I countered the enemy with noble words of defiance.

Bobby: "Up yours, jagoff!"

I was out of ammo. The grueling street-to-street warfare had taken its toll. My only hope of salvation, my two companions, had already become casualties. They had been surrounded and captured. The enemy rifle dug even deeper into my spine.

Enemy Soldier: "This is your last chance, scum!"

With a muffled voice from under my bandana, I uttered my courageous decision. It was my last.

Bobby: "Give me liberty, or give me... "

Gun: "Bang!"

Bobby: "Ow! Son of a... !"

I was shot. The vicious sting of the speeding projectile was too much to bear. I collapsed to the ground in agony. The war was over. It was all over...

Well, at least this game of "War" was over. We were just a bunch of street kids engaged in a make-believe battle for control over the neighborhood. The guns were real. But these "real" guns were actually BB guns. And by our rules of war, only single-pump models were allowed. With just one pump of compressed air power, these older lever-action air rifles were made for plinking empty pop cans.

I was out of ammo. But again, by our official rules of the game, you were only allowed to load your rifle with ten steel BBs. That limited number was determined by countless rounds of play.

And I was actually shot. The little BB hit the back of my left hamstring. The pain was excruciating. Even the slowest moving steel round stung like heck. But once again, by rule, you could only shoot an enemy in the legs or butt. And since I was wearing my thick Wrangler denim blue jeans, the hostile blast that I had suffered barely even left a welt.

It was urban warfare. But we were not roaming the town like wild maniacs randomly firing at each other with air guns. Our combat took place in a well-contained area, an abandoned factory yard. Not that this walled-off "war zone" was a safe space in which to play. In order to access the derelict lot, we first had to carefully traverse over a rusty barbed wire fence. Once inside, there were small graffiti-laden garages with broken glass windows that we used as command bunkers. The boarded-up factory sat in the center. It was surrounded by narrow roadways of sunken cobblestone and clay brick. These skinny paths made navigation treacherous at every turn. But with a scattered mixture of rusted-out vehicles, metal scrap heaps, and overgrown weeds, the deserted mill yard provided the perfect terrain and cover for our armed battles. The old crane served as an ideal lookout tower. I personally liked to hide under a badly corroded pickup truck that was propped up on cinder blocks. It had a small maple tree growing out of its hollow engine compartment.

The battle now over, I met up with my beleaguered squad of defeated friends. Standing in front of the vacant lot, they looked utterly dejected. We hated losing at War.

Bobby: "What happened to yinz?"

Vito shrugged his shoulders.

Vito: "They got all around us somehow. We had to surrender."

While I slung my air rifle onto my back, I threw my free hand up in the air in total disbelief.

Bobby: "Yinz gave up! What the… "

Sal bitterly snapped back at me.

Sal: "We ran outta ammo, jagoff! And we only got surrounded by them connivin' lowlifes 'cause *you* ditched your post like a moron tryin' to beat 'em all by yourself. I saw you runnin' 'cross the lot. Clearly, ya ain't as fast as ya think ya are."

Sal spit on the ground with disgust and continued.

Sal: "You're always tryin' to be a hero, Bobby."

Sal was right. I made a desperate move in a bid to capture the enemy flag behind enemy lines. I was fleet of foot. But it's tough to outrun every problem.

I pointed to where I had been shot.

Bobby: "Donnie hit me in a' leg."

I shook my head in disappointment.

Bobby: "I shouda made it. I just couldn't run fast enough 'cause 'em mossy rocks back 'ere was all slippy."

With a grimace on his face, Sal looked me up and down and reminded me that I was not in the same class as one of the greatest athletes on the planet in 1979.

Sal: "You ain't exactly Bruce Jenner."

Our game of War, more commonly known as Capture the Flag, may seem dangerous and even barbaric compared to the version played in most American towns. However, for us, this was a perfectly normal form of entertainment. Of course, we never told our parents that we ran around shooting each other with BB guns for fun. And worse yet, occasionally there would be inaccurate misfires. I still have a little round scar on my right shoulder that attests to it. Heck, a doctor would probably have prescribed tetanus shots for just entering our rusty combat zone, let alone absorbing the impact from an old steel BB. Looking back, I can't believe that we didn't even wear safety glasses. But we were young and invincible then. Well, that, and we didn't know about paintball guns until the 1980s.

Bobby: "Whatever, Sal. It's over. Let's get outta here."

3

We grew up on a blue-collar block in a blue-collar neighborhood of a blue-collar city during a blue-collar era. My little town of Sharpsburg sat along the Allegheny River five miles from Downtown Pittsburgh. The entire plot was purchased by James Sharp in the 1800s for about $1,300. It was a spartan neighborhood of industrial factories and railway yards. Most families lived in small row houses that were packed with at least three to four children. This paled in comparison to the typical seven or eight children per household in the previous generation.

After we climbed over the fence, we saddled up on our bikes. Sal shook his head.

Sal: "We haven't beaten 'em since summer started. Unbelievable."

Heads down and with our small carbines strapped to our backs, we slowly began to mosey our bikes home like a humbled U.S. Cavalry unit commiserating over a hard-fought defeat. My friend Sal was particularly steamed from losing at War to our archrivals from the neighboring block, especially on this hot summer day. It went against his cool kid aura. He continued to gripe.

Sal: "I'm sick 'n tired o' losin' to them jagoffs. 'Specially Donnie. That snake in a' grass. Always slitherin' around and sneakin' up on you. I can't stand 'at little runt."

Sal would not let it go.

Sal: "I swear, he looks like he could be Danny DeVito's stunt double."

He needed a cold drink to temper his hot ego.

Sal: "Okay, I'm stoppin' home. I need a glass o' ice water."

Vito lifted his head and remarked.

Vito: "I need a whole bucket o' ice water. Think you can fill one up for me with the hose?"

Sal fired back at Vito.

Sal: "No, ya moron! And my mum don't want us drinkin' from the hose no more."

I hung with a tight-knit crew. A trio including Sal, Vito, and myself. We all lived on the same square block in the middle of Sharpsburg. Our game of War was congruent with the true territorial nature of the town. Each block was staunchly defended by its own group of kids. Boundaries were clearly drawn. You owned your block's sidewalk. Four sides. Four Corners. But every inch of concrete beyond that was fought over. Streets were hotly disputed. Alleys were riddled with danger. Parks became minefields. Enemy scouts lurked everywhere. It was a constant battle.

Like field generals planning tactics for a long conflict, we mapped the entire layout of the "battlefield." Sharpsburg is a skinny rectangle of a town nestled between tall cliffs and the banks of the Allegheny River. A highway runs along the cliff wall. Train tracks line the riverfront. The small borough is about 0.3 miles wide and 1.5 miles long. On foot it takes thirty minutes to cross from end to end, but only ten by bike. The flattish floodplain is lined with four horizontal streets that run parallel to the river and about twenty-five streets that run perpendicular, some on a slope. That makes a 4 block by 25 block area. Using the simple math formula, $A = l \times w$, our neighborhood contained 100 square blocks. Factories, junkyards, and warehouses occupied nearly a quarter of that space, leaving us with roughly 75 blocks to navigate.

After we reached our home block, we stopped our bikes in front of Sal's house. His voice dialed down as he glanced up at his front door.

Sal: "I'll put the BB guns in a' basement. Yinz stay here while I go get some water."

After Sal went inside, Vito lowered his head and whispered to me.

Vito: "How come his mum gets so mad about us drinkin' outta the hose?"

Bobby: "I don't know. So does my mum. She thinks we're gonna get sick doin' 'at."

Again, each block had a squadron of kids who vehemently protected their home turf like a swarm of nasty yellow jackets. You never wanted to stir the nest. But in the summertime, collisions with the opposition became inevitable. With young people bursting from row houses onto crowded streets, daily feuds were commonplace. It was a way of life. Rocks, slingshots, and even bottle rockets were fair game. You were just asking for a fistfight if you wandered on foot through rival blocks in Sharpsburg. Therefore, to avoid unnecessary confrontation, Sal, Vito, and I always ventured the neighborhood on our BMX bikes. Strictly adhering to Newton's 1st Law, our wheels in motion stayed in motion.

Like many kids in small towns, we lived on our bikes all summer long. But it always seemed a little different for us. Grueling rounds of urban combat acted like a form of natural selection that hardened any young person left to defend for themself on the streets. Everyone has seen those movies based in the late '70s and early '80s about a bicycle gang of ragtags, misfits, and losers who somehow, by pure serendipity, meet up and join forces to save the world. Well, we were more like a bike gang of brazen punks who all knew each other since birth and had no problem beating up the ragtags, misfits, and losers before they even had a chance to save the world.

Survival of the fittest was a cold reality. Still, the withering heat of late August could weaken anyone. Thanks to Sal, we were zealously gulping down tall glasses of ice water. We straddled our bikes as we discussed school during our water break.

Bobby: "I hope it cools dahn by a' time school starts up again in a couple o' weeks."

Sal: "C'mon, Bobby, what's a matter with you?! Don't remind us about goin' back to 'at dump. It's still summer."

Vito: "I heard there's a lot o' scrapes up 'ere at the high school. Them older kids pick on a' new ninth graders n'at."

Vito took a big gulp from his glass and spit out some water into the street gutter. He wiped off his mouth with the back of his hand and continued.

Vito: "I ain't takin' no crap from none o' 'em jagoffs."

We were not by any stretch pure bullies who went out of our way picking fights with other kids. But we weren't exactly saints either. Also, when we weren't trying to shoot each other with BB guns, we actually played regular sports. We loved alley baseball. Tackle football on concrete was a particularly brutal pastime of ours. Mining out bits of gravel lodged deep into your elbow was a gross, but time-consuming way to combat long sermons in church. You just had to make sure none of the girls from school saw this disgusting self-performed mini surgery during Mass.

We continued to lament about the heat. Vito poured some cold water on his head. He was talking with a big ice cube in his mouth.

Vito: "School ain't so bad when it's hot. You just gotta sit in a' back o' the classroom by the fan. It's football practice 'at stinks in 'is heat. Ya know, Bobby?"

Bobby: "For real. It's horrible. And 'em helmets are the worst. I hate when my eyes start stingin' from the pourin' dahn sweat n'at."

Sal smirked back at us with strong words of encouragement.

Sal: "Then don't play, Sweathogs. Yinz suck at football anyways."

My town had a few grass ball fields to play football on, but they were usually relegated to the older, bigger teens and young adults. By now, all three of us thoroughly understood the town's hierarchy based upon physical size, age, and toughness. Located right in the middle of town next to Kennedy Park, the concrete basketball courts were unofficially off-limits to us as well. We never dared to play there against the ultra-serious neighborhood ballers. At any minute, the pushing and shoving in a hoops game could blow up into a full-fledged rumble.

Of course, we still liked to ride by the arena and watch the show.

Bobby: "Let's swing by the park 'n see what's happenin' on the basketball courts."

Sal: "Okay. Just don't look too nebby."

We slowly rolled around the tall chain-link fences that enclosed the jam-packed courts. I noticed a shifty point guard driving to the hoop. Dribbling through a gauntlet of flying elbows, he was practically mugged as he charged towards the basket. He scored a layup as he was simultaneously hip checked to the ground. Only the most violent of fouls were ever called; there basically had to be visible blood.

Observing the intense basketball games, Vito openly displayed his confidence.

Vito: "I should go show 'em all how to play."

The lead rider in our line of bikes turned around and snickered back at Vito.

Sal: "Yeah, right. You're garbage at basketball."

Vito bellowed out his return insult.

Vito: "So are you, trashball! You couldn't make a layup to save your life!"

During the day, the court had a huge boom box blasting on the sidelines that always seemed to be playing "Runnin' With the Devil" by Van Halen. I swear it was on a nonstop loop. It was our gritty little town's signature tune that summer. It felt like every kid in our neighborhood decided that this new rock band had it all figured out for us. Being bad was the best way to live. As we passed the crowded courts, you could

7

feel the thunder of Eddie Van Halen's electric guitar as David Lee Roth's cavernous voice bounced off brick walls and echoed through the streets.

At night, the courts became a haunt for drug dealers. The kingpin was easy to spot. He had long hair, and a brand-new Sony Walkman attached to the waistband of his red jogging pants. The first portable cassette player sold for $150 in 1979 (and had to be ordered from Japan). Only a teenager with a lucrative business could afford that price in Sharpsburg. Donning bulky foam headphones, the top dog had the luxury of shooting hoops while listening to his mixtape of Black Sabbath and Alice Cooper hits.

After witnessing the main event in town, we began to aimlessly patrol the narrow streets and alleyways. Now we were just spinning our wheels. We still had an hour of freedom before we had to return to our homes for dinner. Sal leaned back and lifted his entire front tire high off the ground. He pedaled slowly while popping a wheelie on his bike. At a low speed, Vito was languidly swerving from one side of the alley to the other like a worn-out sidewinder rattlesnake. I coasted behind them.

I surveyed my friends.

Bobby: "Whadda yinz wanna do now?"

Rolling ahead of us on his back wheel, Sal scoffed at my question.

Sal: "Nothin'."

Still sidewinding, Vito added to the general indolence of my meandering bike crew.

Vito: "I could do nothin' all day long."

As always, Sal punched back at Vito's comment.

Sal: "That's what ya did all *summer* long, Vito."

As I previously mentioned, in the heat of the summer, our crammed town of slender alleys and busy thruways became a battleground even without our BB guns. By the age of 14, Sal, Vito, and I were experienced veterans of the streets. We tried to avoid certain blocks altogether. But sometimes you were just plain unlucky.

Vito pointed up.

Vito: "Hey, look at the new pair o' gold high-tops just hangin' up 'ere on the line."

Sal: "You idiot! It means a drug dealer works this corner."

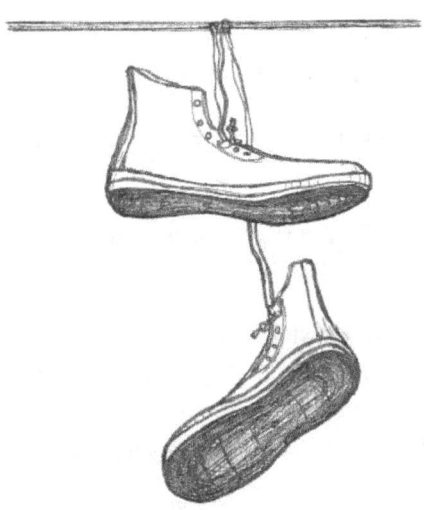

Most street-smart kids were well aware that the calling card of a drug dealer often came in the form of a pair of shoes that were tied together and flung over a telephone or electric line. However, Vito was just admiring the quality of the yellow sneakers as opposed to questioning their presence. The generic shoes imitated his favorite brand. Vito himself always sported a black pair of high-top Converse All Stars.

Vito roared back at Sal.

Vito: "I know what it means, jagoff! I was just checkin' out them kicks!"

Sal looked over Vito's head.

Sal: "Aw crap, the old burnout is comin' outside!"

Our noisy ruckus on the street prompted a large man with a balding head and thick sideburns to come out of the corner row house and greet what he thought were possible customers. Clad in just a tank top and boxer shorts, it was 4 o'clock in the afternoon but the middle-aged man appeared as though he had just woken up. With a lit cigarette in his mouth, the disheveled grump started slowly pacing toward us.

I stood up high and pumped hard on my bike pedals.

Bobby: "Hurry up, let's get outta here!"

The creepy individual stared intently at us as we pedaled away as fast as we could. We burned rubber for two whole blocks. Without thinking, I hastily turned down the next side street. The little alley abruptly halted and was surrounded on three sides by old chain-link fences. I had led us down a dead end.

Unexpectedly, there was a young teenager standing in the middle of the alley with his arms crossed.

Enemy Yinzer: "Well, well, well. What are yinz rats doin' dahn here?"

River Rats. That's what the snobby rich kids up in the affluent hills overlooking the working-class flats of Sharpsburg called us. But this fellow townie clearly spoke straight-up Yinzer and used "rats" as a neighborly term of endearment. I had a prior history with him too. On the last day of school, I completely whiffed at a pitched Wiffle Ball in gym class and my bat errantly flew out of my hands and hit him squarely between the eyes. He fell to the ground right as the bell rang to declare school's out for summer. Everyone cheered while jumping over his body and running to the buses.

From the look on his face, it seemed as though he was waiting all summer long for this very moment. Before I could reply, he squinted his eyes and pointed right at me.

Enemy Yinzer: "I 'member what you did on 'at last day o' school, twerp. And all yinz punks laughin' at me. It's about time you get what you deserve."

He obviously never forgot about the pain and suffering that I had inflicted upon him with that yellow bat. In fairness, those hard plastic Wiffle Ball bats would hurt terribly upon bodily impact. I knew this from experience. The bats made ideal lightsaber replicas for our vicious reenactments of Jedi fight scenes.

My dishonored schoolmate called out to his house for reinforcements.

Enemy Yinzer: "Hey! Yinz guys, come outside! Look who's here!"

Four more enemy soldiers stepped out from the shadows. Well, I mean, his brothers popped their heads through the torn mesh on the screen door of their aluminum-sided row house. This dead-end alley was basically their backyard. To make matters even worse, a random delivery truck stopped directly behind us, closing off the open end of the alley. The brown UPS truck literally sealed our fate.

My eyes flitted around in every direction in order to assess our situation.

Bobby: "Crap! We're trapped!"

Like young bulls to their slaughter, we had steered ourselves into a pen of rusted wire fences. From the loud clamor inside their house, you could tell that the whole family was getting ready for a showdown in the rusty corral.

Sal blamed me and Vito for our rapid turn of misfortune.

Sal: "You boneheads! Why would yinz turn dahn a dead end like 'at?"

I tried one ill-fated attempt at a parley with the enemy.

Bobby: "C'mon, Paulie. Mellow out already. It was on accident. That's all."

But grudges ran deep in our town, and this kid had an old score to settle.

Enemy Yinzer: "On accident, huh? Well, here's another accident!"

Just then, he shoved me. I toppled over my bike. My feet became twisted amongst the pedals and chain. The confrontation swiftly escalated. Vito, the largest and toughest member in our lot, jumped off his bike and pushed my foe. The skinny kid was no match for Vito and fell backwards on his butt.

I yelled as I untangled my shoelaces from my bike chain.

Bobby: "Nice one, Vito! Let's get the heck outta here!"

But there's always a bigger beast in the concrete jungle. After witnessing his brother get tossed, the oldest of the brood aggressively stormed out of the house. The 17-year-old ruffled with intimidation. Along with his ripped-up shirt and tattered jean shorts, this ugly giant had a huge head of dark brown hair and a mangy beard. Behind his back, the neighborhood kids called him "Sweetums" because of his close resemblance to the tall hairy ogre from *The Muppet Show*. Despite his gentle name, the towering Sweetums was by far Jim Henson's most fearsome Muppet character. Tempers were about to flare up in the alley like a deleted scene from the worst day ever on *Sesame Street*.

The bearded creature got in Vito's face. Standing toe to toe, he roared out a question that nearly parroted his younger brother.

Ogre Yinzer: "What are yinz rats doin' on our street?"

Vito: "Whatever we want, jagoff! What are you dirtbags gonna do 'bout it?"

The two largest adversaries in the alley each exchanged a stiff push. Vito spit his gum onto the street. This meant that he was serious. After a more forceful shove was delivered by each rival, the angry banter kept up.

Ogre Yinzer: "What am *I* gonna do? You gotta be frickin' jaggin' me!"

Vito: "Shut up before I mop this street with your hairy frickin' head!"

Vito held a slight resemblance to Lou Ferrigno, the bodybuilder/actor who, at that time, played the massive green superhuman on *The Incredible Hulk* television show. When Vito got mad, we called him Hulk. Like the flip of a switch, one final shove to his chest transformed Vito into his Hulk mode. His eyes turned beady. His fists clenched in fury. Now it looked like Sweetums versus the Hulk on 19th Street.

Ogre Yinzer: "You wanna go, tough guy?"

Vito: "You're done, jagoff!"

Ding! The steel cage match had officially commenced. Vito and the hairy ogre began to clobber each other with pummeling roundhouses. An all-out riot ensued. A line of three younger siblings immediately streamed out of the row house. They pushed out of the door in single file like it was a factory assembly line that produced brand-new Yinzers by the second. The two smallest brothers jumped on Sal's back. He had to spin like a violent tornado to throw them off. Vito's upright boxing bout degraded into a tangled wrestling scrum on the concrete. It became the kind of dirty street scrap where kids were rolling around in balls of fisticuffs like tumbleweeds in the desert. Just after I threw a one-two combo into the gut of the enemy who knocked me off my bike, we heard a loud, but familiar sound.

Police Car Siren: "Woop-woop!"

On this steaming hot day, every Yinzer kid in the alley froze like a bunch of cold popsicles. Sitting at the end of the narrow street was a white Ford Torino police car topped with brightly spinning red and blue lights. The cop probably had no intention of getting out of his car. He just wanted the backstreet brawl to end. Besides, most kid skirmishes at that time were just bare-knuckled and rarely escalated to the use of deadly weapons. But even so, our street-kid instincts were too hard to suppress.

Sal: "SCRAM!"

In a free-for-all, every combatant took off in every possible direction. We scattered like free candy from a busted piñata. Within the chaos, I scrambled over a fence and squeezed through a small walkway between two row houses. The skinny path was blocked by a large, foul-smelling garbage can that I knocked over in a panic. I dashed through sheets pinned on a clothesline, hurdled over a white picket fence, and scampered down an alley. I turned left and kept on sprinting down Middle Street. I looked back and there was no one behind me. I was all alone, but I was safe.

I slowed down to a relaxed pace. That's when my true enemy appeared. My jaw dropped when I saw him. I spoke softly to myself.

Bobby: "Oh, no... Duke."

It was Duke. The bane of my existence since I was a little kid.

And Duke wasn't human. He was a monster in the form of a large stray dog who roamed the streets like he owned them. He was a mixed breed who appeared to be part German Shepherd, part Collie, and part hound from hell. He actually had a nice shiny coat of brown and black fur on him, probably from a well-balanced diet of unfortunate street kids. At first, I thought he didn't notice me. I stood motionless in the middle of the one-way street. But then his ears stood at attention and his eyes lit up. He crinkled his nose and emitted a nasty growl.

Duke: "Grrr!"

    It seemed like there were more stray dogs prowling around back in the '70s. I guess the local police had more important issues to deal with than rounding up loose animals, like keeping an eye on that dude playing basketball with the first ever Walkman. Along with Duke, Sharpsburg was also home to Kinger, an old gray German Shepherd, and Jake, an immense albino shepherd with pink eyes. Everyone in town knew these stray canines by name. We often wondered who even named them in the first place. All the dogs were well known for their nasty dispositions. But by far, the most aggressive stray was Duke. Duke was a predator of kids. Glaring right at me, the big dog snarled and bared his teeth. Then he bellowed out one loud warning call as he pushed off the asphalt with all four legs.

Duke: "Rrrt!"

    The beastly mutt began to race straight towards me down the empty street. He undoubtedly recognized me. His favorite meal. In no time at all, Duke was in a full gallop. His long flowing hair danced around him with each stride. Like a wanted man from a hound, I started booking it in the opposite direction. To Duke, this gesture meant "game on" and he began chasing after me with even more ferocity. The mad dash in full gear, Duke's barks grew even more tenacious.

Duke: "Rrrt! Rrrt!"

An embarrassing inability to properly deal with canines was always the Achilles Heel of my youth. Like young people often do, I blamed my parents for my greatest weakness. In particular, I blamed my incredibly tidy mother for my instinctive fear of dogs. She was a neat freak who never wanted to have pets in her immaculately clean house. My father once brought home a cute Beagle puppy, but it didn't last an hour before she made him return the poor pup. She would never let us keep the feral kittens that we would rescue from our alley either. Even having a pet goldfish was short-lived. For two fleeting days, we had a loopy goldfish with long flowy fins that used to like to jump out of its fishbowl. We named it Sister Goldenhair. Of course, we had no idea if this fish was a boy or girl, but the name seemed fitting. After one unlucky leap from the bowl to the ground below, my mother ran over the family pet with the sweeper (vacuum cleaner). I'll never forget the muffled sound of that poor goldfish being sucked up the hose from off our orange shag carpet. As we sadly emptied out the bag of mangled debris, my little sister cried at the carnage.

At any rate, most children in Sharpsburg knew to never run from an approaching stray dog. My friends all had puppies and learned early on that a dog will naturally pursue anything that rushes away from it. The canine has an innate hunting instinct to chase prey. Whenever we encountered the ferocious Duke, my friends would hold their ground and stand motionless as if a live T-Rex were approaching us. However, unlike Vito and Sal, I would dart away from Duke every time that he made a charge. Duke would always attack the clueless idiot who fled from the safety of the herd. I was that clueless idiot. It was a viciously painful lesson every time. Duke would usually bite my arm or leg. I have a few battle scars from this type of urban warfare as well. Luckily, after a quick taste he would lose interest and move on to his next unsuspecting victim one block over.

Duke was gaining ground on me and woofed out one last mean warning.

Duke: "Rrrt!"

Scientists claim that dogs were first domesticated from wild wolves over 10,000 years ago in East Asia. From these fierce pack hunters, humans have bred many different breeds to serve many different purposes. But Sharpsburg was far from Siberia. And this was not the Stone Age. I had a serious problem right here and now on my own street with a live dog that was selectively bred to chase morons. I continued to motor down Cecil Street towards my house. In full stride, Duke had now made up the difference of one full block between us and I could feel him right on my heels. His nails scraped against the hard pavement. He snarled like a hungry wolf catching up to a helpless fawn on an episode of *Mutual of Omaha's Wild Kingdom*.

Duke: "Clank! Grrr!"

Duke had taken his first chomping bite at me but somehow missed. I heard his razor-sharp teeth clank against each other as his jaw snapped shut. He growled in disgust. I could feel the heat of him breathing down my neck now. I yelled in disdain at Duke as if the vicious dog could actually understand me.

Bobby: "I hate you, Duke! I frickin' hate you!"

As I crossed over 18th Street at top speed, I was almost hit by a white Volkswagen Beetle. As the Herbie lookalike honked its horn and slammed on its brakes, I juked around the Bug and zipped down the home stretch. Using my momentum, I sprang and slid on my hip across the long yellow hood of our parked family station wagon. I was right outside of my row house now. I launched myself off the sidewalk in order to hurdle over my front fence. I managed to swing one leg over the top rail. That's when my archnemesis finally caught up to me.

Bobby: "Owww!"

Duke bit my butt and ripped off my back left pocket as I toppled over the chain-link fence. Luckily, the bite wasn't that bad, thanks again to my thick blue jeans. Part of the standard issue uniform for urban warfare, we wore our jeans even on hot summer days to protect us from air rifle guns, jaggerbushes (Yinzer for thornbushes), greasy bicycle chains, and stray dogs. My leather Nike high-tops helped too.

Speaking of threads, the iconic bell-bottom pants of the '60s and '70s were beginning to phase out of style with young people by late 1979. Most kids wore straight legged jeans that had just a slight flare at the bottom. The status quo ensemble for both Yinzer boys and girls were tight T-shirts, Levi jeans, and an ample amount of hair. Even the shortest haircut for boys sat over the ears. And it was not uncommon for teenage girls to have long hair down to the waist.

As I stood safely behind my front fence, Duke shook his head and spit out some small threads from my blue jeans that were still in his mouth.

Duke: "Pfft."

After another successful hunt, Duke trotted away with his tail wagging. He didn't even look back at me. While he basked in triumphant glory, I quickly regained my composure from the embarrassing chase. I brushed off the dirt from my Pirates T-shirt and marched into my house with what was left of my dignity after a long day of battle. As I flung open the front door, I could smell that dinner was ready.

My mother warmly greeted me.

Mom: "Hey, Bobby. What did yinz boys do today?"

After a grueling day of being shot, pushed, punched, pursued, and bitten, I said what every American kid tells their concerned mother.

Bobby: "Nothin'."

She shrugged and continued.

Mom: "Okay, redd up and worsh your hands. Your spaghetti is gettin' cold."

Ignoring my mother's hygienic wishes, I took off my wristbands and threw them on the kitchen table. I immediately skittered into my regular chair next to my youngest brother. (Without fail, everyone always sat in the same seat at the dinner table. Your spot never deviated.) I began to scarf down my pasta dinner.

My mother cried out with her most oft-spoken phrase.

Mom: "Hey, I didn't raise yinz in a barn!"

She pointed at the dirty sweatbands. After getting scolded for my messy table manners, I promptly followed her orders and swiped them up. Eating quietly, my younger siblings all smiled. Every kid enjoys watching someone besides themself get in trouble with their mother. I lowered my head in apology and mumbled through a mouthful of spaghetti.

Bobby: "Sorry, Mum."

I grew up in a typical household in Sharpsburg. We were above the poverty line, but just by a pinch. My father worked in a small steel fabrication factory that sat just one block away. Sometimes, Vito, Sal, and I would perch on our bikes at the truck entrance and watch him weld together huge industrial fans that were used to ventilate and cool even bigger steel mills in Pittsburgh. We would marvel in awe from afar as large bits of hot molten steel would spray all over him. His welding suit covered in burn marks was evidence of his dangerous blue-collar job. My father was literally a Pittsburgh "steeler."

I guess I should explain the terms "blue collar" and "working class." A blue-collar occupation pertains to manual or industrial labor that does not require a college education. Most blue-collar folks from Sharpsburg worked in a local mill or manufacturing plant of some sort. Some worked down on the railway depot. Others would travel to coal mines in neighboring towns around Western Pennsylvania. Coal was essential. It was needed for smelting iron ore and its carbon used in mixing with the iron to make a harder, stronger substance we call steel.

The working class refers to those who live at a socio-economic level situated below the middle class and far below the upper class. In 1979, Pittsburgh still had a robust working-class community. The steel industry employed a large bulk of these workers. These Yinzer men and women had created the steel used to make everything from the Empire State Building to the Pennsylvania Railroad. At one point, well over half of the nation's steel was produced in the Pittsburgh region alone. Untold legions of laborers worked hard in local factories to manufacture the steel products we needed to win many conflicts from the American Civil War to World War II.

While finishing up supper, I whipped out a penny from my pocket to show my younger siblings.

Bobby: "Hey, guys, look at this penny I got. Pap gave it to me."

My little brother shook his head at me.

Bryan: "That ain't a penny. Pennies are brahn."

My skeptical brother noticed that the penny did not have a typical copper-brown color. I held up the penny and spun it around with an exaggerated display.

Bobby: "It's got Abe Lincoln on it! As yinz can clearly see, it's a penny!"

My brother squinted his eyes at the coin.

Bryan: "Nuh-uh! That ain't no penny, Bobby!"

I held the shiny gray coin right in my little brother's face.

Bobby: "No? Look. This one's made o' steel. Get a load o' this."

I put the penny down on the kitchen table. I quickly got up and yanked a Steelers magnet off our yellow fridge. Then I slowly waved the magnet over the penny.

Bobby: "Abracadabra!"

The little penny leapt up from the table through a full inch of air and stuck to the magnet. My siblings raised their eyebrows. To my younger sister, this was pure magic.

Brandy: "Neato! Can I try, Bobby?"

Bobby: "Whoosh! Here you go, miss."

I handed the coin over to her like a great magician would at his magic parlor. My amazed little sister couldn't wait to test the invisible force of magnetism. At only 8 years old, the simple things in life were often the most fun for her.

Brandy: "Thanks, Bobby!"

She closely inspected the penny and then set it on the table.

Brandy: "Okay, lemme try this. Gimme the magnet."

My favorite keepsake that summer was that penny. I always carried it on me. It was made of pure steel. Why would a penny be made from steel? At the height of World War II, precious copper was conserved for the huge war effort. It was vital in making shells for bullets and wiring for tanks, planes, and ships. So copper was scarce. But steel from Pittsburgh was plentiful. Unlike the typical bronze penny of that time, the 1943 steel penny was silver in color and was magnetic. My grandfather, a veteran of that war, gave me the coin as a gift. He knew that I loved interesting relics of history. I was the kind of kid who liked to keep a small item like this in my jeans pocket, partly as a memento and partly as a self-perceived token of good luck.

My sister picked up the steel penny with the magnet.

Brandy: "Wow, it works! Look, guys!"

My brothers smiled in wonder. My mother grinned at her young daughter. However, after another exhausting day in the mill, my father ate quietly at the head of the table and paid no attention to our impromptu "dinner and a magic show."

Brandy: "Thanks, Bobby. Here's your penny back."

At first cynical about my claim, my younger brother now aimed to conduct a simple science experiment of his own. He wanted to analyze the magnetic steel penny versus a non-magnetic copper penny.

Bryan: "Wait. Lemme try somethin' here. Mum, do you got a regular penny to compare n'at?"

Mom: "Yeah, take one from the Swear Jar up on a' counter."

Due to my father's constant battle with the leaky faucet, a labeled "Swear Jar" over the kitchen sink was packed with a generous portion of pennies.

Bryan: "Oh, yeah! That jar's full 'cause o' Dad."

Pennies were being pinched in almost every home in Sharpsburg. Economists rank the 1970s as one of the poorest times in America outside of the Great Depression. But for kids, it just became the new normal. For instance, most of us never thought twice about having a wardrobe made up entirely of hand-me-downs. It was pretty common for a T-shirt to get passed down from one child to another and another in a family until it basically disintegrated. Many of us sported the same exact outfit every day. My summer uniform included my white Pirates T-shirt with the number 21 on the back, Wrangler jeans, plain white Nike Blazers with a black swoosh, and black Pirates wristbands. I got the wristbands from a free promotional giveaway on "Buc Night" when Pirates tickets were $1 at Three Rivers Stadium. That was the only game of the year that my father could afford to bring his four children. Like most kids in my neighborhood, I had never been to a Steelers game. Tickets for the whole family would be far out of our price range. Only fathers would attend Steelers games with their buddies from the mill, usually by way of tickets that trickled down from the boss.

The average fridge on our block had plenty of magnets on the outside but little food on the inside. We had to scrounge for breakfast and lunch (maybe a chipped ham sandwich), but we usually had a decent meal for dinner. However, supper at my house was almost always spaghetti with marinara sauce. If we were lucky, we would have sauce with actual meat in it. To kill the monotony of spaghetti every night, my siblings and I would try to add anything to spice it up. Garlic salt, red pepper flakes, even Heinz ketchup if my mother wasn't looking. Once in a blue moon we went out to eat. This was only on a special occasion like a birthday. It was typically a stand-alone Italian restaurant in town because – after the Dairy Queen shut down – Sharpsburg had no national chains, and still does not to this day.

After our meal, I asked a loaded question to my mother as I was putting my plate in the kitchen sink.

Bobby: "So, what's for dinner tomorra night, Mum?"

She didn't look at me but responded like all parents do.

Mom: "We'll see… "

Of course, I knew it would be spaghetti all over again. In my house, the after-dinner routine included a short round of playtime for my siblings. At age 14, I would only occasionally check in with my little brothers and sister playing upstairs in the attic of our row house. As I climbed up the steps, I could feel the heat of the attic playroom coupled with the sound of a heated argument.

Billy: "It's your fault, Bryan! You had one o' your bratty temper tantrums and threw the marbles everywhere last time."

Bryan: "That's 'cause Brandy steals all the marbles and feeds 'em hippos with her hands!"

Brandy: "I'm allowed, buttface! I'm younger than yinz!"

Bryan: "Yeah, by two years, not ten! Little baby!"

We had one new game that we loved because all four of us could play against each other at the same time, Hungry Hungry Hippos by Hasbro toys. However, our favorite Christmas present was in disarray after more than eight months of intense use. One hippo's upper jaw had snapped off and gone missing. Likewise, the bulk of the marbles were long lost due to the game's inescapable combination of Murphy's Law and Chaos Theory.

With my hands out, I interjected myself into the family feud.

Bobby: "All right. All right. All right. Then let's play Star Wars instead."

My little sister was excited that I even wanted to play with her.

Brandy: "Okay, Bobby! I'll get 'em out."

In the late 1970s, the *Star Wars* movie franchise exploded into the American psyche. When the original film debuted in 1977, it immediately became box-office gold. From its breathtaking battle scenes to its marvelous musical score, fans became obsessed with the space opera centering around unlikely heroes caught up in a galactic civil war. The immense popularity of Star Wars merchandise created a new crazed demand from kids across the country. The amount of Star Wars toys in a household quickly became a financial metric that you could use to judge a family's wealth. Even working-class kids could afford to have a few Star Wars toys. My younger brothers, Billy and Bryan, and my sister, Brandy, would come to cherish our first four Star Wars figurines. I had Han Solo. Billy had C-3PO. Bryan had Chewbacca. And Brandy had Princess Leia. We were hoping for Darth Vader to join the group after our next trip to Murphy's Mart.

Following our 100th spaghetti dinner in a row, we started playing with our action figures. Like everyone did, we would have make-believe adventures with our little plastic figurines produced by Kenner Toys. We pretended that we were trying to escape from the Death Star. However, after just a few minutes of play, it was obvious that we were trying hard to reenact an epic scene with a noticeably limited supply of Star Wars characters. We didn't even have Luke Skywalker or R2-D2 to round out the flight crew. This gave my siblings something new to lament about.

Brandy: "This stinks, guys. We only got four o' them. My friend Rebecca from school said she's got twelve Star Wars figures already."

I rolled my eyes.

Bobby: "Sure she does. Her name is Rebecca."

"Rebecca" was a rich girl's name. A girl with that birth name in Sharpsburg would be called "Becky" as soon as she stepped off her front porch.

My little brother chimed in next.

Bryan: "Mike and Dave Henderson got a Millennium Falcon. It's awesome. It even makes sounds."

He sighed and continued while staring sadly at the floor.

Bryan: "We'll never get one o' those."

The Millennium Falcon was the tour de force of the Star Wars toy collection. The huge plastic spaceship had a retail price of $29.99 when it debuted that year. That would correlate to well over $100 in today's money accounting for inflation. After a dog-day afternoon on the streets, I had heard enough of their complaints. My frustration boiled over and I belted out at my brother in our hot attic playroom.

Bobby: "Will yinz shut up already?! I'm gonna punch both 'em spoilt rich brats right in a' nose!"

I made one big roundhouse punching motion and punched the support beam in the middle of the attic. Yelling in mumbled Yinzer, it appeared as though I thought it was entirely possible to punch two stuck-up rich kids in their respective noses with just one swing. Even more outrageous would be if the Henderson brothers shared one common nose. But my intentions were fully understood by my Yinzer siblings.

Bryan quickly cheered up.

Bryan: "Thanks, Bobby! I always hated Mike and Dave anyways."

That evening, we got resourceful and managed to construct an improvised model of the Millennium Falcon out of cardboard. Using an old pizza box from our neighbor's trash along with the aid of scissors and masking tape, our spaceship's shape looked surprisingly similar. With a lack of toys, our creative imaginations became an important asset. We all learned how to make do with what we had (or didn't have).

Of course, every working-class Yinzer kid did have one treasured belonging. This was usually a birthday gift or Christmas present that you miraculously received after your father got a nice bonus from the mill. Mine came thanks to the layaway plan at K-Mart. My prized possession was my royal blue BMX. (BMX stands for bicycle motocross.) Currently, my beloved bike sat abandoned on 19th Street after a long day of getting shot, pushed, punched, pursued, and bitten. Not to mention, there was that little brush with the local police. I purposely waited until the safety of near nightfall to retrieve my indispensable bicycle.

I asked my father for assistance. He was a blue-collar man of few words.

Bobby: "Hey, Dad, can we take the car out and go 'n get my bike? It's up on 19th Street."

Dad: "Yeah. Why's it up 'ere, Bobby?"

I had my falsified excuse lined up and ready.

Bobby: "Oh, see, we were playin' a pick-up baseball game dahn at Heinz ball field. And this one kid got all scraped up from slidin' into second. His leg and knee n'at was bleedin' real bad. It was gross. So, I let him ride my bike back to his place."

Dad: "Okay. Let's go now before it gets dark."

Bobby: "Thanks, Dad."

Normally, a street kid would never leave his or her bike lying unattended blocks away in the middle of an alley. It would be stolen within minutes. But a good scare from the cops always had a way of cleaning up a messy street. Everyone involved knew not to return to the scene of the crime, at least for a few hours until the dust settled. So, with the alleyway tainted by the earlier police presence, I assumed that my bike would be left untouched. It was akin to a mother robin not going back to the nest if her eggs were overly handled by a prodding human hand. Contrary to common myth, the bird will return but only if she is assured that the meddling humans are long gone. Like the robin, I was safely waiting until the coast was clear.

As we drove to get my bike, not a single word was said. We pulled down 19th Street and parked at the alleyway entrance in the same spot where the police car siren had broken up our late afternoon melee. Shadows in the alley grew long as the red sun was beginning to dip below the rooftops. I pointed to my fallen bicycle.

Bobby: "There it is, Dad. Right where he said he would leave it."

Dad: "Okay, go and put it in a' back o' the car. Let's get home."

I hopped out and grabbed my bike. After sliding it into the back of the station wagon, I slammed the rear door shut. Relief. I had to fight to contain my smile.

As soon as I jumped back into my seat, I quickly changed the subject to eliminate any further suspicion from my father.

Bobby: "So, who are the Pirates playin' tonight, Dad?"

Dad: "Oh, the Bucs? They got the Phillies tonight. It's away, at Veterans Stadium."

He turned on the car radio and tuned in to the game with a spin of the dial.

Dad: "Let's hear what the score is."

The booming deep voice of Lanny Frattare, the Pirates radio broadcaster, completely washed away the chance of any more discussion about the awkward bike retrieval. Looking back, I'm sure that my father could tell that I was lying. But he seemed simply pleased to be spending a few minutes on a quick ride with his oldest son after a long shift in the mill. After all, he grew up in Sharpsburg too. Just like me, he was a veteran of urban warfare.

Chapter 2: We Are Family

It was a beautiful day in the neighborhood. A chorus of songbirds celebrated the rising August sun. But time was slipping into the future. After enjoying three months of complete freedom, I dreaded the inevitable end of summer break. There was a sense of urgency now with the first day of high school rapidly approaching. I didn't want to waste one precious minute. As warm morning rays shined down upon us, Vito and I were already awake and patrolling the streets earlier than usual. Sal liked to sleep in late, so we forced the issue and rode over to his house.

Bobby: "We only got a few more days o' summer left. Let's go see if Sal's up."

Vito grinned and wiggled his eyebrows up and down.

Vito: "Yeah, maybe his sister's up, too!"

Sal had the only backyard on the entire block with a decent amount of grass, so we liked hanging out there. In contrast, my tiny "yard" was a fenced-in slab of concrete with patches of dandelions growing up through the cracks. We often played highly competitive soccer games on Sal's lush, green lawn. With so many Italian immigrant kids in the neighborhood, the sport of soccer was taken very seriously.

But the star attraction for me and Vito was definitely not soccer, or even our friend Sal. We leaned our bikes against the fence and stepped through the gate.

Vito: "Mamma mia! Look, Bobby! She's layin' out again."

Vito bit his hand like Lenny from *Laverne & Shirley*. My jaw dropped.

Bobby: "Holy crap!"

Sal's older sister, Sofia, was tanning in her bright yellow string bikini. She had olive skin. She had long, wavy light brown hair. She was 18. She was curvy. She was perfect. It was the only thing all the boys in town could agree upon.

Lying out in a folding lounge chair in the center of the grass lot framed by red rose bushes, Sofia bathed in the bright sun wearing oversized sunglasses like the kind TV stars like Farrah Fawcett wore on *Charlie's Angels*. She was listening to Donna Summer loudly belting out "Hot Stuff" from a little transistor radio. In the 1970s, Donna Summer was known as the "Queen of Disco," but this new song rocked more than her earlier hits. With the radio blaring, Vito and I had stopped cold in our tracks and were staring at Sofia in awe. We stood frozen in a trance at the garden gate next to the stone statue of the Virgin Mary. It was as if an artisan had wasted time chiseling lesser statues of two idiot teenage boys.

Sal: "What are yinz jagoffs lookin' at?"

Sal had come up from behind and startled us. In a panic, Vito and I quickly unfroze.

Vito: "Oh… oh nothin', Sal."

Bobby: "Yeah… uh… we just like this song, 'at's all."

Sal was more than skeptical.

Sal: "Donna Summer. Yinz two like Donna Summer's music?"

Without hesitation we both answered him.

Vito/Bobby: "Yeah."

After getting busted for gawking at Sal's sister, I swiftly changed the subject and suggested we head over to Nina's Italian Market for a little shopping.

Bobby: "C'mon, guys, we need our mornin' snack. Let's go to Nina's."

We jumped on our bikes and headed off. Nina, a mousy older woman, was both the manager and owner of the small, well-kept shop. Although it served fresh Italian groceries and deli foods, we always went for the candy. Her prices were hard to beat. Sal lifted his hands from his handlebars and rubbed them together greedily.

Sal: "Nina's got the best five-finger discounts in tahn."

By now you might have the impression that my little neighborhood was nothing but a teenage wasteland of dirty alleys controlled by menacing gangs of street urchins. But this was just a natural part of a seasonal cycle in Sharpsburg. Come late August, the relentless heat coupled with the unbridled freedom of summer break would bring out the worst in the town's large population of young people. However, once school started up again, an unspoken truce was set between each block. The peace treaty lasted all winter, except for the occasional snowball fight. So, unlike the colorful fight scenes between rival street gangs in the 1979 cult classic movie *The Warriors*, our town was, for the most part, a stable home to many extended families.

And most of those families came from one place. We biked past an older man stomping up and down inside a small, wooden barrel in his yard. He was in the process of crushing fresh grapes with his bare feet. As he danced in circles with his pants rolled up to his knees, his wife was handpicking yellow grapes from a garden vine and pouring them into the half-barrel. It was like a scene right out of an old Italian movie.

Sal: "Looks like the Ferragamos are makin' a new batch o' wine."

Vito: "I wonder if it'll smell like feet."

In those days, the borough of Sharpsburg truly was a Little Italy. As a matter of fact, according to the U.S. Post Office, Sharpsburg had the highest percentage of Italian last names of any ZIP Code in America. Most households on my block spoke Italian as their first language. However, being third and fourth-generation Italian Americans, my household spoke only English... well, the Yinzer form at least. When talking to the older, immigrant Italian residents in town, I would improvise and speak the basics like "Ciao" (Hello or Goodbye), "Come stai?" (How are you?), and "Buon giorno" (Good morning). I was decent at faking my limited comprehension of the Italian language. However, when I would go over to visit Vito or Sal, everyone in their homes spoke solely in Italian to one another, and I would have to pick out the important words. "Andiamo!" (Let's go!) was the most common one from Sal after his mother would yell at us in Italian to get out of her kitchen and go play outside.

Like most second-generation Italian Americans, Sal and Vito spoke English at all times outside of the house. That was essential for me because we needed to clearly communicate the details of our elaborate missions, like the one that lay immediately ahead. We were at the deli market now and ready to grab an early snack. We put down our bikes and paused outside of the tiny storefront.

Sal clapped his hands together.

Sal: "Okay. What's our plan of attack today, boys?"

Vito: "Make a big mess and steal everythin' as usual?"

Bobby: "Nah. Nina's on to us, guys. She knows we've been tryin' to distract her by knockin' over stuff."

Sal: "Yeah, we're on the radar. She's seen one too many phony spills n'at. We need a better strategy now."

We would use multiple diversions to trick Nina and lure her away from checking to see if we were stealing candy in her little market on Middle Street. The best distraction technique was what I called "The Accident." For example, Vito would "accidentally" brush over a stocked pile of diced tomato cans in the back of the store. Vito was large and bumbling at times, so this seemed perfectly plausible. The loud crash of the cans on the hard tile floor would frighten Nina, causing pure panic and disorder in her little, well-organized market. This created the perfect cover. While Vito would courteously help Nina restock the tomato cans in the rear of the store, Sal and I would rob her blind up at the front counter. We would quickly fill our jeans pockets with our favorite sweets. Snickers and Clark bars were the easiest to smoothly slide into your front pockets. Hershey's bars, with their big rectangular shape, were a little tougher to conceal. We stayed away from snack-size potato chip bags, like Doritos and Lays, because they made a loud crunching sound when you handled them and tried to stuff them in your pockets. Remember, this was well before security cameras were positioned in every convenience store in America.

But Nina was beginning to catch on and was keeping close tabs on us now. In fact, she would have her husband noticeably reorganize shelves near the back of the store to try and deter "the accident" from happening. We needed a new game plan. Luckily, I had already come prepared by grabbing as many pennies as I could from the Swear Jar at my house before I left this morning. I proposed Operation Money Drop.

Bobby: "Okay. Here's the plan. Yinz go 'n wander 'round the store and look at random stuff. Even pick up cans and act like you're readin' the labels n'at."

Vito: *"That's it?* That's your plan?"

Bobby: "No. That's just a smokescreen. 'At'll get the heat o' Nina's husband off me and on to you guys. He'll follow you two around and hover over yinz like a fly on crap. Meanwhile, I'm gonna grab a Snickers bar from the wall o' candy, go up to the counter all innocent lookin' and pull out my change to pay for it. But I'm gonna act all clumsy and fumble big time as I pull out all o' the pennies from both o' my front pockets. I'll make sure the coins spill over the counter and on a' floor on her side. When Nina gets dahn beneath the counter and picks up 'em coins, I'm gonna swipe two more Snickers bars from the little shelves in front o' the cash register for yinz."

Sal: "Huh. Solid plan, Bobby. It takes care of them two birds with one stone."

Vito was confused.

Vito: "Wait. Who are da two birds?"

Sal: "Them two pigeons over there."

Sal sarcastically pointed at two busy pigeons pecking on the sidewalk.

Vito: "Really?"

Sal flailed his hands up in the air.

Sal: "Mamma mia! You dummy, the two birds are Nina 'n her husband!"

Vito's eyes widened.

Vito: "Oh! Okay, I get it now. We're gonna trick 'em both. 'At is a good plan, Bobby."

I smiled proudly and continued.

Bobby: "The best part is I'm actually gonna pay for my Snickers bar, so it makes everything look on the up 'n up. I came up with a name for this one too. We're callin' it Operation Money Drop."

Sal squinted with devious eyes.

Sal: "Nice! I like it. Let's do this."

With the mission orders revealed and accepted, we all strutted into Nina's Italian Market with purpose. Nina was tending to a customer at the front counter. Her old, bronze cash register made a loud sound as it opened. The high-pitched metallic ring echoed throughout the store.

Cash Register: "Cha-ching!"

The loud ring acted as our cue. Sal and Vito nodded to me and began to randomly trudge around the grocery store like complete idiots. Nina's elderly husband followed them around with a watchful eye. It was terribly obvious that he was faking a sweep up of the immaculate store with his little broom barely touching the floor.

Vito fully embraced his role and acted like a food inspector. He picked up a big metal can from a high shelf in the back of the store. Loudly reading the back label, he pretended like he wanted to be absolutely certain about the contents inside a can of tomatoes.

Vito: "Ingredients: Tomatoes. Okay. Looks good."

I went along with the act. I exaggerated the placement of my hand to my chin as I widely surveyed the big display of candy on the back wall. After pretending like I was making a difficult decision, I grabbed one Snickers bar from the wall of sweets. I went up to the front counter with my candy bar and smiled innocently at tiny Nina. Unlike Vito and Sal, I was shorter and younger looking for my age and the older Italian ladies in town would still try to pinch my cheeks.

Nina leaned over the counter.

Nina: "Hello, young man. Can I help you?"

I politely smiled.

Bobby: "Uh, yeah, I'm just gettin' a Snickers bar."

I nonchalantly put the Snickers bar up on the counter. Then, with both hands, I reached into my front pockets and clumsily pulled out two giant wads of pennies. I had already placed my beloved steel penny in my back pocket so that it would not get mixed up in the scam.

Bobby: "Uh, how much is it?"

As I asked the price, I allowed the coins to spill out over the front checkout. Scrambling after coins that rolled over the ledge of the wooden counter, a disgruntled Nina answered back to me.

Nina: "Twenty five cents."

Suddenly, our well-concocted scheme hit a major snag. Just as the pennies were rolling around the floor in every direction, Father Vasco, the local priest from our Catholic Church, shuffled into the market. As to be predicted, in our small town, he knew everyone well. In fact, he knew just about everything there was to know about my entire family. He baptized me and my three siblings. He presided over the marriage of my parents, and both sets of grandparents. Heck, he probably sat on the boat next to my great-grandfather on the voyage from Italy to Ellis Island. These days, the elderly priest had to rely on the aid of a wooden cane to get around.

Father Vasco immediately recognized me and pleasantly smiled.

Father Vasco: "Hey, Bobby. How you doin'?"

Bobby: "Oh! I'm great, Father… uh, just gettin' a candy bar. How ya doin'?"

Father Vasco: "I'm doin' well. I just need a shaker of parmesan cheese."

I began to nervously nod my head up and down.

Bobby: "Nice. I… I love cheese. 'Specially parmesan. It's my favorite… for sure."

After strangely confessing my fondness for cheese to my priest, there was a long awkward pause. My evil plan of thievery was now straining on me and my Catholic guilt. My priest nodded.

Father Vasco: "Okay, Bobby. Have a nice day."

Bobby: "You too, Father."

As he slowly lumbered away to find his parmesan, I paid for just the one candy bar and legally at that. My nefarious ploy was completely foiled by divine intervention. I hurriedly rushed outside of the store. Vito and Sal exited the market behind me.

Sal: "What happened? Did ya get the candy?"

Bobby: "Are yinz kiddin' me?! Father Vasco was standin' right there. *Steal candy in front of our priest.* I might as well just punch my ticket straight to Hell!"

Even though they understood my predicament, my friends still looked disappointed about the botched mission. Operation Money Drop was a total failure. I shook my head in dismay as I unwrapped the single Snickers bar.

Bobby: "I'm done with stealin' these."

After vowing to stop my thieving ways, I broke the candy bar in half and gave a piece each to Vito and Sal. They both smiled.

Vito: "Thanks, Bobby."

Sal: "You really are tryin' to make a case for them lettin' you into Heaven someday."

After God had intervened Himself into our morning, we decided to be on our best behavior. We stayed on our bikes and reveled in the sun-soaked day on this final leg of summer break. Sometimes, I loved just cruising around and waving hello to all my relatives in town. My entire extended family lived within a ten-block radius from each other. Most were only a stone's throw away. Four generations resided on my street alone. It was here I spotted the most important member of my family.

Bobby: "Hold on, guys. I wanna say hi to my Big Nana."

I stopped my bike to greet my great-grandmother on my father's side. Standing on her front porch, my family's beloved matriarch was gently watering her clay flowerpots that were bursting with black and yellow pansies along with marigolds. Everyone in our town referred to their grandmother as "nana." Pronounced "nuh-nuh" with soft a's, it is the more affectionate variant of the formal Italian word "nonna." In my family, we called our great-grandmother "Big Nana." In contrast to her moniker, she was anything but big. She stood at just 4 feet 9 inches tall. She had a dark olive skin tone and pale white hair. Unlike many Italian widows in Sharpsburg, she did not wear a black dress in mourning for her late husband. She always wore a powder blue dress and a dainty pearl necklace with pure class. From her daily facial treatment with a light layer of olive oil, she had a glowing complexion. She was from another era and obviously spoke full Italian.

Big Nana: "Buon giorno, Bobby. How ya doin'?"

Bobby: "Good. I just stopped by to say hi real fast."

I kissed my great-grandmother on the cheek. By the way, if you don't kiss an older female Italian relative upon greeting them, then they become terribly offended.

Big Nana: "Oh, okay. You be good boys today. Ciao, love you."

Bobby: "We will. Love you, Nana."

Blowing her a playful kiss for good measure, Vito added on.

Vito: "Love you too, Nana."

After the fiasco that was Operation Money Drop, we were acting like little angels. Although he was joking about having a kindred connection with my great-grandmother, Vito and I probably were distantly related. With our Mediterranean looks, Vittorio Calabresi, Salvatore Argento, and Robert Connemara could have easily passed for cousins. All three of us had tan skin and dark hair. Actually, it seemed like half of the town was related to each other. In fact, the majority of Italians in Sharpsburg came from one tiny village in Southern Italy called San Pietro in the region of Calabria. On a map, that's in the toe tip of the boot that makes up the Italian peninsula. I was amazed to learn that my great-grandfather, Big Nana's spouse, sold his small vineyard overlooking the crystal-clear waters of the Mediterranean Sea to move to Pittsburgh. But he saw more opportunity in America than in the Old World.

Sal saw an opportunity of his own up ahead at the park in the middle of town.

Sal: "Hey, look! The sprinkler's on! Let's do a ride by!"

On a hot summer day, the water spray tubes at Gerardi Park would be turned on by the local firefighters who let loose water from a fire hydrant for the little kids to enjoy. Only a few homes in town had air conditioning, so this was by far the best way to beat the summer heat. Masses of tiny barefoot children were frolicking in the cool water of the temporary splash pad. They were stomping and screaming in delight.

Vito: "Look at all them little squirts. They're spazzin' out dahn here!"

We loved riding our bikes through the artificial rain shower. On this scorching hot day, even cool dude Sal didn't mind getting wet.

Sal: "It's already 90 today. We'll dry off in two minutes flat."

Then Sal glared over at Vito.

Sal: "Just don't run over a little kid, Vito."

All three of us slowly glided around the edge of the waterfall on our bikes. We caught the attention of an older Italian lady who sat on a stoop under a big oak tree and watched over the park like a hawk. Always wearing a long black dress, the park's vigilant caretaker kept an eye on the slides and swing sets while also providing free peanut butter and jelly sandwiches to hungry kids which were paid for by the borough.

Clutching a beaded rosary in her hand, the old woman in her dark, flowing dress swiftly swooped over and squawked at us in Italian and Yinzer.

Old Lady: "Santo cielo! Yinz get outta here with them bikes! Get lost!"

Although Sharpsburg is a very diverse community today, back then the town was an enclave for Italian immigrants. Many newly arrived families chose to live with or near their fellow family members from Italy. After several generations, extended families tended to spread out from this one little neighborhood. This has been a common progression for the countless waves of immigrants that have come to settle in America from across the globe.

At this point in 1979, Sharpsburg's Italians had not begun to disperse at all. They were still closely glued to their little hometown, and they all seemed to congregate at two important places: the Church and the Italian Club. We already had our daily dose of religion at Nina's Market, so now we were ready to get our daily dose of entertainment.

Sal: "Let's see what's goin' on dahn the Italian Club. I feel like beatin' yinz at bocce."

Vito was quick to respond.

Vito: "Yeah right! I crushed you last game!"

36

Sal ignored Vito as he led us through a back alley riddled with potholes in between an auto body shop and the post office. We sped our way through the bustle of Main Street. The quaint thoroughfare was lined with small storefronts ranging from butcher, flower, and barber shops to pizza parlors and dive bars. After the short ride from the park, we skidded out on our bikes as we landed at the club.

Sal: "Okay, losers! Let's play some bocce!"

After getting off his bike, Vito forcibly punched his left palm creating a loud smack.

Vito: "Losers? You're gonna lose your front teeth today if ya don't shut up!"

We loved playing bocce at the Italian Club. Bocce is a form of Italian bowling which most Americans are familiar with today. But back then, it was really only found at Italian hangouts. Played on a rectangular surface of stamped sand, your goal is to roll heavy, wooden bocce balls as closely as possible to a little white "pallino" ball. Each ball is worth 1 point, so the main desire is to toss as many of your four bocce balls closer to the pallino than your opponent, scoring up to a possible 4 points per round. You can also knock your opponent's balls out of the way to improve your score. First person or team to reach 16 points wins the match.

We stepped into the crowded, sun-drenched bocce courtyard. Sal cringed.

Sal: "Crap! All o' courts are taken. Don't they know to keep a spot reserved for me?"

Sal's confidence was merited. He was excellent at bocce. Unlike me and Vito who used standard underhand rolls, Sal deployed an overhand grip toss like the professionals do in Italy.

I shrugged and pointed my thumb at the club.

Bobby: "Let's go inside 'n grab a pop, then."

Soft drink beverages are always referred to as "pop" in Pittsburgh and not "soda." To a Pittsburgher, a "soda" was a fizzy glass of carbonated water and flavored syrup served at an Isaly's soda fountain parlor back before there was television.

During a weekday, the club was frequented mainly by older retired men and a few wiseguys enjoying the lazy days of summer. There were always a lot of colorful characters socializing at the Italian Bocce Club. We first ran into Toto and Uncle Mico.

Toto had a lazy eye that spun around like a brown marble in a glass jar. I was always fond of Toto because he would sneak us snacks, like Cheetos, from behind the bar. I also liked to see my Uncle Mico, a World War II veteran who stormed the beaches of Normandy on D-Day. He always greeted us by challenging us to an arm-wrestling match. Even in his ripe old age, we could never beat him. Those old veterans who worked in the mills had freakish man strength that a teenager could only wish for.

During the obligatory arm-wrestling bout, it looked like Vito's bulging eyeballs were about to pop right out of their sockets as he toiled in vain with my great-uncle's massive Popeye the Sailor Man forearm. After a minute of toying with Vito, Uncle Mico took him over the top and loudly slammed the back of Vito's hand on the metal playing card table.

Vito quickly shrugged off his futile attempt as we walked away.

Vito: "I let him win."

Sal: "Sure ya did. Whatever you say, Vito."

After Vito's humbling loss, the head honcho of the Italian Club approached our crew. Sonny Deleone was an imposing monster of a man who stood over 6 feet 5 inches tall and weighed close to 300 pounds. The club's formidable manager was well over 50 years in age, but he looked like he could still physically destroy almost any young man in the prime of his life. He was always clad in a fine Italian suit, even in the summertime. Although on this sweltering day, he did take off his coat and silk tie and just wore the expensive dress shirt (with a huge collar) and slacks. His salt and pepper hair was always slicked back, fine leather shoes always polished, and gold rings always shined. Sonny wore a gold Rolex that looked like it could fit around my neck. That wristwatch alone probably cost more than my family's station wagon.

After wiping away small beads of sweat from his brow, the big boss patted Vito on the back. He knew us rapscallions since we were little kids and greeted us warmly.

Sonny: "How yinz boys doin'?"

Sal: "Good, Mr. Deleone. Just waitin' to get a court to play on."

Sonny: "Well, it's a hot one today. You could fry an egg on a Cadillac out there. Before yinz play, go to the bar and get some cold pops on me, boys."

Sal: "Thanks, Mr. D."

We walked through the cigarette smoke clouds wafting above a crowd of older men playing cards. They played for fun during the day, but for big piles of cash at night. My father and grandfather would sometimes play on Sunday evenings after the Steelers game. A lucky hand and some skill often allowed them to add on some extra money to their finished work week. We sauntered up to the bar.

Bartender: "What are yinz drinkin'?"

Vito: "We'll have a round o' Iron City."

Iron City Beer was (and still is) the beverage of choice in most neighborhood saloons in Pittsburgh. Of course, Vito pronounced iron as "ahrn" in his Yinzer accent. He was also half kidding, as the bartender knew we were well underage. But for Vito, it was still worth a try.

Bartender: "Not for you, Vito. How 'bout an Orange Crush?"

Vito put his head down and replied in a somber tone.

Vito: "Okay, I guess."

Sal, Vito, and I always acted like we were completely oblivious to the illegal affairs going on at the club. Gambling was ubiquitous. Being around it was as normal as breathing in secondhand smoke. There were different levels of it too. We turned a blind eye to the old-timers shooting dice against a wall in the side alley. That was small potatoes. For everyone knew full well that they were operating the biggest sportsbook in town from the back room. Locals would come in and out all day long laying down money bets on the Pirates, the Steelers, the horse races — you name it. I mean, if it was actually listed on the betting slip, the most degenerate gamblers would have bet on a race between two little red ants crawling to a melted Klondike Bar on the sidewalk. Two of those giant black carpenter ants would go double or nothing.

We finally got a bocce court to play on. The midday sun was directly overhead now but we were going to tough it out. We played for small-time wagers.

Sal: "What should we play for today, boys?"

Bobby: "How 'bout for tomorra's take o' Clark bars?"

Vito crinkled his eyes and turned to me.

Vito: "I thought ya said you was done with stealin' those?"

Bobby: "C'mon, Vito! I said I was done with stealin' *Snickers* bars. Not Clark bars."

Vito's eyes lit up as he smiled with mischievous glee.

Vito: "Oh, yeah!"

Just as he was about to roll the first bocce ball, Sal shrugged his shoulders.

Sal: "And besides, tomorra's a new day. We'll all get a clean slate again."

We played bocce with friends and family alike under the hot yellow sun and bright blue skies. During our game, the theme song for the entire city of Pittsburgh in the summer of 1979 began blaring from the outdoor radio speakers on the top of the Italian Bocce Club. The new tune immediately made Vito start to bob his head to the beat as he rolled his luck on the heated sandy court. "We Are Family" by Sister Sledge had just gone gold. A blend of soul and disco, the song had real energy. And it was true to its name. Sister Sledge was an R&B group consisting of a talented family of four sisters from Philadelphia. With its catchy fun-filled chorus, the melody became the town sensation when the Pittsburgh Pirates baseball team adopted it as their clubhouse rally cry. (This after the stadium played it during a long rain delay in June.) Led by the golden smile and strong will of their beloved captain, Willie "Pops" Stargell, the team's magnetic success made the Steel City feel like one big, happy family.

As the quartet from Philly continued to bellow out "We Are Family" from high above, I felt like I was living the dream on that glorious summer day in the Burgh.

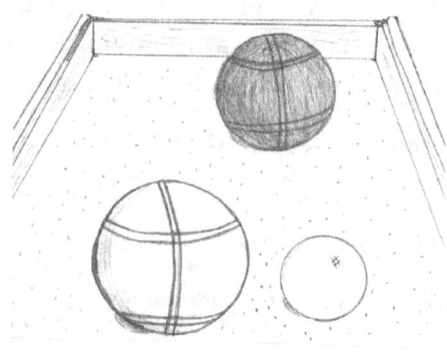

Chapter 3: Native Warriors

After enduring street fights, police lights, and dog bites, there were two places where my friends and I would go to find relief. We had the big river and the calm woods. On the southern side of Sharpsburg flowed the mighty Allegheny River. Originating from tributaries in northern Pennsylvania and the state of New York, it flows downstream past Sharpsburg to Downtown Pittsburgh. The cold water from the Allegheny National Forest churned at the nearby Highland Park Dam into a deep pool that was fantastic for fishing. We would cast our rods for smallmouth bass and catfish. Pittsburgh anglers prize walleye as the best tasting fish in the river.

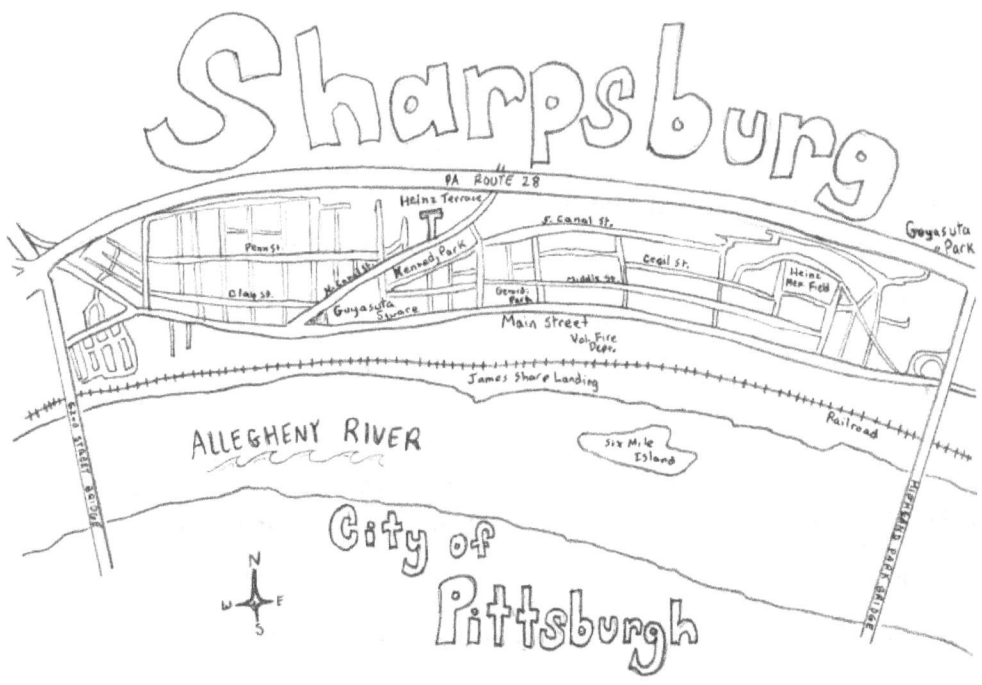

To the northeast side of the small rectangular town was a wooded hollow nestled between steep cliffs and beneath a highway overpass. This small forest refuge is called Guyasuta Park. Sal, Vito, and I would often hang out there to escape the urban warfare. Along with frequent visits from white-tailed deer and raccoons, even an occasional black bear can be seen roaming in this serene slice of nature. A small stream, named

Guyasuta Run, flows through the park. The woodland creek bed was the perfect place to collect bait for fishing at the river.

On this warm, overcast day in 1979, I happened to find an object at Guyasuta Park that would spark our upcoming adventures. We were barefoot in the creek. Vito was skipping stones on the water with sidearm throws like Kent Tekulve. Sal and I were hunting crayfish. I overturned a large rock on the side of the cool, flowing stream.

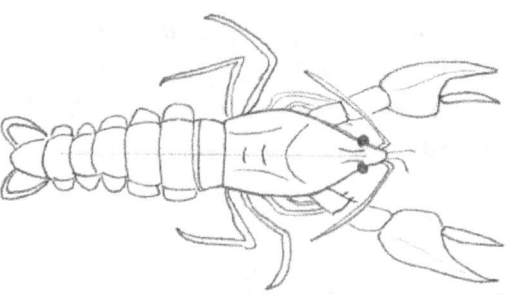

Bobby: "I see one! It's swimmin' dahn a' crick and right at ya, Sal!"

Sal reached into the water. Briskly gliding backwards by paddling its tail, a brown crayfish zigzagged downstream and swam right into Sal's cupped hands.

Sal: "I caught it! I caught it!"

Immediately, the big crawdad fought back for its life in a vicious way.

Sal: "Oww! Son of a... !"

The critter's sharp claws had firmly clamped onto Sal's right thumb. Violently shaking his hand, Sal flicked the feisty creature into the creek and it swam away.

Sal: "That little jagoff bit me!"

Vito: "Yeah, 'cause you taste like your mum's chicken alfredo."

Sal: "Whatever, Vito! Ya hairy oaf! You look like Bigfoot up here in a' woods!"

Vito: "Okay, Salvatore! Ya big wimp! Cryin' over a itsy bitsy crayfish!"

Then Sal looked at his thumb. His eyebrows flew up.

Sal: "What the... ? I'm bleedin' from where 'at little jagoff bit me!"

Bobby: "Actually, they don't bite, Sal. It pinched you with its pincers. They're kinda like mini lobsters. Biologists call 'em crustaceans."

Sal: "Whatever, nerd, with your fancy science words n'at."

Just then, I noticed that the crayfish was not the only thing that was hiding underneath the rock that I had just overturned.

Bobby: "Hey, yinz guys! Look at this! It looks like an arrowhead!"

Vito ran over.

Vito: "Cool! Lemme see it."

Out of the shallow water, I picked up a chiseled stone arrowhead with serrated edges and a notch at its base. It was a little over an inch in length and deadly sharp.

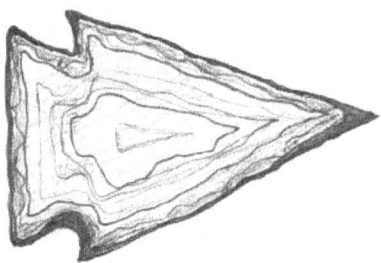

Bobby: "This looks like it's from an American Indian arrow."

Vito: "Whoa!"

Still looking at his bleeding thumb, Sal was only thinking of the here and now.

Sal: "What? There ain't no American Indians in Sharpsburg."

He began to run through our town's ethnic makeup.

Sal: "We only got Italians. Well… and maybe some Irish, Polish, and Germans."

While holding the arrowhead, I reminded him of the African American family that recently moved to town last school year.

Bobby: "There's the Robinsons. They just moved here from the Bronx. They live next to Gerardi Park."

Vito nodded his head.

Vito: "Oh, yeah. The new Black girl in school, Marquita Robinson. She's taller than both o' yinz."

Sal spoke crookedly out of the side of his mouth.

Sal: "Well, it ain't exactly hard to be taller than Bobby."

I quickly snapped back at Sal.

Bobby: "Whatever, Sal. She's taller than you, too."

Sal completely ignored me as he wiped the blood from his wound on his jeans and continued to ponder more about the town's demographics.

Sal: "Oh yeah, I forgot. The Garcia family. They're Mexican. They live over on Middle Street."

Vito tried to chime in with some deep insight of his own. His eyes grew wide like he was having a real eureka moment.

Vito: "Hey! I just realized somethin'! Franky D. lives on Roosevelt Street."

Sal shook his head. He had no idea what Vito was trying to say. Then he pinched his fingers up to his thumb and shook his hand in the air at Vito.

Sal: "So what? And Franky DeLallo is Italian, you pinhead."

Vito tried to further his point. He spun his hand in a big circle like it all made perfect sense.

Vito: "No, I mean put it all together, and you get *Franky D. Roosevelt*. You know, just like the name of 'at president. Get it?"

I laughed but Sal snarked back at Vito as usual.

Sal: "His name was Franklin, idiot! Nobody called him Franky 'cept maybe his mum."

I couldn't help but laugh at Sal's harsh response to what Vito thought was going to be a big revelation. But I actually thought the connection Vito made was kind of clever. Critical Sal always found a way to burst Vito's bubble.

At any rate, I was thrilled by my rare and lucky find in the creek. The stone arrowhead was in good condition. It looked as if it was knapped from a flint rock found in the gravel bar right alongside the stream. Native Americans manufactured bows and arrows by hand for important survival purposes such as hunting for food and protecting one's tribe from harm. This arrowhead served as a connection to the Native Americans who once resided on the land that eventually became Sharpsburg. To this day, it is still one of my most prized possessions. As I spun the gray arrowhead around in my hand, I began to reflect on the depth of my discovery.

Bobby: "This was made hundreds o' years ago. Do yinz ever wonder what it looked like here back 'en? No streets, no buildings, no factories, no ball fields... "

Sal grew a wry grin on his face.

Sal: "No schools... "

Vito became worried.

Vito: "No school lunch?"

His eyes widened with concern.

Vito: "No chicken patty sandwiches?"

I redirected my distracted friends.

Bobby: "No, for real. I wonder what it looked like when Chief Guyasuta called this place home."

Guyasuta Park was named after Chief Guyasuta, the famed Seneca warrior who lived in Sharpsburg during the 1700s. Legends of Guyasuta were a fixture in the town's folklore. Well before the neighborhood was a Little Italy, it was occupied by waves of German immigrants and Scots-Irish before them. However, before the birth of our modern nation, this land along the Allegheny River was originally home to Native Americans. Here, the Seneca Tribe had perfected superior canoes to navigate the region's waterways. They lived in large villages of wooden longhouses and practiced agriculture, growing crops such as corn, beans, and squash.

The area's last Indigenous chieftain, Guyasuta was a well-respected leader. He was famous for his courage to stand up to his enemies and his tremendous bravery on the battlefield. He ruled during a time of ferocious turmoil in the wilderness frontier that is now called Pittsburgh. It was a full upheaval. The Native American civilization that had existed for thousands of years in this region was collapsing under the pressure of foreign colonization and warfare. Land dispute claims between England and France began to drain the lifeblood out of Chief Guyasuta's tribe. The Senecas were under constant pressure to either join sides or be exterminated.

Vito: "What exactly did Guyasuta do, Bobby?"

Bobby: "Guyasuta was a Seneca chief who stood up to the English armies that started comin' here in a' 1700s. He led the American Indians from all over when they fought against the redcoats at Fort Pitt and Fort Ligonier. Back 'en, Guyasuta was the baddest dude in Pittsburgh. He was real tough. Him and his tribe were feared by everyone for their ferocity in battle."

After the French and Indian War, Chief Guyasuta fought to protect his people and their land from a hostile English takeover. This 18th century conflict is well known as Chief Pontiac's War, after the Ottawa chieftain. But some historians call it Chief Pontiac and Chief Guyasuta's War. Under their command, British forts and colonial settlements were attacked everywhere from Detroit to Pittsburgh. Guyasuta became the rallying force at the center of the struggle for control of Western Pennsylvania. He led sieges on Fort Pitt, located at what is now Point State Park. Recognizable by his physically powerful build, his notoriety as a fierce fighter grew from his daring exploits in battle. At the Battle of Bushy Run, Chief Guyasuta and British Colonel Henry Bouquet actually traded point-blank pistol shots at each other.

Vito: "Huh, kinda like a duel. Who won?"

Bobby: "Both shots missed their target. Guyasuta lived to fight another day."

Vito raised his eyebrows.

Vito: "That's crazy!"

Bobby: "Yeah, guns back 'en weren't as accurate as they are today."

Firearms were terribly inaccurate before gun barrels were rifled to project spinning bullets. Besides being a vaunted warrior, Guyasuta was also praised as an outstanding orator and wise political leader. He was able to communicate with the many factions who disputed over the Pittsburgh region. The French, English, Americans, and varied Native American Peoples all fought over the land we were currently standing on.

Vito scratched his head.

Vito: "Wait a minute, Bobby. What side was Guyasuta on, anyways?"

Bobby: "That's real complicated. He did what was best for his people."

War erupted all around Guyasuta. War over land, and war over water. A grand confluence of three rivers to be precise. The world's armies came crashing in on him and his tribe. During the French and Indian War, the Senecas, as part of the Iroquois Confederacy, were officially aligned with the British Empire. However, there are some accounts that, at times, he and his warriors may have flipped alliances and fought alongside rival armies from France and Native American tribes. After England defeated France and seized hold of Pittsburgh, Guyasuta grappled against the massive influx of British troops and settlers in the region. During the Revolutionary War, he reluctantly joined the British cause against the American colonial rebellion. After the wars ended, an elder Guyasuta became a leader in peaceful relations with his new American neighbors in Pittsburgh. As a well-revered political figure by the end of his life, Guyasuta's word was as good as gold.

Vito wanted a more concrete answer from me. His palms faced up in the air.

Vito: "So then what side was he on?"

I looked up at him and answered frankly.

Bobby: "His own side."

During the brutal wars, Chief Guyasuta was forced to switch diplomatic allegiances based upon the welfare of his people. Unfortunately, the Senecas were torn between the unquenchable thirst of two enormous European empires looking to take full advantage of North America's bountiful resources. It was a clash of the titans. When the never-ending quarrel between the kings and queens of England and France moved on to a new continent, his tribe was overwhelmed by a hungry new American nation with its own aspirations to expand in territory. For Chief Guyasuta, it was like getting tangled up in a dirty fistfight between the two biggest bullies on the block and then getting sucker punched by a cocky up-and-comer who came out of nowhere.

47

Vito: "So the chief did what he had to do to clean up his tahn. Kinda like 'at movie *Walking Tall* where the sheriff beats up the whole neighborhood with a wood club."

Bobby: "Kinda like 'at, Vito. 'Cept Guyasuta wasn't just in a scrap with the local tahn scums. He was fightin' against the biggest armies in a' world."

In the end, Chief Guyasuta's valiant effort to preserve the Native American way of life here failed. By the late 1700s, the noble helmsman could no longer stop the westward expansion of the new American nation. His land taken from him, the acclaimed sachem died of old age in a small wooden cabin in Sharpsburg shortly before the year 1800. It was a humble end to a tumultuous life.

Vito: "How's come ya know all this stuff 'bout Guyasuta, Bobby?"

Bobby: "Well, from my Pap Taranto. And 'cause I wrote a book report about Chief Guyasuta in a' sixth grade, too. You had to write about your hero."

Vito's wheels were turning in his head.

Vito: "I don't remember 'at assignment."

Sal had a quick retort.

Sal: "I do. Bobby wrote his on Chief Guyasuta and you wrote yours on Chef Boyardee."

Vito chomped hard on his gum and gave Sal a mean stare. He then began to slowly stomp over to Sal while glaring at him from above. An avid fan of every violent motion picture ever made, Vito acted out his best Robert De Niro impression from the movie *Taxi Driver*.

Vito: "You talkin' to *me*? You talkin' to *me*?"

I quickly defused his anger. Before a fight could erupt, I stepped in between my two taller friends and put up my hands.

Bobby: "Okay. Okay, guys. Forget about it."

Even though he was nearly twice my size, I was always amazed that Vito would listen to me when he got mad. It was like making a wild animal come to heel. My hypothesis was that it was because we became friends at a very young age. It was kind of like how a lion tamer imprints themself on a lion cub right after birth. Except for his mother all of the time and me some of the time, Vito really didn't like taking orders from anyone else. I wished that I had it that way with Duke, the stray dog.

Vito brushed off his chest and composed himself. Still staring over my head at Sal, Vito spat in disgust off to his side at the rocky creekbank.

Vito: "One o' these days I'm gonna deck you, Sal."

I proceeded to talk about a much larger fight in the neighborhood, one that included Chief Guyasuta.

Bobby: "No, for real, guys. How would yinz act if some foreign army marched into our tahn and burnt dahn our homes?"

Still standing in between my two friends, they gave me blank stares and offered no reply. I never accepted how history and cinema regularly portrayed Native Americans as hostile savages bent on bloodthirsty warpaths. In the 1950s, '60s, and '70s, stereotypical depictions of American Indians were constantly rehashed on popular television shows and movies about the Western frontier. Even as a young teenager, this one-sided narrative felt far too narrow-minded and prejudiced for me. I persisted with much more thought-provoking questions for my friends.

Bobby: "What would yinz do if some butthead soldiers from half a world away came in here and hurt your mum, Vito? Or your sister, Sal?"

Now Vito had strong words to say. He scrunched his eyebrows, aggressively clenched his right fist, and spoke in a grizzled voice.

Vito: "I'd be kickin' butt and takin' names until I wiped 'em all out... or they wiped me out."

Sal wholeheartedly agreed with Vito.

Sal: "Yep. I'd be doin' the same thing. But we'd need a lot more than our BB guns."

I got my point across. I especially struck a chord with the ultraprotective Vito. Vito was a tough kid who never backed down from a fight of real significance. And when it came to protecting friends and family, Vito's unwavering loyalty was worth his weight in gold. My much larger friend looked down at me with enlightened eyes.

Vito: "Okay. I get it now, Bobby. Now I see why you chose Chief Guyasuta as your hero. He fought for his tahn and his family just like we would."

Then he directed a nasty smirk over at Sal while we put on our shoes.

Vito: "And I didn't pick no chef 'at cooks his noodles in a can."

Sal didn't look back at Vito and only grumbled out of the side of his mouth.

Sal: "Take a chill pill. I was just jaggin' ya, doofus."

We began to saddle up on our BMX bikes. I still had the arrowhead in my hand.

Bobby: "Let's head dahn Main Street."

Vito: "All right. Why ya wanna go dahn 'ere, Bobby?"

Bobby: "I wanna show my pap this arrowhead. He collects stuff like 'is."

Chief Guyasuta was held in high regard by his neighbors in the region, Native Americans and settlers alike. His reputation as a fair leader, courageous warrior, and skillful scout was legendary. In fact, his knowledge of the forested valleys and rivers of the Pittsburgh region was considered second to none. I was fascinated that the great Chief Guyasuta and his Seneca Tribe once lived here in Sharpsburg. Excited by the tangible piece of history that I had just discovered in the creek at Guyasuta Park, I wanted to show it to a noted town historian, my grandfather. (I always called him "Pap," short for grandpap.) A veteran of World War II, Pap collected relics of warfare. He was especially interested in Native American artifacts.

We decided to ride to my pap's place of work in the center of town. It was about a five-minute bike ride. On the way, we approached Minella's Pizzeria on Main Street. A large sign read "Slice and a Pop – $1" in the front window.

Sal: "A slice at Minella's costs a buck now?! What a rip-off!"

I asked out a question while we rolled by the sign.

Bobby: "Hey, yinz know why our money is called a 'buck'?"

Sal was pedaling slightly ahead of us and snidely replied.

Sal: "No. But I'm sure you're gonna tell us, geek."

Bobby: "Back during Guyasuta's time, people traded deerskin hides like money. Over time, the word 'buckskin' got cut dahn to 'buck'."

Vito: "Huh, 'at's kinda cool to know."

Sal just shook his head.

Sal: "Whatever, dorks. 'At's still *way* too much dough for a slice o' pizza."

The commonly used word for money in America, the "buck," did indeed originate from a widely traded good before the birth of this country, the buckskin. Only the plush, warm, and waterproof pelt of a beaver was more valuable than the hide of a large white-tailed deer. In addition to being a form of currency in the American frontier during the 1700s, both animal skins were used in making clothing both here and abroad.

Currently, we were headed to an establishment that offered a much different type of apparel. Located on Main Street in the heart of Sharpsburg, Taranto's Menswear was a small clothing shop that imported and tailored fine Italian suits from Venice, Milan, and Rome. Owned and managed by my maternal grandfather, Filippo Taranto, the store catered to the older, somewhat wealthier clientele in town. My pap began the small business as a young man and earned a decent living for his skilled services.

A small brass bell chimed as we pushed the door open to my grandfather's shop. My grandfather looked over his shoulder and winked at us. He was in the back measuring out a new suit for the biggest client in town. The tailoring tape was reaching its limit in height and diameter on his huge customer.

In awe of the scene, Vito whispered to me.

Vito: "It looks like your pap is makin' a suit for Andre the Giant."

My grandfather finished his measurements. He reached up high to pat his client on the back.

Pap: "Okay, Sonny. You're good to go."

Sonny: "Thanks, Filip. Lemme know when it's done."

The colossal manager of the Italian Club gave my grandfather a firm handshake, ambled towards us, and grabbed his blazer from the nearby coat rack.

Sonny: "How you doin', boys?"

Sal: "Good, Mr. D. Thanks for the pops at the club yesterday."

Sonny: "No problem. Anytime, boys. Yinz have a good day."

Bobby: "See ya, Mr. DeLeone."

Sonny strolled by us and out the door. Vito was a large teenager but even he felt miniscule compared to Sonny.

Vito: "Yikes! 'At's gonna be one big suit, huh, Mr. Taranto?"

Pap: "Yep, but that's-a good for business, boys. How *you* doin'?"

Bobby: "Good, Pap. I wanted to show ya somethin' we found dahn a' crick in Guyasuta Park."

I pulled out the arrowhead and handed it to him. He spun it around in his hand.

Pap: "An arrowhead! Oh, this is a nice one, Bobby. I told ya I found some too when I was a kid. The Senecas used to live here."

Bobby: "Yeah, maybe it was made by Chief Guyasuta himself. Ya know?"

Pap: "Maybe, Bobby."

Just then, another customer wandered into my pap's little store.

Pap: "Hey, come by my house later this week, after I'm done with work, and I'll show yinz my arrowhead collection. I have some good ones. I got some other stuff, too."

Bobby: "Sure, Pap. Sounds good."

Vito: "See ya later, Pap."

Pap: "So long, boys. Yinz go enjoy that sunshine. It's-a good for you."

In the Italian enclave of Sharpsburg, sometimes a hybrid version of Yinzer was spoken with an Italian American accent. This amalgamation often sounded like a mixture of a Pittsburgh and Brooklyn accent. In fact, my father said that when he served in the U.S. Army many soldiers would ask him if he was from New York City. With a strong emphasis on the "you," "How *you* doin'?" was a common greeting for Italian Americans, as well as all urbanites, from New York to Philadelphia to Pittsburgh. Only when my father used the word "yinz" could the other soldiers determine his true origin.

After we left Pap's store, my interest in historic artifacts of war was piqued. I felt inspired by all the discussion surrounding the newly discovered arrowhead. Vito and Sal seemed to be too. While cycling home, I realized that I had never shown them my father's collection of war memorabilia. I was hoping they would want to look at his personal items from his time in the military.

Bobby: "Hey, yinz wanna come over my house before dinner and check out all the stuff my dad got from Vietnam? It's pretty cool."

Only a few summers earlier, many young Americans were fighting in a long and bloody conflict in Vietnam. And for all youngsters who grew up playing war games on the streets and in the woods, there's nothing more fascinating than looking at awards and authentic relics from actual battles. However, Vito was hesitant with the offer.

Vito: "Sure, I guess. Just as long as your dad ain't home, though."

Bobby: "No, he's gonna be at work still."

Vito reluctantly answered back.

Vito: "Uh, okay. Then let's go."

Like Chief Guyasuta from long ago, my father was a warrior who was native to Sharpsburg. Although nowhere near as famous, my dad also had a reputation for being a tough war veteran. Vito stood over six inches taller than my father but was still intimidated by him.

Vito: "Remember when your pops used his kung fu fightin' skills on those three jagoffs tryin' to break into your car?"

Sal: "Yeah, he looked like Bruce Lee out there. He was crackin' skulls. Bodies hit the floor."

We all still vividly recalled one summer night when we were little kids playing in Sal's yard. Vito noticed three young men attempting to break into my family's station wagon parked in the alley in front of our house. One guy was using a screwdriver and a wire coat hanger to pop open the car door. I ran to alert my father. Skilled in martial arts from his time in the military, he stormed onto the street to confront the thieves. Before we could blink, the three young men were on the cold concrete. Although they were probably just trying to go on a joyride, they ended up going to the hospital. I kept the flathead screwdriver as a memento.

We parked our BMX bikes outside of my house. Concerned, Vito asked me again.

Vito: "Are you sure he ain't home, Bobby?"

Bobby: "Yeah, he ain't home 'til 5. Relax, dude."

Despite their fears, my curious friends were eager to inspect his cache of war artifacts. It was stowed in a shoebox under my parents' bed. We snuck upstairs while my mother was in the kitchen boiling yet another pot of spaghetti. In the concealed box was a small pile of medals along with dog tags that he wore around his neck and on his right boot. These, of course, were for identifying an unfortunate soldier who died or lost a limb. There was also a faded picture of my father in his green army fatigues. And one sheathed knife. I pulled out the most important item first.

Bobby: "This is the Bronze Star. The fourth highest medal awarded by the U.S. Army."

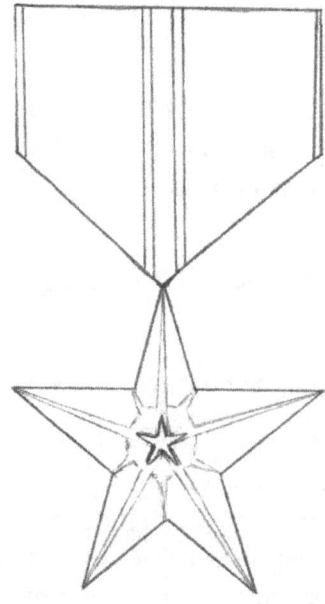

Their eyes gleamed in admiration at the shiny copper star with a red, white, and blue trimmed ribbon. I handed the Bronze Star to Vito. He closely examined the prized medal.

Vito: "Cool."

I grasped the next medal. It was a silver pendant with a large bullseye target.

Bobby: "And this is the Marksmanship Medal for bein' a sharpshooter. He had to hit stationary targets at 200 yards and a bunch o' moving targets with his rifle to get this one. My dad's actually more proud o' this one than the Bronze Star."

Vito: "How come?"

Bobby: "Well, he said he had to work real hard practicin' at the firing range n'at to get the sharpshooter medal. He says he got the Bronze Star for just doin' his job."

Sal: "He musta been real good at his job. So, what'd he do exactly to get it?"

Bobby: "He was a hero in a big battle near the DMZ."

Vito: "The DMZ? What's 'at?"

Bobby: "It's the dividing line between two armies. Kinda like the line o' scrimmage in football."

Vito: "Oh, okay. I get it."

My father served in the 5th infantry of the U.S. Army in the Vietnam War. Robert Connemara Sr. was a decorated veteran who was awarded the Bronze Star after a nightmarish battle on the front line, also known as the DMZ (demilitarized zone). On that fateful day, his platoon walked right into a bunker ambush designed by an entire North Vietnamese regiment. After the enemy opened fire, dozens of American soldiers were quickly killed or wounded. His captain lost an arm, and his best friend lost his leg. The remaining troops were entrapped for hours in a ferocious fight for their lives. Two rescue helicopters tried to land on their position to save the squad, but both were shot down by enemy RPGs (rocket-propelled grenades).

Sal was increasingly interested and demanded more information.

Sal: "You didn't really answer my question, Bobby. How'd he get the Bronze Star?"

Bobby: "Oh, so his whole platoon was pinned dahn real bad in between a bunch o' hidden bunkers. Everyone was wounded bad from the ambush. His captain from Indianapolis had his arm blown right off. His best friend from Michigan lost his leg. His other buddy from Green Bay was killed in action. My dad was desperate, so he ran 'n outflanked the enemy and took out two machine gun nests with grenades."

Sal: "Wow, 'at's crazy! So, your old man really *is* a badass."

In a dire situation, my father realized that his only hope of survival was to outflank the enemy positions. He legged it around the battlefield and circled back to wipe out two machine gun bunkers with a grenade launcher. It was similar to my attempted maneuver during our game of "War" with air rifles two days ago. However, there were three incredibly huge differences. Number one, my father was fighting in a real battle during a real war. Secondly, unlike my failed attempt, my father's daring act actually succeeded. Finally, and most importantly, my father was able to save his friends from being captured. He was a war hero. The battle was even written about in *The Pittsburgh Press*, which was the largest of the city newspapers.

Sal: "Okay, Bobby. Now I see why you tried 'at maneuver against 'em jagoffs we was fightin' the other day. Only difference is, you definitely ain't your dad."

I nodded in sincere agreement with Sal. Vito asked another question pertaining to that era.

Vito: "What was it like gettin' drafted?"

Bobby: "Well, my dad was only 19 and workin' at the broom factory dahn by the river. He said he come home from work one day, and everyone was just standin' 'ere in a' doorway. In his thick Irish brogue, my Pap Connemara says, 'Robert, me lad, there was a letter from the government in the mail today. It's sittin' on the coffee table for ya, boyo.' Everybody knew what it was before he even opened it."

Vito and Sal sat quietly. All working-class kids knew that at any time during the Vietnam War they could find that same letter waiting on their living room coffee table. Unlike our modern-day armed forces composed of volunteers who choose to join on their own free will, many young Americans were simply selected by lottery to serve at that time. Of course, in a time of big crisis this could change, but back during the Cold War era even famous celebrities like Elvis Presley could not escape the draft.

Vito continued in earnest.

Vito: "Then what happens?"

Bobby: "So he said a couple weeks later he had to go to a big meetin' dahntahn with all the new guys who just got drafted into the Army. He said they was all sittin' in a big room dahn the Federal Building and the first guy who got up 'n talked on a' stage was this huge Marine Officer. He shouted, 'I need three men here to volunteer for the U.S. Marines.' My dad said every guy in a' room sunk dahn in their chairs."

Sal: "Yikes."

Like Sal, everyone there knew that the Marines were the first soldiers sent in to the most difficult and bloody of battle situations. I continued.

Bobby: "Of course, nobody volunteered to leave the Army for the Marines. So, this tall Marine Officer comes walkin' real slow 'round the room n'at. He tapped the shoulders of the three biggest dudes there and said, 'Men, stand up. You three are now U.S. Marines.' My dad said the rest of the crowded room sat up in their chairs again and sighed in relief."

Sal patted Vito on the back and started shaking his head.

Sal: "Oh, Vito, you would be done, dude. That Marine woulda picked you in a second."

Our big friend imagined himself in that situation and started crawling under my parents' bed.

Vito: "Ugh! I'd be hidin' under my chair."

Sal then asked a serious question.

Sal: "What would yinz do if you got drafted?"

Bobby: "I would go. My dad and my Pap Taranto both got drafted."

Vito nodded.

Vito: "Yup, I would go for sure."

Sal was straightforward as well.

Sal: "Me too. But it would suck."

There was a price to pay for my father's valor and service. Like many of the men who battled in the jungles of Vietnam, he was diagnosed with a severe case of diabetes. The U.S. Air Force would spray a deadly deforestation chemical, called Agent Orange, over the jungle canopy to reduce tree cover for the enemy. However, a chemical that could eradicate a rainforest could obviously affect a soldier as well. Exposure to the deadly herbicide led to chronic diseases. Agent Orange would end up attacking the pancreas of my father and many like him who fought for our country. It would render them unable to produce sufficient levels of insulin, a pancreatic hormone needed to digest glucose. I would watch in angst as my father gave himself two painful shots of insulin each day to manage his diabetic illness.

Bobby: "Yeah, sometimes he wakes up in the middle o' the night screamin' like he's still in a battle over there."

Sal: "I bet it's real tough for him to forget about it."

A less visible and more detrimental effect of being a warrior was in his head. On some days, he would appear distant and depressed. By night, his traumatic past would manifest itself even more. Often, while asleep, he could be found screaming and swinging at ghosts. In his nightmares, he would relive horrifying battles over and over again. Once vocalizing in his sleep, I vividly remember him yelling, "We're surrounded! They're everywhere... they're everywhere!" It was a small enough row house, so these violent night terrors would easily awaken the whole family and leave us in fear until dawn.

During the day, we kids would keep close watch while surfing all twenty channels on our wooden console RCA television set in the living room. We all knew that graphic war movies would trigger more violent emotions and harrowing nightmares. The past winter, we tried in earnest to conceal from him the release of a disturbingly realistic movie about Pittsburghers who fought in the Vietnam War, called *The Deer Hunter*. For us, this graphic movie hit too close to home. Years later, this type of mental anguish that he suffered from was deemed and diagnosed as a medical condition called P.T.S.D. (post-traumatic stress disorder). Back then, it was just something a war veteran had to live with.

Vito asked another pointed question.

Vito: "What'd he say it was like the first night he had to go walkin' around in 'em scary jungles? I bet you can't see nothin' at night."

Bobby: "He said on his first night in 'Nam, they put him on guard at the barrack perimeter. He was just standin' 'ere in a' dark. Then, he says he heard a big rustlin' sound come out from the jungle in front of him."

Sal: "What was it?"

Bobby: "It was a huge, hairy wild boar with long, sharp tusks and it came runnin' out the woods. The mean-lookin' pig grunted and came chargin' straight at him, so he shot it with his M-16. It died right there on a' spot."

 Sal's eyes widened.

Sal: "Holy crap!"

Bobby: "Yeah, he said besides wild boars he even saw a tiger once. But he don't talk much 'bout the actual battles n'at. Oh yeah, and some poor dude got bit in a' neck by a venomous snake hangin' dahn from a tree. He died on 'at first night, too."

 Sal shook his head.

Sal: "That would suck. Goin' all the way over 'ere and dyin' from a snake bite."

Bobby: "Yep."

 In the end, my father, like most war veterans, rarely discussed what happened during his tour of duty in the Vietnam War. Although he had a visible scar under his left eye and two big scars on his legs, he never made it clear how he acquired them in combat. For a long time, we only had one verbal account of what happened there. Once, at an army reunion, a hulking veteran wearing a Hells Angels motorcycle gang jacket leaned down and told my little brother, "Your dad wiped out a lot of problems for us over there." My father knew that in war, it was kill or be killed. But perhaps the guilt of taking another man's life weighed heavily upon him. I wondered if Chief Guyasuta ever felt the same way.

 I reached into my father's box one more time. I slowly lifted the item I thought would truly impress my friends. I saved the best for last.

Bobby: "Wait 'til yinz see this."

From its golden-brown leather sheath, I carefully pulled out a large, fixed blade knife made of shiny steel. It was a military issue knife that my father kept on his belt side during every mission and every battle. The imposing blade was about six inches in length. The shine of the cold, hard steel was only rivaled by the shine of amazement in my friends' eyes.

I handed the knife to Vito like a knight would be presented a sword. Fully in awe, he cautiously took it and felt its weight.

Vito: "Wow! Think your dad ever killed somebody with this?"

Vito carefully placed the knife down on the bed. Staring down at the sharp blade, Sal answered Vito.

Sal: "He must've. Why else would there be so many medals in 'ere?"

Just then, my father unexpectedly strolled into his bedroom from a long day of work at the mill. As I mentioned, although short in stature, my father was very intimidating. Intense training in the military and a brutal year of combat in Vietnam, followed by many more years of strenuous labor at the factory had hardened my father into a muscular man who all the neighborhood kids feared. My friends quickly stood at attention to salute him.

Vito: "Mr. Connemara. Hi. Uh, we was just... "

Sal sharply nudged Vito with his elbow to shut him up.

Sal: "Hey, Mr. C. We'll see ya tomorra, Bobby."

Vito and Sal scampered down the steps and out the front door. Crestfallen and quiet, I expected a stern reprimand for this invasion of privacy. My father always warned us to never snoop around in his box of keepsakes from the war. He crossed his arms as he looked down at his knife that was set directly on the bed. But when he opened his mouth, he surprised me with a whole new subject altogether. His tone was more inquisitive than angry.

Dad: "So, I hear yinz like to shoot pool and play bocce a lot at the Italian Club while I'm at work. You any good?"

Bobby: "At pool, I'm okay. I'm better at bocce."

Dad: "Really?"

Bobby: "Yeah, my main strategy is to wait 'til the last throw and try to knock out the other guy's best placed ball."

Dad: "Oh, that's good. That's what I always liked to do too."

His eyes focused again on his knife resting on the bed. He paused and continued.

Dad: "I'm fine with yinz hangin' out dahn there. I hang out there. Your pap goes there, your uncles, your cousins… but there's guys there. *Other* guys."

I knew exactly what my father was implying. The "other guys" were local wiseguys with flashy suits and shiny gold rings and chains. They played poker in the front room and ran gambling machines in the back. Most were small-time minnows. However, on occasion, even bigger fish would swim into the Italian Club. A well-connected gangster named Henry Hill would stop by the club to do business and run errands for the big bosses in New York. My father and older cousins would even play pool at the club with this notorious mobster from Brooklyn. In fact, Hill's frequent trips to Pittsburgh were mentioned in the hit movie *Goodfellas*, in which he was portrayed by actor Ray Liotta. Hill used his charisma in attempt to lure in some Sharpsburgers, including my father, to run guns and drugs with him from Pittsburgh to New York City.

Dad: "I want you to stay away from 'em guys who ain't from around here."

Henry Hill and my father shared a lot in common. Both men were of Irish and Italian descent. Both served in the U.S. Army during the 1960s. Both came from working-class backgrounds with a proximity to street life. Both were exceptional talents in the game of pool. But my father knew what an obligation with a New Yorker like Hill would entail and he respectfully declined his business offer. Of course, others from our town were

61

more than eager to cling to this big-time connection to organized crime. The allure of money and power was just too sweet.

However, like my father predicted, it all went sour. Indeed, when he finally got pinched by the F.B.I., Henry Hill ratted out a crew from Pittsburgh who masterminded an illegal NCAA basketball game-fixing scheme. Some local wiseguys had strong-armed a college basketball player from Swissvale into point shaving for them. He and his teammates were forced to miss a few shots here and there to achieve a desired score. The mobsters knew exactly who to bet on and whether they would cover the point spread. It became a cash cow. But after his arrest, Hill blabbed about the racket to the feds. He would end up ratting on a lot more "goodfellas" up in New York City.

My father was serious. He leaned forward and asked for confirmation.

Dad: "You know what I'm talkin' about? Right, Bobby?"

I became slightly defensive.

Bobby: "I know, Dad. I know. We just go there to play bocce and pool."

Dad: "Okay, good."

He paused and went on.

Dad: "Remember, don't ever get into trouble with them other guys hangin' out there. It causes nothin' but grief. Nothin' but headaches."

My father was worried about his son falling into a life of crime. He was speaking from experience. Many years later, I found out that my dad actually was a driver and bodyguard for a local wiseguy captain, or *capo* in Italian. Like many young Vietnam veterans, my father was recruited for his particular skill set. He protected this older gangster who liked to enjoy the local nightlife. My dad took on this moonlight shift on Fridays after punching out from his daytime job at the mill. With four hungry children at home, he saw it as a chance for some extra cash flow.

One crisp autumn evening, after some drinks at a well-known but now long-gone watering hole downtown named Froggy's, my father was escorting the old captain to his Cadillac. A fellow wiseguy began arguing with a large, belligerent bar patron and a vicious fistfight spilled out into the parking lot. From my father's account, with only a handful of spectators, it was like watching the two fiercest gladiators of Ancient Rome fight in an empty Colosseum. But it became a mauling. He witnessed in awe as the stocky gangster gave a bloody beat down to the extremely tall and wiry opponent.

It turned out that the towering fighter who fell back to earth was a star player for the Pittsburgh Steelers. Although he was well inebriated, this famous intimidator had never before lost a big battle, on or off the field. My dad hurried the capo to the Caddy as the oncoming police sirens could be heard echoing through the skyscraper canyons. Not a word was spoken during the car ride home. Sitting in silence, they both processed the shock and brutality of the gruesome bout between two of the most fabled tough guys in Pittsburgh. They were also dreading the likelihood of intense heat from the law. In the ominous quiet, the old capo realized that due to the celebrity status of those involved, the law enforcement aftermath wasn't going to be pretty. *Mob underboss beats up NFL superstar.* Heads would roll. Even bystanders might be pursued by the police. After the short drive home to Sharpsburg, the old man clapped his hands together and said to my dad, "That's it, Bob. I don't want you drivin' me no more. You got little kids at home to worry about now." That was the last night my dad worked for what some would call the Mafia.

My father continued in earnest. His voice grew stern.

Dad: "All the trouble you can get into isn't worth it. None o' that kind o' stuff is worth it. And there's always someone bigger and tougher than you."

My father paused and looked me straight in the eyes. Like many 14-year-old boys, I had a tendency to zone out during a prolonged parental lecture.

Dad: "You understand?"

Bobby: "Yeah, Dad... I know."

The beloved owner of the Pittsburgh Steelers was also well aware of the rough underbelly of the city. Art Rooney grew up in a home that sat above his father's saloon in the North Side. As a teen, Rooney was a tough-as-nails prize fighter who boxed at the highly competitive welterweight level. In his adulthood, Rooney had a penchant for gambling and big cigars. Myth has it, he purchased his professional football team with the winnings from an incredibly lucrative day at the horse races. While yet another common street tale said he won the team in a high-stakes poker game. Urban legends aside, Art Rooney loved his football team. So, after finally reaping the success of winning multiple Super Bowl trophies, the elder Rooney was not about to let a drunken street fight hurt his golden goose.

Ironically, like the well-respected Guyasuta before him, Art Rooney's endearing moniker was "The Chief." And like all tribal leaders, the Chief looked after his toughest warhorse. The old warrior from the ring protected his young warrior from the gridiron. The police would be looking for anyone involved in that rumble and my father quietly drove away unnoticed into the cool autumn night. A smart warrior knows when to retire from battle, won or lost.

Years ago, my father walked away from the heat of those kinds of situations. But at the moment, I was feeling the heat from him. The grilling pressed on.

Dad: "Those wiseguys at the club might have flashy outfits and big wads o' cash in their pockets. But that's all they got. They might look cool to yinz boys now. But they always gotta be lookin' back over their shoulders. That ain't no way to live."

He smirked and laid out one more persuasive point.

Dad: "And most of 'em wannabe big shots don't make any real money anyways. Believe me, it's all smoke and mirrors. It's just a show."

Famous movies in the 1970s, like *The Godfather* starring Al Pacino, had glamorized an extravagant gangster lifestyle. But in reality, most mobster foot soldiers had to hustle hard to make a living. Mob infiltrators like undercover F.B.I. agent Joseph Pistone, who went by the alias Donnie Brasco, found that the vast majority of mob henchmen at that time would have made an equivalent salary working in a steel mill.

By now, like many teenagers would, I looked to alleviate my father's deep-rooted concerns as much as end the conversation. I rolled my eyes and heavily sighed.

Bobby: "Okay. Okay. Okay. I get it, Dad."

My protective father was afraid of his son being enamored by a criminal lifestyle and finding it much more alluring than that of a steelworker at the local mill. He personally knew how easy it was to be enticed by the money, the excitement, the glamor. He gave me a quick nod.

Dad: "Good. Keep readin' all 'em books and gettin' good grades. That's the best way. 'At's how you can get out o' *this*."

By "this," my dad meant the working class. He was referring to one who must scrape every day to stay an inch above the poverty line. He looked down at the dark soot stains on his pants.

Dad: "You don't wanna work in a dirty mill like me. And I'm proud o' all 'em medals yinz was lookin' at. But I don't want you joinin' the Army and fightin' in a war like I did. I want you to go to college."

Like many poor kids back in his day, my father was drafted into the U.S. Army immediately after high school. Unlike many of those kids, my father was fortunate enough to return home alive. He took pride in serving our country. In a war he had not chosen, he was once a great warrior and had the medals to prove it.

He wagged his finger at the items on his bed.

Dad: "Now put all this stuff away, Bobby."

He looked down at his combat knife one last time. During the war, he wore the knife on a belt made of rope. Decades would pass before my father would tell me that he had to use his belt as a tourniquet to prevent his platoon captain from bleeding out when his entire forearm was blown off by an enemy grenade.

Dad: "And never take 'at knife out again."

Bobby: "Okay. Sorry, Dad."

After my father served his tour of duty in Vietnam, he followed in the footsteps of countless young war veterans in Pittsburgh and marched straight into the steel mills. It was another call of duty for these blue-collar Yinzers. But he wanted a different life for his children. He wanted to see his four kids graduate from a local university. Having no direct family member to ever attend college, this was my father's ultimate dream for us. I realize now, this is why he worked so hard to make ends meet.

Dad: "Now let's get ready for supper. Go help your mum set the table."

Bobby: "Okay, Dad."

He paused and added one more thing. This five-minute conversation was the longest talk that I had with him all summer. He didn't talk a lot but when he did, it mattered.

Dad: "Just remember: The best way to make your life better is by gettin' a good education. Only the strong survive. But only the smartest thrive."

Words of wisdom from a warrior.

Chapter 4: Friends in High Places

I was quickly inhaling my breakfast, a half-filled bowl of Frosted Flakes. My spoon clinked on the ceramic as I scooped up and scarfed down the last bits of soggy cereal. I sat alone at the kitchen table while my mother was hand-washing dishes at the sink. Carly Simon was singing about some underworld spy from the little radio with a long antenna on the kitchen windowsill. Like that spy, I was trying hard not to act in a suspicious manner. I picked up my bowl.

Bobby: "Hey, Mum, I'm gonna head over Sal's house today."

I poured the last drops of milk straight from the bowl into my mouth.

Mom: "Okay. What are yinz boys gonna do?"

Like most kids, we often took our mother for granted. Raising four young children, she worked just as hard in that house as my father did in the mill.

Bobby: "We're gonna play some football. Sal got a new Nerf ball."

Mom: "Okay. Yinz be careful. Don't go rippin' your pants again."

I got up from the table and gingerly added one more bowl to her workload as politely as possible. I gave my mom a quick goodbye kiss on the cheek.

Bobby: "Okay. Love you, Mamma."

Mom: "Love you, Roberto."

I was playing my usual "shell game." I had no plans on going over to Sal's house. In truth, I had mapped out a big adventure in the city for us. But my mom would have a conniption if I told her that. So, like every kid in America did before the advent of cell phones and texting, I would lie and say I'm heading to my friend's house. In planned coordination, Sal and Vito would likewise lie to their mothers and say they were going to my house. We would all lie through our teeth to keep our mothers from knowing our true whereabouts. The scam was just like that of a con artist on the street corner moving around three walnut shells with no prize under any of them. Even better, our mothers would never call each other up to verify our stories because they didn't want to deal with the immensely awkward language barrier between Italian and Yinzer English. Today's smart phones, with their tracking capabilities, make these kinds of shenanigans much tougher for kids to pull off with their parents.

Like many married couples in town, my parents were Sharpsburg High School sweethearts. As noted above, my loving little mother of Italian descent (maiden name Rosa Maria Taranto) often called me by the Italian version of my name, Roberto. Caring and sincere, she was a great mother. With a quick sew, she had already mended my back pocket that was torn by my sworn enemy, Duke. I know it sounds clichéd, but my mother was a phenomenal cook as well. On holidays, we were fortunate enough to get a taste of something other than the monotony of spaghetti. Her homemade chicken parmigiana was the gold standard in town. We loved her Italian dishes, like stuffed peppers, just as much as her American classics, like meatloaf and chili.

Speaking of food, today I was leading my crew to a now classic institution in Pittsburgh called Primanti Bros. Restaurant. Surprisingly, none of us had ever eaten at this well-known establishment before. Today, you can find a Primanti's in almost every corner of the Pittsburgh region. However, in 1979 there were just a few of these sandwich shops and they were only located in or around the nucleus of the city.

After filling up my friends with food, I was going to drag them to my desired destination. The top of Mount Washington, the highest point in Pittsburgh. From this commanding view, I wanted to imagine what our city looked like in the age of Chief Guyasuta. I had become fascinated with this era in history; a time when Pittsburgh was still a dense forest of rolling hills and winding river valleys. It was home to many Native American tribes including the Seneca, Shawnee, Mingo, and Delaware. Only a handful of explorers and fur traders from Europe and Colonial America had ever laid eyes upon it.

Our rendezvous point was a gas station at the edge of town near a bridge that heads over to the city. Sal and Vito rolled up to me while I was scoping out the gas station for some cold drinks. They were in mid conversation as Sal continued telling Vito about his latest crush. Sal was the first guy in our circle to start getting phone numbers from girls. Of course, these were the landline numbers to a shared home phone. Today's youths have no idea how scary it was to have to talk to a protective father before he handed over the house telephone to his daughter. Half the time, her nosy mother would be eavesdropping on another line. This kind of nerve-wracking experience has been completely eliminated by modern cell phones.

Sal: "So, I called her up and I says to her I says, 'Wanna hang out at my pad this weekend and watch movies?'"

Vito was finishing up a blueberry flavored Italian ice that he picked up from a vendor's cart on Main Street. His lips were dyed dark blue. Listening intently, Vito was fully enthralled by Sal's story. He spoke with a mouth full of ice shavings.

Vito: "For real? What'd she say?"

Sal: "So, she says, 'Nah, I ain't allowed to hang out with boys from Sharpsburg.'"

Vito's jaw dropped slightly in disbelief. With little blue ice chips falling from his mouth, Vito continued his inquest.

Vito: "But ain't *she* from Sharpsburg?"

Sal: "That's what I said to this chick! Like, so she says to me, 'No, I ain't from dahn Sharpsburg. We live up Sharps Hill.'"

Vito's eyes widened.

Vito: "What's the difference?"

With a sideways glance, Sal answered.

Sal: "It means she lives up in one of 'em houses with the big yards up over our tahn."

Vito nodded back in agreement about the hillside neighborhood above our town. Sal continued in a bitter tone.

Sal: "And it means her snobby mum sticks her nose up over our tahn too."

Vito looked up at the hill. Taking Sal's remark literally, Vito stuck his nose up in the air trying to measure where her mother's nose would be compared to his.

Vito: "Huh, you're right. Her nose sticks up way higher than ours. Sorry, dude."

Sal finally acknowledged me.

Sal: "So where we headin' today, Bobby?"

Vito had just finished off his Italian ice, crumpled up the paper cone cup, and shot it like a basketball into a nearby garbage can.

Vito: "Yeah, I'm hungry. Are we gonna get any grub?"

Bobby: "We're goin' on a little adventure today, boys. Let's branch out and explore the city more. We're gonna go eat at Primanti Brothers and then go Dahntahn and up Mount Washington."

Sal: "How we gonna ride our bikes all the way up 'at steep mountain?"

Bobby: "We can take the incline up. It used to carry up horses so I'm sure it can handle our bikes."

Vito: "Sounds like a plan. Hey, do them Primanti Brothers got Italian food like my parents' place?"

Bobby: "Uh... kind of. You'll see."

Primanti Bros. Restaurant in the Strip District was about a five-mile jaunt by bicycle. It was another hot summer day, so we needed liquid refreshments to stay hydrated for the journey. Fortunately, we didn't need a detailed operation plan to snag "free" goods today. The gas station on the edge of town had ridiculously long lines of customers waiting to fill up their tanks. The worldwide oil crisis that began in June of that summer had led to a severe gasoline shortage in America. Tempers were flaring. The gas station attendant was in a heated argument with a local Yinzer which looked like it was ready to boil over into an all-out fistfight. Bedlam ensued among the long line of cars. Horns were blaring and patrons were shouting profanities from their car windows. With the attendant distracted, each of us were able to easily swipe a Coke bottle from the ice cooler and quickly pedal away with our heads down.

Sal: "Easiest score o' the summer, boys! Nobody even saw us!"

Vito: "Easy peasy! Nothin' like a free bottle o' pop."

At least a few of us were benefitting from an international crisis that day. We laughed our butts off as we bicycled across the 62nd Street Bridge. It spans over the Allegheny River from Sharpsburg to the city of Pittsburgh. Crossing this narrow bridge was a dangerous endeavor. Cars honked at the teenage cyclists who dared to share the road. But like I said before, this summer, we were young and invincible.

To celebrate our stolen bottles of Coke, we started singing "Lola" by the Kinks. The lyrics to this rock song were catchy. Every kid loved chanting the words. We piped the opening lines about Coca-Cola, spelling out the drink at the top of our lungs.

Vito/Sal/Bobby: *"C! O! L! A!"*

We spelled out "Lola" even louder at the end of the verse. Then we vocally imitated the bass riff, wildly strumming our air guitars.

Like many kids, we never put much thought into the meaning behind the lyrics to this popular tune. We didn't realize how progressive "Lola" was, even for the 1970s. It spoke of new revelations with gender identity and preferences for a young person. But that's what made that time period so much fun. A lot of young people started becoming less judgmental of other peoples' lifestyles by the late '70s. After the conservative '50s and the tumultuous '60s, the prevailing attitude for many younger Americans became, "Hey, it's a free country. You can have fun however you want as long as no one gets hurt." At that moment, we were hoping not to get hurt. We were riding our bikes with no hands across a hazardous bridge as speeding cars whizzed by us in both directions. Doing what we wanted to do and having fun, but definitely not telling our parents about it. Probably just like Lola.

After the bridge crossing, we zoomed past a languishing oil refinery. Just then, in the town of Lawrenceville, a brown Chevy El Camino sped by us. The driver threw a McDonald's bag full of trash out of the car window. It nearly hit Sal.

Sal was enraged about the tossed paper bag and screamed at the car.

Sal: "Hey! Your frickin' garbage almost hit me! Ya jagoff!"

I did a bunny hop with my bike over the bag. Vito had a curious cast on his face as he glanced back at the fallen debris.

Vito: "Yinz think there's any fries left in 'ere?"

Sal gave Vito a dirty look. Still fuming, Sal then threw down his glass pop bottle and it broke into a thousand pieces. Vito and I had to swerve around the broken glass.

Vito hated littering. He loudly chirped at Sal.

Vito: "C'mon, Sal! Give a hoot! Don't pollute."

71

Back in the 1970s, it was not uncommon for people to casually litter everywhere. And I mean everywhere. Trash was strewn about the gritty city streets and pretty green spaces alike. In fact, the United States of America brought littering to a whole new level that summer when it dropped the orbiting "Skylab" space station on a barren desert in Australia. Australia charged us with a $400 littering fine.

It took twenty blocks before Sal even spoke again. By then, we were well on our way to the original Primanti Bros. eatery located in the Strip District. The "Strip" is a long stretch of restaurants, markets, and ethnic groceries adjacent to Downtown Pittsburgh. As we hit the Strip, I began my job as tour guide. I pointed to the river.

Bobby: "Yinz know the boat for the Lewis 'n Clark Adventure was built right dahn 'ere? Technically, their big river voyage began right here in Pittsburgh."

Sal quickly replied.

Sal: "Don't be such a drag. Nobody cares about crap like 'at, ya lame-o."

Sal wasn't a big fan of history. In fact, Sal hated school. On the very first day of first grade, he ran away during recess and vowed never to go back. By no means would Sal be considered dumb; he just lacked the motivation to excel at school. This was partly because he knew that after graduation, he would simply walk right into a decent paying job laying concrete for his father. Sometimes, I felt like I was trying to sneak a history or science lesson into our conversation just to try to spark his interest.

Like a lot of 14-year-olds, Sal had recently hit his first real growth spurt and was just starting to stretch into his long and lanky body. He was in good shape. This naturally came from being a cement bag gopher for his dad while they laid new sidewalks. Like many in a working-class trade, Sal only wore sleeveless T-shirts. He had longer, wavy brown hair and he always sported gold framed aviator sunglasses with dark lenses. He wore them day and night, rain or shine. Sal had more swagger than me and Vito. You could tell by the way he used his walk, he was a confident kid. He also had the nicest bike in our pack. I envied Sal's sweet black BMX. It rolled with flashy gold mag wheels as opposed to the cheap-looking thin metal spokes on mine.

Still seemingly worked up over the McDonald's bag episode, Sal had pedaled far up ahead of us. He yelled back while popping a wheelie on his bike.

Sal: "Pick it up, slow pokes!"

Sal would get easily bored and always had the need for speed. His real dream in life was to trade in his BMX bicycle for a sport racing motorcycle one day. Sal idolized Steve McQueen, a brooding actor who starred in hit movies with action-packed car chase scenes like *Bullitt* and *The Getaway*. Dubbed "The King of Cool" by the media, McQueen personally owned over 200 motorcycles.

Fully standing while pedaling, we caught up to the speedster.

Bobby: "Just so yinz know, this place puts fries 'n coleslaw on a' sandwich."

I swerved around a telephone pole and continued.

Bobby: "They started by makin' real fast meals for truck drivers by pilin' up everything in between two slices o' Italian bread. Vito, you can get a capicola sandwich there."

Vito smiled from cheek to cheek.

Vito: "Yum! Now you're talkin'. I love capicola."

Vito's family owned a small Italian restaurant. It was called "Buona Fortuna" meaning "Good Luck" in Italian. They made a fantastic chicken marsala with mushrooms. From birth, Vito never passed on a meal and always left a clean plate. He was the kind of kid at your school lunch table who ate everyone's remaining pear cubes and pineapple slices. In fact, with his healthy appetite and jovial nature, I think Vito was the only kid in the school cafeteria who all the lunch ladies knew by name.

Vito wasn't overweight, but he was a big dude. Standing over 6 feet tall, he was the muscle of our outfit. He was a darker-complexioned Southern Italian with a messy mop of pitch-black scruffy hair. And though not uncommon for an Italian kid at age 14, he was already fully shaving. (He'd have a five o' clock shadow by noon.) Vito always wore tight tank tops to show off his formidable size for a teenager. His imposing man-child looks made him our de facto bodyguard. Of course, his intimidating appearance masked his true fun-loving and lighthearted personality.

Out of boredom from the long haul, Vito started loudly belting out the chorus to his favorite KISS song, "Rock and Roll All Nite." Standing up high on his pedals, he sang like he thought he was Gene Simmons in full Kiss makeup performing at a sold-out concert at the Civic Arena. His booming voice traveled well on the city streets and random pedestrians either eyed him with suspicion or smiled at his antics.

After Vito forcefully repeated the main chorus line three more times, Sal had heard enough. He disliked drawing unnecessary attention. Unlike our earlier vocal celebration on a bridge devoid of people on foot, this was a bustling city street.

Sal: "Will ya shut up, you bozo? Everyone dahn here's gonna think we're nutcases!"

Although Sal always ripped on Vito regarding his intelligence, Vito seemed to know the lyrics to every song ever written. Along with being able to recite every single line, he was excellent at imitating voices too. His vocal range went from as high as Freddie Mercury to as low as Johnny Cash. It was a savant-like skill of his. Vito was never embarrassed about showing off this uncanny singing ability.

After getting scolded on the street by Sal, Vito went on to play the part of an annoying child. Talking in a goofy, high-pitched voice on purpose, a boisterous Vito loudly rang out like a little kid on a long car ride.

Vito: "ARE WE THERE YET?"

Luckily, we had just turned the corner off Penn Avenue, and I spotted the neon sign we were looking for. It hung over the middle of the alleyway.

Bobby: "This is it! Vito, we're here!"

We finally arrived at Primanti Bros. flagship restaurant. At the entrance of the brick building, we set aside our bikes and pushed open the swinging doors. "Just What I Needed" by the Cars was blaring on the radio. A big cook with a curly mustache and a massive head of frizzy hair looked our way. Fully immersed in his craft, the large Italian cook was actively grilling up food right behind the counter. Judging by the picture on the wall above him, it looked like he was an actual Primanti brother. While flipping over a mound of roast beef with a metal spatula, he gruffly called out to us without turning away from the elongated grill.

Big Cook: "What are yinz havin'?"

Bobby: "I'll take a Pittsburgher."

That's a regular beef patty. Vito ordered quickly like me.

Vito: "I'll have a capicola."

Sal looked around the room and measured what other customers were eating.

Sal: "I guess I'll have a capicola… but without the coleslaw. And no fries on it. Oh, and no tomatoes either."

The busy cook gave Sal a disgruntled look. He spoke back in a low, raspy voice.

Big Cook: "Look, kid, obviously you ain't never been here before. You're gonna get everythin' on it and deal with it how ya like."

The place was extremely crowded, and Sal offered no resistance to the surly cook. The smell of steak sizzling on the extended flat iron griddle was enough to make any carnivore's mouth water. In short order, the cook smacked the meat from the long grill onto Italian bread and piled on a heaping layer of fries, coleslaw, and tomatoes.

Sal: "Think 'at's enough ketchup, Bobby?"

Sal teased me as I poured a gratuitous mound of Heinz ketchup onto a napkin to dip my sandwich in, like a true Yinzer. Just as I put the glass bottle down, the cook hustled the steaming hot meals to our tall diner-style spinning seats. We dove into our gigantic sandwiches like starved vultures. While devouring our food, Blondie sang "Hanging on the Telephone" from the old radio above the grill. The phone-inspired tune was just a precursor to Blondie's smash hit "Call Me," a much more powerful pop rock melody which the band would release a few months later. Before the golden-haired lead singer Debbie Harry could even finish her lines, Vito was already done eating his capicola sandwich. However, Sal wasn't enjoying his lunch as much as the other two-thirds of the bike gang. He was dropping bits of the sloppy sandwich everywhere.

Sal: "Aw, now I got coleslaw all over my shoes."

Vito was glaring at the other half of Sal's sandwich with hungry eyes.

Vito: "If you ain't gonna eat that capicola… "

Sal rolled his eyes and pushed his leftovers across the table.

Sal: "Here ya go, Vito."

Vito's eyes became wide in shock at Sal's rare act of charity. Then Vito smiled like a butcher's dog. A nanosecond later, he urgently walked his fingers across the table to swipe up the remains of the sandwich with delight.

Vito: "Yoink!"

Vito gobbled it down in less time than it would take to personally call up Blondie on an old rotary dial telephone. Moments like these were why we nicknamed Vito's gut "The Bottomless Pit."

Vito sat back, lightly patted his stomach, and looked around the restaurant.

Vito: "That hit the spot. I like 'is place, Bobby."

Our hunger satisfied from the classic Yinzer meal, I wanted to push on with my agenda of urban exploration.

Bobby: "Now, let's head up Mount Washington and explore 'round up 'ere."

We paid for our lunch at the register. By the way, we were not full-time crooks who ripped off every store we came across. Despite the horrible impression you may have of our thieving escapades, we actually had some money on us from our little side gigs. Sal made some spending cash laying concrete for his father while Vito occasionally helped bus tables at the family restaurant. Every other week I would cut my paternal grandparents' small yard. Pushing an old rusty reel mower with spinning blades, the little clump of grass took me only ten minutes to finish. Afterwards, I would loaf around for another ten minutes and pull stray weeds by the tomato plants and Virgin Mary statue in my Nana Connemara's garden. This made me feel less guilty when my little nana would hand me a five-dollar bill for the cakewalk job. Still, if I somehow had more than ten bucks in my pocket back then, I felt like I was rich.

Bobby: "Okay, guys. We're gonna ride through Dahntahn."

Rolling on our bikes past long walls of colorful spray-painted graffiti, we came upon Penn Station on Liberty Avenue. The old train station is an impressive structure made of carved brownstone and brick. We wheeled around in its rotunda for fun. Gazing up at the beautifully arched entryway, Vito made a small architectural discovery.

Vito: "Look! "At brick spells 'Pittsburgh' wrong! Whoever built this, forgot to put the 'h' at the end."

Sal: "This place should ask for their money back from 'at brick guy."

For a short time at the turn of the 20th century, the U.S. Post Office forced the city to remove the "h" from the end of its name. A building constructed during that brief era can be spotted by the h-less name "Pittsburg" chiseled on its datestone. Of course, the residents resisted this outside interference and soon went back to the original spelling. Pittsburgh is known for its defiant spirit against federal mandates. The Whiskey Rebellion was a much more notorious case in which the locals revolted against the U.S. government and its attempt to tax their alcohol. Yinzers get dubious credit for America's first armed uprising, all over their precious booze.

Bobby: "Yinz know the Honus Wagner baseball card shows him wearin' a Pirates jersey with Pittsburgh spelled without the 'h' on it?"

A rare Honus Wagner baseball card from 1909 last sold for over $7 million at auction. Wagner was a Hall of Fame shortstop who won the World Series for the Pirates in the card's print year. But the novelty of the "misspelling" of Pittsburgh also adds to the card's value.

Vito: "How come they don't just draw in a little 'h' on a' card with a Sharpie?"

Sal: "You'd ruin the card, moron! It'd be worthless then, ya dunce."

Most of the time, Vito and I simply brushed off Sal constantly ripping on us. He picked on everybody. It was just part of his personality. A master of the art of put-downs, Sal seemed to always be waiting for others to offer up an easy opening for him to take a jab at. Unfortunately, for us, we were often caught with our guards down.

We cycled onto Grant Street, the city's main corridor. The first gray stone building had three huge flags waving high over our heads. The American flag fluttered between the blue flag of Pennsylvania and the black and gold flag of Pittsburgh.

Vito: "What's 'at black and yellow flag?"

Bobby: "At's the city flag. Its design's taken from William Pitt's coat o' arms."

The city is named after William Pitt, a politician from England. The suffix "burgh" comes from the Scottish word for "town," hence Pittsburgh means Pitt's Town. This black and gold banner also provides the color pattern behind the city's three professional sports teams, the Steelers, Pirates, and Penguins.

Sal: "Don't worry, Vito. They don't got no coat of arms for you. You only get that if you're important."

Vito had finally suffered enough of being Sal's punching bag and snapped back.

Vito: "Whatever, jagoff! This is America! Nobody's better than anybody else here."

I added my support.

Bobby: "Right, Vito! That's why we revolted against 'at king back in 1776."

For once, we teamed up against Sal. It was a short-lived mini alliance that teenagers everywhere create within their group of friends. A sarcastic Sal admitted a minor defeat to his patriotic pals.

Sal: 'Okay, I get it. I get it. Yinz two are real American rebels."

We were now bicycling through the heart of Downtown Pittsburgh. Yinzers call it the Golden Triangle. The city streets were lined not with gold, but with majestic skyscrapers. They housed large companies such as U.S. Steel, Alcoa Aluminum, and Pittsburgh Plate and Glass. Although widely known as "The Steel City," Pittsburgh was one of the major world manufacturers of glass as well. Throngs of businessmen and businesswomen in their expensive suits and fashionable dresses were briskly walking by us on the crowded sidewalks. Occasionally, a head would turn to stare at the noticeably out-of-place teenagers on their BMX bikes. We stood out like a sore thumb. All three of us gawked up at the gigantic structures like tourists. The lofty towers of steel and glass seem much bigger when you are riding your bicycle directly beneath them. If you look straight up, you can even get dizzy.

Vito was marveling at the city's tallest building, the U.S. Steel Building, and naturally proposed the dangerous science experiment that all kids want to try.

Vito: "That thing is huge! Imagine droppin' a penny off 'at roof. Yinz think it could kill somebody?"

Bobby: "I bet it would hurt real bad, Vito. 'At thing's like 65 stories high."

Vito: "Whoa! Let's try it. You got your steel penny on you, right Bobby?"

While Vito envisioned an experiment on gravity far more audacious that anything tested by Galileo, Sal was more distracted by the building's unique appearance.

Sal: "How's come 'at thing's so rusty lookin'?"

Bobby: "My dad said it's got a special coat o' rust on the outside that protects the steel beams underneath."

Speaking of pennies, cynical Sal offered his two cents about the tall office buildings of Downtown Pittsburgh. He looked up to the top of the steel skyrise and reflected.

Sal: "Just think, all 'em suits in 'ere thinkin' they're actually doin' work n'at. Pushin' papers from one jagoff to another jagoff."

To a blue-collar, working-class Yinzer kid, "real work" meant hard manual labor. White-collar office jobs were a breeze. Even more so if that office had air conditioning on this hot summer day.

We stopped our bikes at the busy intersection of Smithfield Street and the Boulevard of the Allies to wait for a safe passage. A yellow cab drove by, and Vito extended his hand and called out to it.

Vito: "TAXI!"

Vito turned to us and proudly smiled.

Vito: "I always wanted to do that."

Then the taxi driver stopped his vehicle at the curbside and looked back at Vito as if he was a prospective customer. Big Vito lowered his head in guilt.

Vito: "Oh, crap! He stopped! I didn't think 'at would work."

We crossed the oldest bridge in town, the Smithfield Street Bridge. The ornate steel truss bridge traverses the Monongahela River (called the "Mon" by Yinzers). Pittsburgh is often called "The City of Bridges" as it boasts more bridges than any other city on Earth. With well over 400 bridges, it tops even Venice, Italy.

At the end of the bridge, we crossed over a bustling Carson Street and headed directly into a small red brick building at the base of a steep mountain. It was here that we would hop aboard the Monongahela Incline. Pittsburgh is also famous for its funiculars, better known as inclines. The inclines are like trolley cars pulled by cable chains but at an incredibly steep angle. These vertical railways allow signature red and yellow cars to carry passengers and cargo up and down the precipitous mountainside which lies due south of Downtown.

In the station, Vito questioned us in a low voice.

Vito: "Should we try to sneak on?"

Looking around Vito's wide shoulders, Sal nudged up his sunglasses and whispered calmly under his breath.

Sal: "We got Five-0. Right behind yinz."

Our dreams of a free ride were cut short when we turned around and saw a Pittsburgh Police officer who happened to be strolling by on foot patrol. He was whistling the "Steelers Polka" and spinning his baton while pretending like he was not keeping an eye on us marauding teenagers. In a rush, we rustled up the last bit of change in our pockets to pay the small ticket fee. Like excited riders boarding a roller coaster, we then noisily pushed and shoved each other into the incline car. Fortunately, the double-decker transport had ample room for our bikes too.

The oldest incline ride in the United States would allow us to explore mountaintop views of the city. Overlooking the entire downtown region of Pittsburgh, Mount Washington offers spectacular sights that every American should behold at least once in their lifetime. It rivals famous American sights from the Golden Gate Bridge overlook in San Francisco to the top of the Empire State Building in New York City.

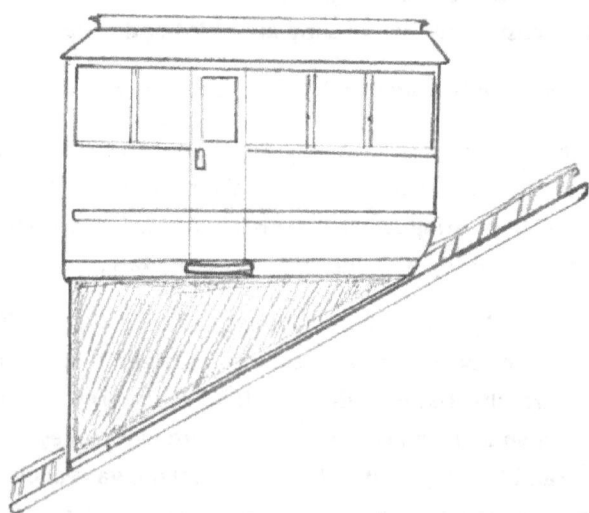

Slowly traveling up the side of the tall mountain, we could hear the large chain and gears loudly clicking beneath our incline car. While enjoying the scenery, I reached into my front pocket and pulled out the arrowhead that I had found in the creek the day before. In a way, I was simply dragging my friends around the city for my own personal reasons. I felt a strong desire to travel in the footsteps of my hero, Chief Guyasuta. He was known to have trekked up this same mountainside. Indeed, the discovery of that arrowhead had inspired me to lead the day's civic excursion.

As I spun the stone arrowhead in my hand, Sal took notice.

Sal: "You really dig 'at arrowhead, don't ya, Bobby?"

I quickly slid the arrowhead back in my pocket and then gazed nonchalantly through the large windows of the incline.

Bobby: "Oh, I just think it's cool 'at Chief Guyasuta used to come up here."

The incline soon came to a stop, and we made our exit. We walked our bikes out to Grandview Avenue at the top of Mount Washington. We gazed down on the triangle of skyscrapers below us. From here, it felt like you could reach out and touch the Steel Building. It sits nestled between the confluence of the city's three rivers. The Allegheny and Monongahela combine to form the Ohio which then flows to the great Mississippi. All four river names have Native American origins.

In fact, it was from this vantage point high over Pittsburgh that the paths of two future leaders had crossed. I gushed with excitement.

Bobby: "Wow! Look at this view! Ya know, they say the last time Guyasuta came up here was to hang out with a old friend."

Vito turned my way.

Vito: "Who?"

I didn't answer him. I looked out over the city and continued.

Bobby: "He could see it. He saw this and knew how important 'is place was."

Vito looked around in every direction.

Vito: "Who? What? Where?"

I turned to Vito.

Bobby: "Oh, George saw it. George Washington. Him and Guyasuta was friends."

It turns out that Guyasuta from the little village of Sharpsburg had friends in high places – the highest position in the country to be more precise. Chief Guyasuta had a long friendship with none other than the first President of the United States of America, also known as the famous General George Washington. Long before the illustrious general heroically led the Continental Army to victory against Great Britain in the Revolutionary War, his monumental military career started with humble beginnings in Pittsburgh. It was here that his legend began.

Bobby: "When George came here for the first time and saw the view from up here, it was nothin' but woods dahn 'ere. A couple days later, he met Guyasuta."

Three decades before America won its independence, a young George Washington was commissioned a major by the English Crown and sent to survey and map the French occupied land in the Pittsburgh region. But the headstrong and youthful officer needed an experienced guide to help him navigate the unfamiliar wilderness. Washington acutely acquired the well-respected scouting services of Chief Guyasuta. Shortly before he met the formidable Seneca warrior, Washington discovered the ideal mountaintop overlook to survey a prized location of both the English and French.

Bobby: "See, Guyasuta took George Washington all 'round here on a secret mission to spy dahn on a' tip o' the triangle and some French forts up north o' here."

Vito: "It's real steep up here. They're lucky they had 'at incline to ride up."

Sal: "They didn't have no incline back 'en, ya numbskull!"

Vito stood up on his toes to see if he could possibly peer into Three Rivers Stadium for a free mountaintop view of a Pirates or Steelers game. He sharply raised his eyebrows and pointed at the stadium.

Vito: "Hey, yinz think they could spy on a game at… "

But before he could finish his sentence, Sal interjected.

Sal: "The stadium wasn't there yet, knucklehead."

Vito bit his lip. I looked out over the city again and smiled. I imagined what Washington thought when he first set eyes on this magnificent view in 1753.

Bobby: "George saw it right away… how special it was here."

My history lesson was finally beginning to pique interest. Vito looked away from the stadium and over at the city.

Vito: "So, Bobby, how's come George and 'em cared so much about this place?"

At this juncture, I had no qualms about being a real tour guide for my friends.

Bobby: "Well, back 'en, whoever controlled the rivers, controlled everything. This was all woods. There was no roads yet. So, the rivers were like highways. The French and the English empires both wanted Pittsburgh so they could transport out lumber and coal n'at. Yinz can travel by river from Pittsburgh all a' way dahn to New Orleans and out into the Gulf o' Mexico."

At only 21 years of age, a raw and ambitious George Washington was dispatched by the British colony of Virginia to head north and meet with French commanders to demand that they vacate a string of forts far up the Allegheny River and on Lake Erie. He was also directed to covertly scout these French garrisons along the coveted waterways. He would draw maps and gather intelligence. The new officer jumped at the chance to make a name for himself by exploring these vast, uncharted forests.

Surprisingly, Pittsburgh was still free from any European presence. Back then, it was known as "The Forks of the Ohio." A pristine triangle of forest. However, its strategic location could be of extreme importance for both military and financial reasons. Here, three major rivers convened allowing a feasible way to transport soldiers as well as the riches of the inner continent to the sea and ultimately back to Europe. Even a very green George Washington had ample vision to immediately recognize this proverbial goldmine of a location and reported this back to Britain.

Bobby: "George told the King o' England they should build a fort here right away."

But France beat Washington to the punch. Not only did the French commanders scoff at the young officer's demands, but they doubled down on their land grab. They too valued Pittsburgh as the crown jewel of the American frontier and soon built a fort where the three rivers meet. Named Fort Duquesne (pronounced Doo-kane), this French military and trading stronghold was positioned at the tip of present-day Point State Park. However, even after France had gained fortified control of the region, the British Empire hotly contested France's presence in Pittsburgh. Outplayed, Washington and a small force of colonial militia and Native Americans returned. To be blunt,

Washington then ignited what is called the French and Indian War when his party opened fire on French soldiers and killed a French officer, Joseph Jumonville, in a battle southeast of Fort Duquesne. In other words, a young George Washington started a major world war between two of the largest superpowers on Earth due to a land dispute over Pittsburgh. His historic military saga began right here in Yinzer land.

Bobby: "Back in 'em days, George was a bad dude."

Sal: "The old guy with white hair on a dollar bill? C'mon, you're jaggin' us, Bobby."

Bobby: "No, for real. George was big. He stood about 6-foot-2."

  Vito stood up straight and stuck out his chest.

Vito: "That's just an inch taller than me, Bobby. He don't scare me."

  I looked up at Vito.

Bobby: "Yeah, but this was back in a' 1750s. That was like a giant back en'. Most guys were like 5-foot-6."

  For once, Sal actually needed his aviator sunglasses. With the bright sun directly shinning in our eyes, Sal looked over the high cliff and continued the conversation.

Sal: "So what? He was still an old geezer."

Bobby: "No, yinz are thinkin' of him like 'at old picture on a' wall in history class. He wasn't no gray-haired old man when he came up here. He was only like 21 when he started scoutin' 'round Pittsburgh for the English."

  Vito began to test the strength of a metal handrail from our fenced-in lookout. While pushing on the rail with full force, he asked a question.

Vito: "What color hair did George have back 'en, anyways?"

Bobby: "Oh, they say it was red. Like reddish brahn."

  Vito nodded his head.

Vito: "Oh, kinda like a cherry from his dad's cherry tree. I get it."

  Sal just shook his head. I continued with my story.

Bobby: "So Guyasuta was George's guide all 'round here and they became friends."

Chomping on his gum in deep thought, Vito asked a more important question.

Vito: "So, how'd George and Guyasuta become buddies?"

Bobby: "Well, they camped out together in a' woods on 'at dangerous mission. It was pretty risky spyin' on a' French and their forts n'at. Crazy stuff happened. George was shot at from real close range and almost got killed. Both o' them was young too, so George never forgot his first real adventure in life with Guyasuta."

A young and impressionable Washington always remembered his first true taste of adventure in the American wilderness. Nights spent sitting around a campfire and talking about one's life stories became a great way to get to know each other. Being able to survive through several life-threatening experiences also tends to form closer bonds among young soldiers. In their brazen adventure, Washington was fired upon from point-blank range and pursued by enemies in the woods north of Pittsburgh. It reminded me of how my father always kept in touch with fellow soldiers from his army platoon in the Vietnam War. Like Washington, my dad was a young man when he and his friends were being shot at by enemies in unknown forests. Vito understood the camaraderie that formed from battle.

Vito: "Oh, I get it. Like how we talk about our first BB gun battles."

Bobby: "Yeah, kinda like 'at. 'Cept way more dangerous."

In fact, a budding George Washington became a minor celebrity when his written accounts of his adventures in the Pittsburgh region were published in newspapers in the American colonies and England. Washington nicknamed Guyasuta "The Hunter" and their historic legends grew both at home and abroad. "The Hunter" had impressed Washington by shooting two large, antlered bucks and three bears for campfire dinners. They had to combat the elements too. The bleak December weather made the mission even more perilous. I continued with one more folk story.

Bobby: "It was late December, so it was snowin' real bad too. On one freezin' cold night, George was tryin' to cross the Allegheny past Sharpsburg and Etna dahn by Millvale. He made this little raft out o' wood and it flipped over in the icy water. Luckily, he swam to 'at little Island they named after him, Washington's Landing. George almost drowned in a' river that night."

Squinting to block out the sun's rays, Vito gazed over the expansive river valley in pensive reflection.

Vito: "That woulda been crazy. Then we woulda never had no first president."

Sal and I looked at each other and smiled at what somehow seemed to be a subtly whimsical yet deep revelation from Vito. Of course, Vito was pondering atop a mountain that was later named after the first president. We took one more look at the sensational cityscape view of Downtown Pittsburgh from the top of Mount Washington. Here, the paths of two great warriors interwove, the American general from Virginia and the Seneca sachem from Sharpsburg. Today, there is a large bronze statue of both George Washington and Chief Guyasuta that stands overlooking the city from where Sal, Vito, and I were straddling our bikes. It depicts the preeminent leaders greeting each other for one last time high above the three rivers. Called *Point of View*, the enormous statue commemorates their pivotal and long-lasting friendship and legacies. Long after the French and Indian War, George Washington made a point to meet here with the Seneca chief and discuss the peaceful progress in the region. Guyasuta even brought George a hefty portion of bison meat as a gift of goodwill. Of course, Vito was most interested in the food choice.

Vito: "Wait a minute! They ate bison? Like buffaloes?"

Bobby: "Yeah, there was still buffalo 'round here back 'en. That was before all them European settlers came in and hunted 'em all out."

Sal: "Yep, 'em big animals was super easy targets."

The Eastern wood bison of Pennsylvania were smaller than their Western cousins on the Great Plains. Due to overhunting and habitat loss, bison became extinct in Pennsylvania in the early 1800s and were almost wiped out across the country by the

1880s. Sadly, the once bountiful population of over 30 million wild American bison bottomed out at an abysmally low level of about 300 animals, including a small herd of only two dozen in Yellowstone National Park. This deplorable plummet helped kick-start the modern wildlife conservation movement. Although he was an avid big game hunter himself, President Theodore Roosevelt set a new priority on protecting American bison, the food and supply source for countless Native American tribes and iconic symbol of the American West.

Chewing on his gum like a meal, Vito asked one last question on the mount.

Vito: "So, whadda ya think them buffalo taste like?"

Bobby: "Uh, probably like a steak. They're kinda like cows."

Sal whispered to me out of the side of his mouth.

Sal: "We better get goin'. *It's* gettin' hungry again."

Of course, in a few short years from our conversation, every kid in America would be hunting big buffalo on a new computer game called *The Oregon Trail*. A brand-new generation of young people continued the American pastime of slaughtering bison for sport in a much more humane way, by simply pressing the "space" bar on a keypad.

After finishing our discussion about the important plans forged by George Washington and Chief Guyasuta at this scenic site, Vito had grand plans of his own up here on the mountaintop overlooking the city of Pittsburgh. He peered over the high cliff that cascades 400 feet down to the rivers. He focused his eyes like binoculars. Then, out of the blue, he heavily slammed his hands down on his handlebars.

Vito: "All right! I say we roll dahn a' bottom o' this mountain to that boat dock and try to jump over the river."

Sal looked over the forbidding cliff. Then he spotted the Gateway Clipper's dock.

Sal: "You go first. I dare you. Nah, I double dare you. We'll watch ya from up here, Evel Knievel."

Evel Knievel. The man, the myth, the legend. The famous daredevil motorcycle driver jumped over everything from river canyons to boxes of rattlesnakes to rows of Greyhound Buses, tallying a world record 433 broken bones along the way. Any kid who ever rode a bike in the 1970s idolized the fearless stuntman. We laughed at Vito's outlandish proposal to jump over the Monongahela and opted to coast down the steep McArdle Roadway instead.

After the long bike ride through the city, we returned back home to Sharpsburg. Rolling down Main Street, we seemed destined to stop our bicycles right in front of the huge bronze statue of Chief Guyasuta. It sits in the main crossroads of town. The noble warrior stands tall holding a large bow and arrow.

As we were bringing our bikes to a stop, Vito called out to me.

Vito: "Yo, Bobby, he's wearin' a cape! He's like our tahn's superhero."

Then Sal noticed the chief's long hair.

Sal: "Man, Guyasuta looks like a badass hippie with 'at hairdo."

We had now parked directly under the statue. While looking up in awe, Vito was thinking about the famous haircut named after the cousins of the Senecas, the Mohawks. He brushed his hand through the hair on the top of his head.

Vito: "I always wanted to get a mohawk."

Sal: "You should get one, Vito. I'm sure your mum would *love* 'at."

In the late '70s, the mohawk haircut was revived by a new wave of punk rock bands. Arguably the most recognizable haircut in American history reached even higher heights of popularity when it was worn by Mr. T on the *A-Team* television series a few years later.

Under the statue was a bronze bust with an inscription. Vito read the end of it aloud.

Vito: "It says, 'Dedicated and paid for by H.J. Heinz.' Huh, the chief musta liked ketchup as much as you do, Bobby."

Although he was much more interested in history than Sal, it was already made clear that Vito displayed a poor sense of historical timelines. Sal made sure to berate Vito once more about his fuzzy concept of time.

Sal: "You're such a imbecile! They wasn't dippin' fries in Heinz ketchup durin' the freakin' French 'n Indian War!"

With a twisted smirk on his face, Vito put his hands up in the air and loudly quipped.

Vito: "Oh, yeah?! Then how's come they're called *french* fries?"

I openly laughed but Sal shook his head and gave up on dealing with Vito's convoluted perception of history. Sal muttered a final surrender under his breath.

Sal: "I give up. The only time you know for sure about is dinnertime."

As Sal turned away in angst, Vito flashed a wily grin behind Sal's back.

Vito: "That reminds me. I'm starvin'."

I smiled at my friends' antics. Although Vito could be an airhead at times, I think he also secretly enjoyed playing dumb just to irritate Sal. One way or another, he would find a way to push Sal's buttons. But their last goofy spat of the day helped me stir up a question of my own.

I looked up at the statue to admire it again.

Bobby: "But for real, how's come H.J. Heinz would build a big statue o' Guyasuta to sit right in a' middle o' tahn?"

Heinz, a mogul of the American food industry, was a well-traveled man who respected the riches of human history and cultural achievement. He explored the world, from the Great Pyramids of Egypt to the Colosseum of Rome. Heinz collected enough artifacts from around the globe to fill a museum. But despite his worldly nature, Heinz was extremely proud of his humble family origin. H.J. Heinz, the "King of Ketchup," grew up in Sharpsburg too. He obviously had great respect for a fellow native of his hometown, Chief Guyasuta. Enough respect to personally finance and dedicate a colossal bronze statue of the Native American warrior. A monument that Heinz wanted to be showcased on Main Street in the middle of the busiest intersection in Sharpsburg. Deep down, I felt there had to be a closer connection between the two.

My friends offered me no reply, so I asked them again.

Bobby: "No, guys, for real. Why do yinz think Heinz put up this big statue?"

At that point, I glanced all around me and noticed that I was parked alone under the Guyasuta Statue. Talking to myself in the middle of town square, I looked like the village idiot. My buddies had already started pedaling away on their bikes. I caught up to them as we reached our block. I got home and took my seat at the kitchen table. Consumed by my thoughts, I sat quietly while we ate our 101st spaghetti dinner in a row.

There had to be more to this story. A lot more.

Chapter 5: The Melting Pot

During the cold winter months of Pittsburgh, my friends and I did what most American kids do to deal with the relentless sleet and snow: we played video games. Sal had an Atari 2600 video game system in his basement along with three games, *Combat*, *Breakout*, and *Outlaw*. With the game controller having just one button and one joystick, trying to control those square pixels on the tiny screen back then was as hectic as herding alley cats. Winter break became an underground Atari-fest where we would bet on who could win the most duels in *Outlaw*, a Wild West shootout game. Of course, the gunslinging image on the game cartridge's box looked much more exciting than the actual graphics in the game itself. At any rate, the head-to-head pixelated contests let us live out our competitive spirit while we waited for the snow to melt for our springtime bocce matches and BB gun battles.

On the other hand, during the summer months, we took full advantage of every warm day that Mother Nature had to offer. We stayed outside of the house from dawn to dusk. We practically lived on the streets. Even a stray summer rainstorm could not deter our constant outdoor existence.

After exhausting all interest in war games and ball games, we would often create makeshift ramps out of spare plywood for jump tricks with our BMX bikes. We played a few rounds of ding-dong ditch almost every day too. But when that got old, we would have to get creative. Sal, Vito, and I liked to play a simple street game that we devised to combat boredom. "Next Car Is Your Car" was the kind of basal game of chance that only working-class kids could make up, let alone enjoy. We would simply hang out on a busy street corner and take turns "getting" the next car that drove by. Today, we were just wasting some time while waiting for my grandfather to finish up work at his store. At the bottom of my pap's street was a thruway that led to the more affluent neighborhoods in the hills above the town of Sharpsburg. It was the ideal spot for "Next Car Is Your Car."

Sal: "My turn. Here comes mine. Aw yeah! A red Mustang! It's a '72 Mach 1 with black racin' stripes!"

The "winner" was picked democratically after about 100 random cars passed by on the street. And there were plenty to choose from in the 1970s. It was the golden era of American muscle cars. Ford Mustangs, Chevy Camaros, Plymouth Barracudas, and Dodge Challengers usually won the game. Occasionally, the owner of the finest Italian restaurant in town would drive by in his bright orange convertible Corvette Stingray. This car would always win straight up by unanimous decision. As trivial as it may seem, the game would get very competitive. In our wishful early teenage years, we played like we actually believed we would be awarded the keys to the cars at the end of the contest.

Vito: "Okay. My turn. My turn. No! Not a Gremlin! I'm gonna puke. Bluh! Bluh!"

To us, the compact Gremlin looked as ugly as its name. A product of American Motors, the small dark green rust bucket appeared to be chopped in half and sealed off with a hatchback. Vito couldn't stomach the idea of scoring a Gremlin. He acted like he was about to vomit. Ironically, the model was said to have been designed by an engineer sketching on a barf bag while sitting on a long airplane flight.

Vito: "Ugh! Put a Mr. Yuk sticker on it! What kind o' jagoff would even drive 'at?"

Still pretending to writhe in agony like he was physically sick, Vito personally blamed the owner of the car for his misfortune. As he continued to groan, I anxiously waited for the next car to drive by us.

Bobby: "My turn. No! A Pinto. With rust all over it too. Whatta piece o' crud!"

Having the bored looking Ford Pinto spin up out of nowhere on you was like scoring a C- on a surprise pop quiz about the states and capitals in social studies class. That plain old family car was not going make the grade needed to win this game. Even worse, the exhaust pipe was clunking under the body of this lemon. In contrast, Sal was cleaning up. It was his turn again and the most coveted car in 1979 was rolling right towards our stoop. Sal smiled and punched both of his fists into the air.

Sal: "Bada bing! A brand-new Trans Am! Blue with a big gold bird on a' hood. Bada boom! It's a convertible, too! In your faces! I win today, losers!"

The Pontiac Firebird Trans Am. My dream car. Commandeered from my little brothers, I kept a miniature Trans Am from the Hot Wheels collection on my nightstand. It was black with a gold decal of a winged Firebird on the hood. The sleek-lined machine had just been showcased in a campy road movie called *Smokey and the Bandit* starring Burt Reynolds and Sally Field as interstate bootleggers. While the head-turning muscle car slowly coasted by us, the owner of the shiny blue Firebird revved up the engine just to impress the gawking teenagers. Acquiring this sweet new ride meant that Sal had easily won this round of "Next Car Is Your Car."

Sal: "Just listen to 'at purr comin' from my souped-up engine, ya dolts!"

As Sal continued to brag about his victory, I could see that my grandfather was slowly approaching us. Today, we were going to check out his Native American artifacts collection containing items that he had acquired as a young boy in Sharpsburg. It was my pap who first sparked my interest in history, particularly military history.

A veteran of World War II, my grandfather served in the U.S. Army during the European liberation campaign. Speaking of classic cars, I still have a cool picture of him in full uniform sitting in his Army Jeep during the war. The original Jeep 4-by-4 was first produced just north of Pittsburgh in Butler, PA. It was prized by the military for its tactical off-road abilities. In that old black-and-white photograph, the name "Lucille" is clearly painted on the side of my pap's mobile Jeep. I always thought it was interesting how the soldiers, sailors, and airmen in that war gave their tanks, Jeeps, boats, and planes feminine names. I guess your vehicle would become your true love after it saved your butt in bloody battle after bloody battle.

Vito: "Nice hat, Mr. Taranto!"

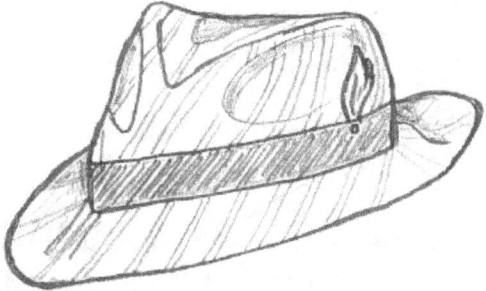

My grandfather always wore a fedora hat with a tiny gold feather nestled in the strap around the base. It was just like the style worn by the singer Frank Sinatra. Pap's jet-black hair in that old wartime photo was now fully white. He had tan skin and blue eyes. He was wearing a nice gray suit with thin pinstripes that matched the color of his hat. His look was from a long-gone era when men and women wore formal dress for every occasion, from shopping at department stores downtown to attending movie theaters or sporting events. His fine suits were in stark contrast to the white T-shirts and jeans worn by most working-class men in Sharpsburg. Unlike my father who had scruffy black hair with thick sideburns and the occasional horseshoe mustache, my grandfather was from the World War II generation and always had slicked back hair and a clean-shaven face. Wearing oversized eyeglasses with thick golden frames, Pap was advanced in age and was walking slowly towards us on the sidewalk.

Bobby: "Hey, Pap. How ya doin'?"

Pap: "How yinz doin'? C'mon, boys. Let's-a go up to the house and see my collection."

My grandfather lived on the top of the nicest street in Sharpsburg, named Heinz Terrace. Decades of hard work and a modest lifestyle allowed him to afford his nice brick home. Contrary to the crowded, aluminum sided row houses that sat within the town's flat streets below, Heinz Terrace was a hilly street overlook that was lined with tall, beautiful sycamore trees and boasted more spacious abodes. A few would almost qualify as mansions at the turn of the century. In fact, the street was named after the ketchup industry magnate, H.J. Heinz, who once resided here along with his top executives. It always felt like an escape from the rest of Sharpsburg. On this quiet and peaceful nook above town, Heinz Terrace was a cool oasis from the hustle and bustle of the hot asphalt streets below. It still is to this day.

We entered his house and immediately felt the much-welcomed temperature drop.

Vito: "Whew! It's nice and cool in here, Mr. Taranto."

My grandfather took his hat off and ushered us ahead.

Pap: "Yinz boys go have a seat in a' kitchen. Let me go find what I'm lookin' for."

Pap's house had old fireplaces decorated with marble slabs and carved oak mantels. Exquisite woodwork adorned the staircases. Hardwood floors made our voices echo. The brick house was built during a bygone era when skilled craftworkers would fine-tune every detail in construction. This was in stark difference to my skinny row house with its cheap shag carpets and faux wood wall panels made of brown vinyl. Those drab, fake wooden walls were a mainstay inside every working-class home in the 1970s. For some reason, even auto engineers picked up on the trend. Our family's yellow station wagon inexplicably had fake wood panels on its sides. We had the same "woody wagon" as The Partridge Family, a '72 Chevy Chevelle Concours.

We sat down at the kitchen table. Leaning on the back two legs of my chair, I was able to peek into the living room and see Pap pull out a box from a secret drawer in the fireplace mantel. He came into the kitchen and laid it down on the dinner table.

Pap: "Okay, boys. Look at this stuff!"

My grandfather opened the box. Our eyes lit up as we gazed in awe at Pap's collection. Vito surveyed the table-top treasure trove.

Vito: "Whoa! 'At's a lot o' arrowheads! And look at 'is big one!"

Sal side-eyed Vito.

Sal: "That one ain't a arrowhead, ya ding-a-ling. That's a spearhead."

There were about a dozen small stone arrowheads in the box. All were made of flint. There was also one larger stone spearhead. Native Americans in the region once used spears to hunt big game such as moose, elk, and bison. Much further back in time, spears were used to hunt even bigger beasts like woolly mammoths. The hairy cousin to the modern elephant, mammoth fossils can be found throughout the Northern Hemisphere. In fact, the most recent mammoths became extinct on the remote Wrangel Island in the Arctic Ocean only about 5,000 years ago. Spearheads found on the island provided evidence as to what caused the demise of the last mammoths. Once thought to be a prehistoric creature, woolly mammoths were still roaming the planet near the time of the construction of the Great Pyramids in Egypt.

Bobby: "Do you think Guyasuta's tribe made all o' these arrowpoints, Pap?"

Pap: "Maybe. But by the time of Chief Guyasuta, all the Senecas were usin' long rifles."

Bobby: "So some o' these arrowheads might be real old, then?"

Pap: "Yep, American Indians lived all 'round here for thousands o' years."

My grandfather then looked down at the collection and smiled at Vito and Sal.

Pap: "Since Bobby's already got one, yinz two pick out a arrowhead for yourselves to keep. Then all three o' yinz will have an arrowhead from Sharpsburg."

Vito became even more excited.

Vito: "Wow! Thanks, Mr. Taranto."

Vito was holding up the big spearhead. It was made from a lighter colored stone than the smaller gray arrowheads.

Sal: "Thanks, Mr. T. And Vito, he didn't say you could take 'at spear point."

As they scrutinized each arrowhead to make their selection, Pap got up and walked into the living room. He came back into the kitchen carrying one more artifact. Indeed, this was by far the most fascinating piece of his collection.

Pap: "Okay, boys. I have one more thing to show yinz."

Vito: "Zoinks!"

Pap held up a large, intimidating tomahawk. It was obviously crafted in a more recent era than the stone arrowheads; it had a silver-colored axe head made of forged steel. Although there were spots of red corrosion on the sharp blade and the long wooden handle was worn, it was clear this weapon could do some serious damage.

Bobby: "Holy crap! That's one mean lookin' tomahawk! Did you find this, Pap?"

Pap: "No. An old man from Sharpsburg gave it to me. He knew I found a few stone arrowpoints and was interested in American Indian things. He gave me some more arrowheads and the spearhead too."

My grandfather handed the tomahawk to Vito. He held it up in awe.

Vito: "Whoa! This ain't no joke. Nobody's gonna mess with you swingin' this scary thing around."

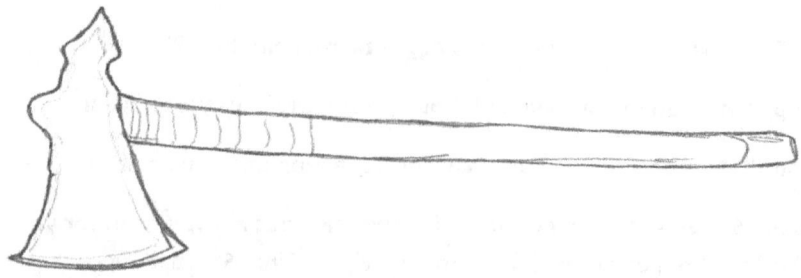

Vito gently placed the tomahawk back on the table. Then Sal and I took turns feeling the weight and balance of the weapon. Legend has it that Chief Guyasuta was laid to rest in Sharpsburg with his personal tomahawk. The Senecas of that era also used a larger ball-headed wooden war club that was equally as lethal. Nonetheless, Pap's tomahawk added a prodigious piece to an already impressive collection.

Bobby: "Thanks, Pap. 'At's a cool collection."

Vito: "Yeah. Thanks, Mr. Taranto. 'At tomahawk's real nasty. It's still pretty sharp too, so you gotta be careful with 'at thing."

My grandfather smiled at Vito's concern.

Pap: "Well, I usually don't carry it under my coat, Vito. It stays hidden in the fireplace."

Bobby: "Huh, I always wondered what was in 'at secret drawer."

My grandfather winked at me and headed to the refrigerator to get us some drinks. After Pap handed each of us a small carton of Turner's iced tea, we started talking about less serious matters and the lighter subject of popular American sports figures came up. We used to like to ask my wise old grandfather his opinion on the best athletes that he had ever seen play professional sports. However, when it came to topics like this, Pap could be biased to an almost comical level.

My grandfather was extremely proud of his Italian heritage. He only drank wine imported directly from Italy. He would only eat prosciutto and provolone cheese purchased from Labriola's Italian Market in Penn Hills. Personally, I always looked forward to the fresh loaf of Italian bread, pepperoni stick, and cured black olives that he would bring us from the market every Sunday after church. He liked to listen to Italian opera music. Either that or his old records of Frank Sinatra or Tony Bennett. Obviously, my pap always wore a fine Italian suit from his store. From food to clothes, from music to culture, he would often say, "Italians do it best."

For the most part, Pap was a rational and level-headed person. But the elder Italian American had his ethnocentric streaks. So, for some entertainment, my friends and I would secretly like hearing his incredibly partisan opinion of America's all-time greatest athletes. Only Italian Americans made his list.

Bobby: "Pap, who was the best hitter ever in Major League Baseball?"

Pap nudged on his glasses in quick thought.

Pap: "Best hitter ever? Joe Dimaggio! Joltin' Joe, for sure."

Vito took his turn.

Vito: "Pap, who was the best catcher ever?"

Like all old Italian men do, Pap started talking with his hands. He shaped his hands like he was about to catch a fastball.

Pap: "Best catcher ever? That's a tie. It's gotta be either Yogi Berra or Roy Campanella."

Yogi Berra was the quirky catcher for the New York Yankees who was famous for absurd sayings like, "If you come to a fork in the road, take it." Roy Campanella was a half African American, half Italian American catcher for the Brooklyn Dodgers. He helped to further break down the racial barriers in Major League Baseball that were initially overcome by his illustrious teammate, the great Jackie Robinson.

Sal: "How 'bout best shortstop ever, Mr. T?"

Pap: "Oh, that's-a easy. It's 'The Scooter.' Phil Rizzutto."

By now, Pap was saying the names in a thick Italian accent. He emphasized the double z's in Rizzutto and put his hand up in the air.

Vito: "Who was the best boxer of all time?"

Pap made a slow roundhouse punch in the air with a clenched right fist.

Pap: "Rocky! There's no dispute. Rocky Marciano's the best fighter there ever was!"

The vast majority of unbiased Americans in the 1970s would claim that title belonged to Muhammad Ali. But I was just glad that he had chosen an actual real person as the best boxer ever and not a fictional movie character. For a second, I thought he was going to say Rocky Balboa. Sylvester Stallone's recent hit movie *Rocky* was still deeply ingrained in our minds.

Sal: "Best pro wrestler ever?"

Pap grinned, crossed his arms, and proudly sat back in his chair.

Pap: "Bruno Sammartino. I made a suit for him once, too."

I fully agreed with Pap about this gargantuan professional wrestler. An Italian immigrant turned Yinzer, Bruno was probably the strongest human to ever walk the streets of Pittsburgh.

Bobby: "Okay, Pap. Who was the best football coach ever in the NFL?"

Pap threw his open hands downward to the floor.

Pap: "Hands down. Vince Lombardi!"

A few years later, we would ask for his opinion on NFL quarterbacks and Pap would always propose a tie between Dan Marino and Joe Montana. Of course, both QBs scored bonus points for doubly being Italian Americans and Pittsburgh natives. But as Yinzers, we saved the most important question for last.

Sal: "Best NFL running back ever?"

Pap clapped his hands together and flashed a huge smile.

Pap: "Franco Harris! Franco is the best running back to ever play the game."

Steelers legend Franco Harris had a special connection with the fans in Pittsburgh, especially Italian Americans. Harris was born to an Italian mother and an African American father. His parents met while his father was serving in the U.S. military while stationed in Italy during World War II. Drafted by the Steelers as a fullback in the first round out of Penn State, Franco made an immediate impact as a rookie. Sporting a cool Afro, Harris overwhelmed opponents with his rare combination of size and speed. The young superhero donned in black and gold was best known for his incredible game scoring touchdown, known as "The Immaculate Reception," that led the Pittsburgh Steelers to their first ever playoff game win. Even "Mean" Joe Greene, the heart and soul of the team, insisted that Franco was the catalyst for the Steelers string of four Super Bowl victories in the 1970s. Obviously, Harris was equally adored by the Black community in the city as well. Of course, my grandfather was a card-carrying member of Franco's Italian Army, a local fan club.

I pointed at my right shoe.

Bobby: "Yinz know Franco stepped on my foot once?"

Vito: "For real? That's awesome."

Once while at Alioto's pizza parlor in Etna, the Steelers running back accidentally stepped on my shoe while he was grabbing takeout. I was trying to liberate some gum from a gumball machine with my little brothers when I felt a crushing pain on my right foot. When I looked up to see who the culprit was, it happened to be the great Franco Harris briskly walking out the door with a large pizza in his hands. He promptly turned around and apologized. I looked up at him but could not reply. I was completely awestruck. To a young Italian American kid from Pittsburgh, the only event that could top that was a handshake from the Pope himself.

As my pap got up from his chair to put away the arrowhead collection, Sal smirked about my story and glared down at my shoes.

Sal: "Big deal, Bobby. Looks like you musta been wearin' a' same shoes 'at day. Least now ya got a excuse why ya never got new ones."

He chuckled about the sad state of my tattered Nike Blazer high-tops. They were in bad shape. The rubber soles were peeling off from the bottom under my heels. My socks were clearly visible through tears in the decaying seams over my toes. Even worse, the shoelace ends had long ago frayed away and resembled drooping feathers.

Sal pointed at the fluffy ends of my shoelaces and continued.

Sal: "They're a mess. It's amazing you can run as fast as you do in those crappy shoes. They look like ya dug 'em up from the bottom of a dumpster."

That was about the closest I came to receiving a compliment from Sal all summer long. It sounded like he was vaguely acknowledging that I had decent running speed. Although he probably just meant to say that I dressed like a dumpster diver.

It was getting close to dinnertime, and we thanked my grandfather for the artifact showcase and his generosity.

Vito: "Thanks for the arrowhead. You're the best."

Sal: "Yeah. Thanks, Mr. T."

Bobby: "Thanks, Pap Pap. See ya this weekend."

Pap gave me a quick pat on the shoulder.

Pap: "Okay, yinz keep lookin' 'round Guyasuta Park. Maybe after the Stillers game on Sundy, I'll show you a couple more things I got in my collection."

By the way, Yinzers typically don't say the entire portion of "day" when pronouncing the days of the week. For example, "Monday" is often contracted to "Mondy." By now, our stomachs were also contracting. We all began to hustle out the door to get home for yet another round of spaghetti. My friends pocketed their small arrowhead gifts, a reward for showing interest in the history of our town. After exiting the house to the tree-lined street, we smiled as we hopped on our bikes.

Bobby: "Yeah, the Stillers got their last preseason game this weekend."

As I mentioned early on, Yinzers pronounce their beloved professional football team as the "Stillers" in conversation. Vito looked over at me as our tires rolled downhill on Heinz Terrace.

Vito: "Who they playin'?"

Bobby: "Dallas Cowboys. But 'cause it's preseason, most o' the starters are probably gonna be rested n'at."

Sal: "Oh, that don't matter to Lambert. If it's 'em jagoffs, I bet he tries to play anyways."

Middle linebacker Jack Lambert, the fearsome enforcer of the Steelers defense, openly hated everything about the flashy Dallas Cowboys. The hard-hitting defender played ferociously against them in two Super Bowl victories. Lambert's gritty persona was always a perfect fit for the blue-collar city that he played for. Due to the team's huge popularity and success, even local churches had to arrange their schedules around the games. However, along with the meteoric rise of the Pittsburgh Steelers franchise came the historic collapse of the Pittsburgh steel industry. Years of foreign imports and high costs had taken a toll on the local industrial powerhouse. In fact, this summer, there were rumors that my father's steel fabricating factory might be closing soon. Sitting just one block away from our row house, small mills like this were the lifeblood of Sharpsburg and the greater Pittsburgh region.

As Vito, Sal, and I were riding our bikes down my street I could hear loud voices emanating from my house. As we coasted closer, the screams were sounding much noisier now and I became a little embarrassed. In a small town of connected row houses, knowing about everyone else's business was commonplace. Dealing with fellow townsfolk who were "nebby" (nosy in Yinzer) was as normal as the sun setting in the west. I recall having a conversation with one busybody neighbor earlier in June that summer.

Nebby Neighbor: "Hey, I heard it's your birthday. Happy birthday, Bobby!"

Bobby: "Oh, thanks, Mrs. Martino. Who told ya?"

Nebby Neighbor: "Nobody. I could hear yinz singin' 'Happy Birthday' to you from outside your kitchen window."

Bobby: "Oh, for sure. Thanks again."

But today, the turbulent commotion from my home traveled well beyond the range of eavesdropping neighbors. It was a full-fledged verbal argument. We could now clearly hear my parents in a heated quarrel from a couple of houses away. Fearing the worst, my friends cringed, put their heads down, and quickly pedaled away. I dropped my bike on the sidewalk out front and darted inside my home.

My parents were screaming their heads off at each other.

Mom: "You knew they were gonna lay you off and ya didn't say nothin' to us?!"

Dad: "I wasn't sure yet! I didn't want yinz to worry. All ya do is worry!"

Mom: "Yeah, I worry about puttin' food on a' table! That *is* all I do! Now how we gonna afford to feed all these kids?!"

At the end of his workday, my father had just been told by his boss that he had lost his job in the mill. He was given his two weeks' notice. My younger siblings were standing against the wall in the living room in fear. Tempers had reached a boiling point. My father's dirty work clothes were sitting in the hamper. My furious mother took his clothes and threw them out the front door and onto the street.

Mom: "You won't need these no more, ya jagoff!"

Bobby: "Mum, don't… "

At that moment, we felt a burst of hot air. A massive heat wave blasted through the front door. The pressure almost blew the screen door completely off from its hinges.

My entire family gathered at the doorway to inspect the cause of the blast.

Bobby: "It's a fire! The Mariuccis' house is on fire!"

The next-door neighbor's house was completely engulfed in flames. A red-orange blaze was streaming from every window and spreading up the side of the house. Within seconds, their entire wooden row house lit up like a candle.

It was an inferno. The heat was unbelievable. Our shock was palpable.

Dad: "Holy crap! Yinz get outta here!"

We all fled out to the sidewalk at once. We knew it was only a matter of seconds before the fire would spread to our adjacent home. My father shouted at my mother and younger siblings as he forcefully pointed down the alley.

Dad: "Get to Big Nana's! RUN! GO!"

My family began sprinting towards our great-grandmother's house. She lived about ten row houses away. Then I heard it. The scariest sound of my youth. The whistles blowing at the Sharpsburg Volunteer Fire Department. The echoes of the winding sirens sent chills down my spine.

More than the howl of a stray dog, my greatest fear in life was hearing the loud ghostly wail of the fire station's rooftop alarm. Not only because of the close proximity of many homes in the neighborhood, but because my father was a volunteer firefighter. Ever since I was a small child, I feared watching him race out the door as the ominous siren would scream over the town.

Unfortunately, he was already at the scene of the fire. It was our house now! Flaming hot embers from the neighbor's house had blown onto our old home's dry, sunbaked shingles and set our whole roof ablaze. It was then that my father turned to me with a steely look on his face that I will never forget.

Dad: "Bobby, you stay out here! I'm gonna go grab some things!"

In the blink of an eye, I saw a different man. A man who fought in countless deadly battles in the jungles of Vietnam. A man who risked his life to save wounded soldiers. A man who risked his life to save fellow neighbors in fires before. He sprinted inside the burning house with no hesitation.

An instant later, I made an unwise decision. I followed him inside. I ran into our house to grab as many items as possible. Smoke had begun to fill up the rooms. I flew upstairs and snatched my backpack from my bedroom closet. In the open backpack, I shoved my mother's small jewelry box that was sitting by the bathroom mirror. I scooted past my parents' bedroom, spun 180 degrees, and whisked back into their room. I reached under their bed and grabbed my father's box of war medals.

As I jetted back down the stairs, thick black smoke had enveloped the entire living room and the front doorway. I had to backtrack and sprint to the side door in the kitchen. I rammed through the swinging screen door and stumbled outside. I was in a daze from breathing in smoke. My eyes were watering. I started coughing up a storm. As I was hunched over, I felt a hand on my back. It was father guiding me to the street. He managed to grab some small items like clothes, his car keys, and some cash. He put it all down on the sidewalk and pointed at it.

Dad: "Take this stuff and get outta here, Bobby!"

I wrangled up all our belongings on the sidewalk and shoved them in my backpack. By now, the fire trucks were pulling up to my house. I looked up and realized the fire had fully engulfed the top section of our home.

Bobby: "Dad, the whole house is on fire!"

Firefighters jumped out and immediately began spraying the houses with water stored in the fire engine's reserve tank. A veteran fireman, my father quickly gripped another hose from the truck and fastened it to a fire hydrant on the street. He worked with feverish determination. It was the biggest stake that he ever had in putting out a fire. I watched as he began directing the water hose on his own enflamed home. While he sprayed our attic playroom, he yelled at me again.

Dad: "I said get out of here, Bobby! NOW!"

By this time, a throng of neighbors filled up the alley. The assembly of onlookers was commonplace in our small town filled with rows after rows of houses. They flocked to witness the incredible scene. They also came to gauge the possibility of the fire spreading on a path toward their own homes. Now standing among the crowd, I heard a loud crack and thud as the large support beam in the attic had succumbed to the fire and fallen. Part of the roof collapsed with it.

I hopped on my bike and began to pedal away. As I rode to my Big Nana's house, the scene was absolute madness. The blistering heat in the smoke-filled alley was hellish. The smell of burnt timber had fully permeated the air. The mixture of cinders and water vapor from the hoses created a thick cloud of wet, floating ash. Everything in sight glowed red from the hue of the flames. Weaving through the hectic crowd, I sped down our narrow street while desperately trying to avoid hitting anyone. Upon arrival, I jumped from my bike and staggered into my great-grandmother's house.

My distressed mother was standing in wait.

Mom: "Thank God you're okay! Where's Dad, Bobby? Where's Dad?"

I coughed and hurriedly spit out my words.

Bobby: "He's tryin' to put the fire out, Mum. It spread to our house. All the fire trucks are dahn 'ere."

I started coughing again. My worried little sister looked up at me.

Brandy: "Are you sure you're okay, Bobby?"

Bobby: "Yeah, I'm fine. Here's the stuff we were able to save."

I set down the backpack full of items salvaged from our burning home. When I unzipped my bag, the contents began to spill into a small pile in the middle of my great-grandmother's entryway. My Big Nana calmly gathered up our things and placed them away for the time being. She wisely knew that human life far outweighed any material possession.

About twenty anxious minutes later, my father walked into my Big Nana's house. He was wearing his gold-colored firefighter jacket. He took his fire helmet off as he crossed the threshold. Behind him swirled the red lights atop fire trucks parked outside in the alley. Shaking in fear, my family sat huddled on the couch in my great-grandmother's living room. My younger siblings had bundled up in my Big Nana's comforting homemade yarn blanket to calm their nerves. Slowly entering the quiet room, my father was disheveled and soaking wet. He had a long face. He brought his helmet to his chest and stared ahead with sorrowful eyes. His melancholic voice dashed any glimmer of hope.

Dad: "It's gone. It's all gone. Our house is gone."

There was a terrible silence. Then my mother and siblings began to cry. I put my head down and sighed heavily in despair.

Two hours later, I couldn't help but wonder about the aftermath. When the smoke finally cleared, I slowly rode my bike down the wet street to see for myself. The little alley was gloomily quiet. I stopped my BMX next to the fire hydrant that my father had used. A tiny stream of water swirled around my shoes and trickled down the storm drain. As I gazed upon the lot where our humble home once stood, I realized that he was right. It was gone. All that remained was a charred ruin. With nothing left to look at, I stared at the gold fire hydrant for what seemed like an eternity.

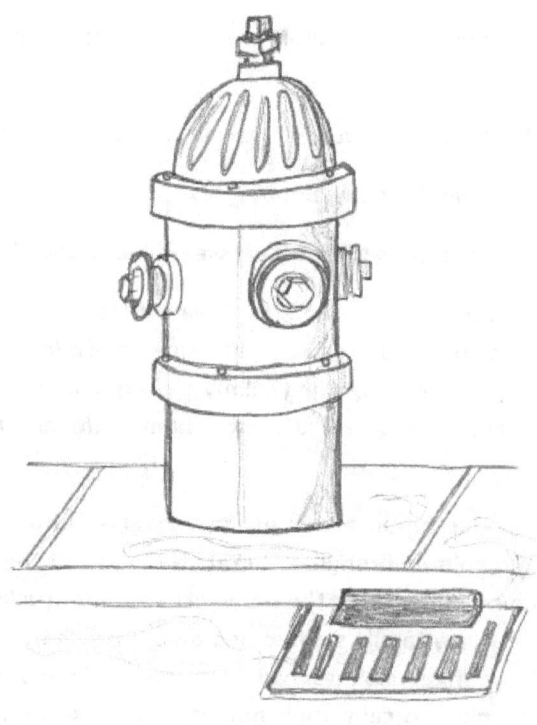

***

The "Melting Pot" is a metaphor that refers to how peoples of different backgrounds have come together to create the American way of life. Our diverse society has long been infused with and influenced by many nationalities, ethnicities, races, religions, and cultures. Like cooking a big pot of delicious soup, our nation becomes richer and richer with each new addition to the stirred broth. The eclectic mixture is part of what makes the United States a unique blend of humanity.

This collective experience continually churns out incredibly novel expressions in music, art, cuisine, and literature. Just look at rock and roll. A quintessential American product, rock and roll music was inspired by a wide fusion of cultural influences. Rock music evolved from African American rhythm and blues. It's sprinkled with a touch of gospel, soul, and jazz and topped with a helping hand of Southern country (which itself morphed from Scots-Irish immigrant folk music). Being equal parts Black and Italian, Franco Harris is the embodiment of the figurative American melting pot. Cities like Pittsburgh had slowly been mixing a giant cauldron of cultures from Africa, Asia, Europe, and the Americas. Sharpsburg, at that time, was more like a little pot of simmering tomato sauce that had yet to be fully stirred. It was heavy on the Italian seasoning but waiting on other ingredients. Today, the town is a much thicker pot of stewed Americana.

Ironically, it was an actual melting pot that started the fire that destroyed our house. Our nice, little old neighbor was warming up a pot in his kitchen to make some pasta. However, he forgot to put water into the heated pot. He only left the pot on the lit gas stovetop for a few minutes unattended. But that was all the time the fire needed. The empty metal pot absorbed the heat energy and rapidly melted into a molten liquid that sparked and caught his kitchen drapes on fire.

Three families on Cecil Street lost their homes that night. Fortunately, no one lost their life. The timely action of my father and the local firefighters stopped the spread of the fire to more homes. Sal's small grass yard provided a buffer that protected his home and Vito's as well.

Later that night, a terrible thunderstorm drenched the town of Sharpsburg. Its pummeling rain was so damaging that it caused scattered flash flooding on the town's streets. Perhaps the torrential downpour could have slowed or even halted the fast-spreading fire that destroyed our home. It came five hours too late.

Chapter 6: The American Dream

The fire had completely destroyed our house. We were homeless. My father and I had managed to salvage a handful of personal items, but other than that, we had nothing left but our family car and my bike. Fortunately, my Pap Taranto had enough room to accommodate our family of six. The very next day, we moved into his white brick house on the top of Heinz Terrace.

After a small spaghetti dinner, my parents went upstairs to organize the sleeping arrangements. Thankfully, my siblings' normal routine of playing after supper remained unhampered. My sister managed to find my Aunt Filippa's childhood Barbie dolls and my brothers were having a war with dozens of little green army men. They were finger-shooting gum bands at opposing lines of plastic soldiers. Lounging in their makeshift bedrooms, I could tell the much-needed playtime helped put their minds at ease. As grateful as we were for my pap's hospitality, it was a somber and strange feeling to have had a house one day and then watch it go up in smoke the next. There is nothing more humbling than losing your home. A huge part of your life seems to disappear into thin air. Poof – it's gone. And you're left standing in the gutter.

Another rainstorm was stirring up and distant thunder could be heard rumbling. Pap and I went to relax in his once elegant but now timeworn living room by the hearth. His brick fireplace stood out because of its ornate wooden mantelpiece and smooth marble base. On top of the mantel sat a small porcelain leopard.

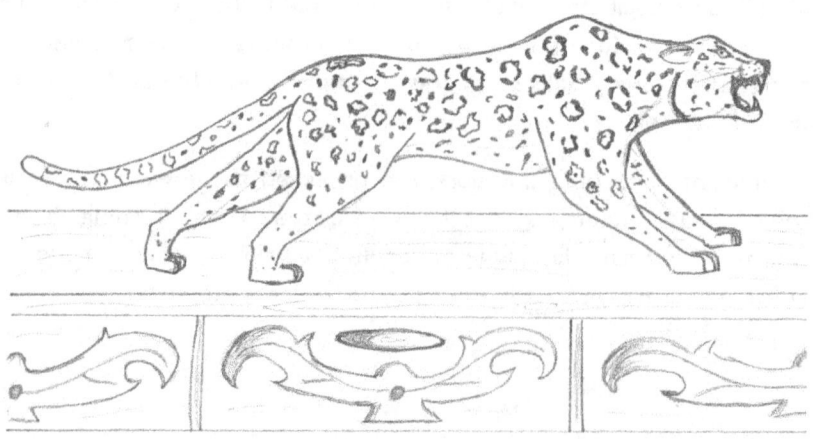

Painted with bright yellow glaze and dotted with black spots, the leopard was frozen in a striking pose with its teeth fully presented. Out of habit, I reached up and touched the cat's sharp pointed canines as I entered the room. I did it for luck, a superstition I had since childhood. The spotted feline stood guard over the fireside. Of course, firewood would not be kindled during the warm nights of August. Yinzers typically don't spark up their fireplaces until the first chilly evenings in October.

Pap: "Is 'at bedroom okay for yinz boys?"

Bobby: "Yeah. It's fine, Pap. Thanks."

After a long day of settling into our grandfather's house, I was finally able to take a load off and try to let go of the tragedy. I plopped myself down on the sky blue velvet couch. Pap sat down in his navy blue upholstered chair by the fireplace. In between us, the hardwood floors were covered with an older decorative rug. On the coffee table, a small jar rested with pistachios still hiding in their shells.

Bobby: "Can I have some, Pap?"

Pap: "Pistachios? You bet. Mangia!"   (Mangia means "eat up" in Italian.)

I grabbed a small handful to snack on and began the tedious process of removing the shells. My grandfather kept his TV in the kitchen, so this living room was set up solely for lounging and relaxed conversation. It had big windows facing the serene, tree-lined street. The calming sound of a ticking grandfather clock permeated the air.

To clear my mind of our loss, I resorted to a time-proven method. I took comfort in hearing stories of "the good old days" from my grandfather. In particular, I wanted to learn more about another native son from our small town. After pausing to allow the clock to chime seven times to mark the new hour, I asked my grandfather a question that had been brewing in my mind.

Bobby: "So, did H.J. Heinz actually live here on Heinz Terrace, Pap?"

Pap: "Yep, for just a little while when he was older. He grew up in a little brick house his dad built in the middle o' tahn. His dad was a brick maker. 'Cause it's on an old flood plain, Sharpsburg was known to have the best clay around for makin' bricks. They did good, but they weren't a real rich family."

Bobby: "Then how'd Heinz get so rich?"

Pap: "'Cause he worked his butt off! Even as a young boy, Heinz had a work ethic that would put most o' yinz kids today to shame."

Henry John Heinz lived the epitome of "The American Dream." The son of German immigrants, Heinz was born and raised in Pittsburgh. He was the oldest of eight children. At age five, his family moved from the crowded tenements of the South Side to the once pastoral fields of Sharpsburg. From his humble roots in Sharpsburg, Heinz went on to become one of the richest men in America.

Pap: "Back 'en, our tahn was nothin' but a little village with some farms and cornfields n'at. The Heinz family had a real big garden."

Heinz was an entrepreneur from the very beginning. As a boy, he would go door to door in Sharpsburg and sell fresh vegetables from his family's garden. By age twelve, his ambitious business grew so much that he used a horse to pull his produce cart around town. Sal, Vito, and I played baseball in a ballpark that was once a vegetable plot of the ketchup maker. If you recall, earlier this week, I had lied to my father and said that I graciously gave up my bike to an injured player at Heinz Memorial Ball Field. Of course, later there was a much larger field with his namesake. The home of the Pittsburgh Steelers on the city's North Shore was named Heinz Field.

Even as a young kid, H.J. Heinz made a name for himself by selling fresh, quality produce. But well before the invention of the electric refrigerator, one needed to preserve food for the long haul. So, Heinz literally started a company from scratch. He used the family kitchen and basement to develop ways to create and store tasty, jarred foods. By the time he was a teenager, he and his mother had developed recipes to preserve their garden's vegetables. Using specially calculated formulas of vinegar and salts, Heinz used trial and error along with some chemistry skills to cure his cucumbers as pickles and turn his tomatoes into ketchup. The enterprising teen also developed a new spicy horseradish dipping sauce from the common root.

Pap: "He'd do experiments with his mum in their little kitchen to figure out all o' the recipes. He kept all his food jars dahn a' cellar. They lived dahn on Main Street."

Bobby: "Where at? Which house?"

Pap grinned at my question and leaned forward in his chair.

Pap: "It's gone. He moved it!"

Bobby: "Whadda ya mean he moved it?"

Pap chuckled and continued.

Pap: "He loved that old house so much that he had it lifted up 'n floated dahn the river to his big factory on a' North Side. Now it's in a museum park of great American homes near Detroit. It's sittin' next to Henry Ford's childhood home."

Bobby: "Huh. We should go see it one day, Pap."

Undeterred after one failed business attempt as a young adult, Heinz exploded onto the international stage during one of the most celebrated commercial expositions in American history. At the Chicago World's Fair in 1893, two Yinzers became world famous: H.J. Heinz for his quality food products and George Westinghouse for his wondrous technological innovations. It was here that the latter introduced Nikola Tesla's newly designed electrical lighting system. Westinghouse, a titan in the field of industrial engineering, allowed fairgoers to bask in the nocturnal glow of electric lights for the first time ever. When he flipped the switch, it was like magic. Some say the modern age began on that illuminated night in Chicago.

Bobby: "So, what's the '57' in Heinz 57 mean?"

Pap: "Oh, it stands for '57 Varieties' of food offered. But Heinz produced way more of a selection than 'at. He thought 57 was a lucky number and it looked catchy on his labels and billboards n'at. He was a heck of a salesman."

Besides being a first-rate food producer, Heinz was a marketing genius. The cheerful man with a huge handlebar mustache always kept a notebook in his pocket to jot down new business ideas or interesting discoveries. He was constantly looking for the next best sales opportunity. At the World's Fair, he found it. Heinz capitalized on the massive crowds drawn to the novel bright lights and first ever Ferris wheel ride to pass out free pickle-shaped pins from his food stand. With over 27 million visitors attending the fair, his newly minted Heinz 57 pickle pins were soon passed along as collector's items around the globe. Heinz had struck gold. The fame of the Heinz brand and its vast selection of food products soon became world renowned.

Pap: "Heinz made sure all his ketchup bottles were made right here in Sharpsburg at his own glass factory. And he had huge tomato patches here and over in Aspinwall. A lot of Italian families came over and settled in Sharpsburg to work for him."

Pap smiled and continued.

Pap: "Nobody loved our little tahn more than H.J. Heinz. But after he became real rich, he moved outta Sharpsburg and over to Millionaire's Row."

Heinz was extremely proud of his Sharpsburg upbringing. After getting married and having children, his family lived in a nice house that sat only two doors away from Pap's place. However, when he really struck it big, he moved to a marvelous mansion in the most exclusive stretch of Point Breeze. Trumpeted as the richest neighborhood in the world at the time, Andrew Carnegie, Andrew Mellon, George Westinghouse, Henry Clay Frick, and H.J. Heinz all lived within several blocks from one another.

Pap: "When I was a little younger than you, Bobby, I helped Mr. Heinz move the last of his stuff outta his old place here and over to his big new mansion. I liked makin' pocket money doin' odd jobs 'round the neighborhood like you do with your grass cuttin'. Anyways, we ended up talkin' a lot and I mentioned that I found a couple arrowheads."

Bobby: "A couple? You showed us a dozen yesterday."

Pap: "Well, I found two of them arrowheads myself. The rest o' my collection was given to me. 'Member how I told ya it was given to me by an old man?"

My eyes widened.

Bobby: "*Heinz* was the old man?"

Pap: "Yep. See, Heinz started farmin' fields here when he was a little kid. His horse plow would dredge up dirt and he would find things all the time. Over the years, his plows uncovered all kinds o' stuff. Beads, pottery, them arrowheads, the tomahawk. He would collect 'ese things. He got real into it."

Pap looked at me, warmly smiled, and continued.

Pap: "You know, you and him both looked up to the same guy from Sharpsburg. That's a Guy with a capital G."

Bobby: "Guyasuta? For real?"

It turned out that H.J. Heinz and I shared a common hero, Chief Guyasuta. From his findings, a young Heinz became intrigued by the vestiges of a Native American civilization that once thrived here. He also became fascinated by the legend of their exalted chieftain. He too idolized Guyasuta for his storied exploits as a bold warrior and strong leader. Obviously, I became excited by these new revelations.

Bobby: "So that's why H.J. Heinz put up 'at big statue for Guyasuta in a' middle o' tahn! He was honoring his hometahn hero. His childhood hero."

Pap: "You got it, Bobby. He wanted to honor the great chief of the Senecas."

As a kid, Heinz tried to learn everything that he could from the older adults in Sharpsburg about Guyasuta, even anecdotal stories. The mythology of Chief Guyasuta still ran strong in the town's folklore. After all, Guyasuta lived here only a few generations before Heinz made Sharpsburg his home.

But time moved on and so did H.J. Heinz. As a wealthy older man, he decided to move to a newer, bigger home across the river. My pap was the perfect kid to help pack up boxes of belongings. It was then that Heinz saw a great opportunity to give away a box or two from his childhood. The famed food giant had a sterling reputation as a caring and generous employer. He kindly passed on his Native American artifacts to my grandfather.

Pap: "So Heinz gave me his arrowhead collection that I showed yinz yesterday. He even gave me the tomahawk."

But apparently H.J. Heinz saved the most important gifts for last. Pap continued his story by extending his hand in order to act out that moment.

Pap: "Then old man Heinz said, 'Here, Filip, you take this now. This'll be the last part of your payment for helpin' me move out.'"

Bobby: "What did he give you, Pap?"

By now, the storm was overhead. Whooshing rain loudly pattered on every angle of the house. Lightning glowed through the stained-glass windows while thunder loudly crackled outside. Pap slowly rose from his chair and walked towards the fireplace. I stood up and followed behind him as he gently pulled open the hidden drawer in the chimneypiece. There sat the secret box with the arrowheads. But behind that was another box. It was small and dusty. Pap lifted out the little box.

Pap: "H.J. Heinz gave me *this*."

He brushed off an old cobweb with his palm and gently opened the lid. It contained a small knife with a wooden handle, a beaded necklace, and polished wood-carved figurines of a bald eagle, red fox, and mountain lion. It also contained a little brown journal.

Bobby: "Cool! I can't believe this. Look at these little animals."

I picked up the mountain lion figurine for a closer inspection. Now extinct in the region, the forested hills of Pittsburgh were once patrolled by a healthy population of mountain lions. My grandfather smiled as I handled the small, wood-crafted animals.

Pap: "I used to like playin' with those animals when I was a kid. I was about as young as your sister when he gave 'em to me. We didn't have a lot o' toys back in 'em days."

H.J. Heinz had found a fellow hometown boy who shared a passion for American Indian antiquities. That little boy from Sharpsburg happened to be my grandfather, Filippo Taranto. By then a millionaire, Heinz had no qualms about giving away his prized childhood collection. The eccentric old man was captivated by the legend of Chief Guyasuta and wanted to pass it on to a youthful spirit. But with his never-ending quest for knowledge, it was his journal records that Heinz valued most.

My grandfather lifted out the journal and wiped the dust off its cover. Then he held it up and lightly shook it.

Pap: "Now here, Bobby. This is the most important thing Heinz gave me. This is what I really wanted to show you. Look at this."

Pap handed me the small notebook. It was a slim, leather-bound ledger. The brown leather cover was badly worn, and the thin pages were turning golden brown from oxidation. I carefully opened it up for inspection.

114

Even in his youth, Heinz was serious about collecting historical artifacts. In the same way that he wrote meticulous notes about ketchup and horseradish recipes, a young Heinz kept a detailed logbook about the Native American archaeological objects that he found. Documenting every single relic that he had unearthed in the fields and creeks of town, Heinz cataloged each arrowpoint, bowl, and necklace.

Bobby: "Huh. It lists everything he found, and where, 'n when. He marked it all dahn. The arrowheads, the beads, the knife, the tomahawk… "

My grandfather curtly interrupted me and pointed at the notebook.

Pap: "But there's more, Bobby! There's more in there."

Bobby: "Really? What is it, Pap?"

I slowly worked my way through the journal. It was a wealth of information. The first half contained itemized descriptions along with the dates and locations of recovered artifacts. Then midway through the ledger, it became a thorough collection of notes about the life of Chief Guyasuta.

Pap: "When he was a kid, Heinz found out everything he possibly could about Guyasuta. He wrote dahn everything from the names of his relatives to his exploits in battle. The stories were still fresh back 'en. There were old people in Sharpsburg who actually knew Guyasuta and talked about visitin' him at his little cabin by the river."

Pap leaned over and continued in a lower voice.

Pap: "There was this rumor. They said there was somethin' Chief Guyasuta said to his family on his deathbed, in the very last moments of his life."

He tapped his finger twice on the notebook with purpose.

Pap: "Go to the back, Bobby. Go to the last page."

Again, my grandfather tapped on the top of H.J. Heinz's little brown journal. I hurriedly flipped to the back of the ledger. To the final yellowed page. Written there in cursive were the fabled last words of Chief Guyasuta. It was one lone sentence.

I slowly read it out loud.

Bobby: "'Beneath the fallen General, marks the spot of hidden gold.'"

I looked up at Pap with astonishment.

Bobby: "Gold? Hidden gold? Whose gold?"

Pap's eyes lit up behind his Coke bottle thick lenses. He grinned like a magician about to reveal his biggest secret. In a gruff voice, he replied.

Pap: "Braddock's Gold. General Braddock's Treasure."

Bobby: "What? What are you talkin' about, Pap?"

I was stunned. As I stood jaw-dropped, Pap was in no rush to reply. He leisurely made his way back to his favorite sitting spot. The thunderstorm was now in full swing. A bright flash came from outside. The room glowed gold from a huge bolt of lightning cracking in the sky directly above Heinz Terrace. Pap slowly sat down in his chair again. By the old fireplace, he began to explain the legend of Braddock's Gold.

Pap: "Long ago, the French controlled Dahntahn. They had a fort... "

In the year 1755, Major General Edward Braddock was the head commander for the British Empire in the American colonies. Two decades before the birth of the United States of America, the Pittsburgh region was hotly disputed over by two of the largest empires in the world, France and Great Britain. Now deeply entangled in the French and Indian War, General Braddock was leading a large British and Colonial American army over the Appalachian Mountains en route to a small French fortress named Fort Duquesne, located in modern-day Downtown Pittsburgh. Two full regiments marched from the southeast out of Fort Cumberland, the remote British outpost in Maryland. A stout army of over 2,000 well-armed troops and dozens of horses pulling cannons and wagons stretched in a column over two miles long. Its huge warpath essentially carved a new passageway in the American frontier, called Braddock's Road. The goal of the campaign was to remove the French and Native American forces from Fort Duquesne and begin a new British stronghold. Once again, both France and England were well aware of the strategic importance of Pittsburgh and its ability to control river commerce and military movements.

Pap: "Generalissimo Braddock made it no secret he was comin' to take 'at fort. Flags flew high. Fifes and drums played loud. He probably thought it would be a piece o' cake with all them troops he had. But that general didn't know how to fight deep in a' back woods o' Pennsylvania. He marched his men in a long, straight line."

Bobby: "You said even in battle they'd march shoulder to shoulder like toy soldiers."

Pap: "Yep. That's how they fought over in Europe back 'en. In tight lines. They'd line 'em up and knock 'em dahn. And them bright red uniforms made easy targets."

General Braddock was accompanied by an unpaid volunteer soldier from Virginia, the now famous George Washington. Braddock considered Washington his right-hand man. Not only was Washington very familiar with the wooded terrain, but also the guerrilla warfare fighting style of the Native Americans. Under his command, the colonial militia gained the reputation of being a formidable force. Unlike the close linear formations used by British redcoats, American soldiers had become accustomed to deploying into the thick forests for a tactical advantage. Trees became shields.

The awaiting clash between Colonial Americans and Native Americans included some of the most prominent figures in early American history. George Washington's company included famed frontiersmen Daniel Boone and John Fraser along with future Revolutionary War hero Daniel Morgan. Much of the logistics and supplies had been organized by the colonial Postmaster General named Benjamin Franklin. The opposing Native American forces included legendary warriors such as Chief Pontiac, Chief

Shingas, and Chief Guyasuta. In fact, Washington may have fought against his friend in this battle. At that time, Guyasuta was caught between a rock and a hard place and often had to switch allegiances to serve the best interest of his tribe.

Bobby: "Do you think Washington 'n Guyasuta saw each other during the battle?"

Pap: "Maybe, Bobby. For all we know, they may have seen each other in the crosshairs o' their pistols."

July 9, 1755. It was a warm day. Fort Duquesne was within reach. General Braddock was confident that his robust army would easily conquer a fort holding only 250 French troops. However, he grossly underestimated the size and strength of New France's allied force – over 600 Native American warriors. Less than eight miles from the fortress walls, Braddock and his marching infantry would be completely surprised. As a long column of British regulars and American colonials was strung out in a forested ravine between the Monongahela River and a steep rock bluff, gunfire erupted. A barrage of bullets whizzed through the trees. Braddock's soldiers were ambushed by a hidden legion of French and Native Americans. A bloody onslaught ensued. Entire rows of redcoats were torn to pieces by unseen rifles. Surrounded by enemies in all directions, General Braddock was struck by a lead musket ball and fell from his horse. Washington scurried to attend to the wounded general.

Pap: "That's when George Washington took charge o' the battle."

Still only 23 years old, Washington made a gutsy move. He jumped in as the de facto commanding officer and bravely directed the remaining British guards and colonial militia. In the chaos, he had two horses shot out from under him. In fact, he was lucky to survive incredibly close calls with enemy fire. After the horrific battle, an unscathed Washington found four holes in his blue officer's coat from missed shots. Although in a losing effort, Washington managed to save many of his comrades' lives and was lauded as the "Hero of the Monongahela." However, the sound defeat became known as an infamous disaster. The Battle of Braddock was a devastating loss for Great Britain. With nearly 1,000 men killed or wounded, the British battalion was crushed and forced to scatter in retreat through the eastern forests. Well over half of the redcoat officers had been killed. In short time, General Braddock died from his wounds. The town that lies on the battlefield site today is known as Braddock, PA.

Bobby: "So what's the story with the gold?"

Pap: "Well, Bobby, that's what I've been tryin' to figure out since I was your age."

This is where the legend of Braddock's Gold begins. Apparently, the British forces had hidden important maps and a treasure chest of gold coins around the timeline of the battle. In those days, armies often carried a large supply of gold to pay their soldiers and scouts. Regular salary payments from this gold bounty were used as a method to preserve loyalty to the English Crown as well as to prevent soldiers from simply deserting into the vast woods of Pennsylvania. However, the chaos caused by the surprise enemy ambush and the confusion caused by the hurriedly scattered retreat meant that the gold was left hidden at a top-secret site. This would have prevented the French and Native Americans from acquiring the golden spoils of war.

For over two centuries, many prospectors searched for the gold. Legend and mystery shrouded the location of the treasure. Scarce evidence had ever been found. But on this fateful night at my grandfather's house, I was given a detailed notebook offering valuable information on the whereabouts of the gold. The clue had long been kept in secrecy until this stormy evening in August of 1979.

Pap: "I want you to have this book now, Bobby. It's yours."

Pap gave me the notebook full of long lists and a short quote. Pap knew that I was just as fascinated with the legend of Guyasuta as he had been. He also knew that now was a better time than ever to allow his grandson to learn about the golden treasure. My grandfather attempted to uncover more information about the mystery behind the hidden gold's location in his youth but made few strides in finding the riches. It was my turn to keep up the hunt. He was passing on the torch that had gone from one Sharpsburg kid to another, and yet another.

Pap: "Remember, Bobby, those last words from Guyasuta are important... he had inside information. Chief Guyasuta was friends with the only man in a' battle who knew for sure where the gold was hidden besides General Braddock himself."

Bobby: "George Washington?"

Pap: "Bingo! George Washington had to tell Guyasuta that."

At this point, I could not control my utter amazement. I sprang up from the sofa.

Bobby: "This is insane! Pap! This is unbelievable!"

I began to pace around the living room. As I walked in circles with Heinz's book in hand, I started piecing through all these surprising revelations that my grandfather had just disclosed to me. It was unbelievable. Apparently, both Heinz and Pap had spent their childhoods trying to track down a storied hidden treasure. Even more amazing, Chief Guyasuta learned about the secret location of the gold from the future first president of the United States. From Heinz's notes, Guyasuta said the gold was hidden at the spot where General Braddock had fallen. I started to tap on the journal.

Bobby: "So, Pap, the gold might be buried beneath the spot where General Braddock had fallen off his horse when he was shot in a' battle. The site o' the battle was named after the general and became known as the tahn of Braddock. Did you ever look dahn 'ere?"

Pap: "I looked all 'round in Braddock when I was young like you. But you got a big advantage over me and Heinz. A huge advantage! You can use somethin' that H.J. Heinz and I could only dream about havin' when we was your age."

Bobby: "What's 'at, Pap?"

Pap: "Follow me, kid."

Once again, Pap got up slowly from his comfortable chair. We exited the front door and went around his house to the detached garage out back. The rainstorm had now weakened, and only a soft drizzle was falling upon us. He hobbled around his long, light yellow Lincoln Continental that was rarely driven. In the back of the garage, Pap reached up to a high wood shelf. He wrestled off a tan cloth tarp and grasped a big contraption that was painted with a matte black finish. It was a long handheld metal detector.

Pap: "This kind o' tool wasn't around until I was in the War. We used 'em over in France to look for landmines. I bought this nifty doodad ten years ago, but I never used it. I'm too old now to go huntin' for gold."

The first metal detector was invented by Alexander Graham Bell in 1881 in a futile attempt to find an assassin's bullet that was lodged in the torso of President James Garfield. The technology had not truly developed into a handheld device until World War II. But by the 1960's, anyone could purchase a decent handheld metal detector. This was well after Pap was an idealistic young kid out searching for a secret gold

120

treasure. But even at an older age, a hopeful Pap bought this gadget from Esther's Hobby Shop in nearby Millvale. After Pap pulled the metal detector down from the shelf, he flipped a switch to turn it on and tested it right there in the garage. He swung the circular bottom end around the shiny metal hubcaps of his elongated car.

Metal Detector: "Beep, beep. Beep. Beeeeep."

It worked perfectly. He handed me the metal detector. The device balanced snuggly under my wrist and forearm. I swung it around and tested it on a metal doorknob. Then I tested an old shovel. Both objects made the metal detector beep.

It was then that Pap set up the real science experiment. While I continued exploring the device's powers inside the garage, Pap made a quiet exit. Slowly walking in between sporadic raindrops, he took off his gold wedding ring. (My maternal grandmother had passed away long before I was born.) Pap slowly bent downwards and placed his shiny gold ring in the wet grass outside of the garage. He pointed down to the ring.

Pap: "This is the real test. Right here, Bobby. Try it on my gold ring."

I walked over to the ring and swung the metal detector over it.

Metal Detector: "Beep. Beeeeep. Beep. Beep."

Bobby: "It works! It works on gold, Pap!"

I spun around and looked up at my grandfather. The thick lenses of his oversized glasses magnified the genuine look of hope in his eyes. He began to nod with optimism.

He was about to offer me the greatest challenge of my young life. Pap leaned over a bit, squeezed my shoulders with his hands, and looked me right in the eyes. He raised his eyebrows and spoke to me in a soft, but decisive voice.

Pap: "Bobby, go and find the treasure. Go find Braddock's Gold."

I had no reply. I stood motionless in the glow of twilight. Soft rain fell from yellow-orange clouds above. Frozen still, I was in the process of digesting everything that Pap had just unveiled to me. *Could I really do something like this? How would I even begin? Were all of these incredible tales even true?* But after one warm raindrop hit me on the top of the head, all my reservations quickly melted away. I realized what I had to do. I had to listen to my grandfather and take advantage of what was literally a golden opportunity.

I wanted to act fast upon receiving these unexpected gifts. At that point in my life, our family's situation was dire. Although we were fortunate enough to stay at my pap's place, we still had major hardships. We had just lost our home. My father had lost his job. We had no money. This could be the solution to all of my family's problems. There was hope.

However, I would need assistance on a mission of this magnitude. I needed Vito and Sal. But in order to persuade my best friends to help me, I would first have to convince them that the treasure hunt was worthwhile. I decided to deal with cynical Sal first. I called up Sal and told him to come over to my pap's house. Sal, the speed demon, got there in no time. He raced up the Heinz Terrace hill like greased lightning. Then he hit a hard brake into a long skid on the wet street while his forward momentum allowed him to smoothly pop off from his bike. We met out by the front steps at dusk.

I explained the entire situation to Sal. I told him about the Battle of Braddock and the possibility of a hidden treasure. I showed him the very last line in the journal.

Sal slowly read it out loud.

Sal: "'Beneath the fallen General, marks the spot of hidden gold.'"

After my full disclosure, Sal seemed even more skeptical than usual. It all sounded far-fetched to him. Cracking his knuckles, he was about to give me a grilling as if I was just picked up by the police. He started shaking his head and crossed his arms.

Sal: "Okay, take a seat. Let's think this through. I wanna get the full skinny."

I sat down on the front porch steps. The drizzle was spotty now. Water drops fell from the trees. In stark contrast to the cool and pleasant atmosphere, I felt like I was under a bright heat lamp in a stuffy back room at a police station. It mirrored a scene out of a '70s cop movie, like *Dirty Harry* starring Clint Eastwood. Sal was the aggressive detective, and I was the nervous suspect. Wearing his aviator sunglasses at night, Sal started pacing back and forth. His interrogation began.

Sal: "Dude, this story sounds crazy as heck. A hidden gold treasure? In Pittsburgh? This is heavy, Bobby."

Sal looked right at me. From the glare of the porch light, I could see my reflection in the lenses of his aviators.

Sal: "Okay, lemme get this straight. First question: Why would Heinz give away all this stuff to your pap in a' first place?"

Bobby: "I thought about that. Heinz was a millionaire by then from his ketchup 'n food business. He was a rich old man who saw a young kid from Sharpsburg, just like himself, who had the same passion he had for collectin' American Indian stuff. They always said Heinz was a real generous man."

Sal nodded his head up and down while still pacing. The interview continued.

Sal: "Okay, I get it. Next question: So why'd your pap stop lookin' for the gold?"

Bobby: "Just like Heinz, Pap searched all over for it 'n hit dead ends. Then Pap got kinda successful himself with his own business n'at. He opened up the Italian suits shop dahn on Main Street. He did good for himself. I mean, look, Heinz Terrace is the nicest street in Sharpsburg. Then he got old and had a family 'n kids. So, he hid the box away just like H.J. did."

Sal stopped in his tracks. He lifted his sunglasses up and rested them on his head.

Sal: "Okay, okay. It still don't add up. Next question: But then *who* went 'n told Guyasuta 'bout the gold?"

Bobby: "I thought about that too, Sal. It had to be someone who was close to General Braddock. Someone important. Someone who actually saw the general get shot and fall dahn in the ambush. Someone who knew the exact spot where he laid. Someone who probably helped hide all the gold there when he knew they were gonna lose the battle. It musta been Guyasuta's friend on the British side... from Virginia."

Sal lifted his hands up high in disbelief. He yelled up into the air.

Sal: "Whoa! C'mon, Bobby! You gotta be jaggin' me!"

Sal looked me directly in the eyes.

Sal: *"George Washington?* You're sayin' George told him about this? Are you freakin' kiddin' me, Bobby? Now you're startin' to sound like a real cuckoo. Why in the heck would he wanna let Guyasuta know about the stashed gold?"

Bobby: "So after the French and Indian War ended, George came back and met up with Chief Guyasuta in Pittsburgh again. I bet George came back here to look for the hidden gold. But he needed someone to help him find it. Nobody knew the woods 'round here better than Guyasuta. And George knew him since he was young. George trusted Guyasuta."

Sal began pacing back and forth again. He scratched his chin and continued.

Sal: "I still don't buy it, Bobby. Next question: Do you really think George would want Guyasuta gettin' a cut of the gold?"

Bobby: "They were old friends. And George probably felt bad about what happened to him after the war. All the treaties were broken. English settlers came in droves and pushed out the American Indians. The Senecas lost all their land. They lost everything. Maybe George wanted to give somethin' back to Guyasuta and his tribe."

Sal started shaking his head.

Sal: "I can't believe it. This is actually startin' to make some sense. So, they obviously didn't find it and Guyasuta told his family about the gold on his deathbed. This is freakin' wild!"

Bobby: "I know! Guyasuta was real old when he told 'em. He said the gold was buried at the spot of 'the fallen General.' The general fell dahn in the tahn they named after him. I know it's a long shot, but it's worth a look. Let's do it, Sal. Let's go dahn to Braddock and hunt for the gold."

With no more questions left to ask, Sal reluctantly put his hands on his hips.

Sal: "Hmm."

Sal was finally speechless. I called up Vito to come over to my pap's house. Sal and I waited on the sidewalk. Loudly huffing while standing up on his bike pedals, Vito rode hard up the hill to meet us. In shorts for once, his long white tube socks almost glowed in the dark. He was wearing an orange peel over his teeth like a mouth guard.

Sal: "Why's 'at orange in your mouth, goofball?"

Vito took out the orange peel and carefully rested it on his handlebar.

Vito: "So I don't lose my gum again."

Ever since it was first introduced by Wrigley when we were in fourth grade, Vito was addicted to the cinnamon flavored bite of Big Red chewing gum. However, he had a bad habit of his gum always flying out of his mouth when he hit a bump with his bike. The orange peel would stop that unfortunate occurrence in its tracks. Only Vito would come up with this kind of unique solution. It was equal parts ingenious and absurd.

Vito lowered his head and continued.

Vito: "Sorry 'bout your house, Bobby. 'At's a real bummer. So, what's up, guys?"

We gave Vito the lowdown. I told him about every detail – from H.J. Heinz, to Chief Guyasuta, to the legend of Braddock's Gold. I showed him the notebook. Vito's eyes widened with excitement.

Vito: "Hidden gold?! Mamma mia! Are you for sure about this stuff, Bob?"

Sal: "Yeah, when you say it out loud again it sounds like a bunch o' baloney. We ain't goin' all o' way over Braddock and lookin' for gold like total wack-jobs. That's nuts."

Vito: "It does sound kinda loony, Bobby… "

Vito and Sal had uneasy looks on their faces. I quickly tried to regain their faith.

Bobby: "But we got somethin' now, guys. We got somethin' today 'at Heinz, and Pap, and tons of people before 'em never had in the old days."

Sal: "What's 'at? Whadda we got now that they didn't have back 'en?"

Vito looked puzzled. Then he quickly raised his hand and called out his answer as if we were in school.

Vito: "Ooh! Ooh! Pet rocks?"

Sal gave Vito an irritated look. Just then, I hopped up the steps to grab the surprise tool that I had placed behind the front door. I scuttled back down holding the long metal detector and swung it over the gold cross and Italian horn on Vito's shiny gold necklace.

Metal Detector: "Beep, beep. Beeeep. Beep. Beep."

Vito was blown away by the incredible powers of the gizmo.

Vito: "Whoa! Way cool! Lemme see 'at thing, Bobby."

I handed it over to my amazed friend. With great enthusiasm, Vito swung the device around and tested Sal's golden cross necklace and mine made of stainless steel. The metal detector beeped as predicted giving Vito a huge smile. Vito gave the metal detector back to me and I set it against the steps. Sal was not as impressed.

Sal: "Yeah, okay, 'at thing's cool 'n all. But what if somebody found the gold already?"

Vito: "Yeah, Bobby, it might already be gone."

I quickly replied with optimism.

Bobby: "But it might still be there, too. What if nobody found it yet?"

My friends grimaced at my idealistic attitude. Suddenly, both Sal and Vito became even more pessimistic. They grew long cynical looks on their faces. Sal lightly shook his head while he crossed his arms. Vito drew a heavy sigh.

I had to rally my troops. I continued by reminding them of my current situation. Standing up a little taller in my Nikes, I raised my voice and became more animated.

Bobby: "C'mon, guys, we gotta try. Look, I lost my home in the fire this week. My dad just lost his job. We don't got no money. We got nothin'. I got nothin'!"

I looked up at both of them and yelled.

Bobby: "NOTHIN'!"

My last word echoed down the empty street. Taken aback by my desperate tone, Sal and Vito became still and silent. They seemed to realize how serious I was about this. I continued to try to persuade my friends into helping me find the gold.

Bobby: "Anyways, this might be our last chance to go on a adventure together. Next summer, we'll all be 15 goin' on 16. Yinz will probably have to go to work for your parents. Vito, you'll be washin' dishes in a' back of a hot kitchen. Sal, you'll be luggin' heavy bags o' dry cement out on a hot sidewalk. Yinz'll be wishin' you'd done one last mission. One last adventure... as a kid."

They both lowered their heads. Vito and Sal absorbed the depressing and inevitable reality of growing up. Soon, they would be working through their summer breaks. Not to mention, we would be starting high school in a week.

Bobby: "C'mon, guys. Let's go have one last... treasure hunt. Who's in?"

We all paused and stood quietly. The light drizzle had finally stopped. A sparse sprinkling of the summer's last lightning bugs began to flash over the street. The only sound was the loud call of annual cicadas chirping high above us in the sycamore trees. The large insect's repetitive chittering is a common sound in the neighborhoods of Pittsburgh by late summer.

My friends were still staring down at the sidewalk, but both started kicking over pebbles. By their lack of words, I was hoping that I had managed to change their minds. While they were quietly digesting my pleas, I actually began to feel embarrassed about nearly begging for their help. My passionate argument was out of character, but it seemed to strike a chord. Vito stopped chewing his gum and straightened his lip. After thoughtful consideration, Vito looked up and firmly replied.

Vito: "All right. I'm in, Bobby. You can count on me."

Then Sal looked up and asked one more probing question.

Sal: "So, for real, how much gold do ya think there is, Bobby?"

Bobby: "Enough to pay a whole army, Sal. Enough to pay a whole army."

Finally, Sal reluctantly decided to join forces with us. He nodded in affirmation.

Sal: "Okay. Me too, Bobby. I'm in too."

Sal then began to shake his head and muttered out again.

Sal: "Yinz crazy jagoffs... "

Sal flashed a crooked smile and continued to comment in the only way that he could.

Sal: "We're all gonna end up on 'em missin' child posters on a' wall dahn a' police station."

A second later, Sal smirked and added.

Sal: "Well, they're gonna need a whole bulletin board for Vito's picture."

We all laughed. The mission was revealed and accepted. We would meet at 9 AM by the Highland Park Bridge and head into the city of Pittsburgh. I hoped that a lost treasure was yet to be found. I dreamed of turning my life around.

High above in the tall sycamore trees, the cicadas continued their urgent night call.

Chapter 7: To the Library

Our mission objective was clear. My loyal crew was going to head across the city of Pittsburgh to the town of Braddock in pursuit of a hidden gold treasure. Well over an hour commute by bike, the daunting nine-mile journey would literally take us over the hills and far away. We planned on making two pit stops along the trek. Our first aim was to gather intelligence at the Carnegie Library in Oakland. There, we needed to inspect detailed maps of Braddock and historic accounts of the battlefield itself. We also planned to stop for field rations in Squirrel Hill.

In a spiral notebook, I had written out the mission plan.

Mission Name:

"Operation Braddock's Gold"

Mission Goals:

1.   Find the gold.
2.   Buy my family a new house.
3.   Buy myself a new Pontiac Firebird.

Mission Destinations:

1.   Oakland (Library)
2.   Squirrel Hill (Pizza)
3.   Braddock (Gold)

Mission Supplies:

1.   Backpack
2.   Notebook/pencil
3.   H.J. Heinz's logbook
4.   Food (Hostess Cupcakes – 3, Fritos chips bag – 1, Slim Jim – 1)
5.   Drinks (Mountain Dew cans – 3)
6.   Money ($7)
7.   Compass
8.   Flashlight

9.   Duct tape
10.   Garden trowel
11.   Map of Pittsburgh
12.   Small shovel
13.   Metal detector

My backpack was bulging with essential supplies that I found in my pap's garage. I also stuffed the front pocket of my backpack with my prized arrowhead along with the eagle, fox, and mountain lion wood carvings. I planned to put Vito in charge of transporting and using the metal detector. Sal would haul the small shovel. Duct tape was imperative. We needed it for securing the shovel and metal detector to the frame and back peg of our BMX bikes. This allowed for safer travel on main roads. Even the most famous adventurers of the century, NASA's Apollo 11 crew, brought a valuable roll of duct tape along when they flew to the moon in 1969. One can only imagine where humans would be now if the Wright Brothers had duct tape available when constructing their fabled Flyer 1 aircraft.

Just as I set off on my mission, the elder of my younger brothers peeked outside.

Billy: "Where ya going?"

Bobby: "I'm goin' to get us a new house."

Billy: "Really?"

I hopped onto my bike.

Bobby: "Yeah. And I'm gonna get yinz a Millennium Falcon."

Billy: "Cool beans! See ya later, Bobby."

I started pedaling down the hill.

Bobby: "See ya. Oh yeah, and don't tell Mum!"

At the onset of our long journey, I met my friends on the east end of town at the Highland Park Bridge. The tall bridge heads over the Allegheny River and into the sprawling city neighborhoods of Highland Park and East Liberty. I handed over the metal detector to Vito.

Bobby: "Here, Vito. You're gonna be in charge o' the metal detector."

Vito: "Awesome!"

Vito excitedly duct taped the device to his bike. Already too big for his undersized black BMX bike, the attached metal detector added even more clutter to Vito's comical appearance. Looking like an alien insect with appendages hanging out in all directions, Vito quickly pulled away from us with noticeable enthusiasm. He loved that metal detector.

Sal questioned my decision to entrust our most essential tool to Vito.

Sal: "Why are ya givin' Vito the metal detector? Don't you wanna be the one who uses it?"

Bobby: *"That's* why."

I pointed at Vito. He was eagerly speeding up the ramp to the bridge.

Sal: "Oh, I see. 'At makes him feel important. Look at the big dork pedalin' away at full steam like a giddy little kid."

Bobby: "Exactly, Sal."

A good mission leader knows how to motivate his troops. As we began biking across the Highland Park Bridge, we could hear roars from across the river at the Pittsburgh Zoo. It was the dominant male lion making his morning wake up call.

A lion's roar can travel over five miles. On quiet weekend mornings, I often woke up in a cold sweat from the call of the lion passing through the screen of my bedroom window. Welcome to my nightmare. My most common reoccurring bad dream as a child was not about running into Duke, but that huge maned cat stalking me down a dark alley in Sharpsburg. Sal shared his opinion on the bellowing beast.

Sal: "He's markin' his territory. 'At lion's tellin' us not to come in a' city today. It's a warnin' call to all jagoffs from Sharpsburg."

I tried to be more optimistic.

Bobby: "Or maybe it's a good sign o' the spoils 'at await us. Like he's cheerin' us on."

Sal rolled his eyes.

Sal: "Always lookin' on a' bright side, Bobby."

At that time, many neighborhoods in the city of Pittsburgh had their own distinct cultural identity. Bloomfield was Italian. The Hill District was African American. Squirrel Hill was Jewish. The South Side was Eastern European. Polish Hill was… you guessed it. These segregated human constructs were also aided by the natural terrain. Rivers, hills, and valleys were everywhere. The topography further separated the towns, creating distinct enclaves. Although less prevalent today, much of Pittsburgh remains noticeably segregated by racial, ethnic, religious, and socioeconomic lines.

Soon after crossing the bridge, we wheeled onto Washington Boulevard and rode right past a six-story building frame where firefighters from the city were training for dangerous scenarios. In fact, the tall building was currently on fire. The top floor was intentionally set ablaze, and a group of brave new recruits was practicing how to direct the water hose at the controlled inferno. Usually an awesome sight to witness, Sal and Vito made no remarks and simply nodded at me sympathetically. Obviously, I tried to refrain from looking at the building engulfed in flames, even if it was artificially ignited for training purposes.

We continued travelling up Washington Boulevard, a valley passageway that traverses through the neighborhoods of Highland Park, Larimer, East Liberty, and Homewood. We tried to ride our bikes on the sidewalks as much as possible. It helped that it was a Saturday morning and there was much less traffic on the main roads. I pointed left down the huge intersection at Penn Avenue in Point Breeze and reminded my friends where Heinz had moved to after leaving Sharpsburg.

Bobby: "Heinz had the nicest mansion on this street, right dahn 'ere. It was called Millionaire's Row 'cause all the big wigs lived there, like Carnegie, Frick, and Westinghouse."

Vito: "After we find 'at gold, we'll be livin' on Millionaire's Row too, Bobby!"

Sal blurted out a laugh.

Sal: "Ha! Dream on! Yinz are outta your minds."

In my opinion, Heinz's opulent estate was the cream of the crop. It was named Greenlawn for it boasted a palatial yard scattered with orchards and greenhouses. The eccentric millionaire even had a museum in the attic for his storied collection of artifacts. Unfortunately, the Heinz mansion no longer existed. Over time, most of the lavish mansions, from those of Richard Mellon to George Westinghouse, were razed. Fortunately, the land plots of the latter two were turned into public parks.

Ironically, one of the only mansions that remains is that of Henry Clay Frick, who was by far the most reviled of all the industrial tycoons in Pittsburgh. His uncompromising persona was given blame for the infamous Homestead Steel Strike in which nine steel workers died while fighting for better work conditions and pay. Although it was often overlooked that he had donated over $50 million to local charities, Frick's ruthless reputation was well known by working folks.

Bobby: "Yinz know Frick was once stabbed and shot by some guy tryin' to assassinate him at his office dahntahn?'

Vito: "For real? What happened to him?"

Bobby: "Oh, he just stayed at his desk and kept givin' orders like nothin' happened."

Sal: "A frickin' grenade couldn't stop 'at jagoff from bustin' his workers' butts."

By now, the sleepy streets had awakened. Among the bustle of honking horns and ambulance sirens, you could feel that the heart of the city was beating loud and strong. Riding our bikes down busy Fifth Avenue in Shadyside, we gazed in awe at a line of large Gilded Age mansions standing behind tall ornate fences. I was always fascinated by the huge financial disparity among the rich and the poor in the city. The striking contrast between the haves and have-nots was never more vivid than when traveling through one neighborhood to the next. The dividing lines between socioeconomic classes were noticeably drawn. While one block swelled with grandiose mansions housing the city's most financially elite residents, only several blocks away sat dilapidated apartment complexes occupied by working-class tenants.

Vito was bowled over by one over-the-top mansion. Its colossal front pillars made this manor stand out from the others. There was a croquet set in the front yard.

Vito: "Holy crap! I swear 'at's where Richie Rich lives!"

Sal: "Go pound on a' front door and see, Vito. Knock yourself out. I'm sure they won't mind a big hairy weirdo in a sweaty tank top comin' in and sayin' hi."

When it came to money, one 5-foot-3-inch Yinzer stood head and shoulders above the rest. This pint-sized businessman had the Midas touch. Of course, we cared more about his accent than his incredible feats in industrial capitalism. After all, linguists believe the Yinzer dialect originated from the Scots-Irish immigrants in Pittsburgh.

Bobby: "Bein' from Scotland n'at, Andrew Carnegie had a Scottish accent. And I'm sure he called his mother 'mum' like we do. But do yinz think Carnegie said 'yinz'?"

Sal: "Who knows? I'm sure none of us poor peasants ever got a chance to even hear one word from 'at rich little Scottish dude's mouth."

Still gaping at the mansions at a slower speed, a distracted Vito was lagging behind us both physically and mentally. He called out to us from the rear.

Vito: "Wait a minute! Are yinz sayin' Carnegie talked like Scrooge McDuck?"

We were about ten blocks away from our first destination, a library that was gifted to the people by the city's wealthiest of residents. Andrew Carnegie emigrated from Scotland to Pittsburgh as a young teen. His life is the original "rags to riches" story. He started out making $1 a week at a cotton factory. He ended up creating one of the largest, most profitable businesses in the world, the Carnegie Steel Company. After selling it in 1901, Carnegie became the richest person in America. He amassed a fabulous net worth of over $300 billion in today's money. Amazingly, upon reaching the golden pinnacle of financial success, Carnegie set about to donate away most of his fortune. He funded a multitude of libraries throughout the city. On this day, we were hoping to take advantage of his great wealth to gain some wealth of our own. I wanted to inspect maps of the Battle of Braddock in the "Pittsburgh Room" at the stately Carnegie Library. Of course, Sal hated this segment of the mission.

Sal: "Like, do we *gotta* go to the library, Bobby?"

Bobby: "Yeah! We gotta see maps o' Braddock. We need to make a plan of attack for metal detectin' where General Braddock fell dahn on a' battlefield. I also wanna find a book 'at shows what 'em English gold coins looked like back 'en."

Sal: "Okay, bookworm. Make it quick in 'ere."

In the year 1979, American teenagers had almost every luxury that we enjoy today. Even working-class families could afford cars, large televisions, video gaming systems, and microwaves. However, there was one major luxury that young people did not have available back then. Not one of us had a handheld portable computer in our pocket. Today's mobile smart phones offer youths the chance to communicate via talk or text to their friends from anywhere and at any time. You also have high quality photo, video, music, and social media applications. In addition, this amazing device offers a compass, maps, global positioning systems, and weather tracking.

But what really sets modern smart phone technology apart from anything we had in the last century is its research capabilities. Today, you can simply Google "Braddock's Defeat" and quickly access detailed maps and information. You can easily find an image of a British gold coin from the 1750s. Heck, by the time you read this book, your phone might have a metal detector app on it. But back in 1979, all this information was stored in one place and one place only: the public library.

The hamlet of Sharpsburg, however, did not have a library. But even local libraries at that time wouldn't possess what we needed. So, we traveled to the biggest one in the city, the main branch of the Carnegie Library of Pittsburgh, in the cultural core of Oakland. We decided to have a quick lunch on the stone steps beneath the Corinthian columns of the Carnegie Museum of Natural History. We set up camp next to the Galileo statue. He sits across Forbes Avenue from a towering limestone edifice, the University of Pittsburgh's Cathedral of Learning. Vito asked a sincere question.

Vito: "Bob, after we eat, can I go in the museum and see the T-Rex?"

Bobby: "It ain't part o' the mission, Vito. We don't got no time for that."

Vito glumly shook his head and pouted.

Vito: "First, no time for Mr. Rogers. Now, no time for the T-Rex. This stinks, Bobby!"

We had passed the WQED studio for *Mr. Rogers' Neighborhood* along the way here. I think that Vito thought he could just walk right in and appear on live television as the special guest for the day. With Vito's goofy personality, it actually might have worked out. He probably would have taken over the Neighborhood of Make-Believe.

Sitting outside of the museum and attached library, we ate some snacks from my grandfather's kitchen pantry that I had shoved into my supply backpack. I packed a few Hostess chocolate cupcakes topped with that squiggly swirl of white frosting. We used to love those ultra-processed cousins of the Twinkie. The fake chemical-like aftertaste of that cupcake is unforgettable, yet incredibly delicious. Vito called dibs on the lone Slim Jim. We all shared a bag of Fritos and washed it down with warm cans of Mountain Dew. More than a decade before every health teacher in the country pinned up a poster of the food pyramid, our pure junk food lunch was the typical nutrition for any American kid in the late 1970s. Vito was talking with his mouth full.

Vito: "What if da gold is rotten by now?"

Of course, Sal quickly snapped back at Vito.

Sal: "Gold don't rot, you dimwit! They're golden coins, not golden delicious apples. You mean *rusted*."

Bobby: "Yeah, that's the thing about gold. Gold don't corrode like copper or iron or just about every metal. 'At's why gold's so valuable. It never loses its luster. Yinz could find a gold coin from Ancient Rome, and it would look shiny 'n new. Meanwhile, 'at steel Tonka truck we played with when we were little rusted out already."

Sal nodded in agreement and smugly cracked at Vito.

Sal: "Yeah. What he said, Vito."

Bobby: "Gold is easy to melt and reshape too. You could find a sunken Spanish galleon at the bottom o' the ocean with a treasure chest full o' gold coins and melt 'em dahn to make new bars o' gold in no time."

Vito looked up into the sky and thought out loud.

Vito: "Just think how much gold is in Fort Knox right now. Thousands of bars o' gold. Just sittin' there waitin' to get picked up."

Sal: "Yeah, just like your mum."

Every young teen would spit immature mom jokes at each other back then. It was a time-honored tradition. But Italian kids tended to be even more offended by the insulting of mothers. After Sal's rude remark, he and Vito began gratuitously swearing at each other in Italian. I only recognized the most vulgar of the curse words. Then they started shoving each other. That's when I jumped in between them and tried to break it up. The scuffle became more physical and the pushing more intense.

Just then, two college girls clad in Pitt tank tops approached us. Both had long, feathered hair. They wore big brown sunglasses, blue jean shorts, and thin foam flip-flops. Every girl wore those flimsy flip-flops in the summertime. Like Jimmy Buffet would lament in song while he was away in "Margaritaville," those cheap flip-flops would easily self-destruct. Between breaking them and losing them, my mother and sister would both go through a couple of pairs each summer.

By now, Vito had wrestled Sal down to the ground and they were rolling around on the sidewalk. Vito had Sal in a firm headlock. I was trying to dislodge his arms from around Sal's neck to no avail. The passing co-eds looked down at the three ruffians who were tangled in a clumsy street tussle. One girl lightly shook her head. The other softly reprimanded us.

College Girl: "Take it easy. Take it easy, guys."

We all froze in embarrassment. Our street-kid nature had reared its ugly head. There's nothing more humiliating for a soon-to-be high school student than getting scolded by older, attractive college girls. At age 14, you truly are stuck between being a kid and an adult. The infantile altercation had revealed the child in all three of us.

Even worse, our rowdy nonsense occurred while literally sitting under the gaze of Galileo within the city's beacon of science and academia. Only a few blocks away, the great scientist Dr. Jonas Salk had discovered a polio vaccine that allowed us to pedal our bikes all summer long with no fear of becoming paralyzed from the wretched virus. I sternly redirected our crew.

Bobby: "C'mon! Let's go, guys! We're on a mission here."

I stationed myself in between my friends. Vito and Sal each murmured one more insult at each other under their breath.

Sal: "Jagoff."

Vito: "Jagoff and a half."

Finished with lunch and recess, we approached the grand, light gray sandstone building that is the Carnegie Library of Pittsburgh. We loudly marched up the long steps with purpose and noisily barged through the tall bronze doors of the arched entrance. It felt like we were entering a palace. A ragtag pack of teenagers wielding a metal detector, we looked entirely out of place in this stoic environment. Our stomping shoes echoed on the fine marble floors. A concerned young library assistant quickly attended to the alien invaders. Although courteous, she emitted a tone that you might hear from a manager at an upscale restaurant that only accepts guests wearing the proper attire. We obviously did not meet the dress code.

But just then an older gentleman sporting a small yellow bow tie started to make his way towards us. Attending to a young girl at the main desk, he was immediately curious of the odd scene that we made when we stormed into the library. His leather Docksides made a loud patter as he briskly treaded in our direction across the marble entryway. He had a short gray beard and wore golden plated eyeglasses that were rounded in the same style as those worn by singer John Denver. After adjusting his bifocals, he politely questioned us with an inquisitive grin.

Librarian: "Can I help you boys?"

His name tag read Frank Greenberg. It turned out that this was the library director.

Bobby: "Yeah. We need some books."

The teenage girl who was standing at the main desk was interested in our group too. She was eavesdropping on the conversation. I noticed that she had just checked out a book on the history of the National Park system. I also noticed that she had a great smile and beautiful auburn hair.

Librarian: "Well, what kind of books are you guys looking for... cars, sports, dinosaurs?"

Vito immediately interjected.

Vito: "Sir, I'll have your biggest dinosaur book, please."

Vito thought he was ordering from a menu at a fine restaurant. I stepped in front of my large friend who was holding a metal detector.

Bobby: "Actually, sir, we need to see a book on the Battle of Braddock durin' the French and Indian War."

The librarian raised his eyebrows in surprised interest.

Librarian: "Oh, really? Interesting. Okay... can I ask what for?"

At this point, the young teen with dark red hair was standing right next to the librarian. She seemed even more intrigued now. Obviously, most teenagers don't barge into the library carrying a metal detector.

Bobby: "Well, we need to see a map of the Braddock battlefield and where General Braddock was, um, mortally wounded. We wanna go look for artifacts."

The director of the library leaned back on his heels. He was politely smiling at what had to be his most peculiar visitors of the day. He softly nudged on his glasses and stammered out of amazement.

Librarian: "Well... well, this *is* interesting. You... you came to the right place."

We followed him and the girl up two flights of steps to "The Pittsburgh Room" where all of the city's important local maps, deeds, and transcripts were kept. Technically called The Pennsylvania Department, the spacious 3rd floor was decorated with huge pieces of artwork and lined with dark wood walls and bookcases. There were several large mahogany wood tables. The librarian spoke to the redhead.

Librarian: "Sarah, can you go and find texts on the Braddock Expedition while I look for the maps of the town?"

Sarah: "Sure, Grandpap."

That cleared up that mystery. The young girl visiting the library was the head librarian's granddaughter. Vito looked up at the artwork adorning the walls. One piece immediately caught his eye.

Vito: "Look at that big picture, Bobby. Looks like 'at redcoat fell on his butt."

Bobby: "That's Braddock! That's the famous *Wounding of General Braddock* painting!"

Vito turned and whispered to me.

Vito: "So under him, they buried the... ?"

I quickly hushed him up.

Bobby: "Shhh!"

The large wall-mounted painting by local artist Robert Griffing portrayed a detailed scene of the Battle of Braddock. A masterful work of art, *The Wounding of General Braddock* vividly depicts the chaotic conflict whirling around Major General Edward Braddock as he is writhing on the ground in pain. The highest-ranking British officer on the continent had just been shot and fell from his horse. In the painting, the fallen general lies surrounded by several redcoat officers and one blue-coated volunteer from Virginia, George Washington. Washington appears noticeably distraught as he holds his hand to his head in despair while leaning on the same tree that General Braddock rests against. As the commanders huddle around the injured general, a hectic battle rages in the background. The forest valley is consumed by smoke from a slew of gunshots volleying between the English and American colonial forces and their French and Native American enemies. A hole in the tree canopy directs sunlight on the injured General Braddock. Of course, the general's wound became a fatal one.

After the librarian and his helper began to diligently search the shelves for our requested resources, I pointed at General Braddock in the very center of the painting and whispered to Vito in a low voice.

Bobby: "'Beneath the fallen General.' And look, that's George Washington next to him in a' blue coat. And there's the wagon that held the treasure chest full o' gold coins. They knew they was gonna lose the battle and they had to bury the gold so the other side wouldn't get their hands on it. George and the redcoats hurried up and hid the gold right at that spot where Braddock fell."

Vito lowered his head and whispered back in contained excitement.

Vito: "Okey dokey, Bobby! Now we just gotta find 'at spot!"

The librarian approached us holding a large parchment. It was a topographical map of the boroughs of Braddock and North Braddock. It showed streets, waterways, and elevation grades. Sarah carried over books about the battle.

Librarian: "Okay. This is a map of Braddock, PA. This should help you boys."

Sarah: "And here, guys, I found two books about the Battle of Braddock's Field."

The librarian turned to his granddaughter.

Librarian: "Okay, I need to head back down to the main desk. Sarah, can you make sure that the map and the books are returned to their proper shelves?"

Sarah: "Sure, Grandpap. I'll put everything back in its place."

The courteous librarian offered us his best wishes.

Librarian: "Okay. Good luck, guys. I hope you find what you're looking for."

Bobby: "Thank you, sir."

Vito: "Thanks."

Vito, Sarah, and I sat down at a large wooden table directly under *The Wounding of General Braddock* painting. We began our research by examining a detailed map provided in a book about the battle site. Sal, the disinterested cool kid, was pacing around the perimeter of the room looking at paintings with his sunglasses on. His excitement level was nowhere near that of his fellow companions.

While analyzing the map of the battlefield, we laid out the plan. I used my finger to point out the military movements and positions of opposing forces for Vito.

Bobby: "Okay. General Braddock and his army marched right through here. They came through this skinny pass between this cliff on this side of 'em and the Mon on the other side. It was all woods. American Indians were hidin' up here in a rocky outcrop and dahn here along the riverbank. French troops were here in the front. Braddock got trapped. They started shootin' from behind trees on the hills above 'em and the river below 'em. It was a complete surprise. Surrounded on three sides... that's how Braddock's Army got slaughtered so bad 'at day."

Vito: "So we wanna go look between the cliff and the river dahn in Braddock?"

Bobby: "Now you're thinkin', Vito. The spot we're lookin' for must be about halfway between 'at hillside and the Mon."

Vito was really taking to his position as head metal detector specialist. Sal remained aloof and continued to meander around the large library room. He was far more concerned with polishing the lenses of his aviator sunglasses with his sleeveless red T-shirt. Sarah, on the other hand, was fully captivated by our research. By then, she could not hold back her interest.

Sarah: "So, what *are* you guys looking for?"

Vito eyeballed me with concern. I concealed our true intentions.

Bobby: "Well, we're tryin' to find old stuff from the battle like musket balls or maybe a bayonet. Who knows, there might even be a rifle dahn 'ere."

Sarah: "Oh, that's neat. So, you guys are really into history, huh?"

Bobby: "Well, we've found some historical stuff before. I come across this old arrowhead last week. Look."

I reached into the pocket of my backpack. I handed Sarah the stone arrowhead that I had discovered in the creek at Guyasuta Park. She held it in admiration and spun it around in her hand.

Sarah: "Wow. You found this? Where?"

Bobby: "Guyasuta Run. It's a little crick in a park in our tahn, Sharpsburg. It's right across the river from the zoo."

Sarah nodded in affirmation.

Sarah: "Oh, I know where it is. I live in Squirrel Hill, not far from here. And obviously you know my grandfather is the librarian."

She warmly smiled and then mannerly held out her hand.

Sarah: "My name is Sarah. Sarah Greenberg."

Bobby: "Oh, I'm sorry. I'm Bobby. Bobby Connemara."

We shook hands. Then an outgoing Vito introduced himself with a firm handshake.

Vito: "Vittorio Calabresi. Head Metal Detector."

Sarah pleasantly giggled as they shook hands. Vito would not part with the metal detector that was clutched in his other hand. He guarded it with his life. Studying the large gadget, Sarah grinned and politely replied.

Sarah: "Oh, I see. I thought maybe that was your job."

Sarah was wearing a pale yellow T-shirt that contrasted with her long, dark red hair. She had crystal blue eyes. They were stunning. Her shirt had a blue owl on it with orange eyes and an orange beak. She had on jean shorts and the obligatory foam flip-flops. *The National Parks* book that she had checked out was nestled in her purple bag which had two brown leather straps. I could not help but notice that she wore a brown leather necklace with a round peace sign pendant made of shiny gold.

Sarah did not have a Yinzer accent. Many middle to upper-class children in Pittsburgh do not speak the Yinzer dialect. She seemed very bright and well read, not surprising for someone who hangs out at the library on a summer day. I thought she was incredibly cute but tried to play it cool by showing hardly any interest in her at all.

Sarah: "So, what grade are you guys going into when school starts up again?"

I remained on task and didn't answer her question. I noticed that she pronounced the word "school" like Marcia Brady, the oldest sister from *The Brady Bunch* television show. It sounded like a two syllable "ski-ool." Vito jumped at the chance to impress her even more.

Vito: "Ninth. We're in high school now."

Sarah: "Cool. I'm going into eighth. I wish I was heading to high school. Allderdice High School is such a beautiful building."

While we exchanged the normal teenager niceties, I hurriedly sketched as much as I could of the maps of Braddock into my notebook. I made sure to highlight the rocky cliffs to the north and the river to the south in my drawings of the battle site. The general fell in the middle of those two geological features. Then I began to flip through the pages of the books and absorb as much information as I could. General Braddock was strict. He ruled with an iron fist. Soldiers who disobeyed his orders would be punished with public lashings. In his army, Braddock reigned supreme.

I also noticed that General Braddock had no problem showboating his superior rank and power. He adorned himself with the most decorative attire a senior British officer could wear. His red coat was fully medaled from decades of military service. It was trimmed with opulent furs and ornaments. A crimson commander sash made of fine silk draped around his shoulder. A silver gorget (armor neckplate) hung across his chest. He always rode a tall horse. He even sat upon a saddle rest made of leopard's hide to set himself apart from the lower ranking officers and common foot soldiers.

Bobby: "Okay, we got our location. Now we need one more thing. Sarah, where would the books on old coins be located? Like English coins from 'at time period?"

Sarah: "Oh, downstairs in the stacks room. There's a section on numismatics."

Vito and I glanced at each other. By the look in his eyes, I could tell that I was not the only one who wasn't sure if "numismatics" meant coins. I shrugged.

Bobby: "Great. Can you show us real fast?"

Sarah: "Sure, let's go."

Sarah carefully returned the map and books to their designated locations. We headed downstairs to get our last piece of information. Remaining incognito with his sunglasses on, Sal nonchalantly lagged behind us. His disinterest was noticeable.

Sarah located a book on English currency throughout the ages. We turned to the section that detailed the coins from the 1700s. By now, Sarah obviously knew that we were seeking much more than metallic war relics. But I was too excited to hide our true intentions at this point. I found an image of the exact type of gold coin that we were hunting for.

Bobby: "Here it is! The English gold coin from the 1750s!"

I put down the book and made a rough sketch in my notepad of what the coin looked like on both sides. The heads side had an imprint of King George II on it. The tails side had a crown symbol and simple markings.

Bobby: "Okay. Now we know what we're lookin' for there."

Vito pumped his fist.

Vito: "Awesome! Let's get dahn 'ere and find 'at gold!"

Unfortunately, Sal had changed gears and once again became hesitant with the idea of prospecting for the treasure. To him, we were hunting for fool's gold. He scoffed at us in a gruff voice like a teenage version of Oscar the Grouch.

Sal: "Yinz are delusional."

Like many locals, Sal's Yinzer accent would get thicker when he was irritated.

Sal: "It don't matter how many maps yinz got. There ain't gonna be no buried gold treasure dahn Braddock, ya chumps!"

I turned to Sal and bargained with him.

Bobby: "C'mon, Sal, we can't bug out now. We came all this way. It's not even 'at far from here."

Sal was not convinced. I attempted to persuade him again. It was a reach.

Bobby: "Sal, you know how your last name, Argento, means 'Silver' in Italian? C'mon, Silver, let's go get us some gold."

Vito appreciated my corny play on words more than Sal did.

Vito: "Yeah! Just like 'at song from Rudolph."

Vito raised his voice even more in the library.

Vito: "*You know*, the 'Silver and Gold' song!"

While awkwardly swaying from side to side, Vito began to sing the main lines from "Silver and Gold," a classic tune from *Rudolph the Red-Nosed Reindeer*. Using a loud purposeful voice, he fully intended to embarrass us in the quiet, sedate library. Everyone was watching him make a scene. But it was pretty funny to see a big hairy dude in a faded gold tank top spinning around like a ballerina in his Chuck Taylors while singing a random song from the stop-motion animated winter special. Vito was great at lightening the serious atmosphere. Sarah and I started laughing. Even a few old folks in the library were giggling at the fool. It was a goofy way to convince him but after fighting with his own facial muscles, Sal reluctantly grew a slight grin. Then Sal tried to temper Vito's enthusiasm as much as halt his absurd song and dance.

Sal: "Okay. Okay. Let's go before ya get sent away to the Island o' Misfit Toys."

Sal scanned around the room and rolled his eyes.

Sal: "For heck's sake, anything beats putzin' around in a lousy library with you turkeys. It's geek city in here. And anyways, if yinz do find gold, yinz need someone who actually knows how to spend it on worthwhile stuff... instead o' borin' books or messy capicola sandwiches."

Sal was finally all in. Better yet, he didn't call me a nerd for spewing an obscure fact about the meaning of his last name, Argento. I was going to add on a note that I remembered from science class about the chemical symbol for silver on "The Periodic Table of Elements" being listed as Ag, from the Latin word "argentum." But I decided to quit while I was ahead.

I cordially thanked Sarah for her assistance.

Bobby: "Thanks, Sarah. Thanks for everything and for helpin' us read the maps n'at."

Sarah: "Oh, you're welcome. I hope you find something over there, guys."

We bounded down the library staircases and back to our bikes outside. Just as we were hopping on our BMXs, Sarah was hurriedly rushing down the main library steps.

Sarah: "Hey, guys! Wait!"

She ran over to us. It was obvious that Sarah was completely enthralled with our mission. Of course, I acted like I didn't want to hear what she was about to say. I kept my head down and tended to my kickstand.

Sarah: "Look. If you're going through Squirrel Hill and into Braddock, then you need a... well, you might need a guide. I can be your guide."

I glanced at my friends and then politely answered her request.

Bobby: "Thanks, we know the way. It's okay."

Sarah took a couple slow steps towards us and continued.

Sarah: "Have you guys ever been to Braddock?"

Straddling our bikes, we stood there in silence. She had a point. We were about to be venturing into an unknown place with unknown foes. We had a rough time just navigating the streets in our own hometown, let alone an unfamiliar one. She gave us a once over and continued.

Sarah: "You guys are going to stand out. I mean, you might look like you're intruding on their neighborhood down there."

Sarah was right. We would definitely look like outsiders. Braddock was a town with a much more diverse population than Sharpsburg. A working-class neighborhood in its own right, it had a larger population of African American kids. She forged ahead with an even more convincing proposition.

Sarah: "Look, I can be like a... Sacagawea."

Vito was perplexed. His eyes darted from Sarah back to me and Sal.

Vito: "The tall hairy guy from *Star Wars*?"

Sal: "That's Chewbacca, ya moron!"

Vito was usually spot on with TV and movie character names. But at the moment, I think he was suffering from an information overload from all of our frantic research in the library. I quickly interrupted my friends.

Bobby: "No, she was from the Lewis 'n Clark Adventure."

Sacagawea was the invaluable Native American scout who helped the famed Lewis and Clark Expedition navigate the uncharted American West. Planned by President Thomas Jefferson, the storied excursion's main purpose was to search for a river passageway to the Pacific Ocean. Sacagawea played an integral role in helping accomplish the mission's journey as the land was inhabited by a myriad of Native American tribes, some understandably adverse to foreign explorers. Fluent in Native languages and knowledgeable of the local cultures and customs, Sacagawea tempered many problems that arose between Lewis and Clark's party and the Indigenous Peoples they encountered on their inland voyage. The Shoshone guide even personally knew some of the Native Americans that the expedition met with, including her long-lost brother who led a Shoshone Tribe himself.

Sarah: "Sacagawea was the American Indian scout who helped Lewis and Clark deal with unknown people in an unknown land. Her presence alone protected the men on their adventure. By traveling with a young woman in their group, they were way safer. Do you know why?"

Vito shrunk down in his bike seat and looked afraid to respond again. Then he began to fasten the metal detector back to his bike. As we watched him fiddle with the duct tape, I replied to Sarah.

Bobby: "They were safer 'cause all the other American Indians knew they weren't a war party out for blood."

Sarah swung her bag around her back, put her hands on her hips, and smiled with approval. She blew away a stray strand of her red hair that had fallen in front of her face and continued in earnest.

Sarah: "Exactly. The Native People knew that a woman would not be coming into their territory with ill will. She provided safety for the men on the expedition. Safety from other men who had no desire for foreigners exploring and hunting on their land."

We all paused and recognized her determination. Then, Sarah looked us straight in the eyes and added one more convincing point to her offer.

Sarah: "And I'm not asking for a cut of the gold, if you find any. But I live in the city and know this area well. I would just be your guide."

The lightly freckled redhead flashed a sincere smile. Now, the wheels in our heads were churning. We realized that she had made a compelling argument. We were heading into a foreign land where we might not be welcomed, especially by other young males. The mere presence of Vito tramping around with his metal detector would turn every head in Braddock. As mission leader, I made the call.

Bobby: "Okay, you got a good point. Sarah, you're in. We could definitely use a guide like Sacagawea. I mean… like you."

To be frank, Sarah's hopeful smile was too hard to turn down. Just as I was starting to feel worried inside about sounding too excited, Sal rolled his eyes and chimed in.

Sal: "Geez oh man! Another boring Lewis 'n Clark story. All's I know is you might o' finally found your match, nerd boy."

I spoke too soon about Sal ending his ridiculing. But I didn't care at all about his teasing this time. I was excited to have another history buff in our search party. And a pretty one at that. I could tell that our goofy sauntering and quixotic ambition was a breath of fresh air to Sarah. She was enchanted by our youthful spirit. Let's face it, not every day do you randomly come across a bunch of young teenagers searching for a hidden gold treasure.

Sarah threw her bag into her handlebar basket as she hopped on to the banana seat of her shiny yellow Schwinn and quickly joined up with our bicycle gang. Her vibrant enthusiasm added even more energy to our optimistic treasure hunt. We were going to head up through Squirrel Hill and grab slices of pizza at both Aiello's and Mineo's Pizzerias on Murray Avenue. We wanted to conduct an official taste test of what many consider to be the best two slices in town. After that, we would head down Forbes Avenue through Frick Park. This would lead us straight to South Braddock Avenue which runs directly to the town of Braddock.

Pedals were spinning. We cruised across the long span of the Schenley Bridge. Then we biked under the green leaves of the tall oaks that line the drive across from Phipps Conservatory. Late season flowers were in full bloom. Our idealistic mission had gained a new crew member. One who possessed valuable knowledge of the locale and cultures that lay ahead in our adventure, the quest for Braddock's Gold.

We made our way past the lily pond at the Westinghouse Memorial. Sarah asked us one more question as we began pedaling up a hill through Schenley Park.

Sarah: "So, what would be the first thing that you guys would buy if you do find the gold?"

We all quickly replied in order.

Sal: "A '79 Ducati 900 SuperSport motorcycle, red with a white racin' stripe on it."

Bobby: "A '79 Pontiac Firebird Trans Am, black with a gold Firebird hood decal on it."

Vito: "A '79 Primanti Brothers capicola sandwich, double meat with a fried egg on it."

Everyone laughed. Then I could feel it. Anticipation. It felt fun and exciting. We were finally heading to our planned destination, the neighborhood of Braddock. A town named after a fallen general from a battle that occurred a very long time ago. Hopefully, the gold was still waiting there for us to discover.

A light summer breeze blew through the towering oak trees. The wind was in our sails now. Our spirit hoisted even higher.

Chapter 8: A Turf War

The bright sunny morning had transformed into a gray overcast Saturday afternoon. Personally, I always preferred a thin layer of clouds to block out the searing sun of late August in Pittsburgh. Sarah turned out to be an excellent guide. She helped us navigate through the tree-lined avenues of Squirrel Hill and to what we hoped would be our mission's final destination. We bicycled past her grandfather's house and then her synagogue on Forbes Avenue. The winner of the debate over the town's best slice of pizza was left undecided. On our trek, we filled her in on all the details of our treasure hunt, including Heinz's journal and Guyasuta's tantalizing clue.

We only had one mishap. Vito's cumbersome metal detector accidentally knocked over a wooden folding chair that was sitting in a parking spot in front of a house in Edgewood. Using chairs to save parking spaces is a time-honored Yinzer tradition. After the old yellow chair fell over, a passing van on the main drag swooped in and took the spot. Witnessing the entire scene from his front porch, a fiery local was livid about losing his prized spot. He ran down the sidewalk and chased after us into the neighboring town of Swissvale. With parking spots in high demand and slim supply, messing with a townie's "personal" spot in a prime location can come at a steep price.

As we biked past a long line of folding chairs saving spots in Rankin, Sal took note.

Sal: "Wow! Look how freakin' hard it is to park dahn here. No wonder 'at jagoff back 'ere tried to kill you, Vito."

Distracted and driven, Vito completely ignored Sal's comment. Vito had only one thought on his mind, the golden treasure. He was daydreaming of our future fame and fortune.

Vito: "What if we do find 'at gold? Yinz think they'll put us on a' cover of *National Geographic*?"

Sal: "Yeah. It'll have a big picture o' you and say: 'World's Biggest Idiot Discovered in Pittsburgh.'"

Vito: "You know what, Sal? They put your ugly zitface on every cover of *Mad Magazine*! Why don't you go find a mirror and pop some o' them pimples!"

I quickly snapped back at my friends.

Bobby: "Quit jaggin' around, guys! We gotta lay low here. This ain't our turf."

My squad was rolling down a big hill and into the town of Braddock, where the historic battle had occurred. From our legwork at the library and the clue left by Guyasuta, we believed we were able to pinpoint the exact spot where General Braddock fell wounded in battle. I drew an "X" there on the map. We assumed the hidden cache of gold coins was buried in the ground directly underneath. Our hope was that we could use the metal detector to find it. The mission was in full swing.

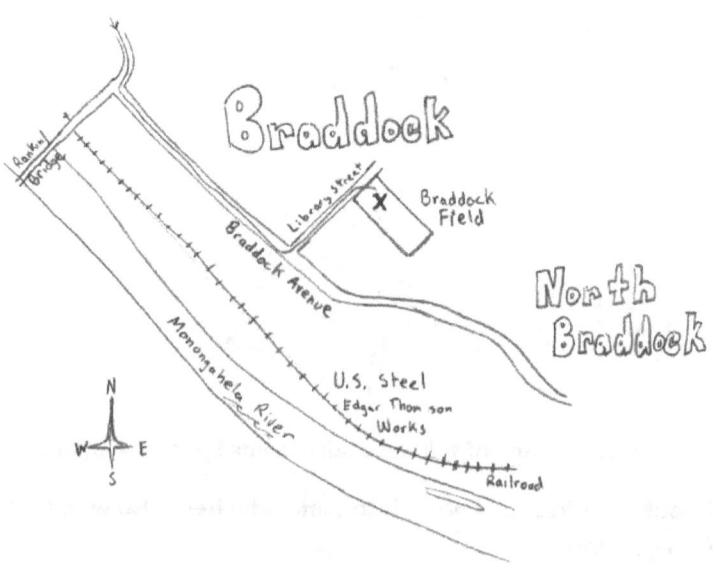

As we rode down Braddock Avenue, the main street of the town, it became apparent that Braddock shared many similarities with our hometown of Sharpsburg. The gritty blue-collar neighborhood was lined with blocks of row houses on a flat flood plain sitting against a large flowing river. It was nestled in between a steep rocky cliff to the north and the colossal U.S. Steel Mill which sat to the south along the Monongahela. Our research indicated that General Braddock was wounded in battle and fell off his horse in a stretch of forest that would be located exactly in the center of the present-day town.

We turned left off Braddock Avenue, passed the local Carnegie Library, and cycled under an old railroad bridge. Finally, our band had reached our desired destination point.

Sarah: "Look, guys! There's a statue of George Washington and a sign up ahead."

It was a large bronze statue of a young Washington in his militia uniform along with a Pennsylvania historic landmark sign. Wearing a three-cornered hat, Washington stood confidently with his sword at his side. An extremely eager Vito rode right up to the marker and read the big blue sign out loud.

Vito: "'Braddock's Defeat. July 9, 1755. General Braddock's British forces en route to Fort Duquesne were ambushed and routed by French and Indians within present limits of Braddock and North Braddock, forcing retreat and failure of the expedition.'"

Sal was mystified.

Sal: "Wow. I can't believe it."

Sarah: "What?"

Sal: "I can't believe Vito could read all o' that."

Sarah giggled.

Bobby: "And look how young George looks in 'at statue. Yinz know when the battle was over, he found four bullet holes in his blue coat? They were from musket balls 'at luckily just whizzed through it without hittin' him."

Vito looked up at the statue in admiration.

Vito: "Awesome."

153

Sal was not impressed.

Sal: "Big wow, Bobby. You keep pushin' 'at crap about how much of a badass George was, but I still don't buy it. I bet it was moths that ate them holes in his coat."

Bobby: "Whatever. So, judgin' by the map, we're halfway between the cliff up 'ere 'n the river dahn 'ere. 'At means Braddock musta fell somewhere right about... here."

I pointed around the statue of Washington and over a chain-link fence. The area behind the statue and marker happened to be a football field. Vito was more than ready to finally use the metal detector for its true purpose.

Vito: "All right! I can't believe the battle happened on a football field!"

Vito was raring to go. He jumped off his bike and ripped off the duct-taped metal detector. He sprinted onto the football field and immediately began to hunt for the hidden gold. Sarah turned to me in disbelief.

Sarah: "Does he really think that this football field was here in 1755?"

Bobby: "Probably. But let's just let it go. He's on a roll."

We soon followed him and began walking around the chalk-lined grass field as Vito scanned the grounds. Vito glowed with enthusiasm and patted his metal detector.

Vito: "Heinz and your pap had no chance findin' 'at gold without one o' these!"

Looking around in all directions, streetwise Sal was much more hesitant about being seen as a trespasser on other kids' turf.

Sal: "Are yinz sure about this? What if, you know, the local kids see us doin' this?"

Sal meant the group of African American teenagers who gave us a curious look as we passed by them on our bikes a few blocks back. From 25 yards away, I replied to his concerns in a louder voice.

Bobby: "Just... be cool."

In the empty stadium, my "be cool" echoed and whirled around us like an eerie breeze. But my words of encouragement rang empty. Heck, even one of the coolest men on the planet in 1979, famous actor John Travolta himself, would have had a hard time looking cool while clumsily swinging around a metal detector over mud patches in the middle of a football field. Of course, Travolta had just recently become immortalized as cool-kid Danny Zuko, the lead leather jacket in *Grease*. Unlike those greasers of yesteryear, at this awkward inception to our treasure hunting quest, my gang looked anything but cool. Caught in a Saturday afternoon fever, we clearly came off as a bumbling brigade of novice gold prospectors. It was amateur hour.

Sal: "We look like a bunch o' dorks out here. There ain't gonna be no gold under this mud pit."

Vito was hopping around in the middle of the grass turf busily searching for buried gold. He swung the metal detector like a pendulum over the ground. Through his aviators, a worried Sal kept his head on a swivel while surveying around the perimeter of the field. Sarah and I were kicking rocks and laying out the mission plan.

I pointed up at the rugged hill overlooking the town.

Bobby: "Look, there's 'at big cliff up 'ere. It could be buried at the bottom of it. If we don't find nothin' dahn here, maybe we should go check it out after this."

Sarah: "Yeah. And there's still all these patches of trees around the field too."

After scanning the entire field with the metal detector, Vito loudly announced his progress. He was shaking his head.

Vito: "I got no hits yet, Bobby! Not one beep! Zilch!"

Sal cynically responded to Vito.

Sal: "Of course ya got no hits, dipstick! You ain't gonna find nothin' here. Yinz are all full o'... "

Then Sal abruptly stopped talking and his jaw dropped a bit. He slowly finished his sentence.

Sal: "Crap."

Sal lifted up his sunglasses revealing a worried look. With wide eyes glued on the street entrance of the field, he lowered his voice to a serious whisper.

Sal: "I knew it."

Sarah and I responded to him at the same exact time.

Sarah/Bobby: "What?"

Normally, Yinzers would playfully call out "jinx" when multiple people simultaneously utter the same word. But this was no time to joke. After only a few hollow minutes of Vito scanning the field, our situation quickly went from bad to worse. Sarah and I turned around as Sal continued in a low voice.

Sal: "We got company."

A tough-looking group of Black kids was fast approaching the field. All three teens were older and bigger than us. They were walking up the street like a determined pride of lions would strut up to a ragged pack of scavenging jackals that made the mistake of intruding into their marked territory. Standing on their football field, of all places, we truly were invading their home turf. Maybe Sal was right about the roaring lion at the zoo this morning.

The leader of their triad cupped his hands together around his mouth like a megaphone. He bellowed out an intimidating warning call from the stadium entrance.

Curtis: "HEY!"

I recognized him. I had played junior high school football against him. His name was Curtis. Curtis Williams. He was a bruising running back who was going into tenth grade. He once busted my nose with a stiff-arm to the face that my thin duckbill facemask could not thwart. But I'm sure that he didn't recognize me. Big running backs usually don't remember the little free safeties that they run over on their way to scoring a touchdown.

We were standing on the 50-yard line. As they reached the goal line, Curtis and his friends picked up their pace. He yelled out again.

Curtis: "YO!"

My crew stood frozen in the middle of the football field. Curtis was crossing the 30-yard line now. He was a step ahead of his friends who flanked him on each side.

Curtis stuck out his chest.

Curtis: "Hey! Who is yinz fools? Y'all must be crazy showin' up here at our field!"

Still briskly walking towards us with purpose, Curtis gave Vito a mean look and pointed at the metal detector.

Curtis: "And what was yinz jokers doin' with 'at thing?"

Vito, Sal, and I all opened our mouths but had no response. We were caught off guard, just like General Braddock's army was right here on this very spot over two centuries ago. In retrospect, by not anticipating this possible scenario in my original mission plans, I may have been as naive as the general himself. By now, Curtis and his friends had met us at midfield. Fortunately, we had Sarah. Just like Sacagawea, she was the first to respectfully speak to the locals.

Sarah: "Oh, that thing. It's just a metal detector. We're collecting coins."

I corroborated her story.

Bobby: "Uh, yeah, we were just lookin' for coins."

Curtis sharply raised his eyebrows in shock. He made himself even taller and loudly blasted back at us.

Curtis: "*COINS?!* You come lookin' for money in Braddock? Now I *know* yinz is crazy!"

Curtis was heated. This was to be expected. He was literally protecting his home ground from outsiders, just like we would if strangers showed up on our block back in Sharpsburg. At this point, we were surrounded in a triangle by Curtis and his two companions. They were twin brothers. One was spinning a football in his hands.

Curtis: "Now, enough of this jive talkin'. For real, what the heck is yinz sorry lookin' White boys doin' here?"

Vito finally spoke.

Vito: "Oh, we ain't White. We're Italian."

Although I could tell that Vito's response was genuine, albeit naive, Curtis and his friends turned to each other and laughed out loud. Then Curtis quickly returned to more serious posturing. He took a step at Vito and continued.

Curtis: "Whateva you say, Fonzarelli. Y'all got three seconds to get your sorry butts off my field!"

He scowled at us with anger in his eyes. His friends crossed their arms with assurance as they fully expected us to oblige Curtis's final ultimatum. But we had traveled too far to come away empty-handed. I glanced at Sarah and then at my friends. I had to do something. Eyeing the football, I made a daring proposition.

Bobby: "Wait. What if we make a wager with yinz? Us verse yinz… in a football game."

Curtis raised his eyebrows, puffed out his chest, and stepped towards me. I nervously stammered.

Bobby: "Uh… uh, yeah. Um… "

I was being distracted by my animated friends who were now standing slightly behind Curtis. Both were silently pleading with me to shut my mouth. Sal was vigorously shaking his head and making a cut-it-out motion with his hand slicing in front of his neck. Vito was clenching his teeth and waving his hands like he was trying to stop a speeding freight train. I ignored them and continued in earnest.

Bobby: "First to 3 scores. If we win, we can… uh, keep lookin' for coins n'at. If we lose, yinz will never see us dahn here ever again."

Curtis stood over six inches taller than me. He looked down at me in disbelief.

Curtis: "Play us in football? Okay, *now* yinz boys for real be trippin'."

Curtis and his friends could have kicked our butts right there and then. But I knew that deep down he was a competitor. He was the toughest football player that I had ever played against. He seemed intrigued by the sport of my offer as much as the audacity of it. For him, and for all of us working-class kids, football wasn't just a game or even a way out of poverty. Football was about pride. And this was a challenge against his pride. No kid from Pittsburgh could walk away from a challenge like this. Let alone Curtis Williams, who was already getting scouted by Pitt and Penn State. I made him an offer he couldn't refuse.

Curtis lifted his chin up and thought about it. After a quick look around at his crew, he appeared to have made his decision. He produced a wry grin and began nodding his head before he spoke again.

Curtis: "All right. All right. It's on! Let's do this."

Curtis flashed us a big confident smile. He grabbed the football from his buddy and flipped it up with a tight spin high into the air.

Curtis: "Put on ya chinstraps, boys."

Curtis and his two friends started laughing again, for obvious reasons. They clearly had a huge advantage in physical size on us. Curtis was even taller than Vito, standing at 6-foot-2 with a solid 200-pound frame. He was a top-notch running back on offense and a stud middle linebacker on defense. He wore a white T-shirt with a Pitt logo on the front and a blue number 33 for Tony Dorsett on the back. His twin brother teammates were bookend outside linebackers who both stood over 6 feet tall as well. I remembered playing against Marcus and Maurice Nelson too. Always swarming around the ball and gang tackling, they were relentless defenders. Both brothers wore matching white T-shirts, while all three wore jeans and high-tops like us. They all sported shorter haircuts. Although hugely popular in the early 1970s, the iconic Afro hairstyle had grown out of fashion by 1979.

The field was a little damp from the severe storms earlier in the week. Our opponents, beaming with confidence, began tossing around some warm-up throws to each other. They continued to laugh it up.

After catching a light toss with one hand, Curtis expressed his self-assurance loud and clear to add even more intimidation.

Curtis: "Can't *nobody* here stop me from scorin'!"

My team was not so upbeat.

Sal: "You gotta be nuts, Bobby. We got no chance. Zip."

Vito: "They was on the best team we played against two years ago, Bobby."

Bobby: "I hear ya, guys. But it's the only thing I could think o' doin'. Let's just play like we always do."

It seemed only fitting that we should be slaughtered at the same exact site that Braddock's army was over 200 summers ago. After setting down the metal detector and huddling together to address our imminent demise, I approached Curtis to discuss the rules of the game. Yinzer street kids knew every parameter that had to be covered.

Bobby: "3 on 3. Full tackle. No blitzes 'til 7 Mississippi."

Curtis nodded and continued with the rules.

Curtis: "4 downs. Ball placed on the 35. First to 3 scores, wins."

Curtis added one more stipulation as he firmly squeezed the football.

Curtis: "Our field. Our ball first."

We shook on it. Sharpsburg, the away team, would start on defense. Whoever scored three touchdowns first, won all the marbles. Of course, by getting the ball first, team Braddock had the clear upper hand over team Sharpsburg. With the odds already stacked against us, this was another huge disadvantage for my team. In the 1970s, it would be like walking up to Bobby Fischer, the U.S. chess champion at age 14, and challenging him to a match on his personal chess board while surrendering your queen before the game even began. But beggars can't be choosers. After all, it was Curtis's turf that we had invaded. I walked back over to Vito and Sal, and we formed a small huddle. Sal had just one line for us.

Sal: "We're gonna get our asses kicked."

Sal was a good athlete. But unlike him, Vito and I actually played organized football together for our school. What's more, years of pick-up games on the streets had allowed us to gain an unspoken rapport. Although linebacker was his forte, Vito was a quality quarterback. He had a cannon arm and he liked throwing long bombs to me. I played wide receiver and free safety. Although I was smaller in stature, I often surprised opponents with my speed. Vito and I always went deep on the first play from scrimmage.

That being said, beating a team of this caliber would be a tall order. They were definitely out of our league. This area of Pittsburgh is well known to be a hotbed of football talent. The local public high school has produced an incredibly high number of alumni who went on to play professionally in the NFL.

To prepare for battle, Curtis tucked his gold chain necklace under his shirt collar. He was more than eager to get the contest in motion.

Curtis: "We about to play here, or what? Let's get this game rollin'!"

By this time, several girls had gathered around the field to watch along with Sarah. It was Cierra Nelson and her best friends. Cierra was the younger sister of the Nelson twins. She also happened to be Curtis's girlfriend. I remembered her from a junior high school track meet that occurred the previous spring. Cierra was the shining star on the track that day. In fact, she was the fastest girl that I had ever seen in my life. Standing on the concrete bleachers, Sarah and Cierra noticeably greeted each other as if they had already been acquainted.

As we started to line up in our positions on the field, Vito turned to me.

Vito: "Should we play man or zone?"

Sal: "It don't matter. Whatever we do, we're still gonna get crushed."

Bobby: "I say we play zone. Vito, cover the middle. Me 'n Sal will play the corners."

See, the game of chess and football actually share a lot in common. Both games require the conquest of an opponent within a limited physical space. Both reward skill of body and mind. And in both, there are moves met by countermoves. Although at first glance it appears to be a brutal scrum of chaos, at its core, the game of football is like a life-sized chess match. No doubt, the team from Braddock had much better pieces.

On offense, Curtis lined up at tailback behind one Nelson at quarterback. The other Nelson split out at wide receiver. On the defensive side of the ball, Vito lined up at middle linebacker. Sal and I played defensive backs out wide. Moments before the first snap, Vito pulled his gold cross necklace up to his lips and kissed it in quick prayer. Then he started chomping hard on his Big Red gum like he usually did when he was putting on his game face or getting ready for a fistfight.

Vito: "Here we go!"

Braddock's ball. Play begins.

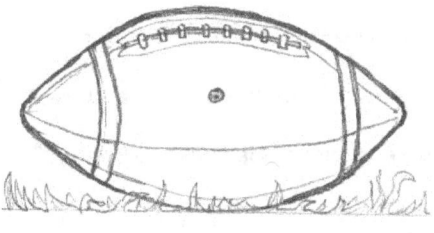

<u>Box Score: Sharpsburg (Away) vs. Braddock (Home)</u>

Score: Sharpsburg 0 – Braddock 0

Braddock Series #1:

Play #1: QB Maurice pitches a toss sweep to RB Curtis. RB Curtis runs wide right. RB Curtis runs over DB Bobby. RB Curtis runs over LB Vito. RB Curtis stiff arms DB Sal and jogs into the end zone for the 35-yard score. Touchdown.

Score: Sharpsburg 0 – Braddock 1

Bobby: "We gotta wrap up 'at big dude!"

Vito: "It's hard to 'cause the field's all slippy."

Sal: "We ain't exactly the Steel Curtain here, Bobby!"

Sharpsburg Series #1:

Play #1: As predetermined, QB Vito throws up a long go-route to WR Bobby on the first play. The other team is caught off guard by the deep throw and speed of the play. WR Bobby hauls in the 35-yard catch in the corner of the end zone. Touchdown.

Score: Sharpsburg 1 – Braddock 1

Curtis: "Okay, so them boys got some game. But next time, move up 'n bump 'em at the line, guys. This ain't no Bradshaw, Swann, and Stallworth we playin' here."

Braddock Series #2:

Play 1: Toss sweep right to RB Curtis who gains 10 yards as LB Vito and DB Bobby cling on to him to drag him down.

Play 2: Toss sweep left to RB Curtis. LB Vito and DB Sal hang on to the ball carrier to make the tackle. RB Curtis gains 15 yards.

Play 3: Dive run to RB Curtis who steamrolls LB Vito for a 10-yard score. Touchdown.

Score: Sharpsburg 1 – Braddock 2

Sal: "We're gettin' rocked. Any more bright ideas, Bobby?"

Bobby: "Let's do our favorite play. The hitch 'n pitch."

Vito: "Okay. Hope they never seen it before."

Sharpsburg Series #2:

Play #1: QB Vito throws a 5-yard hitch to WR Sal. WR Sal is swarmed and tackled immediately. This play is a planned set-up.

Play #2: QB Vito throws the same 5-yard hitch to WR Sal. Sal is surrounded but pitches the ball back to RB Bobby who is running outside from the backfield. RB Bobby hauls in the pitch and runs for a 30-yard score up the left sideline. Touchdown.

Score: Sharpsburg 2 – Braddock 2

Curtis: "Okay! Okay, we got us some hustlers! These cats was thinkin' they can come up in here 'n hustle us. Ain't no way you gonna stop me now!"

Braddock Series #3:

Play #1: QB Maurice pitches a toss sweep right to RB Curtis. DB Bobby and LB Vito sprint up to make the tackle. RB Curtis then stops in his tracks and throws a deep spiral to a wide open WR Marcus for a 35-yard score. Touchdown.

Final Score: Sharpsburg 2 – Braddock 3

Bobby: "The halfback sweep pass! We shoulda expected 'em to run a trick play on us after we ran the hitch 'n pitch on 'em, Vito."

Vito: "Yeah, but it's tough to worry 'bout the pass on first dahn when they got a Mack Truck at running back."

Curtis and his teammates celebrated in the end zone. They were not about to let a ragtag team from Sharpsburg beat them on their own turf. Although we lost the game, we fought hard. In fact, we appeared battered and bruised as if we had just finished fighting in the actual Battle of Braddock. Our mud-stained jeans were a clear sign of our defeat. Exhausted, I bent over to regain my breath. I looked up at Sarah.

Bobby: "We tried, Sarah. We tried real hard to win 'at one."

Sarah smiled and coolly whispered to me.

Sarah: "Don't worry. I know Curtis's girlfriend from running track with her. She's putting in a good word for us right now."

It turned out that Sarah, a long-distance runner, personally knew Cierra from local track competitions. This fact would have probably allowed Sarah, our Sacagawea, to negotiate peace and prevent our rough battle on the football field. But it was too late for that now. However, in a stroke of good fortune, our trusted scout had pulled some strings for us while we were getting our butts whipped by the bruising kids from Braddock. Sarah told Cierra that we were looking for artifacts from the Battle of Braddock. After talking to his girlfriend in the end zone, Curtis slowly made his way over to us. He was still holding the game ball.

Curtis: "Y'all played a good game. My girlfriend told me why you was here and, well, we can help yinz out."

Sal, Vito, and I flashed astonished smiles at each other. Our Sacagawea plan had actually worked. Sarah was pure gold.

Moments later, I turned to Sarah and whispered to her while smiling.

Bobby: "Thanks, Sarah. You're the best."

Vito shook Curtis's hand and thanked him.

Vito: "Thanks, man. You know we played against yinz in school. Well, I mean, we got stomped by yinz."

Bobby: "Yeah, we played against yinz guys two years ago. We lost by a lot more in 'at game."

Curtis smiled at us.

Curtis: "Yeah, I could tell y'all played some ball. That hook 'n ladder play don't just come out from nowhere."

Vito and I smiled proudly at each other. We were happy to get a compliment about our trick play. We gathered up our items for the treasure hunt, most importantly the metal detector. I walked up to Curtis and shook his hand.

Bobby: "Thanks, man. We appreciate it."

Curtis: "Oh, it's all good."

After a round of postgame handshakes, we all introduced ourselves. I should note, Curtis said both "yinz" and "y'all" in conversation. The use of y'all in speech is common among the Black community in Pittsburgh. Obviously, Curtis spoke fluent Yinzer. His father and grandfather both worked in the huge Braddock steel mill. Faster than a juicy rumor, the Yinzer language would spread like wildfire among workers and their families in the mill towns.

Cierra walked up to our team and warmly welcomed us with a radiant smile.

Cierra: "Welcome to Braddock, guys. Sarah says you lookin' for artifacts."

Cierra had dazzling eyes. They were amber. Rare and beautiful, like gold. Held in a high ponytail, she had long braids that hung behind her. Her pretty braids were fashioned at the ends with strings of small purple beads. She wore a purple T-shirt, jean shorts, and purple flip-flops. Having an affinity for gold herself, Cierra styled large gold hoop earrings and a thin gold necklace. It seemed clear that the Nelson twins had no problem with their younger sister dating their best friend, who also happened to be the toughest kid in town.

Cierra was in my grade. From what I saw at the track meet last spring, she was unquestionably faster than just about every middle schooler in the Pittsburgh area. She had long strides, and her form was flawless and efficient. The only thing more likely than getting beat up in a football game with Curtis was getting dusted in a track race with Cierra. She was extremely friendly and knew her town's history.

Cierra put her hand on her hip and smiled.

Cierra: "We can help yinz look around n'at. I mean, we all know about the battle that happened dahn here. We learned all 'bout it in school, too. They was talkin' 'bout it in social studies class last year."

Curtis lightly shrugged his shoulders.

Curtis: "Anyways, this is our tahn. So I wanna know if there's anything here from 'at battle too. I'm from Braddock. My parents and grandparents is from Braddock. Heck, my one grandpa's always talkin' 'bout the battle that went on dahn here. He flew with the Red Tails so he knows his stuff."

It turns out that Curtis was a history scholar himself. He was inspired by his grandfather who was a distinguished fighter pilot in World War II. He flew with the famed Red Tails. This renowned African American flying squadron winged legendary P-51 Mustang fighter planes with red fins. Known for their superior flying skills, these fierce aces of the U.S. Army Air Corps played a paramount role in defeating the Nazis. Of important note, the Pittsburgh area had the highest percentage of Red Tail veterans of any region in the country. Nearly 1 in 10 Red Tails were Yinzers.

As Curtis and Cierra began to lead our pack out of the football stadium, Sarah and I told the teens from Braddock more details about our research. Remaining diligent in his job as head metal detector, Vito's device beeped as he swung it over the metal garbage can by the stadium exit. Vito lifted up the whole bin and checked underneath for good measure. The mission continued as we left the stadium gates and searched other spots in the immediate area. By now, our treasure hunting party had more than doubled in size and looked like a small army itself.

Curtis: "So we should check out Bell Avenue. It was the high ground. There was a lot o' American Indians usin' them rocks 'n trees up 'ere for sniping durin' the battle."

We began to trek uphill into North Braddock. Just as we swept up around the bend, a sweet little old lady was strolling past us while pushing a shopping cart full of groceries. It happened to be Curtis's great-grandmother who was still in superb shape in her golden years. She questioned Curtis.

Gramma Rose: "Hey, Curtis. What are all yinz boys and girls doin'?"

Curtis: "Hi, Gramma Rose. We conductin' a archaeological expedition."

Gramma Rose: "Is that so? Well then, good luck to y'all. I hope yinz kids find what you lookin' for."

She continued on her way and called out to us.

Gramma Rose: "God bless!"

Cierra: "See you in church tomorrow, Gram Rose!"

Curtis made our motley crew smile with pride. Hearing for the first time that we were an actual "archaeological expedition" laid legitimate claim that we were conducting official historical work. The title sounded so formal and made us feel important. With his magnetic personality, Curtis was a confident teen who made everyone around him feel more confident as well.

Funnily, in many Pittsburgh neighborhoods, older residents walked home with their shopping buggy from local stores. Curtis's great-grandmother would simply bring it back during her next trip to the market. It was kind of like checking out a book from the library in those days.

Cierra: "Okay, there could be somethin' up this way. Nobody ever comes up in here."

We were hiking on the hillside road over the town now. It ran along a wooded cliff. Grand View Golf Club sits on its very top. Vito was scanning up ahead with the metal detector. Just then, his device blurted out a short but loud beep. He made a discovery. Vito hollered at the top of his lungs.

Vito: "HEY, GUYS! I found a coin! I found a coin!"

We all froze as Vito hurriedly picked up the coin from the ground.

Vito: "It's got George Washington on it!"

Vito held up the coin with excitement, then turned around and showed it off to the rest of the group. Sal quickly volleyed back at Vito in a scathing manner.

Sal: "That's called a quarter, ya numbskull!"

Vito pulled the coin up closer to his eyes to get a better inspection.

Vito: "Really? What do ya think it's worth?"

Vito was still closely examining what was clearly just a common quarter. Curtis looked with disbelief at the rest of my crew. He whispered to us.

Curtis: "Is he for real?"

Sarah, Sal, and I just quietly shrugged our shoulders and nodded our heads in affirmation. As Vito proceeded to polish the coin with his tank top, there was a quiet pause. Then Cierra took the lead and refocused the group. She turned and looked out over the town from our high vantage point. With her hand on her hip, Cierra continued with her judgment on the mission agenda.

Cierra: "We should go 'n look dahn on the other side of the football field now."

We had explored most of the north side of the battlefield. Cierra suggested that we now check the southern side of town. She pointed down to a spot along the river.

Cierra: "Remember, they walked across the Mon River and came up through there. The river was real shallow back in the day."

The Battle of Braddock is officially known as the Battle of the Monongahela by war historians. A knowledgeable scholar of her town's history, Cierra knew where the British and American troops had entered the area before they were ambushed. She offered more of her educated opinion.

Cierra: "And then we should go check the crick over by the mill."

Cierra pointed to another promising search area. It sat beyond a sprawling, smoky steel mill. The Edgar Thomson Steel Works in Braddock is a gargantuan structure run by the U.S. Steel Corporation. With its towering smokestacks and dizzying maze of steampipes projecting in all directions around multiple blast furnaces, Vito and Sal could not help but notice the hulking structure.

Vito: "Holy crap! 'At's the biggest steel mill I ever seen in my life!"

Sal: "It looks like Willy Wonka's chocolate factory on 'roids."

Hoping to find our golden ticket to the good life, I too saw the resemblance between the colossal steel mill and the fantastical candy manufactory shown in *Willy Wonka & the Chocolate Factory*. Built by the steel industry baron Andrew Carnegie, the immense production plant was one of the first in America to use the "Bessemer Process" of infusing oxygen into the molten steel to make it stronger. It was by far the largest employer in the Mon Valley region.

Curtis: "My dad works there. And all my uncles. My grandpa did, too."

Cierra: "Yeah, my dad works dahn 'ere. So did my mum."

Over the next two hours, we tirelessly sifted through every square foot of the Braddock battlefield in pursuit of the treasure. Any accessible plot of land in town was combed, from the wooded patches along Turtle Creek to the gravel parking lots of the local saloons. With his beloved metal detector, Vito remained in high gear. It was like following a beeping bloodhound dog all around the neighborhood. In fact, while eagerly checking around a tree stump, he managed to sniff out a rabbit hole and sent the rabbits on the run. In his relentless quest for the hidden gold, Vito literally left no stone unturned. Upon hearing a beep, he would flip over everything from rusty brown scrap metal to crusty orange rocks laden with iron ore.

Wiping sweat from his brow, Vito quietly murmured to me.

Vito: "It's gotta be here somewhere, Bobby. It's gotta be."

Bobby: "Just keep scannin', Vito. We can find it."

But despite our optimism, the mission was slowly beginning to fall apart. Bored with the search, the Nelson twins went home to shoot hoops. It was no surprise that Sal wanted to call it quits on the treasure hunt as well. Fortunately for him, Cierra's friend, Rosaria, seemed to be interested in the new boy with aviator sunglasses. Of Puerto

Rican descent, Rosaria Luna was a tall girl with long brown hair. She was one of the best high jumpers in the city. Cierra's other friend, Tina Park, was a Korean American girl who lived only blocks away from Sarah in Squirrel Hill. A gifted sprinter herself, Tina had the longest hair of all the girls and calf muscles that put my skinny legs to shame. Dressed like the stars of *Three's Company*, both Rosaria and Tina were wearing tank tops, running shorts with white trim, and flip-flops.

I overheard Sal talking to Rosaria. Fluent in Italian, he was trying to impress her with his vast knowledge of world languages.

Sal: "You know, Rosaria, 'Sì' means 'Yes' in Italian *and* Spanish."

After running her hand through her hair, Rosaria warmly smiled and asked Sal if he spoke Spanish.

Rosaria: "Sí. ¿Hablas español?"

Sal tried his best to reply.

Sal: "Uh… uh no, I'm good. I just had some pizza."

After two long hours of prospecting, we had collected about $2 in common coins but still had nothing to write home about. We found no sign of the gold. All we found was that Curtis and Cierra were the pride of Braddock. Every teenager that we encountered in town greeted the couple with a "What's up?" and friendly high fives. On the positive side, just being seen with them gave my crew immediate street cred.

But by now, the energy and fanfare of our expedition was beginning to wane.

Sal: "I told yinz, it ain't happenin'. There ain't gonna be nothin' left from 'at battle. It's ancient history."

Although I expected that level of enthusiasm from Sal, everyone else in our unit was becoming frustrated by the lack of results as well. We came to a halt around a corner stop sign. Lightly shaking his head in dismay, Curtis crossed his arms and looked down to the ground. Rolling their eyes at each other, Cierra and Sarah also showed signs of doubt. With our army of archaeologists losing morale, the search for Braddock's Treasure began to look hopeless. Desperate, I tried to rally the troops.

I pointed back in the direction of the stadium.

Bobby: "Look, we came dahn the football field first. I say we go back 'ere and check dahn by the statue and the sign marker one more time."

Curtis: "You right. The sign got put up 'ere for a reason."

We backtracked to the historic landmarks that designated the famous battle. We double-checked the entire area. Feeling desperation in the air, Vito urgently canvassed the grassy knoll around the statue and sign but could only ferret out an old, crumpled Pepsi can. He kicked the can in disgust. Then his shoulders slumped. After embarking on our treasure hunt with such high spirits this morning, he looked wholly deflated from the results of our completely futile search. Ditto for me.

To add injury to insult, I still felt a little battle worn from the football game. From a lone drip of blood on my shirt, I realized that I had a swollen lip. It came from a flying elbow that I absorbed when trying to tackle Curtis. I grimaced when I reached up to touch my small battle wound. Only then did the bruise begin to throb in pain.

My ego was bruised too. I felt embarrassed about the mission failing miserably. I confided in Sarah about the serious doubts that had crept into the back of my mind.

Bobby: "This is way tougher than I thought it would be, Sarah. I don't think we're gonna find 'at gold."

Sarah: "Well, why don't you look harder at the notes that Heinz collected. There might be something else in his journal."

Bobby: "Good point. I'll check through it again. Maybe I missed something."

I riffled through the pages. I found nothing. And with that, our noble treasure hunting mission had fully fizzled in the August heat. The only round gold object to be seen was the warm, glowing sun ironing its way through the stratus sheets in the sky. Bright golden rays were now finding their way through holes in the clouds.

Curtis crossed his arms and spoke to the disheartened squad.

Curtis: "Well guys, I think we checked everywhere 'round here. Y'all did a good search for the gold."

We all paused. My friends and I looked at each other in mild shock. I replied.

Bobby: "You knew we were lookin' for gold?"

Curtis and Cierra smiled at me with wide grins.

Curtis: "Sure. We all know 'bout the legend o' Braddock's Gold. We from Braddock!"

Cierra: "It was worth a try, guys. Y'all was so excited so we had to go 'n look for it."

Sarah and I smiled back at the helpful couple. However, a dejected Vito looked out over the field and hunched his shoulders. He huffed and made his lips vibrate like a motorboat. You could see the disappointment on his face. This was a huge letdown.

Vito: "Now whadda we do?"

Vito asked a deep question. It was not just about what we do next. It was about what we do with our lives now. As for me and Vito, we shared an idealistic vision of riding into the town of Braddock and discovering the long-lost treasure. We would ride off into the sunset as glorious heroes hauling a huge treasure chest full of priceless gold coins. But that was not to be. Now it felt like we were just chasing after a pot of gold at the end of the rainbow.

We stood there by the football field in silence. The audible bustle of the U.S. Steel Works had ceased. Being late Saturday afternoon, the steel mill's vigorous activity subsided for the weekend. Just then, we detected a distinct sound traveling over the river valley. Loudly clicking gears were followed by a rush of thunderous noise accompanied by high pitch screams. From across the Monongahela River, echoed the mighty roar of the wooden rafters from a large roller coaster called the Thunderbolt.

Cierra raised her eyebrows and smiled. Then she pointed across the river.

Cierra: "We could go to Kennywood."

Curtis nodded his head at his girlfriend.

Curtis: "I'm down."

Kennywood Amusement Park sat directly across the river from where we stood. We quickly realized that none of us had even been to our city's theme park yet this summer. We all looked at each other and smiled.

Bobby: "It's right there, guys. Let's make the most o' this day."

Sarah: "Sounds like a good idea to me."

Vito pumped his fist high in the air.

Vito: "Yes! They have primo cheese fries there! And funnel cakes! And pizza!"

Sal: "Calm dahn, Augustus Gloop."

On a whim, our decision to go have fun at an amusement park immediately lifted everyone's spirits. Curtis even offered to drive us over. He pointed to his nearby car.

Curtis: "Y'all can put your bikes in my car. Let's get this show on a' road."

We practically ran our bikes and supplies to the back of Curtis's light blue 1968 Buick Sport Wagon. Curtis just turned 16 and had his driver's license. To his credit, navigating that elongated Buick station wagon down an alley was tougher than steering a coal barge up a river. And good luck trying to park those steel goliaths in the city. They took up two spots compared to today's typical sedan. The one nice thing about the Sport Wagon is that you had a ton of cargo room in the rear. One of the biggest station wagons ever built, our four bikes would conveniently fit under the bubble roof of that spacious back cabin.

As we loaded the bikes, shovel, and metal detector into the back compartment, Curtis laid out a directive to all of us.

Curtis: "Don't none o' yinz make fun of my ride. My grandpa gave it to me."

Bobby: "Oh, no way, man. I'll probably be drivin' a station wagon too in a couple years."

Vito: "That's if you pass 'at drivin' test. I heard it's real hard 'cause them guys who ride with you are real sticklers n'at."

Sarah vouched for Vito.

Sarah: "Yeah, my brother failed the driver's license test the first time he took it. He said they take off points for everything. You even have to make sure your seat is adjusted the right way and your mirrors are at the right angles."

Tina: "My brother said they try to fail everyone on their first time. He heard you should slip a twenty to the driving test guy if you want to pass on the first try."

Vito nodded at Tina.

Vito: "Oh, yeah? I could see 'at."

Most Yinzer teenagers worried about the city's infamously difficult driving license tests. They were conducted at a course on Washington Boulevard in Highland Park, right across the river from Sharpsburg. Sal scoffed at the group's fears.

Sal: "I don't need no driver's license. I already drive my dad's work truck everywhere."

Rosaria smiled again at Sal and questioned him with obvious interest.

Rosaria: "For real? That's cool. Don't you ever worry about gettin' caught?"

Sal: "Nope. Not at all."

Sal smugly smiled. His intentions had hit the mark. Rosaria was now obviously interested in the guy who claimed to live a life of danger.

Finished with configuring the jigsaw puzzle of bikes, Curtis closed the back of the station wagon and continued with a few words of encouragement about the driver's license test.

Curtis: "Yinz just gotta practice, 'at's all. My grandpa would take me to that big parkin' lot dahn by the mill on Sundy nights. He even went 'n set up big orange cones n'at. We was pretendin' like it was the real drivin' test."

Curtis paused to recount one more important point.

Curtis: "Grandpa would tell me, 'I got through a world war 'cause o' God, but I got through a firefight 'cause o' practice.'"

At that moment, I realized why Curtis excelled at football, and everything else for that matter. Sure, he was an intelligent kid and gifted athlete, but it was his work ethic and practice regimen that was second to none.

Cierra added to Curtis's story.

Cierra: "I even sat in the back seat some nights to help critique his drivin' skills."

Curtis smiled at his girlfriend.

Curtis: "Yeah, I know, backseat driver. You was harder on me than my grandpa."

Cierra smiled back at him and added one more piece of advice.

Cierra: "But for real, y'all gotta learn how to parallel park. That's the hardest part. They'll flunk your butt if you can't park right. But once you nail that, you're golden. Everythin' else is easy street."

Obviously, Cierra was smart and blessed with athletic talent as well. I distinctly recollected watching her practice her starting block technique well before the rest of the competition at the track meet in May. She paid attention to detail and possessed the resolute drive to succeed. Glowing with natural chemistry, it was clear that Curtis and Cierra made a perfect couple.

Curtis clapped his hands together and then pulled out his car keys.

Curtis: "All right now. Y'all hop in. We goin' to Kennywood. Let's boogie."

Vito excitedly raised his hand.

Vito: "I call shotgun!"

Cierra looked up at Vito and moved her lips to the side with a smirked smile.

Cierra: "That's cool, man. But the front seat is gonna be me, you, and Tina."

Vito's eyes lit up at getting to sit next to Tina.

Vito: "Awesome."

I was just thrilled that I didn't have to crawl into the back of the station wagon like I had to with my family's car at home. Before the advent of the SUV, an unfortunate but proud group of American kids had the privilege of taking long family commutes while crammed in the back of a station wagon. The absurd situation of sitting within a pile of paper grocery bags while bracing for sudden stops from the moving vehicle was equal parts ludicrous and dangerous. And sometimes you even had to lie down flat on your back. I can remember my father once warning me, "Get dahn, Bobby! There's a cop drivin' right behind us!" This badge of honor from the kids of that era would be deemed wholly illegal by today's car safety standards.

As I sat down on the hot vinyl, I relished simply sitting in the actual back seat for once. With a forceful shove, Sal harshly woke me up from my brief daydream. He, Sarah, and Rosaria were still standing in wait by the car door.

Sal: "Earth to Bobby! Wake up, space cadet! And move over, ya dope. This back seat ain't just for you."

We all crammed snuggly into the front and back seats of Curtis's car and soon began to race across the Rankin Bridge. We looked like packed sardines in a blue tin can on wheels. Surfing for the right radio wave, Cierra was quickly spinning the tuning dial above the 8-track tape player. The crowd in the car cheered when the brand-new hit "Good Times" by Chic popped up on the speakers.

Cierra: "Heck yeah, that's my jam!"

Curtis: "Aw yeah! Turn it up, Cici!"

Cierra turned it to full blast. The blaring music blew out briskly with the wind through all four fully wound-down car windows. The number one song on the pop charts that month, "Good Times" was as much fun as its name. Now considered a catalyst for modern hip-hop, Chic's new R&B sound was a mixture of soul and funk with a solid helping of disco. Although disco music was still hugely popular in the summer of 1979, the golden age of disco was having its last hurrah (and so were we).

We sailed across the bridge. Wind was blowing through our hair. The towering wooden roller coasters were in clear sight now along the Monongahela River. In this free-spirited moment, not one passenger in that station wagon cared about finding Braddock's Treasure. We said goodbye to our yellow brick road to wealth and fame, but we were still young and invincible teenagers.

Rocking high above the Mon, the baby blue car was filled with eight Yinzers blissfully awaiting their next adventure.

Chapter 9: The Merry-Go-Round

Only a group of young Yinzers could plan their whole day around looking for a hidden gold treasure, and instead, end up playing football and riding roller coasters. But here we were at Kennywood Amusement Park, a picturesque paradise in the town of West Mifflin. Widely known for its classic wooden roller coasters, Kennywood has been a fixture in Pittsburgh for well over a century. It started as a small picnic area on the Kenny farm, which was the very last stop for the city trolley line. What was then a scenic countryside bloomed into a recreational playground where Pittsburgh families traditionally visit every summer. In retrospect, this was exactly the kind of fun that my band needed to lift our spirits after a fruitless hunt for Braddock's Treasure.

Cierra hopped out of the car. She merrily snapped her fingers on both hands.

Cierra: "Aw yeah! Let's do this!"

Sarah: "Look at the line to get in. It's packed here today!"

There was a long line of people at the park entrance. Normally in a situation like this, Vito, Sal, and I would have hopped over a secluded stretch of fence to sneak in without paying, but we didn't want to make a bad impression on our new friends. After we scrounged together the rest of our cash to pay the $5 admission fees, we had no more money left between us. Amusement parks back then were different in that you needed to purchase a string of small paper tickets to ride the attractions. The little rides, like the bumper cars, were 3 yellow tickets while the big rides, like roller coasters, were 5 tickets. Completely broke, Vito, Sal, and I started asking people who were leaving the park if they had any extra tickets. However, we quickly realized that we did not have to beg for spares. Fortunately for us, Curtis knew the girls working at the ticket booth, so we ended up getting some tickets at a great price.

Curtis: "Here ya go, guys! 25 tickets each. On the house."

Curtis held up streams of yellow tickets in the air with a triumphant smile on his face. At this point, I started to realize that John Travolta wasn't the coolest guy on the planet. Curtis Williams from Braddock had him beat.

Vito: "Cool! Thanks, man!"

As he happily handed out the long strings of tickets, Curtis grinned and playfully teased us about our loss in the football game.

Curtis: "Y'all deserve it after gettin' smacked on my field today."

Finally, we could enter the amusement park and take in the sights, smells, and sounds. It was a high-quality sensory overload. On this sunny Saturday afternoon, every attraction was jammed with long lines of excited parkgoers. The sweet scent of cotton candy and fresh funnel cakes permeated the air. From all directions, you could hear the roar of free-falling roller coasters and the vibrating beams of their wooden tracks. The swirling echoes of screaming riders and the bells and whistles from the carnival games added to the festive atmosphere.

Leading our flock of friends, a headstrong Cierra was on a mission. She turned around and addressed us with a spirited smile.

Cierra: "Follow me! I don't mess around here. We ridin' every coaster in a' park."

Everyone soon began coupling up for the two-seated rides. Obviously, Curtis and Cierra would be ride partners. Sal and Rosaria immediately hit it off and decided to ride together. Even Vito somehow quickly linked up with Tina. With their new riding companions, they all began to briskly walk away in pairs to the first roller coaster in the park, the Jack Rabbit. None of us ever had a girlfriend before so I was slightly taken aback at how smoothly my best friends had partnered up with pretty girls that they had met only a few hours ago. I overheard Vito talking to Tina.

Vito: "So, yinz should know 'at I'm a treasure hunter by trade... "

It reminded me of how every girl at my junior high school would clamor to meet the new boy that moves into the district in the middle of the school year. The bored coeds all wanted to get to know the new guy. Halfway through the year, most girls are tired of the immature antics of the teenage boys whom they were forced to share a classroom, cafeteria, and school bus with since kindergarten. There is a sort of novelty that stirs excitement and mystery. Vito and Sal with their fresh new faces were quick to seize the opportunity with the girls they met in Braddock.

That left me and Sarah standing alone. Getting ready for the roller coasters, she was pulling her long red hair into a ponytail with a yellow hair tie.

Sarah: "Looks like I'm riding with you."

Bobby: "Okay."

Of course, it was more than okay. I had never even been to Kennywood Park without my family before, let alone with my best friends and a bunch of girls. Usually, my ride partner was my little brother, Bryan. Somehow, today I got to ride with a bright and beautiful redhead from the city that I had just met this morning. As we walked through the crowds at the amusement park, song tracks from the famous album *Frampton Comes Alive!* could be heard blaring on the loudspeakers located on every corner. The best-selling live album of the decade had become the background music of the late '70s.

Cierra: "We doin' the Jack Rabbit first! I love this ride."

Curtis: "Gotta love 'at bunny hop!"

The Jack Rabbit is a vintage wooden roller coaster that has a signature double-dipper "bunny hop" that makes the riders fly out of their seats. Today, the ride is over a century old and is still beloved by young and old Yinzers alike. As we stood in line, Sarah and Cierra chatted about their summer league track team.

Sarah: "Yeah, I got better this summer. I shaved seven seconds off my mile time."

Cierra: "Good goin', girl. I got better too. I fine-tuned my startin' block technique."

I was not even aware that there were summer league track programs for teenagers in Pittsburgh. From my experience, I found that most girls took track much more seriously than their often lackadaisical male counterparts. At practice, my boys track team would find ways to hide from the coaches and get out of running more laps, while the girls tended to be much more disciplined and determined to improve their skills. Of course, this tended to apply in the classroom as well.

Cierra: "The Schenley Park track is gettin' repaved this fall, so it'll be better next summer."

Schenley Park was a large piece of land donated by Mary Schenley to provide a sanctuary from the industrial complex in Pittsburgh's eastern neighborhoods. On our earlier journey, Sarah had pointed out that her grandfather's house in Squirrel Hill sat across the street from the park's golf course.

By this point, we were about to get on the Jack Rabbit. Sarah confessed her greatest childhood fear to me.

Sarah: "For some reason, this tiny coaster scared me more than anything else on the planet when I was a little kid. It's that double-dip."

Bobby: "Yeah, you feel like you're gonna just fly outta the car."

Sarah smiled with nervous excitement in her eyes.

Sarah: "I know! I would close my eyes for the whole ride and hope that I was still alive when it stopped."

I nodded in agreement as we were about to board the very last car on our coaster train. I could not help but razz her.

Bobby: "Crap. We got the back seat. I heard like one kid a day flies off 'is one."

Sarah: "What?!"

Sarah volleyed back at my teasing with some wit of her own. Our two-seated coaster car had a long leather seat belt that both riders must share in order to stay in their seats on this wild ride. Before I could even step into the car, Sarah quickly buckled just herself in with the safety belt. Snugly fastened, Sarah sat back and crossed her arms. She flashed a playful smile at me.

Sarah: "Well then, I guess it was nice knowing you."

She giggled as she undid the buckle and allowed us to fasten up together. As we rolled down the track, the thrilling ride was made even more enjoyable by our playful banter.

Bobby: "Thanks. I was worried back 'ere."

After surviving through the Jack Rabbit's double-dipper, we hopped to another timeless roller coaster. Next up was the Racer. It was just a stone's throw away. The Racer has two coaster trains, one red and one blue, that compete in a race on one big continuous loop. The line was extremely long. This gave me and Sarah plenty of time to get to know each other more. We discussed our likes and dislikes.

Sarah leaned her back against a handrail in the Racer's waiting dock.

Sarah: "So now you know that my biggest childhood fear was the Jack Rabbit. What was your biggest fear when you were a kid?"

Bobby: "Oh, I used to be real afraid o' clowns. They scared the heck out o' me."

Clowns? It sounded like a standard boring response that tons of people give. I just didn't feel like admitting I was horrified by fire whistles, lion roars, and stray dogs. How would I even begin to explain that I had a lifelong archenemy in the form of a savage canine named Duke? Anyways, I quickly asked a new question. I stuck to the early childhood theme. And we did meet at the library that morning.

Bobby: "What was your favorite book at the library when you were little?"

Sarah: "Oh, I loved *Where the Sidewalk Ends* by Shel Silverstein. With its poems and pictures, it was so creative. I would read it over and over again. What was yours?"

Bobby: "I always liked *Where the Wild Things Are*. I wished 'at I could turn my bedroom into a forest like he did."

Sarah: "Nice. I used to like that book, too. So, what's your favorite book now?"

Bobby: "Uh, probably *The Outsiders*. I had to read it for school last year."

The word "read" was loosely applied here. In reality, I skimmed through most of the book and guessed my way through the chapter quizzes. I do remember the impression the novel made on my classmates. For a solid month, kids in the school hallways would say goodbye to each other with a "Stay gold, Ponyboy!"

Bobby: "What's your favorite book?"

Sarah: "Oh, I really love *The Diary of Anne Frank*. It's the only book I've ever read that can be so sad and so uplifting all at once. And she was only 13 when she started writing it. Her writing was so good for someone our age."

I nodded and Sarah continued.

Sarah: "So, what's your favorite quote? Like from an author or a famous person."

I paused as I didn't really have a favorite quote. Poetic novels and colorful memoirs filled with choice sayings were currently not on my reading list. At that point of my life, I was solely scouring nonfiction books filled with facts about the life of Chief Guyasuta or the location of Braddock's Defeat. I quickly thought of a quote from the many posters stapled on the bulletin boards in my eighth-grade reading class.

Bobby: "Oh, I always liked: 'Be yourself; everyone else is already taken.'"

Sarah: "Oscar Wilde! That's a great one."

Frankly, I had no idea who Oscar Wilde was. That was the only quote that stuck out to me while I would daydream during sustained silent reading sessions. I hurriedly asked her the same question.

Bobby: "So what's your favorite quote?"

Sarah: "My favorite one is from Albert Einstein: 'Learn from yesterday, live for today, hope for tomorrow.'"

Bobby: "Oh, 'at's a real good one."

How did I follow up on a quote from the scientific genius behind the groundbreaking Theories of Relativity, one of humankind's greatest minds ever? With an extremely cerebral question of my own.

Bobby: "What was your favorite cartoon when you were little?"

Sarah: "Good question. I loved *Scooby-Doo, Where Are You!* I liked how they all worked together to solve a mystery at the end."

Bobby: "And then they'd always rip a mask off the bad guy's head and he'd say, 'And I woulda gotten away with it, if it wasn't for you meddlin' kids and 'at mangy dog!'"

Sarah: "Ha, I know! What was your favorite cartoon?"

Bobby: "I liked *Spider-Man*. But I think it was just 'cause the theme song was so catchy. The cartoon was just okay."

The highlight of many cartoons and television shows at that time was simply the opening melody. It usually went all downhill after that. Speaking of downhill, we were ready to board the Racer now. Every riding pair was choosing their roller coaster train, either red or blue. Naturally, a Yinzer sparring match began.

Vito: "We got the red coaster. Yinz jagoffs on a' blue coaster are gonna lose!"

Sal: "No way, jagoff! Your weight alone is gonna slow dahn 'at coaster. Blue's gonna win now, ya losers!"

Sarah and I sided with Vito and Tina and picked the red coaster. Curtis and Cierra hopped into a blue car in front of Sal and Rosaria. Vito and Sal continued to heckle each other across the boarding dock as the two competing trains simultaneously rolled out of the station.

Vito: "Yinz are goin' dahn!"

Sal: "It's a miracle yinz are even movin' with you in 'ere, Vito!"

The race was on. Like I said, Vito wasn't overweight, but he was a noticeably big dude for a 14-year-old. The race began as a nail-biter, but our rival blue coaster blazed us in the home stretch. As we pulled back into the station, the blue coaster was already sitting across from us in wait.

Pointing their fingers at us, the ecstatic winners were eager to rub it in.

Curtis: "You lost, suckas!"

Sal: "I told yinz!"

Before we could reply, Cierra chose our next ride of the day.

Cierra: "Let's hurry! The Log Jammer is the next ride over."

Next to the Racer was Kennywood's newest addition, a fun-filled water ride called the Log Jammer. Floating along on a water track, riders sat in drifting canoes shaped like hollowed-out logs which would drop down two tall hills. The giant splashes of cold water that greeted the falling canoes at the bottom provided welcome relief on a hot day.

After watching one falling canoe send a splash of water over twenty feet in the air, Curtis teased Cierra as he put his arm around her shoulders.

Curtis: "You about to get soaked, girl."

Cierra playfully nudged her boyfriend.

Cierra: "Curt, you better not act the fool and rock the boat."

While we each handed over five tickets to enter the Log Jammer line, I spotted a chipmunk holding a peanut that was dropped by a park visitor. I alerted Sarah.

Bobby: "Look. 'At little guy got a free lunch."

Sarah: "Aw, he's cute. Can you guess what my favorite animal is?"

Bobby: "Well, from your shirt, I would have to say... owl. Right?"

Sarah: "Yep. I even have an owl change purse to match."

She pulled out a small yellow coin purse with a blue owl on it.

Bobby: "Cool. I remember goin' on a field trip dahn the Aviary and they brought out this owl and let it fly all 'round the room. You couldn't hear a thing. Their wings don't make no noise. 'At's why they're so good at catchin' mice n'at."

She nodded in interest and continued with the animal theme.

Sarah: "That's neat. So, what's your favorite animal?"

Bobby: "Oh, I like the red fox. I only seen a fox one time, while sittin' on the school bus one morning. It was huntin' for mice in a field. It was so cool."

Sarah: "I saw a red fox once, too. It was in the Schenley Park Golf Course across from my grandfather's home. I was sledding there last winter on a snow day. It was standing on the top tee, and it looked right at me. They are such beautiful animals."

With a continuous flow of floating cars, the Log Jammer waiting line was the shortest of the day. Sarah wisely placed her purse in the wooden cubby at the loading dock before we boarded the ride. We drifted our way through the lazy river and splashed down two wild spills that pummeled us with water. Afterwards, we all were dripping wet. But Vito was even more saturated than the rest of us. Sitting in the back seat, he absorbed the brunt of the waves. Vito slogged out the exit like a shipwrecked sailor who had just survived an epic battle with the most monstrous great white shark on the high seas of the Atlantic.

Bobby: "Holy heck, Vito! You look like ya just got done fightin' Jaws!"

Vito began wringing water from his sopping tank top.

Vito: "I know! I'm freakin' drenched! Even my shoes are full o' water!"

Sal: "Good. You needed to worsh your greasy hair anyways, dirtball."

Everyone laughed as we headed to the biggest roller coaster at Kennywood Park. The main attraction. The Thunderbolt. It was this imposing wooden coaster that we could clearly hear from across the river while searching for Braddock's Gold. The line was by far the longest in the park, so Sarah and I continued our interview. In front of us, a small girl was happily holding a prize from one of the park's games, a plush teddy bear. It sparked Sarah's next question.

Sarah: "So, what was your most prized possession when you were a kid?"

Bobby: "Oh, 'at's easy. My BMX bike. I guess it still is. How 'bout you?"

She answered without delay.

Sarah: "It would have to be my Kodak camera. I treat it like it's made of gold. I hide it in a safe place in my room."

Sarah paused and smiled.

Sarah: "It's just a little easier to find than the gold we were looking for today."

I laughed in agreement.

Bobby: "Yep. Findin' a lost gold treasure ain't as easy as it used to be."

Sarah giggled over my silly claim. Just then, "Take a Chance on Me" by ABBA began to play on the speakers above our queue. Sarah's eyes lit up.

Sarah: "ABBA! They're my favorite! When I was in fifth grade, I played my "Dancing Queen" single so many times that my record player's needle wore out. I even put up a little disco ball in my room. What kind of music do you like?"

Bobby: "Oh, I like a lot o' stuff. I always liked Led Zeppelin. But I really like that new band, the Cars. I heard they're playin' on *The Midnight Special* next month."

Then she asked the most essential question for all teenage girls in the 1970s.

Sarah: "So... I don't know if you believe in this stuff, but what's your sign?"

Knowing your astrological sign in the '70s was more important than knowing your blood type. Every teenager was on board.

Bobby: "I was born in June, so I'm a Gemini. What are you?"

Sarah: "I'm a Sagittarius."

She threw her shoulders back and put a hand on her hip.

Sarah: "They say we're the most adventurous."

Bobby: "Ah! So that's why you joined forces with us goofballs and wanted to come on our quest for the hidden treasure."

Sarah: "Ha! Yeah, I guess you're right."

Sarah warmly smiled. Maybe she realized it was celestial intervention that created the gravity of our treasure hunting mission. A mysterious cosmic force in the galaxy. Somehow, on a random Saturday afternoon, the stars had aligned and Sarah had been pulled into our orbit. Either that or she was simply curious about the wacky teenagers carrying around a metal detector in a public library. No doubt, Sarah was immediately attracted to the unusual bunch of foolhardy explorers.

She continued the light interrogation.

Sarah: "So for real, what got you so interested in looking for treasure?"

Bobby: "Well, I was always interested in history n'at. But I only just found out about the legend o' Braddock's Gold from my pap."

I sighed and continued.

Bobby: "See my house burnt dahn in a fire this week and we're livin' with him right now."

Sarah placed her hand over her heart and gave me a surprised, yet sympathetic look.

Sarah: "Oh, really? I'm so sorry! Did anyone get hurt?"

Bobby: "No, luckily nobody got hurt. My dad's a volunteer firefighter and he actually put out the fire. But we lost our house."

For a second, I remembered my situation in life and slightly lowered my head in self-pity. Sarah quickly tried to lift my spirits back up.

Sarah: "Look on the bright side, Bobby. Your family is okay. That's what matters most. Right?"

Sarah paused and added a sincere piece of advice.

Sarah: "I know it sounds kind of corny, but when times get tough, my grandfather always quotes an old saying: 'The future gains from present pains.'"

I lifted my chin.

Bobby: "Huh, no it ain't corny. I like 'at one."

Sarah continued.

Sarah: "And maybe, one day, you will find that gold treasure too."

We both smiled. I obviously liked this girl. But I realized that I had no idea how to pursue this new-found friendship or the long-lost treasure.

Bobby: "Thanks, Sarah. That would be awesome. But you know 'at's crazy."

Sarah tilted her head and raised her eyebrows.

Sarah: "There's always hope."

The long waiting line for the Thunderbolt was finally starting to move. Sarah changed the subject to a more hopeful tone.

Sarah: "So what college do you want to go to?"

Bobby: "Oh, um, Pitt... or Penn State... or maybe Duquesne."

I simply listed three of the most well-known universities in the region. Like many working-class kids, I had never even visited a college campus before. Sarah continued with her aspirations.

Sarah: "I want to go to Carnegie Mellon. I want to dual major in journalism and photography. My brother's studying there to become an electrical engineer."

Bobby: "Wow. 'At's cool."

I had no clue what an electrical engineer does. I pictured someone in a hard hat removing tangled shoes from a power line. Luckily, Curtis and Cierra joined in with our conversation.

Curtis: "I'm goin' to Pitt. I'm hopin' for a football scholarship and I'm lookin' at gettin' a degree in history. If I don't make it to the League, maybe I'll be a history teacher."

Cierra: "I'm goin' to Pitt, too. I'm gettin' a scholarship for track and gonna be a pediatrician."

Sarah: "That's cool. Pitt has a great med school."

Cierra confidently beamed and added her other lifelong aspiration, a pursuit for gold found not in coin but in the form of a medal.

Cierra: "And I'll be goin' for the gold in the Olympics too, of course."

At that point in the discussion, I realized that kids my age were already thinking about their paths in higher education and beyond. Many working-class young people were not as optimistic about becoming a collegian. Personally, I had given little thought to the matter. My father was adamant that I begin to seriously consider my future schooling. But teenagers often listen to the voices of their peers over their parents. I remember being mildly surprised to find that Sarah, Cierra, and Curtis all had big plans and high hopes for the future.

Speaking of big plans, Curtis heard that a new ride was coming to the park.

Curtis: "They say next year, there's gonna be a roller coaster here that's gonna have a big loop 'at goes upside dahn."

188

Sal shook his head.

Sal: "No way. Never gonna happen. That's impossible, dude."

Of course, a steel coaster called the Laser Loop debuted the following summer at Kennywood Park. While we were eagerly working our way up the long line, I asked Sarah an important question.

Bobby: "So besides college, do you got any other big goals ahead?"

Sarah: "Big goals? Yeah. Actually, I do. One of my main goals in life is to visit every National Park in America."

I remembered the book that she had checked out at the library earlier that day.

Bobby: "Well, 'at book you got today on the National Parks should help."

She laughed and peeked inside her purple purse.

Sarah: "Oh yeah, I totally forgot about that."

She smiled and continued.

Sarah: "So, I have this log book of the National Parks, too. You can get a park ranger to stamp in the park name, location, and date when you visit each park. I have fifteen stamps so far."

Bobby: "That's awesome."

Sarah: "Yeah, I also keep a photo log of each park. I try to find views with my camera that I never want to forget. You should see this waterfall that I found in Yellowstone. I was actually able to snap a great picture of bison standing in front of it."

Sarah paused as a fully loaded roller coaster train loudly swung around us. We both followed the path of the coaster rolling around the track with our eyes. The screaming passengers along with the deafening sound of the churning wheels and vibrating wooden rafters under the elevated rails would have muffled out her voice. After the coaster passed by entirely, she continued in a wistful tone.

Sarah: "I think Yellowstone is the most amazing place on planet Earth."

Bobby: "Cool. I'd like to see 'at one day. Buffalo are my second favorite animal."

Sarah: "Oh, then you *have* to go to Yellowstone. The bison roam free there."

Sarah had a way about her. She was a free spirit who longed to document her exploration of our incredibly vast and beautiful nation. I sensed that she possessed the strong determination of a long-distance runner. She had already set long-term goals and aspirations that went above and beyond those of the typical teenager. It was now crystal clear to me why she so readily volunteered to join us on our expedition today.

I also realized that Sarah and I shared something else in common besides our mutual interest in American history and fandom of the Carnegie Library.

Bobby: "Hey, I got a log book too. Well, I guess it's really H.J. Heinz's. And instead o' stamps, it's got all 'ese cursive notes about Chief Guyasuta and Braddock's Treasure."

Sarah's eyes brightened.

Sarah: "That is so cool, Bobby. I hope you find that gold one day. I really do."

As we moved up one click in the long line, Sal quickly whispered in my ear.

Sal: "See. I knew she would like you, nerd boy."

I shrugged him off and then smiled as I hoped that he might actually be right. We all moved up a ramp and onto the loading dock.

Curtis: "Finally! We made it, guys."

After almost an hour, we had at last reached the front of the line for the largest, most intense ride at the amusement park. Every Yinzer knows about the Thunderbolt. The monster wooden roller coaster was by far the fastest and most exciting ride that Kennywood had to offer in 1979. It still impresses park visitors to this day.

Cierra pointed to the first car.

Cierra: "We call the front seat!"

Vito: "Okay, then we call the back one!"

Sal: "Great, Vito. Then we won't be goin' nowhere."

We were finally funneled into our seats. Sarah and I sat in the second row behind Curtis and Cierra. We clicked on the loosely fitting seatbelt. As we anxiously waited for the final riders to board in the back of the long coaster train, I asked my riding partner a couple more questions.

Bobby: "So which one did ya like the most?"

Sarah: "Which what?"

Bobby: "Which National Park did you like the most so far?"

Sarah: "Oh, Yellowstone, for sure. After Yellowstone, I really like the Sleeping Bear Dunes in upstate Michigan. The sand dunes are so incredible there, like taller than this roller coaster. It's super fun to climb up them. When I got to the top, the view of the sun setting over Lake Michigan… it just blew me away."

A ride worker came by our car and checked that our seatbelts were fastened. She slowly walked her way to the back of the coaster train and closely inspected each car for safety precautions.

Bobby: "Cool. I always wanted to go dahn the Everglades in Florida. And the Grand Canyon. Oh yeah, and I wanna see the Statue of Liberty."

Of course, actually visiting any of these destinations felt like a pipe dream to me. Like many working-class kids in Pittsburgh, I had never even laid eyes on an ocean. Nonetheless, I continued.

Bobby: "How 'bout you? Which park do you wanna see next?"

Sarah: "For some reason, I want to see Mount Rushmore. I just can't believe that someone had the patience to carve those presidents' faces out of stone."

My eyes widened in excitement.

Bobby: "You know, they say there's a hidden treasure o' gold inside o' Mount Rushmore, too."

Sarah: "Then let's go there next… after we find Braddock's Treasure."

She held out her right pinky finger.

Sarah: "Pinky swear on it?"

Bobby: "It's a deal."

Just as the train car began to inch forward, we locked pinky fingers and sealed the deal. Then we both smiled. It was the kind of flippant kid promise that deep down you wished would really come true one day.

Curtis and Cierra yelled back to all of us.

Curtis: "Here we go!"

Cierra: "Aw yeah!"

They both raised their hands in anticipation. Then gravity did its thing. A Kennywood classic, the Thunderbolt starts the fun right out of the gate with an exhilarating drop down a steep hill. As our coaster car began to roll down the first plunge, I felt like this was easily the most fun that I had all summer long. Upon sudden acceleration, came the screams. From there on out, it ran loud and fast. With its walloping curves, it threw us around like rag dolls compared to the smaller, tamer coasters we rode earlier. The Thunderbolt provided the type of spills and thrills worth every cent of the admission price I paid to enter the park.

As we rolled back into the station, the passengers clapped and cheered with delight. Healthy doses of adrenaline and endorphins were pumping through our veins. Cierra was glowing with emotion. She had to wipe a tear from her eye.

Cierra: "Now that's what I'm talkin' about! Best ride in a' park! I love it every time!"

Curtis punched his fist in the air.

Curtis: "Whew! Can't nothin' top that! Beats scorin' a touchdown any day."

After the fun-filled ride, we all exited our seats with wide smiles. Right outside the coaster is a long row of classic carnival games. Curtis pointed up ahead.

Curtis: "Yo, check it out! We gotta go play some games now."

Vito: "I challenge you to 'at football game, Curtis! You ain't seen nothin' yet."

Curtis: "Oh yeah? You about to get whupped again, Vito!"

What makes Kennywood special is that it is an urban amusement park with small town appeal. Like an old-fashioned street fair, parkgoers can test their skills at knocking over a pyramid of milk bottles with a baseball or bouncing a ping-pong ball into a tiny bowl floating within a pool of water. Although many of the contests rely on pure luck, the most competitive of Yinzers will blow paychecks playing the amusing carnival games. Curtis and Vito wanted to show off their athletic prowess again in the Football Toss, a game of skill in which one must throw a perfect spiral through a hanging tire. A confident Vito predicted his victorious future.

Vito: "What prize do you want, Tina?"

Tina pointed at a gigantic stuffed animal hanging on the wall.

Tina: "The big penguin! The one with the gold bow on it!"

Curtis smirked at Vito.

Curtis: "C'mon, man? You sure about that arm?"

Curtis grinned with confidence and asked Cierra the same question.

Curtis: "What prize you want, Cici?"

Cierra bounced up and down and pointed.

Cierra: "Win me that big shark, Curt!"

The game cost only 25 cents for two footballs at that time. But Vito was not about to let go of that "rare" George Washington coin that he found in Braddock. We were still uncertain if he was aware that it was just a plain old quarter from 1972. Luckily, he had found a crumpled dollar bill on the ground while waiting in line at the Thunderbolt. Vito whipped out the money and flattened it out on his leg. After doing the math with his fingers, he heavily slammed the dollar on the counter.

Vito: "Seven footballs, please!"

Curtis: "You mean eight, Vito."

Without hesitating, Vito picked the money back up and slammed it down again.

Vito: "Eight footballs, please!"

The gamers were true to form and gave their riding partners the prizes they had wished for. In turn, Vito was rewarded by Tina with messy Potato Patch cheese fries and a piping hot funnel cake. The food was gone in 60 seconds as every one of us picked at the delicious carnival meal. After devouring the grub like a pack of starving wolves, I heard Vito whisper to Sal.

Vito: "Hey Sal, Kennywood's open."

Sal: "No duh, dingus. We're here ain't we?"

"Kennywood's open" was secret Yinzer code for "Your zipper is down." Assuming that Vito was kidding, Sal initially ignored the warning. However, moments later, he nonchalantly looked down and checked just in case since he didn't want to embarrass himself in front of his lovely riding partner, Rosaria. Realizing that it was just a prank by Vito, Sal quietly mumbled to himself.

Sal: "Jagoff."

Having enjoyed the big-ticket rides along with the games and snacks, Rosaria and Tina made plans to head back to Braddock with Rosaria's older brother who worked at the bumper cars. Countless teenagers from the Mon Valley earned their summer spending money by working at Kennywood Park. Vito and Sal hugged their ride partners and thanked them for a fun time. While we watched kids joyfully jump up and down on the huge, foam tongue laying inside the whale's mouth entrance for Noah's Ark, Cierra made the last call for the day.

Cierra: "Okay. Last ride, y'all. Let's do the merry-go-round!"

Curtis: "All right. Let's hit it."

As we were heading to our last attraction, we spied Kenny Kangaroo lumbering on the path up ahead of us.

Vito: "Look! There's Kenny!"

Sal: "C'mon! Let's go step on his tail!"

Kennywood's version of Mickey Mouse, the giant Kenny Kangaroo mascot was adorned with a long, foam-stuffed tail which dragged on the ground behind him and was just begging to be stepped on. Trampling on Kenny's squishy tail was a rite of passage for every bad kid in Pittsburgh. Vito and Sal immediately started to jockey through the crowd for position to be the first to apply the winning step. Sal won by a leg and managed to deploy the perfect stomp, causing poor Kenny to trip and spill over onto the concrete walkway. From under his heavy costume, we could hear his muffled scream.

Kenny Kangaroo: "Hey! Who did that?"

As bystanders stopped to help poor Kenny get back on his feet, Sal played it cool and acted like he had no idea of what just happened. He called back to us.

Sal: "Let's move it, guys! We don't got all day."

After briskly walking by the havoc, Cierra shook her head and laughed as she scolded us for our childish antics.

Cierra: "Dang, yinz is some rude boys."

While hustling away from the scene of the crime, we happened to pass yet another statue of George Washington right in the middle of Kennywood Park. The tall bronze statue depicts a confident, young Washington pointing his high sword forward in the direction of the ill-fated march through Braddock that lies ahead of him. Inscribed on a plaque is the phrase "George was here!" The marker tells how Braddock's army passed through this site before crossing the shallow river to the battlefield where they were ambushed by French and Native American forces. The big display even had British, Colonial American, and French flags from that period.

Everyone breezed right by the monument except for me. I slowed to a halt. I stood alone and stared at the statue of Washington. His shadow had grown long in the late day sun. He served further reminder of my failed search for Braddock's Gold. It was as if I was being taunted, challenged even. I thought once more about that mysterious clue. That real enigma. I whispered Chief Guyasuta's final words to myself.

Bobby: "'Beneath the fallen General, marks the spot of hidden gold.'"

Just then, Sarah rushed back and broke me out of my trance.

Sarah: "Bobby, are you okay?"

Bobby: "Oh, yeah... I'm fine."

Sarah: "Okay. Well, everyone's getting ready to go on the merry-go-round."

Bobby: "Oh, for sure. Let's go."

We hurriedly jogged the short distance to the ride where all our friends were already waiting in line. Like eager little kids, everyone in our group was pointing out which horse they were going to ride once the spinning merry-go-round stopped for new passengers. In order to be heard over the thunderous pipes of the Grand Carousel's band organ, Curtis and Cierra mightily called out their dibs.

Curtis: "I call the big horse with the American flag on it!"

Cierra: "I call the gray horse right next to it!"

Besides horses that rise up and down with the music, the historic landmark merry-go-round also has two large felines that sit along the outside perimeter of the spinning amusement ride. Sal and Vito were clamoring for a chance to ride on these big cats. Sal eyed up the big yellow lion with a golden-brown mane.

Sal: "I call the lion! I knew it was a good sign this mornin' when we heard 'at lion roar from the zoo."

To Sal, this morning's bad omen had magically transformed into this afternoon's fortunate prophecy come true. But just then, we were struck with true serendipity. Vito claimed the remaining wild cat on the carousel.

Vito: "I call the leopard!"

Sal verbally pounced on Vito.

Sal: "That ain't no leopard, you idiot! That's a tiger!"

Vito stuck out his chest.

Vito: "That's a leopard!"

Sal: "Leopards got spots, ya moron! Tigers got stripes like 'at!"

Sal quickly turned to me for affirmation.

Sal: "Tell him, Bobby. Is 'at a tiger or a leopard?"

At that moment, our entire crew turned and focused on me. However, I was once again trapped in a trance. The large cat was quite obviously an orange tiger with black stripes, but I was staring at the horse behind the cat in question. It was the horse that

Curtis called for – a white steed with red, white, and blue stars and stripes painted on its back. It was going up and down ever so slowly now as the spinning ride was coming to a stop. I stood there mesmerized. The steel horse draped with an American flag went up and down one more time in slow motion.

Sal nudged me with his elbow.

Sal: "Well, Bobby? What kind o' cat is it? A tiger or a leopard?"

Everyone stood in silence while waiting on me to answer Sal's simple question and put an end to their goofy argument. Curtis crossed his arms and smiled at Cierra as she rolled her eyes over our childish squabble. The merry-go-round came to a complete stop. The big, striped cat was standing right in front of us.

Tiger or leopard? Tiger or leopard? The wheels in my head were spinning in high gear. I remembered one nugget of information from a book at the library. A distinct picture of General Braddock's personal items. Then, it hit me. It hit me like a bolt of lightning. It hit me like I was run over by that thundering stallion being ridden by George Washington himself. I blurted out what my brain was processing.

Bobby: "Leopard!"

Vito slapped Sal on the back.

Vito: "See! I told ya, Sal!"

Sal: "No way! Yinz are crazy!"

I repeated myself loudly and with purpose.

Bobby: "LEOPARD! IT'S ON THE LEOPARD!"

Everyone gave me strange looks.

Sarah: "What, Bobby?"

Bobby: "The leopard skin! The one that General Braddock sat on before he was shot dahn in battle! 'Beneath the fallen General, marks the spot of hidden gold!'"

Curtis: "Say what? What you talkin' 'bout, man?"

Bobby: "Listen! In a' library today, I saw a picture o' General Braddock's horse saddle pad 'at he rode on. It went over his horse's back. It was made from a leopard's hide. After the battle, George Washington made sure he got this leopard skin saddle pad. How's come Washington would want General Braddock's leopard skin so bad?"

Curtis: "Must've been real important to him."

Bobby: "Right! Washington kept 'at leopard skin on his horse for the rest of his life. He even rode on it durin' both the French 'n Indian War *and* the Revolutionary War!"

My friends got closer in a huddle as they realized that I was on to something.

Bobby: "For real, why would George wanna always have 'at leopard skin under him?"

Vito: "'Cause it was real soft on his butt?"

Cierra and Sarah both giggled.

Bobby: "No! Well, maybe, Vito. But just maybe he kept it so close to him 'cause it had somethin' real important written underneath it!"

Sarah's eyes lit up.

Sarah: "'Beneath the fallen General, marks the spot of hidden gold!'"

Curtis sternly looked me right in the eyes.

Curtis: "You sayin' there might be a *map* for the gold on the back o' that leopard skin?"

Bobby: "Yes! The general was sitting on a treasure map! That's what Chief Guyasuta was tryin' to tell his tribe!"

Sal lifted his sunglasses up revealing the surprised look in his eyes.

Sal: "So that's how the chief knew about the gold. George showed Guyasuta the map on the back o' the leopard hide. And that's why George never let go of 'at thing."

Bobby: "Exactly! George always held it real close to him 'cause it has a treasure map on it. So, the marked spot of the hidden gold literally was *beneath* the general!"

Vito: "Under his butt?"

The girls laughed again. I shook it off and continued.

Bobby: "Well, yeah, General Braddock sat on it. Like, they marked it on a map under the leopard hide he rode on. George was a mapmaker. He must've drawn it on the reverse side o' the fur. You know, on a' leather underside."

Curtis started nodding his head.

Curtis: "I got you. That's the best spot to put a treasure map. Under your most important guy, with tons o' bodyguards around him. Like Capture the Flag."

Bobby: "Right. Them British redcoats probably thought there was no way the French or American Indians could ever get their hands on a map placed under the general on his horse. He had a huge army with him. Thousands o' soldiers. And he was bein' heavily guarded by dozens of his best men!"

Curtis: "But then he went 'n ran into some real trouble waitin' for him over in my hood."

Bobby: "Exactly!"

Sal: "That's when the crap hit the fan."

Sarah: "And that's when the general fell... "

Bobby: "And George got the leopard skin!"

Cierra cut to the chase.

Cierra: "Okay. So now we gotta go and find this leopard skin then!"

By this time, the line had passed over us and a new group of passengers was boarding the merry-go-round. Parents and their children were staring at us. Now, we truly resembled the foresaid Scooby-Doo gang working together to decipher a cryptic riddle based on local legend in hopes of solving a historic mystery. I guess zany Vito with his boundless appetite and sniffing metal detector was the closest one of us to being Scooby. In fact, Vito helped me sum up the whole conversation.

Bobby: "If we find 'at leopard skin... "

Vito: "Then we can find the gold!"

We all wildly cheered. Again, parkgoers glared at the rowdy bunch of teens who were celebrating in line. But there was one very big question remaining.

Sarah put her hands up in the air and asked.

Sarah: "Okay. But where is this leopard saddle pad?"

Bobby: "Sarah, your grandfather might know. He's the head librarian at the Carnegie Library. He can call 'round all the museum directors, right?"

Sarah: "Well, I guess so. I can ask him. Where's a phone?"

Sarah looked around in every direction. Cierra pointed ahead.

Cierra: "Up front! By the ticket booth!"

Bobby: "Let's go!"

In a flash, Cierra took off with her blazing track speed. She literally hightailed it out of there. Her long ponytail flew up in the air. We all galloped after her. It looked like a herd of wild horses had been released in Kennywood Park. Every parkgoer we passed gave puzzled regard to the crazed bunch of teenagers in full stampede. Urgently pulsing from the park speakers, a screaming panic from the Ramones punk rock anthem *Blitzkrieg Bop* added to the chaos. As we dodged through the crowds, Curtis hurdled over an amazed child sitting in his stroller. The little toddler looked up in awe like Kermit the Frog gazing at a rainbow overhead. Vito bumped into an unlucky man eating a corndog. The meal on a stick fell to the ground and Vito looked back in grief.

Vito: "What? They got corn dogs here?"

Of course, Cierra toasted all of us and was leisurely standing at the telephone booth well before we all caught up to her. Unlike us, she wasn't even out of breath. She was holding up the attached receiver in wait. Sarah hurriedly popped in a dime and dialed up her grandfather. As she excitedly explained the situation, we could hear his bewildered voice sputtering over the phone.

Librarian: "Uh, this... this is quite a story, Sarah. But... but I can make a few calls. Stay by the phone. I'll call you back as soon as I find out where it is."

Sarah gave her grandfather the payphone's number. Before the advent of cell phones, these were the kind of phone tag games that teenagers, and everyone for that matter, had to play. As we anxiously gathered around the phone booth, Vito went foraging. He tried to coax some cotton candy from a nearby vendor.

Vito: "This one looks kinda old. If yinz're just gonna throw it away, then I can make it easy for yinz and take it off your hands."

The phone rang. We all jumped. Sarah spoke in earnest to her grandfather, while we huddled around her.

Sarah: "Yeah. Okay. Okay! Yeah! Thanks, Grandpap! Bye!"

She hung up the phone. We waited on edge for her informed response.

Sarah: "Okay, so the leopard skin is not at the Carnegie Museum in Oakland."

We sighed in collective disappointment, but she continued with a smile.

Sarah: "It's Downtown at the Fort Pitt Museum!"

Cierra swiftly responded.

Cierra: "Then we gotta go Dahntahn!"

We all cheered loudly with excitement. Once again, Yinzers enjoying the amusement park casted curious looks at the raucous bunch of teenagers jumping up and down in fevered exhilaration. But Sarah tried to bring us back to earth. Although she glowed with elation, she calmly addressed our frenzied crew.

Sarah: "But it's about to close soon."

Sarah paused. Then she grew concerned.

Sarah: "And how would we get a good look at what's underneath the leopard hide anyways?"

She put her hands on her hips and continued.

Sarah: "We can't just go in there and... steal it."

Vito, Sal, and I looked around at each other. Devious smiles stretched across our faces. Sal spoke for all of us.

Sal: "Where there's a will, there's a way."

Chapter 10: The Point

It was only fitting that we were traveling to the place where this whole legend began. Point State Park is the small and scenic triangle of grass and trees at the end of Downtown Pittsburgh where the three rivers meet. At the very tip of the city's Golden Triangle, lies a beautiful vista that Yinzers simply call "The Point." This was the very spot where Fort Duquesne once stood, the same French fort that a headstrong Braddock and a young Washington so badly desired. Three years after General Braddock's brutal defeat, a much larger army of British and Colonial American forces, led by General John Forbes along with a now battle-hardened Colonel George Washington, finally conquered the French stronghold here. Gruesome clashes raged throughout the foothills leading to the riverside garrison. Ironically, after all the bloodshed, on the day that Fort Duquesne was finally captured, not a shot was fired. The French had abandoned it and set it ablaze. Britain subsequently built a much larger fortress in this strategic location. They named it Fort Pitt. Today, there is a small museum built on site that highlights these important events.

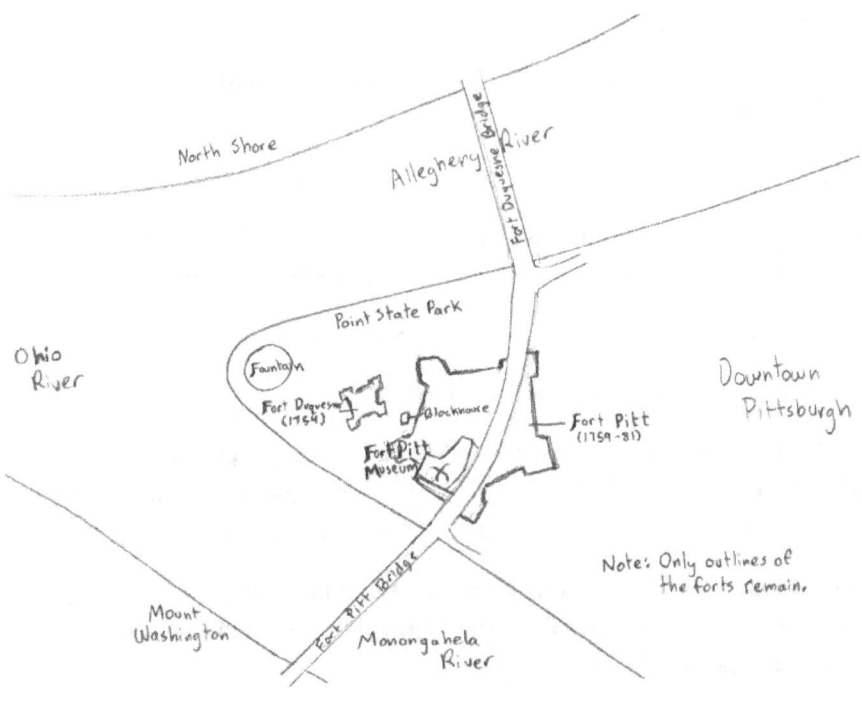

On exhibit at the Fort Pitt Museum, was the leopard hide saddle pad that was ridden on by the fallen General Braddock and then inherited by George Washington. Washington held close to this exotic saddle rest and rode on it during two major campaigns, the French and Indian War and the American Revolutionary War. We were hoping that this leopard skin had a map on its underside, a treasure map to be more precise.

We parked across from the Hilton Hotel right in front of Point State Park. The sun had set during the drive from Kennywood to Downtown Pittsburgh. We huddled outside the car to discuss our strategy for accomplishing the enormous task ahead.

Vito: *"Beneath the general.* Oh, I get it now. See, I was right. It *was* under his butt!"

Sal: "Shut up, you butthead. Okay, so what do yinz think should be our plan of attack dahn here?"

I was about to reveal the mission plans when Curtis and Cierra harmoniously voiced their wise intentions.

Curtis: "I'm about to sit this one out, boys. I ain't lookin' to risk no football scholarship here tonight."

Cierra: "Same here, guys. I don't wanna play with losin' a scholarship neither. But good luck to y'all."

Curtis: "Yeah, we gonna chill here by the car. Y'all be cool in 'ere."

I understood their smart decision and gave them a nod of respect. With that, I was ready to propose the grand plan that I had hatched on the ride here from Kennywood.

Bobby: "Okay, I call this mission Operation Leopard Lift."

Sal and Vito's faces glowed with devilish grins.

Bobby: "So the museum just closed. That means the night janitor's gonna come and start reddin' up the bathrooms n'at. Meantime, we're gonna hide and wait outside by the back door. You know, where they take out the garbage to the dumpster."

In the late 1970s, it seemed like almost every adult smoked, and heavily at that. I knew the janitor was bound to take a smoke break out behind the museum and enjoy the nice summer night.

I turned to Sarah.

Bobby: "Sarah, I'm not gonna ask you to break 'n enter or steal stuff like us idiots. But we do need your help."

Sarah: "Sure. What do I do?"

Bobby: "Okay, listen carefully. So eventually the janitor's gonna come out the back exit and take a smoke break. Soon as the janitor lights up his cigarette, act like you was just walkin' by and ask, 'Scuse me, is the museum still open?' and distract him. After he says no, ask, 'Oh, what are the hours?' just to continue with the ruse. This will give us guys enough time to sneak in the propped open door behind him."

Sarah: "Okay, Bobby. I can do that."

Then she paused and grew a look of concern. She tilted her head.

Sarah: "It sounds like you guys have done something like this before. Have you?"

Sal: "Oh, no. We don't go runnin' around stealin' stuff like this n'at."

Sal was right. We never stole "stuff like this n'at." This was not a 25 cent Snickers bar at Nina's Market. This was a priceless historic artifact which was securely guarded in a locked museum and happened to be a cherished military keepsake of the first President of the United State of America. This heist would bring our thievery to a whole new level. It was like going from junior high to Harvard in one week.

Bobby: "Well anyways, we ain't stealin' it. We're just gonna borrow it for a few minutes so I can sketch a copy o' the map into my notebook."

Vito and Sal nodded their heads in affirmation convincing themselves that we were not about to commit a serious crime.

Bobby: "Okay, so the leopard hide should be hangin' in a frame next to a big diorama o' the Battle of Braddock. After we grab 'at thing, we ain't gonna be able to make a copy of the map in 'ere. So, when the janitor comes back inside, we hide until he goes in a' bathrooms and then we sneak back out the dumpster door."

Vito and Sal nodded their heads again.

Vito: "Sounds like a plan, Bobby."

Sal: "All right. Let's do this."

The mission plan was revealed and accepted. It was a terrific, warm summer night, so the park was teeming with visitors. Whirling around small herds of young people strolling on the concrete paths was a meandering pack of roller skaters gliding and spinning with delight. All this commotion provided great cover for our mission. On the contrary, we would have looked highly suspicious as the only visitors in a desolate park if this were a cold winter night. And remember, we didn't have to worry about security cameras monitoring every angle of the park and museum back in 1979.

My fearless friends began tramping through the park with real swagger. We had the biggest heist of our lives ahead. In what seemed like a slow-motion walk, Operation Leopard Lift was now in full effect. We marched side by side into the night. Sal put on his aviator sunglasses for no reason other than to look like a badass. Vito popped in two new sticks of gum with true purpose. He heavily chomped on the giant wad of Big Red on the side of his mouth like a professional. I pulled up my black wristbands a little higher on my wrists to get to work. Even Sarah prepared for her part by pulling off her hair tie that she wore at the amusement park. Shaking out her long ponytail, her once straightened hair had become wavy from the water ride at Kennywood. We were on a mission. A real mission this time.

Only the most observant soul in Point State Park noticed us walking through the crowd. He got up from his park bench. Closely watching over his backyard, the elderly homeless man in a tattered Terry Bradshaw jersey somehow suspected that four young teenagers were on a clandestine operation with a brazen plan. He flipped up his pillbox Pirates hat and called out to us with slurred words of wisdom.

Homeless Yinzer: "Hey! It's a long road 'til the top if yinz wanna rock 'n roll!"

We looked at each other and him and roundly nodded our heads in agreement. Vito gave him an assured thumbs-up. It was like that wise old sage with a scraggly beard knew exactly what we were up to. That or he simply mangled the main line from AC/DC's hit song "It's a Long Way to the Top." Either way, my friends and I still say that all-powerful line to each other to this day just for fun.

We stepped over the outline of the walls of the old fort and under the Fort Pitt Bridge overpass that every Yinzer knows has the best acoustics in the city. Under this concrete tunnel was a band of older hippies listening to music from a huge silver boom box. They were clad in tie dyed shirts and sprawled out on a blanket. Within a floating cloud of their own smoke, the long-haired hippies were deep in the process of making a large pyramid out of empty Iron City Beer cans. They were listening to "Miss You" by the Rolling Stones and Mick Jagger's softly whispering voice was echoing through the tunnel. The new song was different from the Stones' hard rock hits of the early '70s. In the middle of the melody, Mick uses a quiet, rhythmic voice to create a scene of a crazy man singing to himself in a city park late at night.

At that very moment, I realized the levity of this situation. What we were doing was completely crazy. It was sheer lunacy. We were attempting to break into the Fort Pitt Museum in hopes of finding a historic map that could lead us to a fabled gold treasure. We weren't even sure if it would even be there. Our day had gone from idealistically optimistic to categorically insane and it took Mick Jagger, of all people, to remind me of this. Oddly, I couldn't help but smile.

I cased the museum as we passed directly by the main entrance. Through the glass doors, I noticed a security guard sitting at the front desk with his feet up and reading a newspaper. He appeared perfectly relaxed, but my eyes zeroed in on one thing – the revolver on his side. Our daring scheme had just become a downright dangerous one.

Bobby: "Sarah, after you distract the custodian, come out front here and just keep a lookout in case things get dicey. Okay?"

Sarah: "Gotcha. You mean keep an eye on that security guard, right?"

Bobby: "Exactly. Have *you* done this before?"

Sarah flashed a cunning smile. By the gleam in her eyes, I could tell that the thrill of our sophisticated mission was much more exciting than she had anticipated. That said, I did not want her to be involved in the physical theft inside the museum. I couldn't imagine how bad I'd feel if she were to get nabbed. As for myself, I didn't feel too guilty about attempting to rob a museum on a Saturday night.

We arrived at our appointed mission positions. Sarah stood about thirty feet from the back door. Vito, Sal, and I hid behind a large garbage dumpster. We all waited.

Vito grimaced and waved his hand in front of his nose.

Vito: "Eww, it smells back here."

We stuck our noses deep inside the collars of our shirts to filter out the foul aroma of the putrid rubbish. Sal shot a cutting whisper at Vito.

Sal: "That's you, scuzzbucket. You smell like 'at stank water from the Log Jammer."

It only took about five minutes for the janitor to need his first smoke break. He moseyed outside and casually lit one up. If I recall correctly, he was rocking one of the first ever mullet haircuts in Yinzer history. As he began puffing away on his cigarette, a determined Sarah bravely initiated the mission. With a confident strut, she sauntered right up to the night janitor.

Sarah: "Excuse me! Excuse me, sir. Is the museum still open?"

That was our cue. We snuck in through the out door behind the unsuspecting custodian while the pretty redhead began to ask him a slew of distracting questions. It worked like a charm. I whispered to my team of thieves.

Bobby: "Okay, the Braddock room is right up the hall and around the corner."

Sal: "Let's move."

We began to sneak in the shadows of the museum. There was just enough extra light to see what we were doing. As we stealthily tiptoed along the wall of a dark hallway, Vito began to softly hum the theme music to *The Pink Panther*.

Vito: "Hmm-hmm. Hmm-hmm. Hmm-hmm-hmm-hmm-hmm-hmm... "

Sal elbowed him and whispered.

Sal: "Shut up, you frickin' moron!"

I knew we were close when I spotted the large tabletop diorama of the Battle of Braddock. It depicted a small-scale layout of the battlefield and the position of the opposing armies with tiny soldier figurines.

With my eyes on the prize, I pointed and whispered with excitement.

Bobby: "That's it! There it is!"

We had turned the corner and sure enough, high on the wall above a statue of Washington on his horse, was the coveted leopard skin saddle pad. It was mounted under glass in a polished wooden frame. Showcased under a small spotlight, the fur shined with a golden hue which contrasted with its darker spots. The leopard saddle pad was about three feet long and two feet wide. It was uniquely shaped to rest over a horse's back and under a riding saddle.

Bobby: "Vito, you can you grab it, right?"

Vito looked up at the leopard hide and confidently nodded one time.

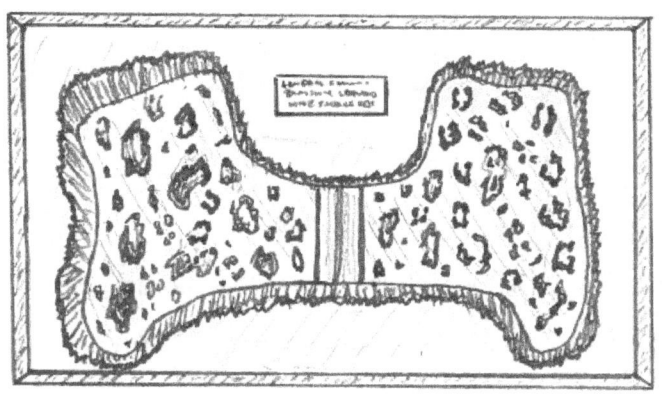

As Sal and I kept a close eye on the doors, Vito was in charge of swiping the framed feline fur. Only Vito was tall enough to reach the object and bring it down. With true determination in his eyes, Vito began sizing up his important task. He wiped his hands on his jeans. He took one deep breath and slowly exhaled. Then he reached up and delicately hoisted the exhibit from its hooks on the wall.

Firmly holding it in his hands, Vito proudly whispered.

Vito: "Target secured! We're good to go!"

Bobby: "Great work! Let's hide behind a' horse until the janitor comes back inside and goes in to clean 'em bathrooms."

We quietly waited with fiendish grins on our faces. The museum heist was halfway completed. That's when we literally hit a snag. As we were crouched behind the full-sized replica of George Washington on his horse, Vito's back hit the blade of George's cavalry sword. It was as if Washington himself was still guarding his hallowed leopard saddle. Poked by the sharp point on the tip of the saber, Vito yelped loudly.

Vito: "OUCH!"

I whispered in fear.

Bobby: "Oh, crap!"

Hearing this, the lounging security guard threw down his newspaper and shot up from his seat. Luckily, we had our lookout scout up front. Noticing that the night watchman quickly got up from his chair, Sarah hurriedly bustled up to the museum's front entrance. She innocently knocked on the glass door and waved her hand in order to grab his attention.

Sarah flashed her freckled smile as he opened the locked door.

Sarah: "Excuse me, sir. Can I use the restroom?"

The guard took off his hat and scratched his head.

Security Guard: "Um… well, the museum is closed for the night, miss."

Sarah: "Oh please, sir? I'm just here with my family and I promise it will only take a second."

Sarah pointed at the ragged bunch of hippies who were building the beer can pyramid. The armed guard became befuddled. But the batting eyelashes of a damsel in distress subdued any suspicions.

Security Guard: "Well… okay, miss. Just try to be quick."

Sarah gushed.

Sarah: "Thank you so much!"

Security Guard: "Oh, sure. It's… groovy."

Sarah's quick thinking was just what we needed. The distraction preoccupied the security guard just long enough to allow us to sneak closer to the rear exit. Another thing, the word "groovy" was no longer widely used by young people by 1979. Right on the cusp of the 1980s, saying "groovy" and "far out" had become as out of style as wearing bell-bottom jeans. The older security guard's attempt to sound in touch with the current lingo was clearly a reach.

210

As we hid by the back door, I could hear footsteps. I whispered to my crew.

Bobby: "Get ready. Here he comes."

The oblivious janitor walked back through the dumpster door from his cigarette break. After he pushed his cleaning cart into the men's bathroom, Vito, Sal, and I hightailed it out of the museum. We tore across the big grass field where the fort once stood. Once we felt we were in the clear, we began to loudly celebrate our successful heist. We really whooped it up. Vito raised the framed leopard hide over his head like a newly crowned heavyweight champion holds up the title belt. Just like Rocky Balboa, he held the prized artifact up high as he yelled out in triumph.

Vito: "Woo! We did it! We freakin' did it!"

Sal was hopping up and down.

Sal: "Just like 'at! Just like 'at, suckers!"

I pointed to the Point State Park Fountain.

Bobby: "Let's take it dahn to the fountain! There's more light dahn 'ere!"

While still howling about our museum robbery, we dashed like wild bandits down to the huge fountain at the bottom of Point State Park. The water was spraying up over 100 feet in the air. Sarah sprinted down to meet us.

She was overcome with joy.

Sarah: "You got it! You got it!"

I pointed to the flat base that encircles the fountain.

Bobby: "Okay, let's put this dahn right here. We gotta be careful and get this thing outta the frame without breakin' the glass n'at."

Vito nodded as he gently put down the loot.

Vito: "Okay. Take it easy. Take it easy."

We delicately popped open the framework that protected the leopard saddle pad. The spots on the fur were noticeably faded due to the rigors of time and wear. Slowly, we slid it out from the glass. Vito raised the yellow leopard hide up with great hope.

He spun it around. He stiffly straightened out both arms and held it over his head. We all looked upwards with our eyes wide open. It was the moment of truth.

Of course, Sal was the first to notice the results.

Sal: "What? There's nothin' 'ere! There's no map, yinz jagoffs!"

On the other side of the spotted coat, there was nothing but a swath of tan hide. It was just a blank piece of leather.

Bobby: "Son of a... !"

Vito brought the blank hide to his face for a closer examination.

Vito: "What the... *nothin'*?"

Sal pointed his finger at us and snarled.

Sal: "I told ya, idiots! You yo-yos wouldn't listen to me!"

Vito thundered back at Sal.

Vito: "Screw you, Sal! You've been a real jerk from the start!"

Vito and Sal began to shove each other. They were angrier than I had ever seen them in my life. Still holding the leopard skin, Vito violently pushed Sal into the fountain with a massive one-handed shove. Then Sal grabbed Vito and used brute leverage to pull the big guy into the circular pool of water with him. Vito dropped the leopard skin in the water, and they began throwing punches in an all-out fistfight. They were sloppily hitting each other while standing knee-deep in water in the Point State Park Fountain. The splashing water and swinging fists created a whirlpool of mayhem. The towering spray from the fountain overhead soaked them even more.

I shaped my hands around my mouth like a bullhorn and shouted at them.

Bobby: "QUIT IT! Knock it off and get outta there before the cops see yinz! We're gonna get busted!"

My pleas were ignored. The loud smacking sound of clenched fists striking faces and torsos was disturbingly palpable. To be honest, this vicious fight between these two life-long buddies had been brewing all summer long. In the fountain's choppy waters,

212

the agitated froth of their friendship had finally come to a head. Vito landed a hard roundhouse to Sal's left eye knocking off his beloved sunglasses.

Sal: "You son of a... !"

Sal responded with a clean uppercut to Vito's jaw. Vito's precious wad of gum flew right out of his mouth. After hopelessly watching his gigantic red ball of chewing gum plop into the fountain water, Vito looked like he was about to have a nuclear meltdown worse than Three Mile Island. I think it was his last piece.

Vito: "That's it! You're dead meat!"

Vito flexed his muscles with rage. His radioactive temper had reached critical mass. Overflowing with fury, he transformed into his Hulk form. Wound up punches flew with even more tenacity. Opposite him, Sal boxed like a soggy Aquaman. The ferocious brawl was reminiscent of the countless battles fought over this small triangle of land. Centuries of violent history had all led up to this crazy scene.

Momentarily forgotten in the chaos, the yellow leopard skin was floating on top of the rippling water in the fountain. Its faded spots facing up, the famed saddle rest gently rocked from side to side in the turbulent waves. With fear in her eyes, Sarah called out to me.

Sarah: "Oh no, Bobby! It's getting soaked!"

In a panic, I snatched the leopard hide out of the fountain and inspected it again. After flipping it over to assess the damage, I held it up and froze in shock. It was the craziest thing that I had ever witnessed in my life. My eyes lit up like gold.

Bobby: "Guys! Look! Look at this! Look at this!"

My hands began to shake as I held up the leopard hide. Then my knees shook too. Talk about a big break. On the leather underside opposite the spotted coat, the faint gray lines of a drawing had miraculously appeared. *Lo and behold, it was a map!*

Bobby: "We found it! We found it!"

With one glance at the map, Sarah's bright blue eyes twinkled in amazement. She screamed at Vito and Sal.

Sarah: "WE FOUND THE MAP!"

The fight stopped. Sal and Vito slowly put down their clenched fists and looked over at us in disbelief. Both had battle wounds. Sal's nose was bleeding, and his eye was badly bruised. It was entirely red. Vito's lower lip was swollen and bloody. They sloshed out of the fountain and scampered over to us.

Bobby: "Look! We got it! Here's the map! We were right!"

Sal was shaking his head.

Sal: "No way! Lemme see."

Then his eyebrows flew up and his jaw dropped.

Sal: "What the... ? You gotta be frickin' kiddin' me!"

Vito's eyes were popping out of his head.

Vito: "Holy smokes! It *is* a map!"

It just so happens that George Washington was a master at writing with invisible ink. He perfected this craft so that he could send out top secret dispatches on what appeared to be blank papers. Undercover agents would carry orders in plain sight. Real cloak-and-dagger stuff. The special skill aided his long streak of wartime success.

Bobby: "The map was done with invisible ink! The warm water in a' fountain musta made it appear!"

The invisible ink was made with a foundation of sodium bicarbonate, better known as baking soda. To be seen, the map drawing had to be activated in a warm, mildly acidic solution. The tepid, chlorinated water of the Point State Park Fountain created the perfect conditions for revealing the concealed map. It was a stroke of serendipity that every good treasure hunter hopes for.

Bobby: "George *did* tell the secret o' the treasure to Chief Guyasuta! 'Beneath the fallen General, marks the spot of hidden gold!'"

Sarah: "I can't believe it! We actually figured it out!"

Fully astounded, Sal and Vito glowed with newfound pride. Seconds after trying to kill each other, they quickly turned back into best friends. As they were getting their acts straight, I began to feverishly sketch out a duplicate of the map into my notebook.

Laid out on the leather underside of the leopard saddle rest, the map was divided into two separate sections. The map on the left clearly showed an "X" drawn a good distance from the triangle where the three rivers meet. At the Point, was the outline of a small fort that was labeled "Fort Duquesne" in an old style of cursive.

Bobby: "Look! Here's the fort. "At's where we are right now."

In a hurry, I made no attempt at copying the decorative cursive from the 1700s and simply printed the few words found on the map instead. I was far more concerned with the twisting lines that represented large rivers. The bends and curves of these waterways would direct us to the location of the elusive treasure.

Bobby: "Oh, we were way off, guys. The gold ain't buried dahn in Braddock. 'At's for sure."

We had been hunting in the wrong place. The gold was definitely not holed up in the modern town of Braddock. Judging by the great distance between the X and the Point, it was now clear that the treasure was nowhere near where General Braddock had fallen in battle. Instead, the gold was hidden much farther from the French fort and present-day Downtown Pittsburgh. Braddock and Washington must have buried the gold at their distant campsite on the night before their ill-starred march down to Fort Duquesne. This was a common preemptive practice used to prevent the gold from being stolen by the enemies during battle. Fortunately, they created a secret map that pinpointed the gold's exact location. George Washington was a skilled cartographer. He had been surveying and mapping land since he was a teenager. His ability to draw maps was highly regarded, especially by General Braddock.

Obviously, the map was believed to be safely hidden under the saddle of the heavily guarded general. But their plan hit a major snag when they were surprised by the French and Native American forces awaiting them in the woods along the Mon River. Braddock and Washington did not expect to get ambushed. Even more shocking, they surely did not expect to lose General Braddock himself.

Using the flat limestone base around the huge fountain as my drawing table, I copied every feature into my notepad. I sketched like a madman. My ecstatic friends were hovering over me while I marked down every inch of the treasure map with my yellow No. 2 Ticonderoga pencil. Even a curious pair of mallard ducks slowly paddled up to us from within the fountain basin to watch me at work.

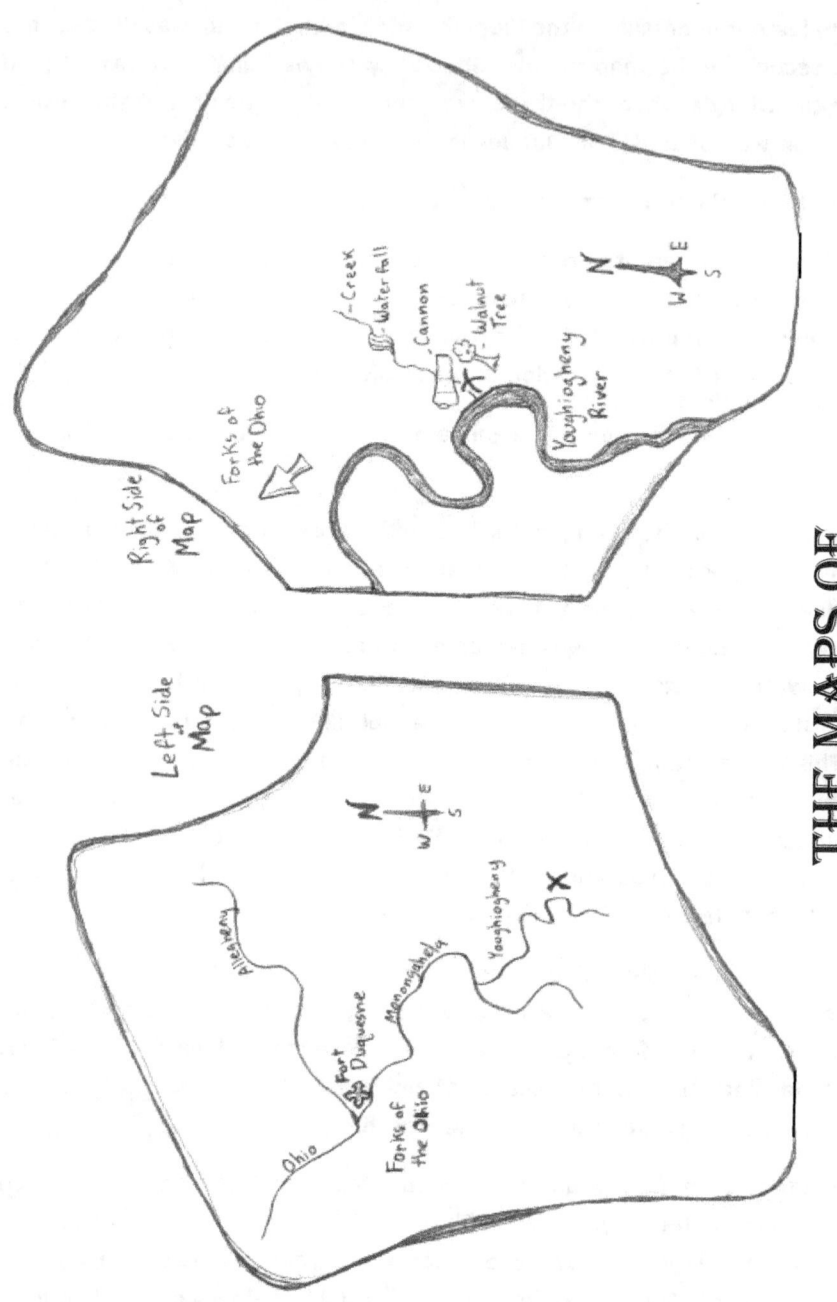

THE MAPS OF
BRADDOCK'S TREASURE

Sarah put her hands on her hips and smiled.

Sarah: "You were right, Bobby! This is why George Washington held on to this leopard skin for his whole life."

Vito: "'Cause it had the treasure map!"

Vito ran his fingers over the tufts of fur on the top edge of the leopard hide.

Vito: "Woah! And it's real nice and soft too, just like I said it'd be! I wish I had one o' these on my bike to sit on."

Sal: "Here we go again with you and your butt!"

I pointed down at the sprawling treasure map.

Bobby: "Look, there's actually two maps. One shows the location o' the gold from Dahntahn Pittsburgh, where the fort was. And the other map is a closeup with more detail. It shows a small cannon over a big X. There's a waterfall, and a crick that leads into a river, and then it says 'Walnut' next to a tree by the X."

Sarah energetically pointed at the big X on the map to the right.

Sarah: "That's it! Right here! We have to go *right here*!"

Sal and Vito fixed their heads directly over the spot where Sarah pointed. Their astonished eyes somehow grew even larger.

Sal: "Holy crap!"

Sal put his hands on his head in disbelief.

Sal: "This is freakin' unreal! We found it!"

Vito began dancing in the moonlight. He pumped his fist high in the air.

Vito: "Woohoo! We're gonna be rich!"

The map on the right was clearly a more detailed description of the secret location of General Braddock's Gold. This section depicted a small creek which led to a bigger river. About halfway down the line of the creek was a drawing of a waterfall. At the end of the creek, positioned over a large X symbol was an outline of a small cannon without wheels. Next to this X marking was a drawing of a tree with the word "Walnut" written in cursive.

My writing hand was getting tired and started to cramp up. I paused to shake around my fingers while holding the pencil. The once sharp point was now dull and rounded. In only a matter of minutes, I had diligently transcribed every minute detail that George Washington must have drawn on that leather hide over 200 years ago. As I finished up drawing the final touches of the two maps into my notebook, Sal added one more important question.

Sal: "Hold on! Where are my shades?"

As he began to look around feverishly, Vito answered him with a mischievous grin.

Vito: "Over in a' water, where I punched 'em off your face, ya jagoff."

Sal laughed.

Sal: "Thanks, jagoff."

We began the careful process of putting the soaking wet leopard hide back into its frame. As it laid flat on the outer concrete ring of the fountain, Sal was firmly pressing down on the hide and trying to push off excess water to its sides. Vito was blowing on it like his mouth was a hairdryer. Sarah looked a little worried.

Sarah: "Are you sure about this, guys? It's still soaking wet."

Bobby: "It's gonna be 90 degrees tomorra. It'll dry out. We'll just hide it back behind 'at dumpster. The janitor will find it."

Of course, unlike Sarah, we had no concern about the treatment of a precious artifact of American history. After thinking about it, Sarah reluctantly shrugged in agreement with my cavalier attitude.

Sarah: "Okay, I guess that works. Just make sure you hide it well, guys."

As we gingerly placed the glass over the leopard skin in its frame, Sarah quickly changed gears. She lightly spun around in a circle. Widely scanning the nocturnal backdrop with the keen vision of a photographer, she voiced an elated revelation.

Sarah: "Wow! I didn't even notice how gorgeous it is tonight!"

After all the commotion, Sarah was the first to realize that it was easily the most glorious night of the summer. A calm west wind blew up the Ohio River valley. Her long, wavy red hair lightly floated in the pleasant breeze. She looked up at the clear sky full of stars. Her vivacious eyes sparkled as they captured the starlit scene.

I gazed up at the stars with her.

Bobby: "Aw yeah, it's a great night."

I slowly rolled up my thin notebook until it was a tight tube. This mere act made me finally register the magnitude of our discovery. I was holding a treasure map! Elation. I couldn't contain my smile. Not after this incredible turn of fortune. I felt like I was an actual treasure hunter living in a real adventure.

Proudly standing tall in the night was the colossal water tower produced by the Point State Park Fountain. The whooshing sounds from the spraying fountain muted the bustle of a warm Saturday night in the city. Cool, splashing water created a wonderfully serene atmosphere to revel in our triumphant accomplishment.

As we were wrapping up our mission, my partners in crime and I lingered to appreciate the picture-perfect panorama of the city skyline from the fountain. I realized something. I had been at the Point at nighttime on only one other occasion, Independence Day in 1976. When I was 11 years old, my family attended the huge 4th of July fireworks display. It was so crowded with Yinzers enjoying the Bicentennial celebration that I could not fully appreciate the scenic vista. In our brief break to relish what was a special moment in time and place, I turned to Sarah.

Bobby: "I never really seen the Point after dark like 'is. At night, it looks even nicer dahn here... I mean *down* here."

I quickly corrected my Yinzer accent pronunciation of "down." As a cool cloud of mist from the fountain surrounded us, Sarah agreed with me.

Sarah: "I know! I've actually never been down here at night either. It's incredible. The fountain, the trees, the rivers. Even the moon looks bigger and brighter here. It's like we're in a whole different world compared to the city all around us."

Turning towards the confluence, we paused to admire one last magical view of the meeting of three rivers at the Point. Calmly flowing downstream, the mighty rivers

219

were topped with tiny waves that crashed softly in the night. The rolling black water shimmered with gold light reflected from the lit-up skyscrapers behind us.

Looking down the Ohio River, I shared what was on my mind.

Bobby: "Just think, everyone from Chief Guyasuta to George Washington fought here, for this little triangle o' land in between a' three rivers."

Sarah smiled as she looked down the river from her spot on the most prized parcel of land in Pittsburgh.

Sarah: "Yep. Standing here now, you can see why they all fought over this place."

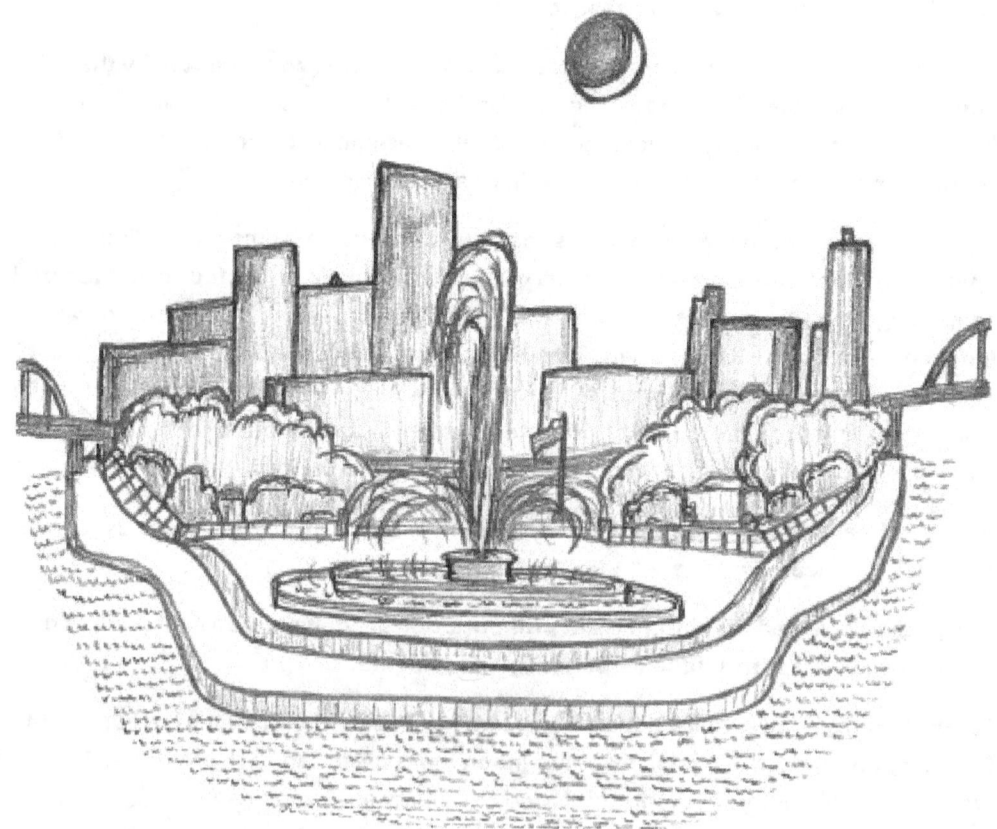

We snuck back up to the museum and gently placed George Washington's belongings back by the janitor's door. And that was that. Mission accomplished.

We then excitedly raced at full tilt up through the park. Vito high-fived the homeless Yinzer as we streaked past him. Our crew hurriedly rushed towards a relaxed Curtis and Cierra who were coolly resting alongside his Buick station wagon. Leaning against the car with big smiles, the good-looking couple appeared to be posing in a photo shoot for the latest *Sears Roebuck Catalog*. In stark contrast, the museum thieves looked like a wild bunch of disheveled lunatics.

As we approached Curtis and Cierra, Vito shouted out to them.

Vito: "We found the map!"

I proudly held up my tightly rolled notebook that contained the sketches.

Bobby: "It was there! Underneath the leopard saddle!"

With a surprised face, Curtis pushed himself off his car and stood up straight.

Curtis: "Hold up. Is yinz for real?"

Curtis didn't even wait for us to respond. After swiftly swinging both fists across his body, he firmly nodded his head and grew a joyous grin on his face.

Curtis: "I knew it! I *knew* yinz was crazy!"

We met them with proud smiles. Cierra's reaction was much more reserved than that of her boyfriend. Lightly tapping her long fingernails on the hood of the car, Cierra looked up and down at Sal and Vito and the small puddles of water that were pooling at their feet. She shook her head at both of them. With a smirk on her face, she playfully scolded them with a question.

Cierra: "So how's come yinz two sorry lookin' fools is all soakin' wet?"

We all laughed.

Bobby: "We'll tell yinz in the car. Let's get outta here!"

We jumped into the station wagon and relayed the whole story to Curtis and Cierra. As we gloated over our success, we planned out our mission for tomorrow. Curtis dropped Sarah off at her house in Squirrel Hill. From there, Vito, Sal, and I rode our bikes past where the Heinz Mansion once sat on Penn Avenue, down an empty Washington Boulevard, and across the Highland Park Bridge back to Sharpsburg.

I got home well after midnight, but fortunately all eyes were glued to the little TV in the kitchen. The Pirates were playing a late West Coast game versus the San Diego Padres that started at 10 PM. Thick in the 1979 pennant race, the Bucs held the attention of everyone in town, including my parents and grandfather. The ball club always seemed to play great out west, especially Willie Stargell. As team captain, he would award gold stars to players for feats on the field that led to wins. Every player in the dugout wanted their black Pirates pillbox hat to have as many "Stargell Stars" as possible. Of course, Willie had the most gold stars sewn on his cap; he was in the midst of a mythic season that would outshine his already monumental decade. The Hall of Fame slugger had hit more home runs than any other Major League Baseball player in the '70s. In Los Angeles, "Pops" Stargell belted two mammoth blasts that completely exited the park over the spacious outfield bleachers at Dodgers Stadium. Stargell was so highly esteemed that the Dodgers actually placed a plaque for an opposing team's player at the point where his longest home run ball had landed.

With the game tied in the 9th inning, my captivated family didn't even notice me sneaking through the front door of my grandfather's house on Heinz Terrace. Even better, during a commercial break they flipped over to a rerun of *Saturday Night Live*. The loud laughter of the studio audience from the antics of Dan Aykroyd and John Belushi concealed my speedy tiptoeing up the creaky wooden steps. Plus, with a Steelers game on tomorrow afternoon, I was hoping that nobody would notice if I skipped town and headed out to the country in search of Braddock's Gold.

Like a cat in the dark, I had quietly scurried up the staircase and jumped into bed. Just as I slid under my covers, I heard a low voice. My dad was standing at the door.

Dad: "So, any luck? Did yinz find the gold?"

My father somehow always knew what I was doing.

Bobby: "No, Dad. But we got some good leads."

Dad: "Okay, just be safe. The Bucs are tied 2-2 goin' into extra innings. Night."

Bobby: "Good night."

After my long and adventurous day, I was beat. I closed my eyes and was out like a light. The ball game was one for the ages. It lasted well over six hours as the Pirates eventually won 4 - 3 in 19 innings. I missed every second of it.

Chapter 11: A Real Cliffhanger

It is one thing to discover a secret map that discloses the location of a hidden gold treasure. It is an entirely different thing to successfully find said hidden gold treasure. We knew that we had our work cut out for us. But our crew was determined to find Braddock's Gold.

It was by far the hottest day of the summer, well over 90 degrees Fahrenheit. We all met at Sarah's house in Squirrel Hill at 11 AM and Curtis picked us up in his big Buick wagon. Of course, we had promised Curtis a fair share of the treasure by now. We excitedly hopped into his car to begin our quest for the gold. The big guys sat up front, while Sal, Sarah, and I took the back seat. Vito clung to his trusty metal detector.

Although Sal, Vito, and I were wearing the same outfits as yesterday, Curtis was sporting a royal blue Pitt T-shirt with a gold 33 on the back. Sarah wore a powder blue shirt with a golden owl on its front center. She had a big yellow flower pinned in her hair like Linda Ronstadt. It was also evident that Cierra was not with Curtis.

Sarah: "Where's Cierra?"

Curtis: "Oh, she always goes to church with my mum and Gramma Rose on Sundys."

Curtis paused and nodded to all of us in the car.

Curtis: "Y'all don't worry now. She said she gonna pray for all our sorry butts."

Sal chimed in from the back seat.

Sal: "Good. We need all the help we can get."

We laughed as we rolled along the urban avenues. I began riffling through my notebook sketches and deciphering the final details from the maps that we had discovered under the leopard saddle rest. My calculations showed that the gold was hidden east of the city and just outside of Allegheny County. Judging by the location of the X along an oxbow river curve, I deduced that the treasure was buried along the Youghiogheny River, upstream from McKeesport. Comparing this information with a modern map, it appeared to be located on the edge of a forested park in neighboring Westmoreland County. The park was quite fittingly named Braddock's Trail Park.

Apparently, this was where Braddock and his army camped the night before their doomed attempt to take Fort Duquesne in present-day Downtown Pittsburgh.

Eventually, city streets became country roads. We meandered onto an open stretch of the famous Abraham Lincoln Highway that traverses the nation from coast to coast. As we rambled down the freeway, Vito sailed his long right arm out the window and caught air with his cupped hand like the wing of a bird. For what seemed like the span of a good mile, his hand flew carelessly up and down from the wind currents like a free bird that had finally escaped the city. He expressed his delight.

Vito: "I love road trips. Well, actually this is my first one."

For a bunch of city kids, this certainly was a big trip out to the country. Like many urban Yinzers, we had our worries about leaving the comfort of our familiar concrete streets and brick buildings. We discussed these innate fears on the car ride. We passed a sprawling farm topped by a big red barn on a hill.

Vito warily surveyed the vast green cornfield that was blessed with a bounty of tall cornstalks. He shuddered in his seat.

Vito: "Zoinks! For some reason, farms give me the creeps. They're spooky."

Curtis: "For real. Cornfields is creepy. I'm actually more scared o' bein' lost in a big cornfield at night than bein' lost dahn any alley o' Picksburgh."

Sal: "Yeah. They freak me out, too. Like, it feels like Michael Myers and Leatherface are just waitin' in 'ere for ya to step into the cornfield to get slaughtered. I can see 'em two deranged psychos right now, spinnin' 'round the butcher knife and revvin' up the chainsaw n'at."

Vito: "Yikes!"

In the 1970s, the slasher horror film genre bloomed. Teenagers across the nation would love going to the movies and getting scared to death from gory hits like *Halloween* and *The Texas Chain Saw Massacre*. We especially enjoyed sneaking into drive-in theaters and catching a free scary movie. Of course, witnessing the ghastly bloodbaths orchestrated by masked murderers made us all lose some sleep.

Curtis added to the worried tone of the conversation in the car.

Curtis: "And y'all is forgettin' 'bout zombies. Zombies freak me out real bad. Ain't nothin' freakier than a bunch o' zombies walkin' real slow outta them cornfields and comin' right up at you."

Sal: "Oh yeah, man. You're right. Zombies are way worse than psychopaths."

America's original zombie horror movie, *Night of the Living Dead*, was shot in the hinterlands north of Pittsburgh at a farmhouse and cemetery in Evans City. Its sequel, *Dawn of the Dead*, was filmed at Monroeville Mall. Watching flesh-eating corpses overrun our city in these movies made a zombie outbreak seem almost feasible.

Vito woefully expressed his fears of the undead.

Vito: "Them slow walkin' ghouls scare the crap outta me. And how's come us humans taste so good to them zombies anyways? Wouldn't they rather eat a cheeseburger?"

Sarah giggled at Vito's questions. However, most teenagers passed along an oral history of widely accepted beliefs, secondhand accounts, and common logic when it came to the supernatural, especially the walking dead. Of course, these ingrained folklores remain today for everything from vampires and werewolves to superheroes. I replied to Vito as if I were offering a serious scientific answer backed by evidence.

Bobby: "See, it's 'cause they need to eat our brains n'at to stay alive. I heard they can't go on for more than a week without a fresh brain to eat."

Sal quickly alleviated Vito's fears.

Sal: "Don't worry, Vito. They ain't gonna want *your* brain."

Sarah laughed again at the playful banter but agreed with the summative fear of her fellow passengers.

Sarah: "To be honest, guys, I can't even watch those scary zombie movies. When my brother dragged me with him to go see *Dawn of the Dead* last year, I hid under my coat the entire time. I got so creeped out that I didn't even want to go trick-or-treating last Halloween. I was afraid a mob of zombies might start chasing me."

Curtis: "I ain't gonna lie. I'd rather fight five livin' dudes than one dead one."

By now, Vito seemed to believe that our next back-alley brawl in Sharpsburg would be with a swarming horde of Yinzer zombies. He swung and punched his open palm.

Vito: "I'm with you, man. I wonder if their bodies are all squishy when you sock 'em real hard in a' guts."

Then the gears in his head truly started turning.

Vito: "Wait a minute. So, if they eat us and our brains, would 'at mean zombies are cannibals?"

At this point, the eldest teen on our mission took charge of the frivolous adolescent conversation. Adjusting up from a relaxed position in his driver's seat, Curtis quickly redirected our crew.

Curtis: "Okay, y'all better start gettin' *your brains* ready to hunt for that gold. Let's lock in now."

Vito immediately forgot about zombies and became focused on the treasure hunt. He heavily nodded his scruffy mophead.

Vito: "Heck yeah! I'm psyched!"

He shouted while slamming his meaty fist down on the car's front dashboard.

Vito: "Let's do this!"

The glove compartment drawer popped open from the strike and Vito lowered his head in an apologetic fashion.

Vito: "Oops. Sorry, Curtis."

To get into the right mindset for the mission ahead, Curtis searched the radio stations for some motivational music. Scanning with the dial, he quickly found a melody that suited our road trip to the rural outskirts of Pittsburgh. It was the perfect song for cruising down an empty highway through the green farmlands.

Curtis: "If we drivin' in the country, then we gonna need the right kinda tunes."

Curtis blasted the speakers and coolly leaned back while the rest of us immediately began chanting the chorus of "Take It Easy" with the Eagles rock band. It was a huge hit. Every kid who grew up in the '70s knew all the words. Our enlivened group sang away, with Vito loudly leading the vocals. Even Sal strummed along on his air guitar as he now had a good feeling about our mission. Cynical Sal finally believed in the legend of the lost gold of General Braddock. The incredible discovery of George Washington's secret map lifted all our spirits to a whirling level of high hope.

After the song ended, we were well within reach of our targeted destination. But as we rolled into the vicinity of Braddock's Trail Park, we needed just a little assistance to pinpoint its exact location. On the side of the road were a couple of local teenagers leaning against their big white pickup truck. An old flatbed Ford F-100. The mud-streaked truck had a large, rusty grille guard and huge off-road tires. The front bumper plate depicted a black flag with a skull and cross bones, a common fixture in a region home to a professional sports team named the Pirates.

The relaxed pair appeared to be brothers. Both had blond hair. They wore sleeveless white T-shirts, faded blue jeans, and leather work boots. They looked like real country boys to us city kids. As we slowed to a stop beside them, the larger of the two acknowledged the car full of out-of-towners. His shirt read, "Keep on Truckin'."

Country Yinzer: "Yinz look lost. What brings yinz to this neck o' the woods?"

Even rural kids in Western Pennsylvania speak fluent Yinzer. In fact, the accent is often thicker in the countryside than in the urban or suburban portions of Pittsburgh.

Curtis: "Yinz know where Braddock's Trail Park is?"

The tall, older teen pointed back down the road in the opposite direction.

Country Yinzer: "It ain't far. Turn 'round and go back 'bout a half mile 'n make a right dahn Turner Valley Road. Yinz'll run right into it."

Curtis: "Thanks, man."

Country Yinzer: "Good luck, guys."

It seemed strange to me that he wished us good luck. But sure enough, we came to a large wooden sign that read "Braddocks Trail Park." A patch of yellow wildflowers swayed beneath it. As we parked next to the sign, the collective enthusiasm of our crew had reached its peak level. We swiftly popped open the doors and jumped out of the car. I left behind my backpack of supplies. All I needed now was the map.

Vito was in overdrive. He ran to the back of the car to get Sal's shovel out.

Vito: "All right! I'm ready, ready, ready! Ready to get rich!"

A warm breeze blew atop the tree canopy, gently rocking high branches full of green leaves. The sprawling trees offered us a much-needed reprieve from the baking sun above. Sarah noticed the immediate temperature drop from the sweltering highway to the shade-covered forest.

Sarah: "Oh, it's so nice and cool back here."

Bobby: "Yeah, this breeze feels real good."

Curtis was stretching out his legs from the long car ride.

Curtis: "For real. It was crazy hot dahn in a' city today."

A crow resting high in an oak tree urgently alerted the quiet forest of our presence.

Crow: "Caw! Caw! Caw!"

As the watchful warden flew away from its treetop lookout post, I half-expected Sal to mark the bird as another bad omen. But like the rest of us, Sal was locked in on the mission objective and eagerly grabbed his shovel from Vito. At last, Sal had caught our contagious gold fever.

Sal: "Man, I'm pumped! Let's go find 'is gold!"

Everyone was on board now. This was a treasure hunt. I couldn't have asked for a better team of intrepid explorers to embark on our quest. We were undaunted.

Curtis: "All right. This is it. My grandpa always says this one line his flying squadron would shout before a big mission: 'Ain't nothin' to it, but to do it!'"

Bobby: "Huh. My dad's army platoon had a chant like that too. It went: 'Do it! Do it! Do it! Put your mind right to it!'"

Vito nodded and flipped his device on. He swiped it over the steel doors of the station wagon. As expected, it beeped loudly. He smiled with an optimistic glow and faced the group. The final leg of the mission had officially begun.

Vito: "Operation Braddock's Gold is a go!"

Sarah: "Here we go! Where do we start looking, Bobby?"

I earnestly referred to the map for an answer. Everyone followed along intently as I traced each geological marker on the prized map with my index finger.

Bobby: "Okay, first we need to find this crick. It leads to this waterfall and then it runs dahn to this river. At the end o' the crick, there should be a walnut tree. There's a picture of a cannon here on a' map right over the X. I think maybe the gold was stashed in the cannon and buried under 'at tree. It'll be along the river. Right here."

After all the hard work from yesterday, it seemed like we were on a trip with destiny. We were going to find that treasure. Our venture into the woods would begin with Sarah's keen sense of hearing. She pointed the way.

Sarah: "I hear a creek flowing over there, past those evergreen trees."

Bobby: "Nice! Let's go!"

We were off to a good start.

The little creek ran down a gentle slope into a thickly forested hillside. In some spots, mature trees stopped the sunlight altogether. Hiking here was a welcome contrast to the congested avenues we would normally be roaming on a summer day. The forest's fresh air was nothing like that of the smoggy urban river valleys. Far from any smokestacks, these types of serene, wooded vistas inspired a Pittsburgh scientist named Rachel Carson to spearhead the modern-day environmental movement. Carson was a biologist who bravely stood up to industrial pollution and widespread use of pesticides. Another fan of nature, Sarah was admiring the pristine forest too.

Sarah: "Wow, this park is so beautiful. I feel like we're a thousand miles away from the city out here. And it seems like we're the first people to visit this park in forever."

Just then, Curtis pointed up to the sky.

Curtis: "Yo, check out the hawk."

I gazed up in awe at the majestic bird sailing directly above us. With this happening only moments after Curtis mentioned his grandfather's flying days with the Red Tails, I was secretly hoping that this was a sign of good fortune.

Bobby: "It's a red-tailed hawk."

The large bird of prey screeched as it soared over the treetops. It was circling upward in a thermal convection current that rose high above the forest.

We hiked onward. The entire park was green. The mixed wood forest included oaks, maples, and scattered groves of pine and hemlock trees. Trillium and fern made up the lush underbrush. Deep within the rolling foothills of the Appalachian Mountains, you could vividly see why this state was named Pennsylvania, meaning Penn's Woods. It was established in the 1600s by an English Quaker named William Penn as a place where people could enjoy religious freedom without persecution. Far from any judging eyes, we happened to be in about as remote of a woodland spot as you can find and still only be forty minutes from Downtown Pittsburgh.

Sal: "Now I see why 'at general decided to hide the gold here. Who the heck would ever come lookin' for it way out here in a' sticks?"

About twenty yards down the creek, a white-tailed deer and her spotted fawn stared at us like they had never laid eyes on humans before. After a prolonged study of the visitors to her park, the doe scampered away into the brush. The curious little fawn gathered in one last glance at us before it followed its mother.

Vito: "Look, there goes Bambi and his mum."

Sarah: "Aw, it's so cute."

As we trekked onwards, the tranquility of the deep woods created an almost alien world for us city kids to explore. I found myself looking up at the gigantic trees that stood around us in every direction. The steady breeze in the treetops along with chittering insects and chattering birds added to an atmosphere that was completely unlike the bustling streets that I was accustomed to. Personally, I needed the sound of car traffic and chugging trains to lull me to sleep at night. The remote forest reminded me that at the time of Chief Guyasuta, the entire region (as well as most of the continent), was just one big wilderness.

We entered an opening in the trees where the creek moved over a rocky outcropping creating a tiny waterfall. Limestone slabs were hanging over a pool in the creek like a shelf over a sink. The flat gray rocks were in direct sunlight. Vito was exploring the stone protrusions with the metal detector.

Sal: "Get off o' them frickin' rocks, ya moron! Rattlesnakes might be sunbathin' on 'em."

With Vito busily prospecting up ahead, Sal jokingly whispered to the rest of the crew.

Sal: "There ain't no way we're gonna be able to lug 'at meathead outta here if he gets bit."

It was the first time in a long while that Sal had openly displayed his scientific knowledge. He knew that on this hot morning, cold-blooded reptiles might use the warm rocks to ramp up their metabolism. Copperheads and timber rattlesnakes are venomous species common to the region. Besides sunbathing on the rocks, snakes often sit near bodies of water waiting for small prey like field mice and chipmunks to stop for a drink. Although he often teased me about my passion for history and science, Sal would conceal the full depth of his knowledge. It was definitely not cool to appear to be book smart in our neighborhood. But today, in a distant forest among the great outdoors, Sal had no qualms.

At the shallow creek pool, I bent down to feel the cool water flow through my fingertips. I noticed a few tiny minnows dart away in fear. The soothing sound of the creek flowing over the cascading waterfall was a peaceful gift from the forest. After all, it was a similar creek in Guyasuta Park that ignited our treasure hunting expedition and led us all here in the first place. I wiped the water from my hand onto my jeans and double-checked the map to confirm our path.

Bobby: "Okay, guys. So far, so good. We just gotta keep followin' the crick. Eventually, we're gonna come to a big waterfall. Like way bigger than 'is one."

We kept hiking down a mild slope that started to turn into a steep grade. Twigs and dried leaves on the forest floor crunched beneath our feet as we trampled with more force heading down the steeper stretch of the hill. Over our thunderous marching, we failed to hear the faint sound of softly falling water.

Catching a glimpse through a cluster of hemlock trees, Curtis spotted it first.

Curtis: "Look! That's it. There go the big waterfall!"

Vito: "Wow! Look at it!"

Sarah: "It's beautiful! I wish I would've brought my camera. I love waterfalls!"

I said nothing. But secretly, I was thrilled. The map was completely right so far.

We stopped at the top of the graceful waterfall. It fell about thirty feet over a tall cliff of layered shale. Water splashed at its base. Normally, that view alone would be worth the trek. But this mission was much more than a sightseeing stroll in the park.

Curtis looked out over the waterfall and nodded to us.

Curtis: "All right. This gold ain't gonna find itself. Let's shake it."

Sarah: "I can't believe this, guys! We're almost there!"

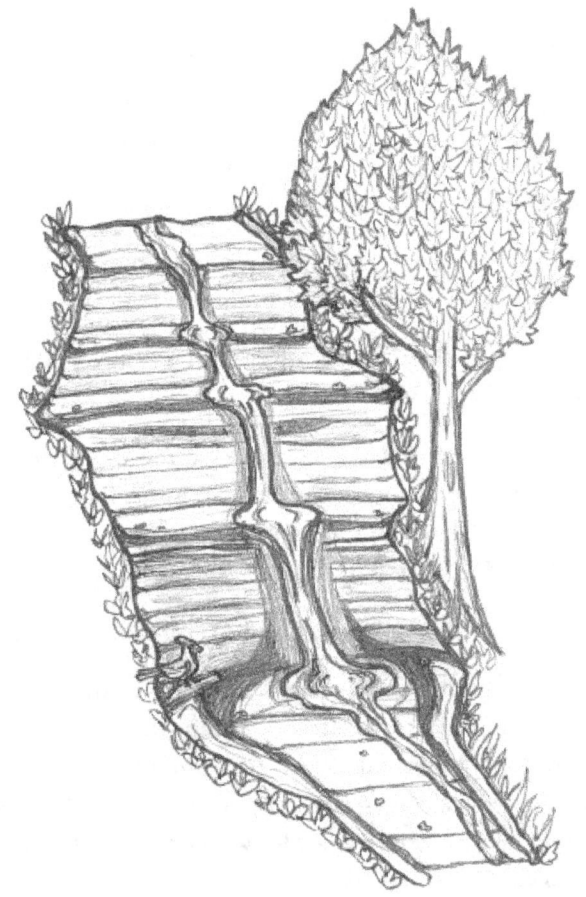

Walking alongside the waterfall was invigorating. We became even more fired up. What began as a seemingly whimsical fantasy had somehow turned into a real, live search for a historic buried treasure. Even Sal couldn't hold back his enthusiasm.

Sal: "I can't freakin' believe this is happenin' to us bums! Is this for real?!"

We could almost smell the gold. It had to be close now. Our pace picked up. We circled around to the base of the waterfall and advanced along the bank of the rippling creek, following its flow. We hopped over some mossy rocks that led into a gully. It was here that we hit our first snag in navigation.

Curtis: "The crick splits up right here. Is 'at how it look on a' map?"

My eyes flew back down at the map.

Bobby: "No. It don't got a split like this. Crap! What should we do?"

Although the stream on the map was represented by just one long and curvy line, the one we were following split at a fork into two different directions.

Vito: "I say we go dahn 'at way."

Vito pointed down the creek path that was shallow and narrow. Curtis then motioned to the wider, more rapidly flowing branch of the creek.

Curtis: "Nah, I say we go the other way. It's steeper 'n probably heads dahn to the river. Man, we gotta go with gravity here."

We all paused and looked around at each other. At this point, no one had the energy to bicker about which direction to take. Along with the long hike through wooded terrain, the brutal football game and violent slugfest in the fountain yesterday had taken the fight out of all of us. Sarah offered a wise suggestion.

Sarah: "Why don't we vote on it? There's five of us, so there can't be a tie."

We all nodded in agreement. We had come too far to argue, so we decided to cast a vote instead. Once again, our trusted scout, Sarah, brought peace to the mission. Ironically, some historians believe that the first woman on record to have cast a democratic vote in America was Sacagawea on the famous Lewis and Clark Expedition. Unimaginably, it would take 115 more years for women in the U.S. to finally achieve the constitutional right to vote.

Vito raised his hand straight up like he was in elementary school.

Vito: "I vote for the littler crick this way."

He eagerly pointed left at the smaller of the two stretches of water. None of us seemed to mind that no one ever uses the word "littler."

Curtis: "I vote to follow the steeper crick."

Curtis confidently pointed down the hilly waterway that veered to the right.

Bobby: "I agree with Curtis."

Sal: "I don't vote for nothin' that Vito votes for."

Sarah: "Sorry, Vito. I'm with them on this one."

Vito nodded at the results.

Vito: "Ten-four, good buddies! Here we go!"

Without hesitation, the head metal detector specialist gladly accepted the results of our democratic vote and started briskly tramping alongside the steeper stretch of the creek. As he gleefully bounded down the hillside, Vito began to loudly belt all the high-pitched "La's" strung in a row from his favorite song when he was a little kid, "Crocodile Rock" by Elton John. His high voice echoed through the woody hollow.

After he took off, the rest of us looked at each other and laughed at the singing goof. Even Sal chuckled as he lightly shook his head. After we caught up to Vito, we hiked about fifty more yards along the winding stream and then we saw it through the trees. We all stopped in our tracks. Sarah wildly jumped up and down.

Sarah: "There it is! There's the river!"

Up ahead, was the Youghiogheny River. The "Yough" is a long tributary of the Monongahela. General Braddock and his army made their campground along this river corridor on the night before they planned to overwhelm the French and take Fort Duquesne. As was tradition right before a big battle, the head officers hid a chest of gold that was hauled along to pay their troops. Of course, the following day, the British would suffer an unexpected defeat at the hands of their enemies. After the general's demise, the gold became an afterthought. Even in 1979, this remote wooded location looked like a great place to hide a golden treasure.

Curtis: "So here's where they was camped the night before they all went 'n got jumped dahn in my hood."

Bobby: "Yep, right around here. And they hid the gold that night, too."

Curtis: "Then 'at gold's gotta be real close now."

Vito could no longer contain himself. He started to pump his fist in the air and yell.

Vito: "It's here! I can feel it! I CAN FEEL IT!"

As he shook like a firecracker about to explode, I directed what I hoped would be the last mission orders for Operation Braddock's Gold.

Bobby: "Okay, now we gotta find a walnut tree."

Vito: "What's 'at look like?!"

Sal: "A tree with walnuts on it, ya rockhead!"

Vito: "Can we eat 'em?"

Sarah chimed in with her voice of reason again.

Sarah: "Walnut Street in Shadyside is lined with them. Walnut trees have round, green fruits that start to fall this time of year. The walnuts are tucked in a shell inside. Let's look for a tree down by the end of the creek that has walnuts underneath it."

Bobby: "Good thinkin', Sarah. Let's go, Vito! Get your metal detector ready!"

We were only a few yards away from the creek's end now. It was spilling out over a high cliff and into the surging river. This waterfall was not on the map, but over 200 years of weathering and erosion may have caused it to form naturally. We scoured the grounds for walnut seeds. I even looked for squirrels or chipmunks that might lead us to them. Vito was lumbering up ahead.

Vito: "I don't see no walnuts, guys."

Sal: "Keep lookin', ya Sasquatch!"

We abruptly found ourselves toeing on a high rockface. Our mission came to a screeching halt. With his head down and metal detector swinging, Vito would have tumbled over the cliff and fallen fifty feet into the river had I not grabbed a fistful of the back of his sweaty tank top. We looked around with feverish haste like gold prospectors have done for millennia.

Curtis: "Is we at the spot? Where's 'at tree?"

There was no walnut tree in sight. Only some scattered pines around the cliff's edge. Then I noticed a huge tree stump on the bluff. I pointed right to it.

Bobby: "Look, guys! 'At walnut tree would be over 200 years old by now. It probably grew old, died, and fell dahn over the ridge in a' river. But this stump is right where it's supposed to be."

Sarah: "Vito! Vito, come scan around this stump!"

Vito vaulted over a fallen branch and barreled towards the old stump like a maniac. He lowered his metal detector and began to sweep around it. He circled it once and then we heard the sound that we were all waiting for.

Metal Detector: "Beep. Beep. Beeeeeeep. Beeeep. Beep."

We all began to freak out. Everyone started screaming in excitement.

Vito: "Woohoo!"

Sal: "Holy crap!"

Curtis: "This is it!"

Sarah: "I can't believe it!"

I pointed to the spot.

Bobby: "Sal, dig right here! Right here!"

Sal whipped out the shovel and plunged it in the ground where Vito's gadget was beeping. Sal dug like his life depended on it. Then we heard another sound that we all so desperately wanted to hear.

Shovel: "Clink!"

Sal: "I hit something! It sounds like metal!"

Sarah and I froze in complete shock. A normally cool, calm, and collected Curtis started to jump up and down like a little kid.

Curtis: "What is it?! What is it?!"

Sal and Vito dropped to the ground and began to dig like badgers with their hands. As they scraped away more dirt, we could see a metallic object shining through the debris. It was the exact color that we were all looking for.

Vito: "It's gold! It's gold!"

Sal: "HOLY CRAP! It *is* gold!"

Vito pulled up the metal artifact from the dirt and held it up high. It was gold. It was shiny. And it was round. Our jaws dropped. Sal was the first to speak.

Sal: "That ain't no buried treasure! That's a hubcap!"

Our coveted hidden gold treasure turned out to be a gold-colored hubcap lost from the tire of an old car. Even worse, the wheel cap looked like it was poorly coated with gold spray paint that was peeling off from the edges. In search of a priceless bounty of gold, we instead found a rusty hubcap that was as cheap as they come.

Curtis: "What the... ? It's junk!"

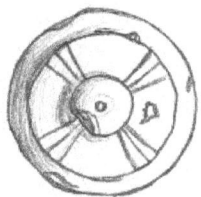

Still holding up the hubcap, Vito fell to his knees and screamed in despair.

Vito: "Nooooooo!"

Sal was steaming. He clenched his fists in disgust.

Sal: "This has gotta be one big flippin' joke!"

As they loudly lamented, Sarah and I just stood there. She was speechless. I was completely floored.

Sal became flushed with ire. He started breathing heavily. His face turned bright red. Veins in his temples were throbbing.

Sal: "I've had it with this bullcrap! I'm sick of it!"

238

Then Sal went berserk. He jumped over the hole that he dug. He was spitting fire.

Sal: "GIMME THAT! GIMME THAT FRICKIN' WORTHLESS PIECE O'… !"

Sal violently ripped the old hubcap out of Vito's hands.

Sal: "YOU MOTHER… !"

Grunting in fury, Sal spun and hurled the hubcap off the steep cliff. The round metal disc whirled like a Frisbee as it fell fifty feet to the river. It made a loud splash upon impact with the water. Leaning out over the high overhang, we watched it slowly sink beneath the surface. We were left in stunned disbelief. Our dream of finding Braddock's Gold sank into the depths of the river with that busted hubcap. It was about to meet me at rock bottom.

We sulked upon the edge of the precipice in a collective sullen silence. The shock and anger subsided. Now we were gripped with an abysmal feeling. Utter disappointment. Long faces hung in the bright sunlight. Disillusioned eyes stared down at the swiftly flowing water. A lone blue jay swooped over our spot on the tall cliff and landed on a nearby treetop. From its perch, it snidely taunted us with three mocking chirps that echoed over the river valley. After the bird's call faded away, it became deathly quiet.

That's when we heard a truly shocking sound. It came from right behind us.

Shotgun: "Click, click."

Chapter 12: X Marks the Spot

We all froze in fear. The alarming broadcast of a 12-gauge shotgun being prepared to fire has that effect on you. Just like at the beginning of my story, I had a loaded weapon pointed at my back. But this was no BB gun. This was an oversized pump-action shotgun. The kind that would make a snowman shiver. Its long barrel was aimed and ready. Behind us came a loud, gruff voice.

Old Man: "What are yinz kids doin' on my property?!"

Still facing the river, none of us dared to turn around from the cliff overlook. We were completely petrified. With his mouth wide open from fright, Vito's gum fell out and rolled onto the ground. Harsh demands came next.

Old Man: "Every one o' yinz put your dang hands up! RIGHT NOW!

We shuddered with horror. Then we quickly lifted our hands up in the air. Vito had raised his hands while still holding the metal detector.

Old Man: "You there, with the metal finder... drop it!"

Vito promptly obeyed the command. The metal detector fell to the ground. At this point, none of us had even spun around yet to look at him.

Old Man: "Now, real slow-like, I want all yinz to do an about-face."

We all slowly turned 180 degrees and faced a burly old man. The business end of his long gun was pointed directly at us. Well, at me to be more precise. I was standing in the middle of my crew. He sternly growled his next orders.

Old Man: "With your hands up, we're gonna take a walk up to my house right over these here woods. Straight up through there."

He pointed with the shotgun. Up on the hilltop, sat a small home. It was nestled in a clump of dark green spruce trees. In our great excitement, we obviously failed to notice that we had wandered out of the park and onto his property. He nodded up towards his little cabin in the woods. Then he barked at us.

Old Man: "Now git goin'! MOVE IT!"

We jumped. Then we began to march. This guy was dead serious. The aged country man had a crooked scowl beneath his long white beard. He was wearing a white T-shirt, blue denim overalls, and tan leather work boots. A red bandana hung from his side pocket. His white hair was topped off with a mesh cap that had a faded John Deere patch. We were city Yinzers, but we knew that country folk protected their turf with the same tenacity that we do, maybe even more so. Only minutes after the incredible elation of thinking that we had struck gold, we hung our heads in great despair as we slowly trudged up the hillside to his house. The dream was over. Now our lives were at risk.

As we worked our way through a thicket, we started whispering to one another.

Sal: "Great. Now we *are* gonna end up in a cornfield. Uncle Jesse Duke here probably has ditches already dug up for us."

Everyone grew terrified looks on their faces.

Bobby: "You're right. These kinda guys don't like city kids."

Vito: "He probably don't like Italians either."

Sal: "Or Catholics."

Sarah: "Or Jewish girls."

We all looked over to Curtis. He was next in line. We expected a reply to continue our string of worries. Instead, he whispered out of the side of his mouth.

Curtis: "I know what all yinz is thinkin'. But I ain't gonna say it."

I smiled with respect for Curtis's strong resolve. But then we were scolded again by the cantankerous old codger.

Old Man: "Yinz better quit that jabberin'! I done got no problem usin' a shotgun on trespassers!"

We had reached his humble abode. White paint was peeling off from its thin wooden panels. Two weathered flags flew over the small, rickety porch. One was the American stars and stripes while the other was a yellow "Don't Tread on Me" banner with its ominous rattlesnake. Next to the wooden porch swing, there were two signs that read

"No Trespassing" and "Beware of Dog." Of course, with my innate fear of canines, I attempted a final plea bargain before he marched us into his house.

Bobby: "Sir, we don't gotta go inside. Let me explain."

Old Man: "Shut your yapper, Roberto!"

I was dumbfounded. I wondered how this old man could possibly know the name that only my Italian mother called me by. Curtis read the perplexed look on my face and in a low voice reminded me of my attire.

Curtis: "Brother, you wearin' a Clemente shirt."

In fear for my life, I completely forgot that I was wearing my number 21 Clemente T-shirt that I wore almost every day that summer. Roberto Clemente was a Puerto Rican Hall of Famer who led the Pirates to two World Series Championships. Blessed with incredible speed and a rocket arm, the star outfielder won 12 Gold Glove Awards. His athletic talent was topped only by his desire to help others. The benevolent Latino legend had sadly perished that decade in a plane crash while trying to deliver humanitarian aid and medical supplies to Nicaragua after a devastating earthquake there. To the people of Pittsburgh and Puerto Rico, Roberto is known as "The Great One" or "El Magnífico." Along with Chief Guyasuta, Roberto Clemente was my hero.

Old Man: "Now, yinz kids git inside and go sit dahn on them couches. None o' yinz better think o' makin' any dumb moves."

We entered through the squeaky screen door of his bungalow. Lying down by the wooden console television, was a big old hound dog which did not even lift his long ears off the floor to give us a bother. His hunting days were far behind him. The rustic living room was decorated with taxidermy in the form of stuffed pheasants, quails, and mallard ducks. There were old military pictures hanging on the walls along with one gold Terrible Towel. The old man sat us down on his faded fabric sofas. He still held the shotgun on us.

Old Man: "I'm goin' in a' kitchen. No funny business. I don't wanna hear a peep!"

He slowly shuffled around a corner wall and into the kitchen. On impulse, Sal sat up and urgently whispered to us.

Sal: "This is our chance. Let's split. Like, now!"

We all flinched forward in our seats. Just then, the old man yelled back at us from his kitchen.

Old Man: "Don't none o' yinz move a muscle in there!"

We all sank back into the dusty couch cushions. Sal whispered again.

Sal: "Crap."

Sitting there in silence, the only audible sound was some clanking from in the kitchen. Then Sarah began to lightly tap her sandals on the hardwood floor in nervous fear. There was a soft glow projecting from the old black-and-white TV. The Steelers game was turned on with no volume. Vito and Curtis glanced over at the game. Vito whispered.

Vito: "Franco ain't playin'. He musta got hurt."

Curtis whispered back.

Curtis: "No. They restin' Franco today."

Sal added to the muted conversation with scorn directed at Vito.

Sal: "It's a preseason game, stupid. They ain't gonna make Franco play."

Vito: "Oh, yeah. I forgot."

Vito had commented at normal voice level and the old curmudgeon in the kitchen heard him. He hollered in a loud, harsh voice.

Old Man: "QUIET IN THERE!"

We zipped our lips. While being held captive at the mercy of a scary old man toting a 12-gauge shotgun for the crime of trespassing while searching for a historic gold treasure, only a bunch of Yinzers would be arguing over a meaningless Steelers preseason game. Actually, I think I may have finally explained what a Yinzer is to those of you who were not fully aware yet.

Just as it seemed like the end of our young lives was near, the old man turned the corner from his kitchen. Instead of wielding a shotgun, he was holding a large metal tray with a big glass pitcher of pink lemonade. He had poured five tall glasses, one for each of us. We looked at him with baffled expressions. He placed the tray on the coffee table in the middle of the living room. Then he sat down in his upholstered Archie Bunker chair by the television and now sleeping dog.

Old Man: "Okay. Now, tell me why yinz was trespassin' on my property."

We all looked around in bewilderment. Maybe he was not going to kill us after all. An instant later, we jumped at the chance to answer the old man's question.

Vito: "We found a map!"

Sarah: "A treasure map!"

Bobby: "A *hidden* treasure map!"

Curtis offered a much calmer explanation.

Curtis: "We got us a map for Braddock's Treasure. It led us right dahn here in a' woods."

The old man raised his eyebrows with interest. He calmly surveyed the room. Scrunching one eyeball closed, he keenly examined the goony bunch of teenagers sitting on his living room couches. Then he focused on the only crew member who didn't jump to answer his question. He spoke to Sal with an inquisitive voice.

Old Man: "Well, you're awfully quiet, son. What do *you* think about all this?"

Sal slowly removed his aviator sunglasses and hung them on his T-shirt collar. Today, he wore them in part to cover up his badly bruised left eye that got slugged by Vito in the Point State Park Fountain. Sal spoke in a manner as clear and blunt as the big black eye on his face.

Sal: "I think I'd have a hard time believin' this crap if I was you."

Sal paused and continued.

Sal: "But it's true. We found a map 'at George Washington made o' Braddock's Gold. It said the gold was buried dahn on 'at cliff by the river."

The old man sat back and crossed his arms. He began to nod his head up and down while digesting Sal's sincere explanation.

Old Man: "Hmm. I see. I see."

I felt it was my duty to apologize to him. After all, I had gotten us into this mess. From my seat, I showed him the sketches in my notebook.

Bobby: "We're real sorry, sir. But look, here's the map we found."

The old man lifted his head and nodded. While squeezing his left eye closed, he could clearly see the big X next to the cannon on the map.

Old Man: "Oh, I see it now, young fella. X marks the spot, huh?"

Bobby: "Look, sir, we apologize for trespassin' on your property. We just got real excited 'cause we worked real hard to find this map and get this far. We didn't mean to hurt nothin'. We just hoped… "

Old Man: "You hoped to find yourselves a buried treasure."

I lowered my head and slumped my shoulders.

Bobby: "Well… yeah."

My gloomy eyes looked down at the floor. Then we all drooped our heads down low. All hope was lost. Our mission was a complete failure. We weren't going to be rich. I wouldn't be able to buy a new house for my family. And I definitely wouldn't be getting a brand-new Pontiac Firebird. (My mind was set on a T-top convertible by then.) The fantasy had ended.

And that's when the old man began talking again.

Old Man: "Well, I reckon I do believe yinz kids."

We all looked up. At least he believed our crazy story. After scratching his bushy beard in thought, he continued.

Old Man: "Yinz came here lookin' for a treasure. Well, maybe I got one for you."

At this point, the aged man slowly stood up and hobbled back into the kitchen. We all looked at each other with puzzled faces. Of course, Vito broke the ice and reached for a cold glass of lemonade from the tray sitting on the coffee table.

Sal threw up his hands to stop Vito.

Sal: "Don't drink that, dummy! It's probably poison!"

Vito was too thirsty to care. He put the glass to his mouth and the pink liquid slid down his throat. After downing the entire cup, he licked his lips and burped.

Vito: "Aaahhhh. That stuff's DYN-O-MITE!"

We all waited about three seconds. Nothing happened. After realizing Vito wasn't going to die, the rest of us dove in and started chugging the pink lemonade with huge ice cubes. Delicious and with the perfect amount of sugar, I'm sure that it tasted just as good as the pink refreshments that the Eagles drank while being held prisoner at the Hotel California.

Now in a pleasant mood, the old man came around the corner again carrying a large chest made of wood and dark leather. It appeared heavy. He placed it on the floor with a loud clunk. Using the armrests for support, he slowly settled back down on his well-worn orange chair. He leaned forward and opened the lid of the trunk.

Old Man: "You see, I been livin' here for a real long time. And over the years, I found me some things that might interest yinz. Let's take a looky here."

He carefully pulled out a long metal bayonet. The steel blade was over a foot long and could be fixed at the end of a musket. It had some corrosion, but it was still silvery in color and its sharp point looked lethal.

Vito: "Whoa! Look at that thing! Imagine somebody chargin' at you with 'at."

Curtis raised his eyebrows.

Curtis: "For real, that'd wreck your day. I ain't never seen one o' them up close."

The old man continued with his show-and-tell.

Old Man: "When I was a kid, I heard about the legend o' Braddock's Gold just like yinz. I spent entire summers lookin' all 'round here. I knew his army camped in these parts the night before they went and got themselves ambushed. Look at this."

He pulled out a metal belt buckle and some ammunition, two large lead balls that would be shot from a musket or long rifle. He also had a two-pronged metal fork. He passed the relics around the room. We inspected the items closely. Then he whipped out the big gun, literally.

Old Man: "Then, one day, I found myself this."

He slowly lifted out a small bronze cannon that had corroded entirely green. A little over three feet in length, it was a compact piece of artillery that could be easily transported and used by soldiers to shoot flares or small shot.

Bobby: "The cannon! It's the cannon from the map!"

Sarah and I both scooted to the edge of our seats.

Sarah: "Was there anything inside of it?"

He slowly raised it above his head and turned it vertically. All at once, we held our breath and rose in our seats with anticipation. We half-expected a river of gold coins to spill out from its barrel. He flipped the cannon completely over for us.

Old Man: "Nothin' but dust in the wind. Sorry, kids."

Some dust fell out of the small cannon's muzzle and onto the floor. We let out a collective sigh and fell back into our seats. He put up an index finger and continued.

Old Man: "But I did find somethin' buried near the cannon."

He reached into the brown leather trunk again and slowly removed another item. Once again, the entire room of hopeful teenagers rose a little in their seats. He held it up for all to see.

Old Man: "A small cannonball. It's about a three-inch diameter."

We fell back in our seats again. This was a cool artifact on its own. But this was not what we came for. The solid iron cannonball appeared slightly rusted and very dense.

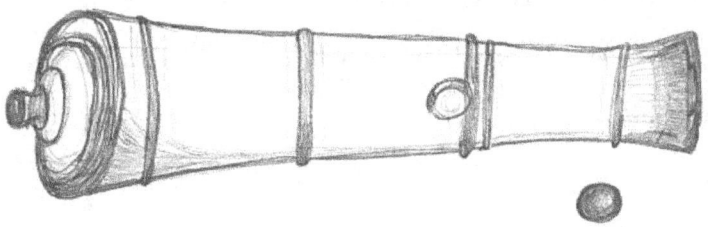

The old man handed the small cannonball to Vito. He lifted it up over his head.

Vito: "Whoa! This thing's heavier than it looks."

Vito passed it to Curtis. Curtis weighed out the cannonball in his hands.

Curtis: "Yo, it feels kinda like a shot put do at track."

Vito: "Yeah, it does."

Both big guys threw the heavy shot put ball as a field event for their schools' track and field teams. Just as we finished passing around the small cannonball, the old man started rubbing his hands together. Then he began to nod his head. He wanted to add one more artifact to his show.

Old Man: "Oh yeah, kids, there's one last thing."

He leaned forward in his seat. He spoke dramatically and in choppy segments.

Old Man: "One day, a long time ago, dahn where the cannon was, I went lookin' 'round with my dog, and found somethin' else."

We all picked up our heads. The old man paused and looked over the room. With his audience held captivated, he waited like an experienced magician who had one last trick up his sleeve. He carefully reached into the front chest pocket of his overalls.

With pride in his eyes, he slowly pulled out a small, solitary item.

Old Man: "I found *this*."

He held it up high. It was clamped between his index finger and his thumb.

Our jaws dropped to the floor. We sat frozen in absolute shock. We felt ten times more astonished than we were when we had a loaded shotgun pointed at us just thirty short minutes ago. We stared at the object in complete and utter awe.

The old man was holding up one shiny yellow coin. It was Braddock's Gold.

Bobby: "You found the gold!"

Sarah: "You found it!"

Curtis: "That's what I'm talkin' about!"

Sal: "Holy crap!"

Vito: "Whoa!"

We all clamored for a good look at the glistening coin. It was identical to my sketch. This was English gold currency from the 1750s.

Curtis: "You did it! You went and found Braddock's Treasure!"

Old Man: "Well, I just found this. One gold piece. Dahn by that cliff where yinz was diggin'."

He warmly smiled at all of us.

Old Man: "But I suppose you could call it a treasure, if yinz want to."

He gently handed the gleaming coin to me. I took a good long look at the target of our mission. I checked both sides. It was in brilliant condition. Not a scratch was on it. I handed the coin to Curtis and we passed it around the glowing living room. The gang finally got up from our seats and congratulated each other.

Vito: "We found gold!"

Sal: "I can't freakin' believe it!"

Curtis: "I'm tellin' the whole tahn o' Braddock!"

Sarah: "We did it! We did it, Bobby!"

Sarah hugged me. High fives flew around the joyous room. Vito even wrapped Sal in a big bear hug and lifted his feet clear off the floor. This wasn't exactly the gold rush we dreamed about, but we didn't care. Heck, the single gold coin may have simply fallen out of a soldier's pocket. None of that mattered. We found a piece of Braddock's Treasure.

After celebrating our triumph, the old man brought us back down to earth.

Old Man: "I'm glad yinz are all so happy. But it belongs dahn in a museum. At my age, I just don't feel like goin' all o' way Dahntahn Picksburgh no more."

Sarah politely gave a suggestion.

Sarah: "My grandfather works at the Carnegie Library in Oakland. The one that's attached to the Carnegie Museum. Want me to call him up and see if we can donate all of these things in your name?"

The country man grew a big, wrinkled grin on his face from Sarah's cordial offer. He had no intention of bringing these artifacts down to a museum himself. For many rural Yinzers, a trek into the busy city is a huge ordeal that's largely disdained.

The old man's eyes crinkled at the corners.

Old Man: "Sounds like a swell idea to me. That would be splendid, sweetheart."

By now, the old man had formally introduced himself. Randall P. Ferguson was a U.S. Army veteran who served in Europe during World War II. Under the command of General George Patton, Private Ferguson fought in one of the fiercest woodland battles in military history: the Battle of the Bulge. It took place in the frigid forests between Belgium and Germany. In fact, he had some really interesting artifacts around the living room. One was an old, weathered map of Pittsburgh in a frame. It was marked with German words and had a small Nazi symbol in the corner.

Sarah was taken aback.

Sarah: "What's this? Were you a… "

Old Man: "Ha! No way, miss! I hated every last one of 'em. I found this map at a little abandoned airfield when we was headin' to Berlin back in the War."

Bobby: "It's a map o' Pittsburgh!"

Old Man: "That's right. An aerial map."

Bobby: "Oh, yeah. The Germans wanted to bomb Pittsburgh 'cause we had more steel mills than Germany and Japan combined. The steel mills made the backbones of all the ships, planes, tanks, and trucks."

Vito was intrigued.

Vito: "Wow. So, the English, the French, and the Germans all wanted to take Pittsburgh. Who ended up gettin' it?"

Sal: "The jagoffs got it. And you're the leader of their army, Vito."

We all laughed the afternoon away looking at Mr. Ferguson's World War II relics, watching the Steelers game, and drinking ice-cold lemonade. When the sun began its slow descent behind the tallest trees, Sal and Vito double-timed back down to the cliff's edge to retrieve the shovel and metal detector. Curtis located his car and parked it right in front of Mr. Ferguson's house. Using the home phone, Sarah called her grandfather up and he was on his way from Squirrel Hill. Mr. Greenberg intended to pick Sarah up and garner the French and Indian War artifacts for the museum. After that, Curtis called Cierra and joyfully told her about our successful treasure hunt. Remember, back in those days, you had to memorize everyone's phone numbers. Every kid had at least 10 phone numbers memorized in their heads. For teenagers back then, forgetting your friend's phone number was equivalent to the modern dilemma of your smart phone running out of its battery charge.

Sarah made sure that I wouldn't forget her phone number. She wrote it down for me on a small slip of paper. Well, I had to return the gold coin to her somehow. Mr. Ferguson gave me permission to take the prized coin home first to show my family.

While waiting for Sarah's grandfather, we played a couple rounds of horseshoes in Old Man Ferguson's backyard. In a way, the timeless game of horseshoes resembled our familiar bocce matches back home. Tossing the steel shoes for sport, Vito and Curtis found yet another fun way to compete against each other. It turned out to be an ultimate last weekend of summer. When Mr. Greenberg arrived, we all greeted him from the front porch. He even had a gift for Vito from the library.

Librarian: "Here you go, big guy. We had some extra copies lying around. You can keep it."

Vito: "A dinosaur book! I knew you had one there."

251

Sarah's grandfather nodded to all of us.

Librarian: "I'm very proud of what you did this weekend. All of you. The museum will be thrilled to showcase these artifacts."

Of course, Sarah had not fully informed her grandfather about the dirty details of our covert operation at the Point. The story of a soaking wet leopard hide was for another day.

After being elated one moment, Vito grew a genuine look of concern the next. He chewed on his bottom lip.

Vito: "Will I... I mean... will we... get credit for it?"

Sarah's grandfather smiled and patted Vito on the back.

Librarian: "I'll see what I can do."

Vito pumped his fist in the air.

Vito: "Woohoo! It's official! I'm a real treasure hunter now!"

Whether we got credit or not mattered little to me. Technically, it was an old man named Randall Ferguson who had discovered and donated the small treasure trove of relics. But we would not come home empty-handed. Beyond the cherished coin, we helped deliver valuable historic artifacts from the French and Indian War to the museum for all to enjoy. Without our hard work and determination, none of this would have ever happened.

To all of us, one piece of gold was better than nothing. The gold coin was slightly bigger than a quarter and noticeably heavier in weight. It was stamped with King George II facing to the left on the heads side and an English crown on the tails side.

Sal spun the coin around in his hand. He faced the two astute adults on the porch.

Sal: "So how much do ya think this gold's worth?"

Old Man: "Well, I weighed it myself at just a hair under a third o' ounce o' gold."

The elderly Mr. Ferguson proudly raised his eyebrows and flashed a sunny grin.

Old Man: "That would fetch ya 'bout 75 bucks."

Sal lightly tossed up the coin and caught it. Eyeing the gold in the palm of his hand, he smiled with satisfaction.

Sal: "Decent. Not a bad score."

Mr. Greenberg then added a bit of his wisdom.

Librarian: "But that coin is worth far more than that for its historical value."

Mr. Ferguson crossed his arms and nodded.

Old Man: "Yessiree. No doubt about it. And it's in mighty fine shape too."

Vito plucked the gold coin right out of Sal's hand and positioned it inches away from his squinting eyes for a close inspection.

Vito: "Who's 'at lady on the coin? She's got the same hair as Miss Piggy."

Sarah's grandfather lightly chuckled.

Librarian: "That's King George the Second. He was known for wearing long curly wigs. He set the fashion in England in his time."

By the look in his eyes, Vito had come to a revelation.

Vito: "Oh, I get it. Kinda like how David Bowie used to have all 'em wacky haircuts when we was little kids."

Sal winced at Vito's response. Then he realized that Vito was basically correct in that the famous British rocker of the 1970s and the British king from the 1750s both shared a taste for flamboyant hairstyles. Sal reluctantly agreed with Vito.

Sal: "Ah... yeah. Vito's... kinda right."

Sal and I all looked at each other and smiled. It was the first time in a while that Sal had not ripped on Vito for a goofy remark. Only the discovery of a historic treasure was rarer than Sal agreeing with Vito.

Sarah's granddad added one more interesting fact about the gold.

Librarian: "You know, that coin is the same type of coin found in the book *Treasure Island*."

Bobby: "For real? That's crazy."

Vito: "I used to love 'at movie. I always wanted to be pirate. I wonder how they get them parrots to sit on their shoulders n'at."

Sal: "You should go practice with pigeons when we get back to Sharpsburg, Vito."

The coin that we had stumbled upon was a British gold guinea produced by the Royal Mint circa 1750. Amazingly, it happened to be the same exact type of gold coinage found in Scottish author Robert Louis Stevenson's famous novel about an epic treasure hunting quest set in the Caribbean Sea. *Treasure Island* is the original "X marks the spot" adventure story. The classic saga includes a band of colorful pirates, most notably the one-legged Long John Silver, who seek to find a buried treasure that was hidden on a remote island.

Sarah turned to her grandfather.

Sarah: "Grandpap, wasn't that your favorite book when you were a kid?"

Now a seasoned librarian who tended to tens of thousands of books, Sarah's grandfather grew a genuine smile. Adjusting his gold-framed reading glasses, Mr. Greenberg warmly replied.

Librarian: "Yes. Yes, it was."

Coincidently, along with the same gold currency, the lavish tale was set in the same era as the Battle of Braddock and included a young man who discovered a coveted treasure map. These parallels to my quest were uncanny. Believe me, even if I tried, I could not have made up these connections.

While we loaded up the back of Mr. Greenberg's old yellow Jeep Wagoneer with the artifacts, Mr. Ferguson watched from his front porch. He put his hands on his hips.

Old Man: "Gosh, I sure am surprised. Here I figured kids these days didn't care much about historical things like this no more."

After he finished loading in the cannon with Vito, Sal wiped his hands off on his jeans and pointed at me with his thumb.

Sal: "Well, only squares like Bobby here get their kicks from history stuff n'at. But trust me, we all still care 'bout findin' gold. 'At's for sure."

Before Sarah was about to leave with her grandfather, I hurried to Curtis's car and grabbed my backpack. I reached into the front pocket to find one of the three wooden animal figurines that my grandfather had given to me from his collection gifted to him by H.J. Heinz. I jogged back bearing a special gift created by a Seneca artisan from Sharpsburg. I thought it was the perfect memento.

I met Sarah alongside the fake wooden panels of her grandfather's Jeep. Two giant sunflowers stood over us by the mailbox.

Bobby: "Here ya go, Sarah. It's for helpin' us."

Sarah: "A fox! Your favorite animal. Thanks, Bobby."

We hugged each other goodbye.

Bobby: "Thanks for everything, Sarah. We did it. We found Braddock's Gold."

Sarah got into her grandfather's car. She looked up and winked at me.

Sarah: "We sure did. We made a great team."

Her car pulled away. I stood alone by the country road. The skies were clear, but I was on cloud nine. I took out the gold piece from my pocket, felt its weight in my hand, and flipped it high into the air. After twinkling in the light of the late day sun, the spinning coin landed right back in my palm. I beamed from ear to ear. Jubilation.

My friends were already waiting by the station wagon.

Sal: "C'mon, loverboy! You got her number already!"

I blushed. All the guys laughed, even Old Man Ferguson. He was a proud old war veteran. He valued the legend of Braddock's Treasure just as much as we did. And underneath his intimidating persona and gruff exterior was a heart of gold. It goes to show that you should never judge a book by its cover.

As we opened the car doors, Mr. Ferguson called out to us from his porch.

Old Man: "Hey! If there's ever a next time, then yinz kids just knock on a' front door."

We all jumped into the wagon and yelled out our final words of gratitude.

Bobby: "Thank you, sir! Thanks for everything today!"

255

Curtis: "Thanks, Mr. Ferguson!"

Vito: "And thanks for the lemonade!"

Sal stuck his head out the window.

Sal: "And thanks for not shooting us!"

We celebrated the whole way home as we recounted our weekend exploits. Curtis even drove us back across the Allegheny River to Sharpsburg. The Sunday night streets were almost entirely clear of traffic. Curtis pulled over in a corner spot on 18th Street to allow us to pull our bikes out from the back of his station wagon.

With all four of us standing beside his car, I offered Curtis some money.

Bobby: "Hey, Curt, thanks for all the lifts. Can we pay for the gas?"

Sal: "Yeah, gas prices are through the roof right now."

Curtis shook his head.

Curtis: "Nah, you good. It was a fun ride. And I can't wait for my grandpap to hear 'bout all this. I'm tellin' you, he gonna flip."

Curtis flashed a gigantic smile as he envisioned his grandfather's reaction to our historic find. Curtis truly valued the history of his hometown and the legend of Braddock's Treasure. We all felt the magnitude of our accomplishment.

Vito and Sal shook Curtis's hand as we kindly thanked him.

Vito: "Thanks, dude. You're the man."

Sal: "Yeah. It's been a trip. And thanks again for those tickets at Kennywood."

Bobby: "Thanks, Curtis. I have somethin' here for you."

For his instrumental and generous role in the mission, I wanted to give Curtis two parting gifts. From my backpack pocket, I pulled out the remaining two animal figurines from the time of Chief Guyasuta.

Bobby: "This mountain lion figure is for you 'cause you're gonna be a Pitt Panther one day. And this bald eagle is for Cierra 'cause she runs like the wind."

I handed Curtis the wooden carvings.

Curtis: "Right on. Thanks, man. She gonna dig this. She thinks all y'all is crazy, but she likes yinz."

Curtis lightly nodded as he looked us up and down.

Curtis: "Yinz guys is solid."

We all smiled at the compliment. After a pause, my head sank slightly as I spoke.

Bobby: "I hate sayin' this, but school starts soon and we probably won't be… "

Vito: "Yeah, if we don't see you… "

Curtis shook his head and interrupted us.

Curtis: "Oh, don't sweat it. Yinz boys will be seein' me again."

I looked up.

Bobby: "When?"

Curtis slowly got back into his station wagon and coolly replied out of the window.

Curtis: "Y'all be seein' the bottom o' my cleats when I stomp on yinz in a high school football game one day."

He turned the car on and nodded at us with a big grin.

Curtis: "Peace."

He slowly pulled away in his behemoth Buick with one quick wave out the window. We were all smiles. Obviously, we couldn't wait to get ourselves trampled on again by Curtis Williams.

The long car sailed away like a trusted vessel at sea passing over the distant horizon.

Chapter 13: Home Sweet Home

My friends and I stood on the street corner of our old block back in our little hometown. Finding out that there is a whole world to explore outside of its confines somehow made our neighborhood feel exponentially smaller. Hanging overhead was the glow from a waxing crescent moon. On this clear summer night, the stars shined upon us. I leaned on a telephone pole on 18th Street and my friends relaxed against a parked car with their arms crossed. Although we were visibly exhausted from the long weekend, we all felt a deep sense of satisfaction.

Bobby: "Well, guys, 'at was a real stellar adventure we had this weekend."

Vito: "Yup. I'm glad we listened to you, Bobby. 'At was the best weekend ever."

Sal: "I have to be honest with yinz, I don't even care we didn't find 'at treasure. It was worth it. The whole thing was worth it."

Bobby: "So you're sayin' you do like history and science and... "

Sal put up one hand like a big stop sign.

Sal: "Whoa! Let's not go 'at far, nerd. I meant it was worth it 'cause Rosaria gave me her number. She's a knockout. That chick's foxier than Wonder Woman."

I lowered my head.

Bobby: "Oh. Cool."

Then Sal smiled and gave me a pat on the back.

Sal: "Aw c'mon, Bobby. I'm just jaggin' ya. This weekend was a blast. I might even read a history book when yinz ain't lookin'."

We laughed under the moonlight. Three kids as thick as thieves. After reminiscing about the escapades of our exciting weekend, Vito had one last question.

Vito: "Uh, Bobby, can I keep the metal detector for just a little while longer?"

Sal and I smiled at each other. Vito had grown attached to his newly acquired superpower and was having trouble letting it go. It would be like telling Spider-Man that he could spin webs and swing from tall buildings for only one weekend. I answered sincerely.

Bobby: "Sure, Vito. You made a great Head Metal Detector."

Vito: "Thanks, Bob."

Vito smiled and clutched the device. You could see in his eyes that he was planning to sweep the entire neighborhood by lunchtime tomorrow.

Sal: "All right. Catch ya on the flip side, Bobby."

Bobby: "Okay, see yinz tomorra."

My solid gold friends began walking their bikes to their nearby homes. Vito was struggling to hold both the metal detector and the dinosaur book in one hand while steering his bike with the other. I slowly walked my BMX bike away and towards the charred remains of my old house on Cecil Street. Then I turned around and yelled back to both of them.

Bobby: "Oh yeah… and 'at was a tiger on the merry-go-round! Not a leopard, Vito!"

Vito called back to me.

Vito: "Oh, I know! I was just jaggin' with all o' yinz!"

Our voices echoed down the empty alley. The triumph of our adventure made us glow with pride. A bunch of street kids had actually accomplished something of value. Something of importance. Something bigger than us. On the last weekend of August in the summer of '79, we were young and invincible.

I watched my compadres until they disappeared into the blanket of darkness. Alone, I hopped on my bike and began breezily pedaling to my grandfather's house on Heinz Terrace. I couldn't wait to show my family the golden bounty that we had scored. I was especially eager to let Pap see the precious coin from Braddock's Treasure. My bike coasted at a pedestrian speed as I relished the memories of our adventure. Fully immersed in my reverie, I took the gold coin out of my front pocket to admire it again. It had a lustrous golden shine under the soft yellow buzz of the sodium streetlamp above. I lightly tossed it up in the air one more time and caught it. I slid it back into my pocket. I gave it a quick pat. *Wow. We did it.*

I was over the moon. My smile matched its crescent in the night sky. The Sunday evening streets of Sharpsburg were calm and quiet. And I had a pocketful of gold. Euphoria. Mission accomplished. I thought I was home sweet home.

Just then, a big pickup truck with no headlights on slowly turned the corner from 17th Street and headed down the single-laned alleyway in my direction. I couldn't see the driver behind the steering wheel. The haunted automobile eerily cruised in the darkness at a lazy speed. Its tires sluggishly rolled on the concrete ahead of me. The truck crept down the moonlit alley like a zombie in the night.

Taken aback by the strange scene, I whispered to myself.

Bobby: "What the... ?"

The truck stopped. Its engine revved. And revved. In a flash, the trucker flipped on the headlights and stomped on the gas pedal. The vehicle's back tires loudly peeled out like it was in a drag race. The huge pickup accelerated at full throttle towards me. It flew down the dark alley like a screeching bat out of hell. Stuck in the middle of the narrow street, I had no time to maneuver my bike. Without hesitation, I dropped my BMX to the pavement and jump-rolled onto the sidewalk to avoid being roadkill.

As I got up from my log roll, I looked over my shoulder and witnessed the speeding truck smash my bicycle to bits. Shrapnel flew in every direction. I screamed in fear.

Bobby: "HOLY CRAP!"

I immediately began to sprint up the sidewalk and down a side alley. I quickly wrapped around the block to try to lose my pursuers. However, as I turned right on to a wider street, the pickup truck was speeding at me from behind this time. Its blazing tires ate up the ground between us. It swerved right in front of me and with a loud skid, cornered me alongside the old Fort Pitt Brewery building. Boxed in against the brick wall, I instantly realized that I had seen this truck before. I recognized the front bumper plate as it came flying towards me. It was the Jolly Roger. This was the same white Ford pickup that the older teenagers were driving near Braddock's Trail Park.

The truck's doors shot out like cannons opening fire from the sides of a pirate ship. The two country boys leaped out of the tall, mud-stained vehicle like raiding pirates making landfall on a distant sandy shore. They came to pillage and plunder. Stranded in one of Sharpsburg's darkest alleys, I got jumped.

The captain of the crew hollered.

Country Yinzer: "Give us the gold, kid!"

Stunned, I quickly realized that they were probably spying on us at Old Man Ferguson's property. I remembered flipping the coin high in the air outside of the nice old fellow's house. Perhaps while passing by us out on the gravel road, they caught a glimpse of that flash of gold. They must have followed us all the way here from the distant countryside. Glowing from our success on the lively car ride home, there was no way that we would have noticed that we were being tailed by another vehicle. Not to mention, they obviously didn't want to mess with the brute size and strength of both Curtis and Vito. Biding for their easiest opportunity to pounce, the two marauding teenagers strategically waited until I was all alone for their ambush.

After hopping out of the passenger's side door, the smaller of the two country boys lunged at me and grabbed my right arm. He kept me in place while the much bigger teen ran around from the other side of the pickup. I tried to wrestle away from him, but his calloused hands held fast. It was hopeless.

Just then, I heard an unexpected but familiar voice.

Duke: "Rrrt! Rrrt!"

The monstrous hound came out of nowhere. He sprang up and sank his sharp teeth into my attacker's forearm, instantly freeing me. I couldn't believe it! It was my life-long nemesis, Duke. The vicious stray dog that had tortured me since I was a little kid had now come to my rescue. Snarling with ferocity, Duke pulled my assailant to the ground and chewed on his arm like it was a fresh rack of lamb. It sounded as if Duke was growling, "Nobody hurts Bobby 'cept for me! He's mine!" My beast of burden had finally paid me back for all those years of pain and suffering.

261

That grisly distraction gave me a split second to dash around the truck and keep running towards my grandfather's home. The bigger teen immediately chased after me past an old auto garage. I was fast for a 14-year-old, but this guy looked to be four years older and at least a head taller than me. I could hear his steel-toed work boots pound on the pavement as he gained ground behind me. The thumping boot soles echoed down the empty street. Then he yelled.

Country Yinzer: "Just give me 'at money, kid!"

While under hot pursuit, I realized that I didn't want to lead him to my family's place. I cut through the Kennedy Park grass and sprinted right past the bottom of Heinz Terrace. I threw my backpack under a tree to improve my agility. Being a Sunday night, the unlit basketball courts sat vacant and silent. Everywhere was dark. Quiet. It was dreamlike. The park, the courts, the alleyways, the entire town was now liminal space. I began to race straight down the middle of North Canal Street to the safest place that I could think of. The only place I could think of.

Three blocks away from my destination the farm boy caught up to me in the empty town square. Right in front of the Guyasuta Statue, he managed to swipe me with a strong push to my back. Like a swinging scythe in harvest, his long arm cut me down. My body tumbled over like a fallen crop on to the hard concrete. The tall teenage nightmare from the distant cornfields stood over me like the Grim Reaper coming to collect. His skinny, sunken-in face had a menacing glare. While I was still sprawled out on the ground, he violently grabbed me by the shirt collar and shouted in my face.

Country Yinzer: "All I want is 'at piece o' gold! Now, gimme it, kid!"

Firmly holding on to my collar, he managed to lift me cleanly off the sidewalk. It was like a street cleaner scraping off a piece of discarded chewing gum from the gutter with one quick sweep. For a second, I thought about surrendering the gold coin to save myself from a sure beating. But in this jolting moment, I somehow found clarity. I realized that I had worked too hard to obtain that coin, only to just give it away. We *all* worked hard for that coin... Sal, Vito, Sarah, Curtis, Cierra. No way I would let them down. Not now.

Standing in the shadow of Chief Guyasuta, I did what I had to do.

Bobby: "Okay, okay. Lemme get it. It's in my pocket."

Slowly, I reached into my back pocket. I grabbed the lone coin that was inside. With a somber face, I reluctantly offered it up to him. He released the firm grip he had on me. He quickly swiped the shiny coin out of my hand. Letting down his guard, he closely inspected his pirated prize. His pale green eyes glowed with greed. He even let out a villainous laugh.

Country Yinzer: "AHAHAHA... wait. What the... ?"

My last con job of the summer. It was a coin all right, just not the coin that he was looking for. It was a fugazi. A fake. A switcheroo. I had handed him the steel penny from my back pocket. The precious gold coin was still tucked safe and sound in my front pocket. The trick gave me a split second of freedom that I used to position myself like I was about to punt a football. I proceeded to kick the tall teen straight in the groin.

He howled in agony.

Country Yinzer: "OWW! You son of a... !"

I took off. My cheap shot made the country boy boil over with anger. He threw down the penny in disgust and reached into his back pocket. I looked back over my shoulder and saw that real trouble was coming for me now. The furious teen had quickly pulled out a large pocketknife, unfolded it, and began chasing after me again. Now, I was running for my life.

I bolted up 10th Street. Whipped around the corner. Flew by my church. Terror. My heart was racing. I could hear him shrieking in fury.

Country Yinzer: "You're dead meat now, kid!"

Two blocks to go.

Country Yinzer: "Drop the gold or I swear you're DEAD!"

One block to go.

Country Yinzer: "Gimme the money, kid!"

There.

I made it!

I turned toward the brick building, leapt up the steps, and burst straight through the front doors. I ran right into the Italian Club. Seconds later, the country boy came hurtling through the doors while firmly holding up the large hunting knife. He screamed at the top of his lungs.

Country Yinzer: "GIMME THE MONEY!"

Everyone in the club froze. Then their heads swung in the direction of the main entrance. The smoke-filled room was jam-packed with Italian Club members playing cards at round tables. In the center of each fully seated poker table was a big pile of cash. I scurried to a table near the middle of the room where my father and grandfather were playing five-card draw with my uncles and older cousins.

All eyes were on the tall teenager brandishing a long steel blade. Every man in the room slowly rose to their feet and began a calm, heavy walk towards the bold intruder who had the audacity to barge into their private party with a weapon and loudly demand money. The titanic skipper of the Italian Club, Sonny, angrily arose from his chair in the smoky lodge like a slowly erupting volcano. Sonny was so big that he clearly stood out in the middle of the pack of over thirty working men, war veterans, and wiseguys. This mass of humanity slowly enveloped the outsider.

Now, the entire club was facing the tall blond trespasser. The room grew completely quiet. Then, from the old jukebox, came the sound of a softly strumming guitar and a gently blowing trumpet. Frank Sinatra began smoothly singing the entire first line of "The Girl from Ipanema." The delicate guitar accompanied Sinatra as he crooned over the room. The light, relaxing tone of a song about a carefree girl strolling on a tropical beach created a surreal, almost comical scene.

Sonny had worked his way to a commanding position at the forefront of the small army of men. He and the party crasher now stood face to face. After a long awkward pause, Sonny tilted his head to the side and curtly spoke out of the side of his mouth. The big man was serious.

Sonny: "You look lost, pal."

Sonny's left hand then slowly pulled his suit jacket to the side to reveal a concealed handgun in a shoulder holster.

Sonny: "Do we got a problem here?"

At that instant, you could visibly see that country boy's heart sink to the floor. Judging by the fear in his eyes, this kid knew perfectly well that he had just stepped foot into the wrong poker parlor. I will never forget the look on his face. After a nervous pause, he was finally able to stutter out a response.

Country Yinzer: "Oh, no… no. No… no problem here, sir. I'm… I'm good. Sorry for botherin' all yinz."

His hands began to shake like leaves on a tree. He quickly folded up his knife and slid it back into his pocket as he started to slowly back-pedal towards the doorway behind him. Sonny spoke in a calm, low voice.

Sonny: "Okay, that's a good thing. Now… this is a *private* club."

After another short pause, Sonny nodded to him and curtly spoke one word.

Sonny: "Capisce?"   (pronounced "kuhpeesh")

The unwelcomed guest slunk back three steps toward the door.

Country Yinzer: "Oh… sure, okay. Sorry, mister."

Even if he didn't know that "Capisce?" meant "Got it?" in Italian, that country boy fully understood Sonny. The young fellow with hair colored yellow nervously caught his foot on a chair while stepping backwards to the exit, spun around and ran outside as fast as he could. At this point, the old guys were laughing their heads off and most of them spilled out onto the street and watched him sprint away into the dark.

Standing like a mountain among the crowd on the street, Sonny turned to me.

Sonny: "Whatta jagoff. Who was 'at guy, Bobby?"

I shrugged my shoulders like I wasn't just running for my life through town.

Bobby: "Oh… that guy? He ain't nobody. Thanks, Mr. DeLeone."

Sonny: "Sure, kid."

Sonny turned around and leisurely strolled back to the club. He called out in a matter-of-fact tone.

Sonny: "All right, fellas! Show's over! Let's play some poker here!"

The aroused crowd slowly headed back into the Italian Club. Sonny yelled as he lumbered through the door.

Sonny: "Hey, Gino! You better not be touchin' my cards!"

The only people left standing outside of the Italian Club on 8th Street and Clay were me, my father, and my grandfather. We stood under a flickering streetlamp by the fence of the empty bocce courts. My father looked inquisitive. He crossed his arms.

Dad: "So, what happened? Did yinz find the treasure?"

I slowly reached into my pocket.

Bobby: "We found *this*."

I pulled out the lone gold coin. I held it up high in the palm of my hand. It shined bright under the golden beam of the now steadily glowing streetlight.

Bobby: "We found a map, but this is all the gold there was. A single coin."

My father and grandfather looked at the radiant gold coin with proud smiles.

Bobby: "It's authentic. A King George mint from the 1750s. We got a small cannon too. And a bayonet and some other artifacts that are gonna go in the museum."

I paused and looked at the sparkling coin in my hand.

Bobby: "Well, I'm gonna give this to the museum, too. I just wanted to show it to yinz first."

My father simply nodded his head and smiled.

Dad: "Well, 'at certainly looks like a golden treasure to me, Bobby."

Like typical war veterans, my father and grandfather were not interested in the details of our adventurous mission. They only cared about the final results. Pap clapped his hands two times in the air to applaud the spoils of our treasure hunt.

Pap: "Bravo, Bobby! Bravo! I knew it. I knew yinz kids would find gold."

Pap smiled with great satisfaction at our success. To further savor the moment, he pulled out a small Italian cigar that was hidden in the front pocket of his suit. You could tell that he was saving the cigar for a special occasion. He lit it up and took in two quick puffs. After blowing out a huge cloud of smoke, his grin widened even more and he continued.

Pap: "Okay, boys. C'mon now, let's-a go play some cards."

One gold coin was good enough for them. It was good enough for me too. I put the small treasure back into the front pocket of my jeans. For good measure, I reached in and double-checked that it was safely in my possession.

Pap wrapped his arms around our shoulders, and we all walked back into the Italian Club together. All the commotion had stirred up the joint like a disturbed beehive. The heightened buzz made the Sunday night card games even more entertaining. I drank a cold bottle of Dr. Pepper from a tall bar stool and watched over the action.

On the walk home, I retrieved my backpack from Kennedy Park in the flats under Heinz Terrace. I would wait until tomorrow to check on the carnage of my BMX bike. After all, its smashed frame was sitting right in front of my Big Nana's house on Cecil Street. And I already had a new mission lined up for tomorrow for Vito and his trusty metal detector. My lucky steel penny was lying somewhere in front of the Guyasuta Statue in town square.

That night, before I went to sleep, I emptied out my pockets. On my nightstand, I set one stone arrowhead from Chief Guyasuta's Tribe and one shiny gold coin from General Braddock's Treasure. Oh yeah, and from my back pocket, I placed down a small slip of paper with Sarah's phone number.

On the last weekend of August in the year 1979, we found Yinzer Gold.

Afterword: A Pocketful of Gold

One gold coin can never truly quench the thirst of a real treasure hunter. Historians continue to debate the whereabouts of the bulk of Braddock's Treasure. Some believe that the French forces discovered the hidden gold shortly after the Battle of Braddock and simply melted the precious metal down into their own mint. Others claim that a famous American folk hero like Chief Pontiac or Daniel Boone may have found the gold bounty. Still, others think the treasure was buried under General Braddock's grave. A few maintain that the gold never existed in the first place. Of course, I believe there is hope that a large treasure remains undiscovered somewhere in the vast woodlands of the Appalachian Mountains. At any rate, the mystery and legend of Braddock's Gold remains unsolved. The saga continues to this day. If you do some research like my friends and I have done, then maybe you can find the historic treasure and beat Vito to the cover of *National Geographic*.

My adventure was inspired by true events and involved many great figures in the annals of American history. However, this novel must be regarded as historical fiction. While every iota of the history chronicled here is authentic and many of the urban legends have been passed down for generations, some of my firsthand accounts are a product of confabulation. In light of this, I want *Yinzer Gold* to be treated as it should: a mythology of a metropolis. I wish not to offend anyone with my portrayal of preeminent American icons ranging from President George Washington to Chief Guyasuta to H.J. Heinz. Furthermore, all other characters in my story should be considered strictly fictional in nature. If there is a conflict in name or likeness for any non-historical character, then this is purely coincidental. I should note that I did use the real names of the dogs that roamed the streets of Sharpsburg when I was a kid. I hope Duke would be okay with this.

The small town of Sharpsburg is no longer a Little Italy. Although many Italian American families reside there, it is a much more diverse community today. The club that I mentioned throughout the book no longer exists. The bocce courts are long gone. They paved our summer paradise and put up a parking lot. But what remains the same is still the great thing about Sharpsburg. The parks, basketball courts, and ball fields are packed with young people having fun. I would like to dedicate this book to all kids from Sharpsburg, young and old.

As it happened, 1979 was not just a successful year for a few teenage treasure hunters in Pittsburgh. That season, the Pirates won the World Series and the Steelers won the Super Bowl, thus solidifying Pittsburgh's '70s nickname: "The City of Champions." For those who bleed black and gold, it was a magical time. I tried my best to capture the spirit of '79. I was tempted to write that a new single by Styx called "Renegade" could be heard playing from a nearby saloon at the start of our hard-fought football game in the town of Braddock. But the insertion of the more recently anointed rally song of the Steelers would simply be embellishing my tale.

On that thread, I do want to admit to using some artistic license in timeline regarding my favorite historical painter, Robert Griffing. *The Wounding of General Braddock* painting was not showcased in the Carnegie Library in 1979. This incredible work of art had not yet been completed. A resident of Western PA, Griffing has created scores of fantastic paintings that portray the American Indian experience in the Eastern Woodlands, particularly the Senecas during the French and Indian War. I wanted to pay tribute to Griffing for his inspirational artwork depicting the great legacy of Native Americans in the region. Often highlighting the struggles threatening the American Indian way of life, Griffing's sense of realism and respect is nothing less than brilliant. His remarkable artwork is now displayed in numerous museums and libraries across the nation, from the Seneca-Iroquois National Museum to the Smithsonian Museum of Natural History to the Fort Pitt Museum. Griffing's classic *On the Trail to Fort Pitt*, which features Mingo warriors stoically overlooking the fort from what is now Mount Washington, is the centerpiece painting in my living room.

Speaking of artwork, my favorite illustration that I made for this book is the large tiger on the historic merry-go-round at Kennywood Park. I drew every picture by hand with my trusty Ticonderoga pencil on my dining room table. I even used a big candle on the table to trace the circular shape for the steel penny, quarter, and gold coin. Surprisingly, the most difficult drawings for me were lone, inanimate objects such as my BMX bike and the folding chair. Somehow, the large panorama of Pittsburgh from Point State Park was a piece of cake. Incidentally, many Yinzers may have noticed that I left out the distinct spired silhouette of PPG Place in that drawing. This beautiful glass skyrise did not yet exist in 1979; it was completed in 1984.

As for the big picture, I hoped to create an inspiring novel that young adult readers can both relate to and learn from. Growing up isn't easy. It never will be. But this

270

challenging time shapes us all. Trials and tribulations become blessings in disguise. I also wished to tell a story that portrays adolescents who are not often showcased in writing. We need to share more quality narratives about those who live and thrive in real working-class neighborhoods. Our most unique young people reside outside the castle walls. In this real world, ordinary kids can do extraordinary things.

I do have a few messages that I feel are important for younger readers. Please do not attempt to conduct or reenact dangerous or illegal acts from my story. Do not shoot BB guns at each other. Do not steal from convenience stores. Do not rob museums. Do not dig on private or public property without permission. And do not step on Kenny Kangaroo's tail. For all readers, I give one golden rule: Judge people by their actions, not their accents.

Here are some random factoids to ponder:

1. The King George II gold coin of the 1750s contained about 8 grams of gold. Slightly larger in diameter than a modern American quarter, this British gold coin was commonly referred to as a guinea. King George II ruled over the American colonies during the French and Indian War. He is famous for being the last sitting English monarch to lead an army into battle. Of course, on July 4, 1776, the Unites States of America officially declared its independence from Great Britain and the aforementioned king's grandson, King George III.

2. The zinc-plated steel penny of 1943 was not the only product of the war conservation effort. Adult men were even on short supply during World War II. The Pittsburgh Steelers and Philadelphia Eagles had to merge as the "Steagles" during the 1943 NFL season due to lack of players.

3. The Pontiac automobile brand that produced my favorite car model, the Firebird Trans Am, got its namesake from Chief Pontiac of the Ottawa Tribe. While on the subject, my family's string of station wagons would stall out and break down so often that we nicknamed them "The Pittsburgh Stallers."

4. Thunderbolt was ranked #1 coaster in America by *The New York Times* in 1974.

5. John Fraser was the first settler to build a cabin in the Pittsburgh area. The Scottish frontiersman set up a fur trading post where the mouth of Turtle Creek spills into the Monongahela River. Amazingly, Braddock's Defeat, the high tide

of the Whiskey Rebellion, and the construction of Carnegie's Edgar Thomson Steel Works would all eventually take place in what was this Yinzer's back yard.

6. The famous workhorse helicopter of the U.S. Army in the Vietnam War was called the "Huey." However, staying in line with the tradition of Native American titles, the helicopter was officially named the UH-1 Iroquois.

7. For the record, 33 Americans lost their lives in the horrific battle in Vietnam detailed in this novel. After this, my father was awarded a Bronze Star. In fact, he was awarded a total of three Bronze Stars for heroism in combat during the Vietnam War. Also, his war medals are no longer hidden away in a shoebox. I created a decorated display case for my father's medals and memorabilia.

8. Shortly after his rookie season, Steelers halfback Rocky Bleier was drafted into the U.S. Army. He served in the 31st Infantry in Vietnam and was badly wounded during an ambush; after being shot in the left leg, an enemy grenade sent shrapnel into his right leg and foot. Awarded the Bronze Star and Purple Heart, doctors told Bleier that he would never be able to play football again. Of course, Rocky recovered and won four Super Bowl titles.

9. The great Roberto Clemente was a U.S. Marine. While playing for the Pirates, he was drafted into the armed forces and enlisted in the Marine Corps Reserve. At the notoriously grueling boot camp at Parris Island, Clemente set the Marine record for most chin-ups and fastest time in the obstacle course.

10. Although the Red Tails are widely recognized by their nickname acquired from the crimson rudders of their fighter planes, the famed African Americans of the 332nd Fighter Group are also well known as the Tuskegee Airmen. These storied heroes of World War II trained at Tuskegee Army Airfield in Alabama.

11. On everything from classroom posters to coffee mugs to internet memes, Oscar Wilde is credited with the quote, "Be yourself; everyone else is already taken." However, there is no clear evidence that the Irish author-playwright ever wrote or said this line. It remains my favorite saying.

12. Bald eagles are once again a common sight in Pittsburgh. They are often seen gliding high above the rivers and hunting large fish. They tend to nest in sycamore trees along steep wooded cliffs overlooking the waterways.

13. During the time of Chief Guyasuta, mountain lions (also known as cougars, panthers, or pumas) were the apex predator in the Pittsburgh region. Although their numbers remain steady in the American West, they were hunted to extinction in Pennsylvania. The vast, wooded mountains made a perfect habitat for these large cats. They remain famous in name as mascots for both the University of Pittsburgh and Pennsylvania State University.

14. Unlike most of America, many Yinzers in the late 1970s were unaware of the "Blues Brothers" or the "Coneheads." The first few seasons of *Saturday Night Live* were not even aired in Pittsburgh. The local NBC affiliate chose to continue showing a Yinzer favorite instead: *Chiller Theatre*. It was a double feature of classic sci-fi and horror movies hosted by "Chilly Billy" Cardille. He is most remembered as the reporter in George Romero's *Night of the Living Dead*.

15. The childhood home of H.J. Heinz was in fact moved by boat a few miles down the Allegheny River from Sharpsburg to the Heinz company headquarters in the North Side of Pittsburgh. His cherished home later joined a famous collection of nearly 100 historic American buildings and replicas at Greenfield Village in Dearborn, Michigan. Established by Henry Ford, the outdoor museum includes the childhood home of Orville and Wilbur Wright, the laboratory of Thomas Edison, and the courthouse where Abraham Lincoln began his law career.

16. When Heinz made his first profits from his food business, he made sure to buy gifts for his parents. He bought his mother a horse for $10. He also built a new home for his parents right on Main Street in Sharpsburg. The house still sits next to the fire hall where my father volunteered.

17. When H.J. Heinz moved from Sharpsburg to his palatial mansion on Millionaire's Row in Point Breeze, he became next-door neighbors with George Westinghouse, the engineer and entrepreneur. Each of their homes took up one large city block. Heinz's estate, called Greenlawn, had a library and numerous greenhouses for growing fruits, vegetables, and exotic plants. The "Pickle King" turned his upper floor into a personal museum that showcased his most prized archeological artifacts and artwork from around the world.

18. The large urban oasis that is Schenley Park marks only one of many important spaces Mary Schenley donated for Yinzers to enjoy. In staunch support of

preserving the region's rich history, Schenley refused to allow a small brick building that she owned be demolished by industrialists and railroad developers at the Point. She donated the historic Fort Pitt Block House to the Fort Pitt Society, a branch of the Daughters of the Revolution. Constructed in 1764, it is the only structure that remains from the original British bastion.

19. Pittsburgh is now officially recognized by the federal government as the starting point of the famed Lewis and Clark Expedition. The National Park Service marks it as the beginning of the 4,900-mile westward journey that makes up the Lewis and Clark National Historic Trail. (Their keelboat went in the Allegheny River at Fort Lafayette near the modern-day David L. Lawrence Convention Center and Rachel Carson Bridge.) Officially named the Corps of Discovery, it was led by Army Captain Meriwether Lewis and William Clark who sought to explore the Louisiana Purchase and find a route to the Pacific Ocean.

20. Sacagawea was with child when she joined the Lewis and Clark Expedition. She later gave birth on the trek. The Shoshone guide is said to be the first woman on record in American history to cast a democratic vote. The exploration team voted on the location for building a fort for the winter.

21. Washington was with the acclaimed frontiersman Christopher Gist when he first met Guyasuta in Logstown, a trading post along the Ohio River near modern-day Ambridge. Washington garnered Guyasuta's invaluable services for a dangerous trek through the wilderness to meet French officials at Fort Le Boeuf, near Erie, Pennsylvania. Commissioned a major at only 21 years of age, Washington was sent in the name of the British Crown by the Virginia colony's lieutenant governor, Robert Dinwiddie, to demand that the French forces abandon their forts and land claims along the Ohio and Allegheny River Valleys. Washington personally handed the diplomatic letter of request to the French commandant. Of course, the French refused the British demands. After Washington surveyed and documented the strategic position of the Point in 1753, the British set up a tiny outpost there called Fort Prince George in 1754. Only a few months later, the French captured it and then built Fort Duquesne.

22. Washington's firsthand account of his dangerous expedition from the Forks of the Ohio to Fort Le Boeuf and back, *The Journal of Major George Washington*, made him an international celebrity after it was published. Even the man

stamped on the heads side of our hard-earned gold coin, King George II, was said to have enjoyed reading the memoir of the young soldier's great adventure in the unforgiving December forests of Western Pennsylvania.

23. In the journal, Washington nicknamed Guyasuta "The Hunter" because of his prowess in harvesting bucks and bears during the mission. Both were young men when they first met. Guyasuta was the lowest-ranking Seneca in the diplomatic mission to meet with the French. The superior Seneca leader in the small party was Tanacharison, also known as Half-King. Tanacharison was as serious as Washington about removing French forts from the region and even carried a wampum (war belt made of shells) warning of a possible war.

24. On his way back from Fort Le Boeuf, Washington was nearly assassinated near modern-day Evans City in Butler County. He was directly shot at by an enemy from only fifteen yards away and felt the bullet whiz by his body. After this near-death experience, Washington and Gist raced back to what is now Pittsburgh. Days later, Washington again almost lost his life while attempting to cross the icy Allegheny River in late December of 1753. Shortly after launching from where Pine Creek spills into the river in Etna, their raft capsized and tossed George into the treacherous waters of the Allegheny. Wet and frozen, they fortunately made their way to a cluster of small islands. The largest remaining island in this vicinity is now called Washington's Landing.

25. George Washington was a 22-year-old lieutenant colonel when his small unit accompanied by Tanacharison ignited the French and Indian War by opening fire and killing a French officer, Joseph Coulon de Jumonville, at The Battle of Jumonville Glen near Uniontown, PA. After the skirmish, Washington was hotly pursued by French and Native American forces. He built a makeshift fort, called Fort Necessity. After a bloody battle at the small outpost, Washington eventually submitted to his enemies. Upon surrender, Washington apparently was forced to sign a peace treaty written in French that admitted his group's responsibility in the assassination of the French officer and declared that England would give up its land claims in Western Pennsylvania.

26. Not all Seneca chieftains were male. Indeed, historians consider Queen Aliquippa a very powerful Seneca leader of the Pittsburgh region. Aliquippa remained staunchly loyal to the British and Colonials during the French and

Indian War. George Washington considered her to be one of his strongest allies and friends. In fact, the female Seneca warrior and her son led a small party to help reinforce Washington's beleaguered forces at Fort Necessity.

27. Washington would continue to return to Southwestern Pennsylvania to keep tabs on his more well-known treasure, a large acreage of land. He owned property in parts of Washington and Fayette County and operated gristmills that turned farmed grain into flour. He also attempted to collect rent from settlers who lived on the land. Of course, the early Yinzers vehemently refused his request, and Washington ultimately gave up on his demands.

28. Chief Guyasuta was obviously not pleased with the westward expansion of settlers after the French and Indian War. However, after leading various sieges against the British and American forces, he finally decided that peace was needed in the region. He promised to end the attacks on forts and settlements and to return all captives. At the peace treaty that basically ended Pontiac's Rebellion, Guyasuta exchanged handshakes with the same man he had exchanged gunshots with at the Battle of Bushy Run, Henry Bouquet.

29. Late in his life, Chief Guyasuta of the Seneca Wolf Clan passed down most of his leadership duties to his nephew, Cornplanter. Chief Cornplanter was a vaunted warrior himself who would become a spokesman for the Seneca. As an aside, Guyasuta's name has several spelled variants including Kiasutha and Kayahsota. His name has been translated in the Seneca branch of the Iroquoian language as meaning either "Standing Paddle" or "He Stands Up The Cross."

30. Today, the Seneca Nation has over 10.000 citizens from three main tribal branches. Most have historically lived in Western New York. (Guyasuta was born in this region along the Allegheny River upstream from Pittsburgh.) The Great Council of The Iroquois Confederacy or Six Nations includes the Seneca, Mohawk, Oneida, Onondaga, Cayuga, and Tuscarora Nations. Presided by over 50 leaders, this democratic government of the Iroquois, or Haudenosaunee, predates that of the United States of America by over 500 years.

31. After America won its independence, Revolutionary War officers were often paid with land grants. Colonel James O'Hara, the quartermaster general of the war campaign, purchased a large swath of land north of the Allegheny River that

was once home to the Seneca People. The area included modern-day Sharpsburg and Aspinwall, then called Guyasuta Bottom. Out of respect, O'Hara allowed the well-revered Chief Guyasuta to stay in his small home in Sharpsburg. Upon a regular visit to his cabin, it was O'Hara who was the first to receive the news of the chief's death.

32. H.J. Heinz did indeed finance the original Guyasuta Statue on Main Street in Sharpsburg. Unfortunately, two car accidents at the busy intersection toppled the original in 1930 and the replica in 1983. The latter of which I remember witnessing the aftermath. Prominent in the main crossroads of the town, the current "Guyasuta" statue located in Guyasuta Square is not molded in the true likeness of Chief Guyasuta. Although a beautiful piece of artwork, it is simply a general depiction of a Seneca hunter. (Personally, I believe that a true to form monument of the great Native American leader should be added to represent and honor his legacy.) For example, unlike the existing statue, most accounts depict Guyasuta with a traditional Seneca hairstyle from that period consisting of a clean-shaven crown with a long ponytail. I should also add that the town "square" is really shaped like a triangle.

33. Along with the Seneca, the Pittsburgh region was also home to the Shawnee, Mingo, and Lenape, formerly known as the Delaware. Before the French and British arrived, the Lenape had a settlement called Shannopin Town along the Allegheny River where Lawrenceville and the Strip District are today. Also, the most common Native American trail from present-day Pittsburgh to Lake Erie was called the Venango Path after a Lenape village. A young George Washington used much of this well-traveled route while exploring the wilderness of Western Pennsylvania with Guyasuta. The famous path of his first adventures in the American backcountry is now known as Washington's Trail. It roughly follows U.S. Route 19.

34. Grant Street in the heart of Downtown was named after Major James Grant, a British officer who was captured during the Battle of Fort Duquesne. The vicious battle occurred only one month before the French fort fell. The British were routed yet again. Years later, Chief Guyasuta told George Washington that Grant was drunk as a skunk when he was captured. Guyasuta said Washington, ever the serious military leader, was infuriated after hearing this.

35. Originally called the Forks of the Ohio, the city of Pittsburgh was given its name by British General John Forbes after the capture of Fort Duquesne in 1758. (Forbes pronounced it "Pitts-buh-ruh" in his Scottish accent.) It was named after William Pitt the Elder who served as Prime Minister of Great Britain during its arduous victory against the Kingdom of France in the French and Indian War. Upon learning of the toughness of the American frontier and its people, the highly regarded politician accurately warned England that it could suffer defeat before the American Revolutionary War. I should add, the Commonwealth of Pennsylvania was named after British Admiral William Penn Sr. who was the father of the state's Quaker founder William Penn.

36. The name Pennsylvania literally means Penn's Woodlands in Latin. It has been said that at the time of Chief Guyasuta, a squirrel could travel from tree to tree across the entire state without touching the ground. Barring rivers, this may have been more fact than fiction.

37. Mount Washington was originally called Coal Hill. It contained one of the largest coal deposits ever discovered in America. The coal was used over the centuries to fuel everything from British soldiers' campfires at Fort Pitt to blast furnaces at Andrew Carnegie's steel mills.

38. The French and Indian War is known as the North American segment of the Seven Years' War in both Europe and Canada. From 1754 to 1763, this global conflict involved fighting in regions of North America, Europe, Asia, and Africa. It is for this reason that Winston Churchill referred to it as "the first world war."

39. Most soldiers used smooth-bore muskets during the French and Indian War. Although it could be equipped with a bayonet, the 5-foot-long, muzzle-loaded flintlock musket was not very accurate. The war introduced a much more renowned firearm, the Pennsylvania long rifle. Developed in eastern PA in the early 1700's, the rifled bore barrel allowed the long gun to shoot a spinning projectile with much more accuracy. It became the weapon of choice for sharpshooters in Washington's Virginia Regiment and frontiersman like PA born Daniel Boone. The famed long rifle is even carried by Hawkeye, the hero in James Fenimore Cooper's classic tale about the era, *The Last of the* Mohicans. Hawkeye is amply nicknamed "The Long Rifle" because of his superior shooting skills. Both muskets and long rifles shot heavy balls made of solid lead then.

40. In May of 1755, The Braddock Expedition to the Ohio Country to take Fort Duquesne was one of the largest military campaigns ever in Colonial America. When the British army first set out from Maryland it included a string of over 2,000 soldiers, 10 large cannons, and dozens of wagons that stretched over two miles long. It took six grueling weeks for hundreds of axmen and engineers to cut a path for the marching troops through the heavily forested mountains and valleys of the Appalachians. Following a trail of the Lenape Tribe called Nemacolin's Path, Braddock's Road spanned over 100 miles from Fort Cumberland to within ten miles of Fort Duquesne. (The road is now roughly paralleled by U.S. Route 40.) General Braddock assumed his British army boasting thousands would easily conquer a French fortress holding hundreds.

41. A historical marker in North Huntingdon sits at the likely spot of Braddock's campsite two nights before his army's final march. Down the road is a wooded park with a waterfall and river overlook. It's called Braddock's Trail Park.

42. The Battle of Braddock's Field, also known as the Battle of the Monongahela, occurred in the afternoon of July 9, 1755. Historians say it was more of a surprise collision than a planned ambush. Strung out in a long column, Braddock's army and its artillery was rendered useless by dense forest. Unlike the British redcoats that clumped tightly together in squares and traditional firing lines, the opposition stealthily spread out and used the trees and terrain to their advantage. Stationed on three sides, the ravine became a shooting gallery for the smaller band of French regulars and Canadian militia at the front and larger groups of American Indians on the flanks. The battle was a complete rout. The French and Native American forces lost fewer than 40 men while the British and Colonial American contingent suffered close to 1,000 casualties in soldiers and staff. Braddock himself was said to have been shot in the lung.

43. General Braddock was not the only highest-ranking field officer to lose his life from the battle. The opposing French commander, Monsieur Daniel Liénard de Beaujeu, was among the first to perish when gunfire erupted. He was killed while leading the charge at the head of the battlefield. In fact, after receiving news of the large size of the approaching British army, Beaujeu rallied hundreds of his American Indian allies at Fort Duquesne by removing his officer's coat and applying traditional warpaint on his face. Racing on foot to confront the enemy,

the captain's shirtless act of solidarity helped kickstart the fight. But without dispute, the American Indian forces deserve the lion's share of the credit for the resounding victory that sent shockwaves around the globe.

44. Following the British defeat and retreat from the Battle of Braddock, the deceased General Edward Braddock was first secretly buried under the road that was created by his army on its march to Fort Duquesne. Washington even presided as chaplain at the general's funeral. Braddock's remains were later moved to a more visible location and are now marked with a large stone memorial by the Great Meadows near Fort Necessity in Fayette County, PA.

45. Along with the leopard hide saddle rest, Washington inherited General Braddock's brass-barreled pistol and red commander sash. Washington highly prized these gifts from the dying general and fondly held on to these items for his entire life. The red officer's sash has been displayed at the museum gallery at George Washington's Mount Vernon in Virginia. The flintlock pistol with Braddock's initials (E.B.) has been shown at the National Museum of American History in Washington, D.C. It is said that Washington rode on the leopard saddle pad while commanding from horses throughout the remainder of the French and Indian War and the American Revolutionary War. The leopard skin is noticeably worn from years of use on horseback. Once preserved and displayed by the Society of the Sons of the Revolution, the leopard saddle pad was recently sold at auction for $150,000. I have no idea who bought it.

46. In his autobiography, Benjamin Franklin wrote that he explicitly warned General Braddock about the possibility of being attacked by Native Americans while marching to take Fort Duquesne. Braddock scoffed at the advice. He felt they posed no threat to a large army of British regulars. In fact, Franklin said that Braddock disrespected both his Native American foes and his Colonial American allies in a single breath. Franklin documented the general's reply.

General Braddock: "These savages may, indeed, be a formidable enemy to your raw American militia, but upon the King's regular and disciplined troops, sir, it is impossible they should make any impression."

47. After suffering through years of horrible defeats, no man was said to have been more jubilant about finally capturing Fort Duquesne from the French than

George Washington. Shortly after celebrating this achievement, Washington made a point to return to the banks of the Monongahela and bury the remains of hundreds of soldiers lost during Braddock's Defeat.

48. In the wake of his daring exploits and military accomplishments in newly named Pittsburgh, Washington expected to be rewarded by King George II and commissioned a high-ranking commander in the British Army. Instead, he was passed over by far lesser soldiers who the king perceived had higher pedigrees (read as born in England). The lowly farmer from America learned a humbling lesson on how the British Empire's class system really worked. Scorned, he quit the army. Don't for a second think a man as driven as Washington would let this slide. Over a decade later, he found work as the head commander of a brand-new army altogether. With his new position, Washington returned the English monarchs a lesson in humility.

***

Braddock's Defeat was a watershed moment in military history. It has become a cautionary tale for soldiers of all ranks. A bedtime story told on the night before a big battle. But first and foremost, it emerged as a learning point for both Native and Colonial Americans. They realized that the British Empire and its elite military was not so invincible after all. It set the stage for the American Revolution.

I believe no leader has done more for our country than President George Washington. His phenomenal feats on the battlefields of two bloody wars have been unrivaled. His tremendous resolve to lead our country to independence and beyond will always remain unparalleled. He was a true revolutionary. Washington defines the American patriot.

Historians maintain that Washington earned his stripes in Western Pennsylvania during the French and Indian War. Lessons learned from fearsome battles in the forests of Pittsburgh molded a fledgling scout of the Virginia militia into the indomitable General of the Continental Army. In the epic struggle to control the strategically positioned Point, the foundations of a brave military commander and future president were laid. Along the way, Washington gained invaluable experience and knowledge from his encounters with Native Americans, such as Chief Guyasuta. Washington's last meeting with Guyasuta in 1770 was just a short distance down the Ohio River from what is now Mount Washington (and not on the mount itself as I erroneously told my friends in my story). By this time, Guyasuta was now the most powerful American Indian sachem in the region. Washington said Guyasuta seemed very happy to reunite and once again share stories over the fire. Both had survived through many years of brutal warfare since they had first met. Although they came from two disparate cultures, their shared experience forged a unique bond.

After becoming president, Washington gifted Guyasuta a silver gorget (decorative military neckplate) as a symbol of their friendship. But as we all know, even the storied, albeit tepid, relationship between Washington and Guyasuta did not stop the inertia of western expansion in America. Following even more horrific warring and strife, however, Guyasuta's final quest for peace with his neighbors ultimately succeeded. Under President Washington, a peace treaty was signed between the Six Nations of the Iroquois Confederacy and the United States in 1794. The Canandaigua Treaty has recognized the ancestral lands and government of the Six Nations for well over two centuries. Although he was too old and frail to physically sign this peace treaty, Guyasuta had left his mark. The largest delegation in attendance was that of the Seneca Nation. It was led by Guyasuta's nephew and close protégé, Cornplanter.

A major strain in the treaty occurred in the 1950s when Seneca land was taken to construct the Kinzua Dam to prevent flooding on the Allegheny River. Although officials claim the Canandaigua Treaty remains honored, contentious projects like this continue to cause acrimony. Unfortunately, many Native Nations have also suffered from broken promises. Time after time, countless treaties and agreements between European and American governments and Indigenous Peoples were not upheld. Case in point: the Mount Rushmore National Memorial exists on sacred land reserved for the Lakota, or Teton Sioux, as stipulated in the 1868 Treaty of Fort Laramie.

More than five centuries of conflict over territory have left a painful legacy. Indeed, my story was born from a triangular slice of land hungered by kings living in castles halfway around the globe. From the very beginning, whenever land was disputed over in the Americas, violence and bloodshed became the norm. Far too much of this horrid past has been omitted or sugarcoated by history. Whether by force or by treaty, millions of American Indians surrendered ancestral lands and were often relocated to reservations. Make no mistake, when writers (including myself) refer to land as "frontier," "wilderness," or "uncharted," this grossly overlooks the fact that this very same land had long been home to Native Americans.

Of course, it is also widely known that George Washington and many of his contemporaries earned considerable wealth from the inhumane act of forced slave labor. This despicable treatment of fellow humans in America must never be forgotten. A grotesque institution supported by the U.S. government, slavery in America was driven by disgraceful greed and abhorrent injustice. Without doubt, the slave trade was fully entrenched in a diabolical world economy devised by European kingdoms and colonial empires that was based upon the conquest, bondage, and mass exploitation of Africans and Native Americans.

Although Sacagawea has been celebrated as a heroine in American history for her incredible acts during the Lewis and Clark Expedition, she was never duly rewarded for her services. Again, her life was much more tragic than is commonly purveyed. After being kidnapped at a young age, she was basically purchased by a French fur trader to be his wife. She died at age 25 most likely from typhoid fever. Sacagawea (variants include Sacajawea and Tsakakawias) means "Bird Woman." The lasting legacy of the Shoshone explorer has been honored with a beautiful image of her and her infant son on the U.S. dollar coin. Four mountains and two lakes are named after Sacagawea.

An unsung hero of the Lewis and Clark Expedition was named York. The first African American frontiersman to cross the continent, York played an integral role in providing food, supplies, and shelter. York hunted big game with firearms, parleyed with Native Americans, and casted an equal vote along with everyone else in the crew. He was also a slave of Clark. Sadly, after returning home from the arduous mission, York was denied his payment and his freedom. Today, he is venerated as a great American explorer with statues across the country just like Sacagawea.

I would like to acknowledge all men and women who have served in the U.S. military. All battle accounts in my novel were diligently researched for accuracy. We must always remember the Red Tails, revere the Navajo Code Talkers, and honor the Unknown Soldier. We should never forget the sacrifices they made for us. It should be known that Native Americans have comprised the highest percentage of service of any race or ethnicity per capita in the U.S. Armed Forces. From World Wars to today, these courageous warriors have continued to protect and defend their homeland.

I especially want to acknowledge my hometown hero, Chief Guyasuta of the Senecas. During a time of great turmoil in the Pittsburgh region, he bravely fought to preserve his peoples' sovereignty and way of life. The profound change that Guyasuta witnessed during his lifetime is mind boggling. The largest transformation occurred where the three rivers meet. Here, a serene triangle of forest became a small frontier outpost that would eventually blossom into a large urban settlement. Tall trees turned into tall buildings and narrow streams into narrow streets right before his eyes. As a young scout, he would often be out hunting big game in the quiet woods in and around the Forks of the Ohio. As an old sachem, he would occasionally be seen walking down the busy avenues of the fast-growing city of Pittsburgh. Incredibly, a warrior became a peacemaker, and a Seneca became a Yinzer.

We should remember the legacy of Guyasuta in both local and American history. Part of the rich cultural fabric of this country has been stitched by the Native American Peoples who have inhabited this beautiful land for many millennia. The United States of America will reach its full potential when we all fully accept the vast diversity and deep history that makes this nation like no other.

***

In the 1970s, an infusion of talented artists and groundbreaking performances propelled pop culture to new heights. The decade produced iconic stars in music, media, sports, television, and movies that remain highly recognizable to this day. I always felt like our modern culture was galvanized during this era. Simply walk through a department store today. From the toys to the clothes displayed, you soon realize just how much imaginative films like *Star Wars* have become forever engrained in our collective psyche. To this day, we remain fascinated by the life of Michael Corleone and frightened to death by Michael Myers.

Looking back, it seems television sitcoms had the biggest impact on me and my family. From *The Muppet Show* to *The Jeffersons*, our world revolved around making sure that we didn't miss our favorite programs. (Of course, we all can still recite every line from the opening theme songs.) Our favorite show was *Three's Company*. John Ritter, who played goofy Jack, and Suzanne Somers, who played bubbly Chrissy, were geniuses of slapstick humor. The talented cast seemed to magically whip up hysterical comedy out of thin air; almost every episode was simply based on the wacky hijinks swirling around one big couch in the middle of a small apartment. (Watch the episode "Handcuffed" and I dare you to not laugh out loud. Jack and Chrissy accidently get handcuffed to each other, and Jack still tries to go out on a date with another woman.) We loved Arthur Fonzarelli on *Happy Days*. Played by the beloved actor Henry Winkler,

"The Fonz" defines coolness to this day. My favorite TV star, Danny DeVito, became a household name from his role as the surly and obnoxious Louie De Palma on the hit show *Taxi*. To be honest, John Travolta's portrayal of the loveable airhead Vinnie Barbarino on the show *Welcome Back, Kotter* may have subconsciously mixed in with my good memories of my fun-loving friend, Vittorio.

In the field of cinema, the newly released *Rocky II* cemented my dream car's status in the summer of 1979. The movie showed "The Italian Stallion" zooming around the streets of Philly in his brand-new Pontiac Firebird Trans Am. It was fast. It was shiny. It was black and gold. It was awesome. To me, that car remains the epitome of all that was cool in the '70s.

My favorite movie made that decade is a classic road comedy. Set during the Great Depression, *Paper Moon* stars the real-life father-daughter tandem of Ryan O'Neal and Tatum O'Neal as traveling con artists. They have natural chemistry and give indelible performances as lovable crooks. Of course, Tatum O'Neal went on to play the gifted pitcher in my second favorite 1970s flick, *The Bad News Bears*. No movie better portrays the hardships and joys of life for an American kid in the late '70s than this comedy about a diverse Little League Baseball team full of ragtags and ruffians.

The incredible diversity of new music produced during the 1970s may never be matched. From the stirring country rock of Lynyrd Skynyrd to the urgent punk rock of the Ramones, new sounds popped up everywhere. As I wrote, the #1 single on the Billboard Hot 100 chart during the week of my August adventure was Chic's huge hit "Good Times." Reflecting on the optimistic feel of the day, the high-spirited song was the perfect score for the summer of '79. Chic was able to blend funk, soul, R&B, pop, and disco into one new and unforgettable sound. Chic oozed with energy and was loaded with talent. One tidbit: Chic's guitarist and bassist, Nile Rodgers and Bernard Edwards, also composed "We Are Family" for Sister Sledge. Even more eyepopping, "Good Times" served as the replayed sample melody for hip-hop's first mainstream rap hit. "Rapper's Delight" by the Sugarhill Gang dropped that same August.

Of course, the signature music of that era was disco. Its worldwide popularity peaked in the spring of '79 when Gloria Gaynor's "I Will Survive" topped every chart imaginable. The year before was dominated by the Bee Gees. In the late '70s, everything they touched turned to gold. The group's smash hit songs "Stayin' Alive" and "Night Fever" still resonate today. I still love the decade's rock music. My favorite group was Led

Zeppelin. The English band stirred rock and roll up from its solid roots in African American rhythm and blues and made it transcend to modern heavy metal. Zeppelin's final studio album, *In Through the Out Door*, was released only two weeks before my treasure hunting adventure in August of 1979. (My story is loaded with hidden eggs in reference to their songs along with many other '70s classics.) My favorite car radio band has always been The Doobie Brothers. I can't help turning up "China Grove" to full volume if I'm driving to the city down Route 28. I should add that KISS did perform at the Civic Arena in the summer of 1979. The main theatrics involved Gene Simmons attached to high wires and flying across the stage.

My favorite album to drop in the late '70s was by the Cars. Their self-titled debut record *The Cars* blew my mind. It rocked. Powerful synthesizer. Clean bass and guitars. Great intros and vocals. They were ahead of their time. Their synth style paved the way for the new wave sound of the 1980s. I think they hold up better today than most any other rock band from that age. Songs like "Just What I Needed" and "My Best Friend's Girl" get more airplay than almost anything else released in 1978. *The Cars* will always be my "stranded alone on a desert island" album.

When it comes to my favorite songs from the '70s, "Lola" by the Kinks always topped the list. I can vividly recall belting out the lines while riding down the alleys of Sharpsburg with my BMX bike gang. Of course, the controversial song made strong allusions to gender identity and personal preferences. But ironically, with strict product placement rules back then, radio stations were even more worried about the song's reference to a name-brand soft drink and often played a watered-down version of "Lola" in which Ray Davies sang "cherry cola" instead of "Coca-Cola."

Coincidently, the most iconic television commercial of 1979 showed "Mean" Joe Greene joyfully chugging a bottle of Coca-Cola and throwing his game jersey to an admiring young fan. Jack Lambert, Jack Ham, Mel Blount, Mike Webster, and all the '70s Super Steelers will never be forgotten. The Immaculate Reception. The Steel Curtain. The Levitating Leap. This is NFL lore. I used to dream of playing like Lynn Swann. In my mind, Swann's acrobatic athleticism was only eclipsed by Spider-Man himself. However, my all-time favorite Steeler was the quintessential big-game wide receiver John Stallworth. His go-ahead touchdown to win the Super Bowl that season, by way of a long bomb from Terry Bradshaw, is forever ingrained in my childhood memories. I remember jumping higher than our wooden console TV in celebration.

By all measures, Willie Stargell was the best baseball player on the planet in 1979. The Pirates slugger won both the regular season and World Series MVP awards. He capped his storybook season by hitting a 2-run homer to beat the Orioles in Game 7. However, the top Major League Baseball player throughout the late '70s era might have been his teammate, Dave Parker. Nicknamed "The Cobra," the huge right fielder from the "We Are Family" team belongs in the Hall of Fame with "Pops" Stargell. While I'm on my soapbox, I want to add that MLB should retire the number 21 worn by the great Roberto Clemente. He was the first Latino player inducted into the Hall of Fame. But more than that, he lost his life while trying to help others in need.

In my humble opinion, one of the greatest tales ever written was penned during the 1970s, a short story called *Rita Hayworth and the Shawshank Redemption* by Stephen King. Although published in the early 1980s, King wrote the classic novella piece behind the acclaimed movie *The Shawshank Redemption* in the mid to late '70s. This dark yet uplifting narrative is about a wrongfully imprisoned man who never gives up hope and finally escapes jail to achieve his rightly due freedom. Subtitled *Hope Springs Eternal*, the short story and movie have long influenced my optimistic outlook in life. From our darkest nights to our brightest days, it is hope that makes life special.

I want to thank the Carnegie Library of Pittsburgh and all its branches. They are sanctuaries of learning that I cherish to this day. If you live in Pittsburgh, make it a point to visit and explore the many neighborhood libraries. A generous gift from our great philanthropist Andrew Carnegie, the library system is a true gem of the city. I am thrilled that the town of Sharpsburg finally received a local branch library.

In closing, the Yinzer language is alive and well today, both in speech and in spirit. If you were flustered by dialogue written with eye dialect ("dahn" replacing "down"), then I should remind you that door was opened long ago by a good friend of Andrew Carnegie. His name was Mark Twain. Frankly, a true depiction of the Yinzer dialect is almost unreadable in print. For example, a framed picture in the original Primanti Bros. Restaurant in the Strip reads "Jeet jet?" which is how a Yinzer would pronounce "Did you eat yet?" Travel to Pittsburgh and you'll hear it spoken everywhere, from the parks to the sporting venues. Also go to enjoy the sites, the food, and the culture. Check out the Carnegie Museums of Art and Natural History, the Carnegie Science Center, the Heinz History Museum, the August Wilson Center, the Andy Warhol Museum, and the Frick Art and Historical Museums. Heinz Hall is the world-class home of the Pittsburgh

Symphony Orchestra. There's the Benedum Center, Byham Theater, City Theatre, and Carnegie Music Hall too. Ride on an Incline or Gateway Clipper. I'm a huge fan of the Pittsburgh Zoo & PPG Aquarium, National Aviary, Phipps Conservatory, and Beechwood Farms. (This is not a paid ad. I love these places.)

There are also smaller museums in the region that highlight action in my book such as Braddock's Battlefield History Center in North Braddock and the Bushy Run Battlefield Museum in Westmoreland County. Of course, I highly recommend that you (legally) visit the Fort Pitt Museum and Fort Pitt Block House at Point State Park. Witness the spectacular sight from the *Point of View* sculpture of Chief Guyasuta and George Washington meeting at the top of the Mount Washington overlook. Crafted by artisan James West, the colossal bronze monument is a fitting tribute to the great chief and the great commander in chief. If you really enjoy Colonial American history, then take a day trip to scout out Fort Ligonier and Fort Necessity. You may also want to learn more about Guyasuta, Washington, and early American history by reading the incredibly insightful books written by author Brady J. Crytzer.

When it comes to exploring Native American history in the region, you should take a walking tour of the Meadowcroft Rockshelter and Historic Village in Avella, PA. Sponsored by the Heinz History Center, this large outdoor exhibit and archaeological site displays one of the earliest known Native American homesteads in the United States, dating from well over 10,000 years ago. At Guyasuta Park in Sharpsburg, Camp Guyasuta offers fun year-round activities from STEM camps to Halloween hayrides. Try to attend the annual festival held by the Council of Three Rivers American Indian Center in Dorseyville. This fun celebration of culture and tradition is a great way to appreciate and support the local Indigenous community. Indeed, many are surprised to learn that Pittsburgh has always had a proud Native American population.

I am proud to have family roots in Sharpsburg, a small neighborhood with a big heart. So much history is packed into this one tiny town. I also feel it was truly an authentic Little Italy, one of the last of its kind in America. If you want to learn more about the town's unique Italian American culture from firsthand experiences, then check out *Always on Sunday; Memories of an Italian Childhood*, a book written by Marcia Russotto. You might also enjoy viewing the award-winning documentary *il Messaggero*, a film by Peter Ferraro. The colorful stories of Sharpsburg live on.

***

In my life, Pittsburgh has undergone a remarkable transformation. I witnessed the shuttering of factory after factory. The city didn't just lose its industry, it lost its identity. It was a gut punch for us all. But we Yinzers pulled ourselves up by our bootstraps. Many Americans might consider Pittsburgh a crumbling "Rust Belt" town full of vacant lots and abandoned dreams. However, visitors are amazed to find that it has evolved into a thriving hub of medicine, technology, robotics, engineering, and education. Civic pride is sky-high. And although the city has reinvented itself, the blue-collar work ethic remains. Its landscape has endured through it all. We have been blessed with beautiful natural vistas and an abundance of trees. To me, the most wonderful sign of its strength is simply the return of bald eagles flying high above the revitalized waterways. Chief Guyasuta would be proud to see these majestic birds soaring once again over our wooded hills and winding river valleys.

I wrote this novel so that important history will not be forgotten. A lot of people say Pittsburgh likes to live in the past. They're right. But many great cities do. Does not Rome? Does not London, Paris, Athens, Tokyo, and New York? It is only natural to revel in our achievements from yesterday as we hope for even better things to come tomorrow. Life goes on, and so will the Steel City. Our always humble hero and the city's greatest ambassador said it better than anyone:

Franco Harris: "Believe in Pittsburgh."

I have but three more important points to make.

Bobby: "The Log Jammer ain't there no more at Kennywood. They took 'at dahn and put up a new coaster called The Still Curtain. Yinz gotta ride 'at thing. It's real good."

Of course, most people would call it "The Steel Curtain." Speaking of the Steelers...

Bobby: "So, they went and changed the name o' Heinz Field. C'mon, man! The Stillers won two Super Bowls playin' dahn 'ere! Every Yinzer in tahn is still gonna call it Heinz Field, ya morons."

In all fairness, Heinz remains an official partner of the Steelers and the newly renamed stadium. Finally, if you think that my Yinzer tale is too outlandish for you, then go start fact-checking the history for yourself. And if for some reason you still don't buy it, I have just one last thing to say.

Bobby: "Up your nose with a rubber hose, ya jagoff!"

YINZER

GOLD

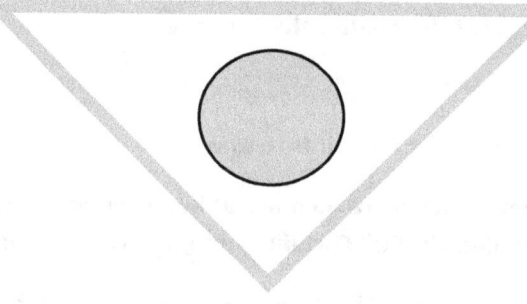

ROBERT EMMET

CONNEMARA

Roberto Clemente: "Any time you have an opportunity to make a difference in this world and you don't, then you are wasting your time on Earth."

Proceeds from this novel will be used to provide funding for public athletic facilities and playgrounds in Pittsburgh and Puerto Rico.

Remaining proceeds will be donated to the Pittsburgh Promise.

I'm not pocketing a single penny. I already have one.

This work of art is a product of

Steel Penny Books LLC